White River
Brides

White River Brides

Missouri Couples Find
Unexpected Love
in Three Historical Novels

FRANCES DEVINE

BARBOUR
PUBLISHING

Print ISBN 978-1-63058-177-0

eBook Editions:
Adobe Digital Edition (.epub) 978-1-63058-542-6
Kindle and MobiPocket Edition (.prc) 978-1-63058-543-3

Published by Barbour Books, an imprint of Barbour Publishing, Inc., P.O. Box 719, Uhrichsville, Ohio 44683, www.barbourbooks.com

Our mission is to publish and distribute inspirational products offering exceptional value and biblical encouragement to the masses.

ecpa Member of the
Evangelical Christian
Publishers Association

Printed in the United States of America.

Frances L. Devine grew up in the great state of Texas, where she wrote her first story at the age of nine. She moved to Southwest Missouri more than twenty years ago and fell in love with the hills, the fall colors, and Silver Dollar City. Frances has always loved to read and considers herself blessed to have the opportunity to write in her favorite genre. She is the mother of seven adult children and has fourteen wonderful grandchildren.

White River Dreams

Dedication

Lovingly dedicated to those early settlers who paved a path to a world they couldn't have even imagined. Thank you for Branson and for my favorite theme park, Silver Dollar City. I wish to thank my friends and family who encourage me every day. Thanks to Aaron McCarver. What would I do without your excellent editing? Special thanks to my editor, JoAnne Simmons, for being so supportive.

Chapter 1

Missouri Ozarks, May 1889

Alexandra Rayton tilted the tin dipper and poured lukewarm water down her parched throat. She glanced across the half-plowed field to make sure her brother and aunt weren't looking her way, then unfastened the top button of her dress and poured the rest of the tepid liquid down the front, not caring that it soaked through her chemise. A shiver passed over her skin, scorched from the hot sun. Too hot for the end of May in Missouri. She would love to push her cotton sleeves up more, but Aunt Kate would be shocked and let her know about it, in no uncertain terms. She looked up and lifted her hand against the glare of the noonday sun. If only the tiniest of clouds would cast its shadow even for a moment.

"Lexie! Bring me some of that water. What'cha tryin' to do? Keep it all to yerself?"

"Oh hush up, Will. Give me time." Lifting the heavy bucket, she carried it over to where her brother leaned on the plow and handed him the dipper.

He took a long drink and refilled the dipper, frowning at Lexie's soaked bodice. "What did you do, take a bath in it? We better not run out of water before we're done planting these tomater seedlins', or you can go to the creek and fetch more."

"Humph. I wonder what Miss Sarah Jenkins would think if she heard you talking to me like that. Think she'd still want to marry the likes of you?"

Will snickered and upended the dipper, sending a cascade of water over his sweaty shirt. "My sweet Sarah Jane's mighty took with me. Ain't nothin' I could say or do would change her mind."

"Is that so? All I can say is the woman must be mighty desperate for a man." Grinning, she bolted down the row and into the woods before her brother could drop the dipper back in the bucket and take off after her.

"Alexandra Marie Rayton, stop that tomfoolery and start doing your job." Aunt Kate's voice, carried by the wind, rang familiar and safe to Lexie's ears.

"All right, Aunt Kate. Be there in a minute." Her voice echoed through the tall oaks that circled the field on three sides. Dropping onto a carpet of thick, green grass, she leaned back against an ancient tree trunk. The sounds of the nearby White River rippled over her mind, and birdsong mingled with the rush of flowing water. She should get back to the field, but the tomato seedlings would wait a few minutes. She closed her eyes, surrendering to the wave of drowsiness. She'd just rest for a moment. She wouldn't daydream.

Will would be getting married soon, and they wouldn't really need her on the farm, would they? Of course, Uncle James's death last year had hit Aunt Kate really hard, but she was doing well now and didn't really need Lexie. Wasn't this the perfect time to leave? Surely she could find a job in a café or boardinghouse. She could cook and clean as well as any other woman she knew. Of course, Aunt Kate would be sure to throw a fit if she went to work at Marmoros with the rough miners running around the place. Besides, no woman in the Rayton family had ever worked outside the home. Not Aunt Kate and not Mama.

Lexie flinched. Would the pain ever go away? Eight years. She'd been nineteen and Will fourteen when Mama and Papa died in the accident. The sheriff said something must have frightened the horses, causing them to bolt and run. There wasn't much left of the turned-over buckboard they'd found at the bottom of a ravine. Funny how little she remembered about the trip by wagon and steamboat from Oklahoma.

A sigh pushed its way out from way down inside her, and she clenched her teeth against the pain. Aunt Kate and Uncle James had been wonderful to her and Will. But Lexie didn't want to spend the rest of her life on a farm. And she wasn't getting any younger. Twenty-seven in two months. She reached up and ran a hand across her cheek. Did her face show her age?

"Alexandra Marie!"

Lexie jumped up and crammed her bonnet back on her head, confining the thick black curls once more. She walked back to the field and threw what she hoped was an apologetic smile at her aunt. She'd done it again. Gotten lost in daydreams.

The earth felt cool against her hands and fingers as she packed it around the tomato plants. Not like it had been in the hot, dry dirt of Oklahoma. Oh, but she'd trade it in a minute if it would bring Mama and Papa back.

The planting went quickly with all three of them working, and the afternoon sun was still halfway up the horizon when the two women headed for the house, leaving Will to take care of the mule.

Lexie sniffed in appreciation at the aroma that met them as they stepped up on the back stoop of the log cabin. The stew had simmered on the stove since noon and would be perfectly tender and succulent in another hour.

They went into the small mudroom, and Lexie's thoughts wandered as she poured water from a pitcher over Aunt Kate's hands.

The little patchwork bag in her bedroom had been Mama's, but now it contained all the money Lexie had managed to save from the tomato canning over the past few years. Surely it was enough to give her a start. . . .

"Lexie, pay attention. You're spilling water," Aunt Kate sputtered. "What in the world is wrong with you?"

"I'm sorry. Here's the towel."

Lexie washed up and followed her aunt into the kitchen.

"Aunt Kate…" Lexie cleared her throat. "I've been thinking maybe I should get me a job in Marmoros."

"What?" The apron her aunt had picked up slipped from her fingers. "Why would you want to do that? This farm provides a good enough living without you working for someone else, doesn't it? More than enough for the three of us and Sarah, too."

"Yes, of course it does."

"I can give you more money from the tomato sales this summer."

"Oh no, I have plenty. It isn't that at all…you know I appreciate all you've done for Will and me since Mama and Papa died. And I think it's wonderful of you to add Will's name to the farm deed. But I can't let you or him take care of me forever, and now with Will getting married soon, I want to be on my own." This wasn't coming out right. How could she put something in words she didn't really understand herself? "I wouldn't be that far away."

Aunt Kate opened her mouth then clamped it shut. Oh dear, she wasn't happy at all. Would she forbid Lexie to get a job? "That there mining town isn't fit for a woman to walk in, much less work in. Saloons and such. The very idea. Why, I can hear their drunken brawls every Saturday night."

"I've never seen a saloon there. I think that's just a rumor someone started."

At her aunt's stare, Lexie swallowed. The noise from the saloon had carried, no denying that. The men who worked in the Marble Cave frequented it. And that was no rumor. "Well then, perhaps when I go into Forsyth for supplies next month I could check things out there."

"Forsyth? Why in the world would you want to go there? You can get everything we need at the general store."

"Now, Aunt Kate, you know the mining town cleans out most all of Mr. Hawkins' supplies."

Aunt Kate sighed. "Why can't Will fetch the supplies? I don't like the idea of you going into Forsyth alone." A worried frown puckered Aunt Kate's face. "Not that it's a bad town, but it has its share of riffraff."

"You know Will is going to be busy in the fields. I won't go near the boat landing. I'll wait until they unload and supply the stores. I promise, although it would be faster and cheaper to buy directly from the boats."

Lexie cringed as Aunt Kate sighed deeply. "You're a grown woman. I can't tell you what to do. But I wish you would think about this job thing."

"I have thought of it." Thought of nothing much else lately, in fact. "And I truly think this is what I should do."

Aunt Kate peered at Lexie, who lowered her lashes and bit her lip. "Humph. It sounds to me you have your mind made up already."

Warmth flooded Lexie's face.

Her aunt nodded. "Uh-huh. Well, like I said, you're a grown woman. I can't tell you what you can or can't do." She shook her head. "I don't know why you can't just marry Dan Wells or Tom Powers. They've been nosing around here long enough, and Lord knows you aren't getting any younger."

Lexie stiffened. She'd be hogswaggled if she'd marry the likes of one of those two and end up on a farm the rest of her life. She'd rather be an old maid.

Aunt Kate sniffed. "Sure hope you don't make a mistake."

A niggle of doubt wormed its way into Lexie's thoughts. What if she was making a mistake? She pressed her lips together and lifted her chin. So what if she was? What did she have to lose? She could always come back if things didn't work out. Lexie shuddered. No, that didn't bear thinking of. This was probably her last chance for a life of her own.

⚬⚬⚬

The morning air, caressing Lexie's face, was deliciously cool for the month of June. The fragrance of summer flowers wafted from the fields as she drove along beside the White River. Her favorite time of the day. And how she loved being so close to the rushing water. She'd like to take her time and enjoy the sights and scents of the countryside, but she couldn't dally if she wanted to get to Forsyth, buy supplies, and make it back before dusk.

She flicked the reins, and Jolly, their little gray mare, picked up speed. The mule would have been better for pulling the wagon over these hills, but Will needed Old Stubborn for the work.

She guided the mare away from the riverbank around a grove of walnut trees, and Mr. Hawkins's general store came into view. Should she stop or not? It wouldn't hurt to look and see what was still on his shelves. If she hurried, she could still make good time. Mr. Hawkins's prices were sometimes lower than the ones in Forsyth. Maybe she could save a little.

Urging Jolly toward the store, she pulled up in front of the long, unoccupied hitching post. She gathered her skirts, climbed down, and tied the horse to the post.

A bell over the door clanged when she walked into the building. A little shiver of pleasure rippled through Lexie at the spicy scent of cinnamon and cloves blended with the aromas of cedar and oak. Mr. Hawkins wasn't in sight, so she weaved her way through barrels of flour and sugar. Buckets labeled LARD stood in an aisle to her left. The very idea. It was sheer laziness to buy lard when anybody could render their own hog fat.

"Well, Miss Lexie, enjoying the nice day?" The proprietor limped a little as he made his way from the rear of the store and stepped up to her.

"Yes, Mr. Hawkins. How is business?" As if it wasn't obvious.

"A little slow today, but I've been busy all week, in spite of the mine closing down."

"The mine is closing? I hadn't heard."

"Yep. Guess they're tired of mining bat manure." He chuckled. "They must have been mighty disappointed when the cave didn't have the marble they expected to find. 'Spect Marmoros will be a ghost town within a week.

No one is likely to stay."

So, the job in Marmoros was no longer an option. At least Aunt Kate would be able to sleep on Saturday nights. "Would it be all right if I look around a little?" she asked then hastened to add, "Of course I'll purchase something."

"Please browse all you like. Call me if you need anything." He smiled, then turned and headed back to the rear of the room.

Mr. Hawkins was a good man. She'd pray that his business would prosper even if the mine was closing. After all, more settlers were moving into the area all the time since free land came up for grabs.

A splash of bright plaid caught her eye, and she glanced at the bolt of cloth expecting to see calico. Her breath caught in her throat. Silk. Real silk. She reached out and ran her hand gently across the smooth fabric. She swallowed past a lump in her throat and closed her eyes against the memory of the dress her mama had worn to the last harvest ball before the accident. Tears burned her eyes, and she jerked them open at the same time she yanked her hand away from the cloth.

"Pretty, isn't it?" She hadn't heard Mr. Hawkins walk up, but there he stood, an open wooden crate full of tall bottles in his hands and a curious look on his face.

"Yes, sir. Very pretty." She straightened her back and lifted her chin. "But dress goods aren't on my list today."

He nodded and walked behind the counter where he proceeded to place bottles of vanilla extract in a line on a narrow shelf. Now that was something that was on her list.

She continued through the store, checking prices, finding most of them lower than she was likely to find in Forsyth. "Well, thank you for allowing me to look, Mr. Hawkins. What time do you close today?" Lexie laid her hand on the counter, mentally tallying up what she'd need to buy in Forsyth and what she could get cheaper here.

"Five o'clock." He raised his eyebrows. "Where are you heading?"

"I'm driving to Forsyth to get some of my supplies." She blushed. "You don't seem to have everything I need. But I'll be back before you close and pick up what I can here."

"Good. See you then." He smiled warmly as he came from behind the counter and opened the door for her.

She started to follow, and her glance fell upon a notice on the wall behind the counter. HELP WANTED. Her heart jumped. Was it a sign? She gave a little laugh. No, of course not. If she worked here, she'd have to live at home and that would defeat her purpose. She headed toward the door.

"Miss Lexie."

At the store owner's voice, Lexie stopped and turned around.

"I noticed you looking at the sign. Would you by any chance know someone looking for part-time work?"

"What kind of work? You mean here in the store?"

"Yes, I expect to get mighty busy once tourists start flocking in."

Tourists? Whatever was the man talking about?

"What tourists?" She frowned, hoping he wasn't daft.

"Why, for the tours at Marble Cave. A man named Lynch bought the mine and all the land roundabout, including the town."

"Humph. Why anyone would travel to see a cave is beyond my understanding. Especially that one." She wrinkled her nose. "Bat manure."

Mr. Hawkins laughed. "I think they made a pretty good profit off the manure harvest. But they'll be harvesting history now. People are very interested in the story of Devil's Den, as the Indians used to call it."

"You may be right." She shook her head and opened the door. "Sorry, I can't think of anyone right now."

Lexie climbed into the wagon and waited while Jolly drank from the trough beneath the hitching post, then she flicked the reins and turned onto the road that led to Forsyth. A part-time job at the general store might not be too bad for a while. But she really had her heart set on working in town. And Mr. Hawkins probably wouldn't hire a woman anyway.

Chapter 2

Jack Sullivan planted his feet on the wet deck of the *Julia Dawn* and narrowed his eyes at Bull Thompson, his second-in-command. "Now, Thompson, keep the men in line. I don't want them half-drunk and surly when we're ready to push off downriver again. Those shoals need steady hands and minds."

"You can count on me, Cap'n." Thompson leaned on his mop. "They'll be on deck a full day before you get back here and are ready to shove off."

Jack nodded. He hated to leave the steamer even for the three days he reckoned it would take to wrap up Uncle Pat's business. Too bad the old guy hadn't had any children to leave his farm to. He sighed. Surely there would be someone who'd like to buy the land.

He mounted the chestnut mare he'd rented from the livery and rode through the teeming crowd of shoppers who'd come to the landing for supplies.

Suddenly a flash of blue caught his eye and the horse reared. A scream rent the air, and Jack struggled to bring the animal under control. Its hooves landed hard within a few inches of a huddled form on the street.

In seconds, Jack dismounted and ran to where the woman lay, looking stunned, amidst packages and folds of skirt and petticoats. "Ma'am, are you all right?" He gently tried to lift her, and she scrambled to her feet.

"Stop. What do you think you're doing?" A heavy reticule slammed against his shoulder and pain shot all the way to his elbow. Stormy blue eyes cut through him.

He grabbed her wrist before she could swing the bag again. Jack glanced over her swiftly with a practiced eye.

Black curls tumbled from beneath her bonnet, and frown lines creased her forehead as she jerked away from his grip. She planted her very pretty hands on her hips, and the glare from her deep blue eyes announced her displeasure.

Hmmm. Didn't seem to be any damage. "Only trying to help, ma'am. What were you doing walking out on the street in front of my horse?"

"Why I. . ." She sputtered then glared at him. "He wasn't there when I stepped off the curb."

Not wanting to call her a liar, he bit his lip and scowled. "Well, since you aren't hurt, I guess I'll be on my way." He gathered up her parcels and shoved them into her hands, then tipped his hat and started to remount.

"Wait a minute," her voice lashed out. "What about my ripped dress?"

Jack let his gaze run down the blue and white bodice of the dress to a small tear in the skirt that she was gripping with her free hand. He removed his small money bag from his jacket and held a gold coin out to her. "Here, this should cover the expense."

Slapping his hand away, she bit her lip. "Never mind. I don't want your money. But you could at least say you're sorry."

He grinned and bowed with a flourish. "Ma'am, I am very sorry my horse was in the way when you wanted to cross the street." He swung up onto the mare's back and tipped his hat, leaving her with her mouth hanging open.

Now, that was an interesting way to start the day. Too bad such a pretty little lady had an unreasonable temperament. Still, there was no denying she was very attractive standing there with her hands on her hips, anger darkening her lovely azure eyes. Just about the color of a clear October sky, in spite of the storm that had flashed from them. The picture stayed with him as he urged the horse into a canter, kicking up dirt as they left the town behind.

Jack whistled as he rode, surveying the countryside. Rolling hills, studded with oak and cedar trees, met his surveillance. Fog hung over the higher mountain ridges in the distance. Things hadn't changed much in the Missouri Ozarks. The place wasn't home to him, never had been from the day he went to live with his uncle. The past fifteen years the river had claimed that title and that was okay with him. It was a stroke of luck the telegram had finally caught up with him when he docked in St. Louis last month.

A pang of sadness pierced Jack at the thought of his old bachelor uncle's death, even though they hadn't gotten along from the minute Jack came to live with him at the age of twelve. He gave a short chuckle. That had been Jack's fault, more than likely. Looking back, he could still feel the pain and resentment. He must have made things really rough for Uncle Pat, his pa's only brother, the only family he had when his parents were killed in the barn fire. His uncle was more than likely as relieved as Jack when he took off at the age of sixteen.

He topped a hill and pulled up in surprise. A large, square building stood alone near the bank of the river. Now why hadn't he noticed it when they'd come downriver last night? The grove of walnut trees must have hidden it from view.

He clicked at the horse and headed down the hill, glancing at the sign as he passed by the building. HAWKINS'S GENERAL STORE. There must be a lot more people here than when he left to support a store.

A man stepped out on the porch carrying a broom and lifted a hand in greeting.

Jack nodded and rode on, mentally filing a reminder in his head to check with the man later. Could be a potential business deal there.

The sun had nearly sunk behind the hills when he pulled up in front of the still familiar farmhouse. The weathered logs were a little grayer than he remembered, but otherwise, the house looked pretty much the same.

Jack dismounted and led the mare to the new barn that overshadowed the side yard where the old shed used to stand. According to the telegram, the livestock, consisting of two mules, two goats, and a yearling steer, were being cared for by a neighbor named Jacob Williams. After caring for the horse, he walked back to the house, half expecting Uncle Pat to hobble out onto the porch.

Jack winced as he opened the front screen and heard a familiar squeak. Some things never changed. He stepped into the front room and took a deep breath. It didn't surprise him that the room was still neat as a pin. His uncle never could tolerate a mess. A framed photograph of Jack's parents greeted him from the mantel, and the old horseshoe still hung over the fireplace. He'd never known for sure if Uncle Pat was superstitious or just liked seeing the horseshoe hanging there.

The door shut behind him with a thud. As he stepped across the bare boards, a scurrying sound came from the direction of his uncle's bedroom. Frowning, he went to see what had taken up residence. He'd need to put some traps out if rats had taken over the place.

He pushed the door open, expecting to see a rodent run across the floor, but perfect stillness met him. Lifting his foot, he stomped once. Still nothing. He shrugged and headed for the kitchen.

Dishes with half-eaten food stood on the table. Jack tensed and glanced around, scanning the room. He walked softly over to the iron cookstove and touched the top. Warm. Someone had been there. And not long ago.

Jack picked up the broom from the corner and kicked open the pantry door. Jars of vegetables and preserves stood on the deep shelves and bins full of flour and sugar lined the back wall. Otherwise, it was empty. He backed out and retraced his steps to the bedroom where he'd heard the sounds earlier.

Taking a deep breath, he crashed through the door yelling at the top of his lungs and swinging the broom in an arc. Screams reverberated from wall to wall, and two small figures darted from behind the bed. Jack reached out as they tried to shoot past him and grabbed one in each hand. He yelped in pain as teeth clamped down on his hand. "Why you little. . . Hold it! Stop your squirming. No one is going to hurt you."

The struggling stopped, and Jack stared in amazement at two identical little overalls-clad girls shivering with fear before him.

oⅢ0

"Now let me get this straight." Jack paced up and down the floor in front of the brown horsehair sofa where the two wide-eyed girls perched. "You've been staying here since your pa died in a mining accident?"

Two blond heads, covered with dirty tangles, bobbed in unison.

"Where's your ma?"

The girls eyed each other.

"Well?" How was he going to get to the bottom of this if they wouldn't tell him what was going on?

"Ma died in Kentucky when we were two. We had a stepma named Bella, but she ran off with the doctor last year." Jack stared at the little girl who'd spoken in such a matter-of-fact way.

"The doctor?" Sympathy washed over him.

"Yep, you know, the one who sells elixir from the gods and all that other stuff."

A traveling huckster. He looked at the beautiful little motherless girls. His stomach tightened and he clenched his teeth. How could a mother walk out on her children?

"How did you know the house was empty?" Good, his voice was almost normal. *Lord, keep them talking until I can figure out what to do.*

The other twin spoke up. "Well land's sake, our pa knew old man Sullivan. Told us if anything ever happened to him to come here. So we did."

"You walked?"

"Naw. Rode Pa's old mule, Buzzard Bait. But then we knocked and we knocked but no one answered, so we sat on the porch and waited for him to come home. But he didn't. Our old stupid mule took off, and we sure didn't want to start out walking to nowhere, so we stayed. Finally we got hungry and went inside."

"We didn't break in though. The door wasn't locked."

"We didn't know the old man was dead though. Just figured he went somewhere."

Jack ran his hands through his hair. The story sounded a little bit far-fetched, but why would they lie about it? The question now was what could he do with these girls? It would be a shame to send them to an orphanage, but they sure couldn't stay here alone. They couldn't be more than seven or eight. "How old are you girls?"

"We'll be ten next year." The girl showed no sign of humor as she spoke.

"So that would make you nine, right?" He tried not to grin.

The other girl frowned. "Stop lying, Abby."

Tuck shrugged. "We just turned eight last month."

Jack turned to her sister. "I guess you must have a name, too."

"Sure, it's Adeline. But Abby calls me Addy. She's really Abigail."

"No, I ain't." The girl stuck a grubby paw in his direction and shook his hand soundly. "The name's Kentucky. You can call me Tuck if you like."

Addy rolled her eyes and shook her head but didn't say anything.

This was getting stranger by the minute.

"And a last name, please?"

"Flanigan," Tuck replied then grinned. "Pa said it used to be O'Flanigan, but our grandfather lost the *O* in a game of cards on the way over from Ireland."

He hid a smile, wondering how many times he'd heard the same joke with a different name. "Okay. Well, Addy and Kentucky Flanigan, we seem to have a bit of a problem here."

Both girls stiffened. "Can't we live here with you?" Addy's blue eyes brimmed with tears.

Jack's stomach churned. "Honey, I wish you could. But I'm going to have to sell this place. You see, I own a steamboat and that's where I live—on the river."

"Oh." Tuck's eyes lit up. "That's all right. I always wanted to go on a riverboat. Couldn't we live with you there?"

Jack flinched as he thought of the innocent little girls in the midst of the rough and brash swabs that worked up and down the rivers from here to the Mississippi. "Sorry, that won't be possible."

Jumping off the sofa, Tuck stomped her foot. "Well, why not? Don't you like us?" Addy joined her sister and they stood, hands on hips, brows wrinkled, reminding him of the young woman he'd nearly run over that morning.

"Of course I like you. But, you see, it's a working boat, and besides there's no place on there that's suitable for girls."

"Huh! I'll bet you just don't like girls." Addy's bottom lip thrust out and she frowned.

Tuck stomped her small foot again. "And just what's wrong with girls?"

"Never mind, Tuck. I don't think a riverboat would be a very nice place for girls to live, anyway."

Her sister rolled her eyes. "Don't be such a sissy."

Jack gulped then took a deep breath. He'd faced drunken sailors and shoals that threatened to tear his boat into pieces. Two little girls weren't going to get the best of him. "Well, for one thing, females are unreasonable and throw tantrums. I said I can't take you with me. And that's that."

Tuck's lips quivered then Addy's did the same. A sob erupted from one throat then the other. Before he knew it, both girls were squalling like a thunderstorm on the river.

Now what could he do? "Hey, don't cry. Let me think about it. I'll figure out something."

⚓

The embers in the fireplace sputtered, spewing sparks onto the ashes. Jack sighed and leaned forward in the ladder-backed rocking chair, his head in both hands. Tuck and Addy lay curled up together in the feather bed in the small bedroom that Jack had called his own until he was sixteen. He'd tried to go to sleep in Uncle Pat's oversized bed, but thoughts whirled in his mind. Of course, there was no way he could take the girls with him on the steamer. It was a shame that the sweet-faced twins would have to end up in an orphanage after all, but there was no other solution.

Unless. . . Maybe the storekeeper would know of a family that might take them in. Surely someone would have compassion for two little motherless girls. Jack didn't have to tell them about their tempers. Yep, that was the answer. He'd ride over there tomorrow and have a talk with the man. Then he'd get his uncle's business settled. He could be back on the *Julia Dawn* and ready to head downriver toward Batesville, Arkansas, with a load by the end of the week.

Chapter 3

Lexie sighed. Should she take the job at the Hawkins store or not? She had been crushed when she hadn't found suitable employment in Forsyth. Then after spending so much time searching for a job, she'd broken her word to Aunt Kate and hurried to the docks to do some fast shopping.

The incident with the horse had slowed her down as well. Now she found, to her chagrin, she couldn't get the face of that rude, impossible man out of her mind. There was no denying he was handsome with those dark-brown eyes that seemed to stare into her soul, but oh how cocky and egotistical. If she ever saw him again she'd give him a piece of her mind that he'd never forget.

"Lexie, you just kicked the corn seed right out of the furrow."

Startled out of her disturbing thoughts, Lexie threw an apologetic glance at Will and dropped to her knees. She packed the dirt carefully around the seed. Without corn to harvest, Jolly and Old Stubborn would be mighty hungry when last year's feed ran out.

"Lexie." She looked up in surprise at the worry in Will's voice.

"Wh–what's wrong?"

"You've been acting strange ever since you got home last night. Did something happen in Forsyth?"

"Oh, it was nothing." She tossed him a grin. "Except a horse nearly ran me over down at the landing."

"Landing?" Aunt Kate stood at the end of the row, her hand inside a small bag of seed corn. Lightning flashed from her eyes. "You promised you wouldn't go down by the boats."

Uh-oh. Lexie cringed at the accusation and guilt squeezed her middle.

"Well, Will Rayton? What do you have to say to your sister? I can't do anything with her anymore." Her frown washed over Lexie. Then she looked back at Will. "You need to take over the buying from now on."

Will winked at Lexie, then coughed and covered his mouth, hiding a smile. "Don't worry. I'll get onto her good when we're done with the planting today."

Lexie ducked her head to hide a grin and scooted down the row, pressing the dirt over the seeds. As if he could tell her what to do. She'd been bossing him around all his life.

"I'm sorry, Aunt Kate. The stores weren't stocked yet when I arrived in town. I wouldn't have made it back before dark if I'd waited." She bit her lip. Well, it was probably true. She would have been pushing the limit. It was easier to go ahead and buy from the boats.

"Humph. Well then. I wouldn't have wanted you to ride back in the dark." The familiar worry lines creased her forehead. "But I think maybe you'd better let Will go to Forsyth from now on."

"Maybe we'll both go." Will raised an eyebrow in Lexie's direction.

"Good idea. I wouldn't mind being escorted by my handsome brother."

"Oh, you two. I know when I'm being hogwashed." A glimmer of a smile started in Aunt Kate's faded blue eyes, made its way to the corner of her lips, and was soon a full-blown grin. She folded the empty seed bag and stuck it under her arm. "Let's get supper on the table, Lexie. It's almost sundown."

They walked arm in arm, bathed in the soft glow of the setting sun. Lexie sighed. Her second favorite time of day.

$\sim$

"Lexie, wake up, wake up!" Will's voice invaded Lexie's dream, and she sat straight up in bed. "Get up, Lexie. There's a fire somewhere. They may need our help."

In a flash, Lexie jumped out of bed as her brother rushed out of the room. She dressed quickly and hurried to the kitchen. The door of the mudroom stood open and she hurried outside.

Will rode out of the barn on Jolly.

She wrinkled her nose at the acrid smell of smoke. What could be burning? "Can you tell what it is?"

"Can't see any flames, but it could be the mine or the town." He mounted the horse. "I'm heading in that direction. Sure hope I'm wrong."

"Wait, I'm coming with you." She started to put her foot in the stirrup.

"You'd better let Aunt Kate know. She'll worry if she wakes and finds us gone."

"Don't you dare leave without me." She ran inside, wrote a quick note that she left propped up on the kitchen table, then grabbed a bonnet and tied it on while running back outside.

Lexie clung to Will's shirt as Jolly galloped up the hill toward Marble Cave and Marmoros. *Dear God, please don't let anyone be hurt.*

"It looks like the whole town is in flames!"

Fear stabbed at Lexie's heart at her brother's frantic words. She didn't know anyone in Marmoros, but her throat tightened at the thought of people being trapped inside the buildings.

"Hurry, Will. Go faster." But what could they do if the fire was out of control? Were there children living there, families? Or had they already left? Mr. Hawkins had said everyone would be clearing out. She prayed he was right.

Lexie grabbed tighter to Will's shirt as Jolly sped up. She coughed as the smoke got thicker.

"Maybe I better let you off here, Lexie. The smoke's really getting bad."

"No, I can stand it if you can." She gasped and yanked her skirt up to cover her face.

"Okay, but it's gonna be hot in there. I can feel the heat already."

So could she, even through the long sleeves that covered her arms.

They saw the roaring flames long before they reached the top of the hill. Jolly reared and tried to turn.

"We'll have to walk the rest of the way!" Will was already off the horse, holding his arms up to her as the mare shied and reared once more.

Lexie fell into Will's arms, gasping as Jolly ran down the hill, hopefully toward home.

"C'mon." Lexie scowled as Will started up the hill, leaving her to make her own way. Well, she'd do just fine on her own.

The incline wasn't that steep, but her breathing came in short gulps in the smoke-thickened air. She came over the rise and froze.

Will and another man stood side by side watching the roaring flames destroy the town. Why were they just standing there?

"Come on. We have to help." She grabbed Will's arm and tried to drag him toward the burning buildings.

"No, Lexie." He jerked back, almost causing her to fall. "Look around. Do you see anyone? Or even an animal?"

Lexie stood, gasping from the heat. Nothing moved except the flames and falling stores and cabins, and there wasn't a sound besides the roar of the fire and the crash of burning logs and shattering glass. Fear shot through her. Was everyone dead? Or had they all left?

She turned toward her brother and took a sharp breath as her gaze fell on the man standing beside him. In spite of his smoke-blackened skin, she didn't doubt his identity for a moment. The cad from Forsyth. What was he doing here?

Tearing her gaze from him, she blinked her eyes against flying ash and looked at Will. "Maybe someone is alive in there."

"Lexie, the town's been emptying out all week. There's no one there. We need to get away from this heat."

"But what could have caused the fire?"

Will shook his head and leaned over, coughing.

The other man cleared his throat and swayed, then caught himself. "It was arson. Men were riding off just as I got here. One of them shot at me as he passed."

"Who?"

He swiped a sleeve across his eyes, smearing the soot, then winced as though in pain. "I've no idea. They wore hoods."

Lexie glanced quickly at Will. Bald Knobbers. It had to be.

"They didn't hit you, did they?" Will asked.

"Just a graze." He swayed again and would have fallen if Will hadn't caught him.

"Whoa there, mister. Let me take a look at that shoulder."

Nausea rose in Lexie's throat. Blood was trickling down the man's forearm to his fingers.

※

Jack let the young man ease him down onto the log. He tried to protest as he saw the boy poised to tear his shirt away, but he couldn't seem to get a sound past his throat. He must have lost more blood than he'd realized to cause this much dizziness. No wonder he was hallucinating. As if that woman would be here.

He clenched his teeth as probing fingers examined the wound.

The young man whistled. "Looks like a bullet went right through your shoulder."

Jack nodded. He had to get back to the farm before the twins woke up and thought he'd run out on them. He'd awakened Addy and told her what was going on, but she'd just grunted and turned over. He had no idea whether she understood. He tried to rise, and a wave of dizziness hit him.

"Don't try to move. I'm going to bind this up until we can get you home." The boy worked as he spoke. "Do you have a horse nearby? I didn't see one when I came in."

"He's tied up over there." He waved toward a grove of trees then closed his eyes.

"Okay, easy now. Maybe you'd better try to stay awake."

A groan was the only thing he could manage. His head swam but he forced his eyes open.

"Lexie, come here a minute, please."

Jack attempted to focus on the figure of the girl coming toward them, but everything was a blur.

"Lexie, I hate to ask, but would you mind fetching this fellow's horse from the grove yonder? Ride him to the farm and fetch Old Stubborn. I'd go, but..." He glanced at Jack and shrugged at the young woman, who had averted her face.

Of course he'd send her. He wouldn't leave his wife or whoever she was with a perfect stranger. Even if the stranger was threatening to fall over at any second.

She turned and Jack blinked. He must have already passed out. This had to be a dream. The woman was the same one he'd nearly run over in town. He chuckled and everything went black.

※

Humph. Not only was he a cad, he fainted over a little lost blood. Lexie rode the stranger's horse and led Old Stubborn, who carried Will and the injured man. Will held onto him with one hand and the mule's harness with the other. Remorse ran through her. Will thought it was a pretty bad wound. So maybe the man wasn't such a weakling after all.

It was a lucky thing he'd revived long enough to tell them he lived on

Sullivan's farm. He must be the nephew who'd run off years ago. Way before she and Will had moved here. He'd probably been bumming around the country ever since. Although, he hadn't seemed like a bum when she'd seen him in Forsyth—just a cad.

The first rays of dawn were painting the sky when she turned the horse into the Sullivan yard. With a sigh of relief, Lexie dismounted and hurried over to help Will.

The man, who'd been unconscious since they'd left the burned-out town, moaned and woke as Will lifted him off the mule's back. He grabbed Will's arm and steadied himself.

The screen door flew open and a little girl in overalls ran out, her shoulder strap hanging loose and hair streaming around her face. "Pa! Pa!"

Pa? Surprise knifed at Lexie's mind while a niggle of disappointment bit at her. She brushed it aside.

Before the child reached them, her double shot through the door. Twins?

The man wobbled, and his eyes narrowed as he opened his mouth to speak to the girls. Then he fell over, hitting the ground at Lexie's feet.

Lexie headed for the girls while Will picked the man up and carried him toward the house.

"Don't worry." She leaned over until she could look in the girls' eyes. "Your pa was shot, but he'll be all right. My brother will fix him up as good as new. Where is your mother?"

They glanced at each other.

"She run off with a doctor. A huckster kind." The girl spoke matter-of-factly, while her sister gave a nod.

"Oh, I'm sorry. Well then, could I speak with whoever is taking care of you?"

"Ain't no one. Just Pa." The little girl grinned and glanced at her sister.

"Yep. Just Pa." She sighed. "Now that our uncle Pat died."

The poor little things. And the poor man. But then, where were the girls when she saw him in Forsyth? Surely they hadn't been here all alone after Mr. Sullivan had passed away. That was weeks ago.

She forced herself to speak calmly. "I'm Lexie. What can I call you?"

"I'm Tuck." She motioned to her sister. "That's Addy."

Tuck? What sort of name was that for a little girl? Lexie stood and held her hands out toward the girls. "I'm happy to meet you, Tuck and Addy. How about if we go inside and find something for breakfast?"

"That would be nice, Miss Lexie." Addy cast a sweet smile at her and reached for her hand. "Oh, and my sister's name is really Abby."

Tuck frowned at her sister. "Yes, ma'am. I like Tuck best, but you can call me Abby if you want to." Tuck took her other hand and smiled, too.

The little darlings. Surely they deserved better than to be abandoned by their mother and raised by a cad like their father. She'd be sure to have a talk with that man as soon as he recovered.

Chapter 4

Jack groaned and opened his eyes. Severe pain shot through his arm and shoulder, and his whole upper body was one big burning ache. He blinked and shook his head, then tried to sit up. Agonizing pain gripped him and he gasped.

"Whoa there, pardner. I wouldn't try to get up just yet if I was you."

A blurry face bobbed in front of Jack's eyes, and he blinked to try to clear his vision. "The fire. You were at the fire." The words weren't much more than a croak escaping Jack's raw, sore throat.

"That's right. You were shot. By the Bald Knobbers, I'd guess. My sister and I brought you home after you passed out."

A flash of blue and a cascade of black curls assaulted Jack's memories. Sister. So she wasn't just a dream, and she wasn't the man's wife. Confusion swirled around his mind. Somehow he'd linked the woman from last night with the one who'd stepped in front of his horse.

Jack resisted the heaviness that pressed against his eyelids. There was something else he needed to remember. What? "The twins," he whispered.

"The girls went home with my sister. Don't worry. They'll love our farm. Lexie and Aunt Kate will take good care of them."

A niggling worry wormed its way around in Jack's head. He wasn't sure why.

~~~~

Lexie knew her own eyes were as round as those of the twins as she listened to Addy's frightening tale.

Aunt Kate had gone to bed hours ago, and Lexie had brought Addy and Tuck out on the front porch for some fresh air, planning to put them to bed shortly. But two hours had passed as the girls told one horrifying tale after another about their time alone after their great uncle died.

"So what did you do when you came face-to-face with the bear?" Lexie's voice trembled.

Addy glanced at her sister, who was telling the story. "Yep, Ab. . .er, Tuck. Tell her what we did."

An owl hooted somewhere in the darkness and Lexie jumped, placing her hand to her chest. One thing was sure. They knew how to make someone's hair stand on end.

Tuck sucked on her top lip and looked up at the sky. "Well now, I'll tell you. It was mighty scary. And I thought we were prob'ly gonna end up tore to pieces. But I remembered I had a slice of sweet tater pie in my pocket, so I grabbed it and held it toward that bear so's he could get a good whiff. Then

I threw it over his head as far as I could. It landed up on a tree limb, and that ole bear took off after that pie lickety-split. Then I grabbed Addy by the hand, and we ran fast as we could back to the cabin."

Lexie frowned. "Really?"

"Yep." Tuck's blond curls bobbed up and down. "Everyone knows the bears around here love sweet tater pie."

Lexie bit her lip. Okay, this was too much. Especially after the tale about the Indians who had tried to scalp them. She'd been here long enough to know there weren't any wild Indians in Missouri anymore. She didn't want to think the girls would lie, but this was ridiculous. "Are you girls making up tall tales?"

"Oh no, ma'am. We wouldn't tell lies. Especially after you've been so nice to us."

Lexie sighed. "All right. I think it's time you two were in bed." She led them to the spare bedroom and found that Aunt Kate had already turned down the covers and laid out nightgowns for them. After helping them with their prayers, she tucked them in and blew the lamp out, then went to her own room.

Bothered by the obvious falsehoods the children had told, she lay awake for a long time. They seemed so sweet otherwise. Addy, who could be very straitlaced with her sister even while mischief danced in her own eyes, and Tuck, whose misplaced sense of fun probably got them both in trouble quite often.

But what could one expect after what they'd been through? After all, their father had left them in the care of an old man while he pursued his adventures. Then the time they'd spent on their own... She shuddered. Even if none of the horror stories they'd told her were true, anything could have happened to two young girls living all alone, not to mention the fear they must have endured.

She would simply have to be patient with them and teach them right from wrong while they were here. She'd start with a Bible lesson in the morning. She thumped her pillow and settled in for what she hoped would be a good night's sleep.

While they were cleaning the kitchen after breakfast, she informed the girls of her plans.

Tuck handed the plate she'd just dried to Addy to put on the shelf. She placed both hands on her hips and frowned. "But you said you'd take us to the river."

"And so I will. But not today."

"But you said." Tuck stomped her small foot.

"Young lady, I said I would take you there one day. I didn't say today. And please don't stomp your foot. That's very rude."

The girl opened her mouth but clamped it shut when her sister shook her head. The girls stood side by side, looking at her.

"You'll like the Bible stories. I promise." She paused, and when the girls both looked unconvinced, she quickly changed plans about which lesson she'd teach. "The first one we'll read is about lions."

"Lions? Really?" The sudden animation on the twins' faces sent a wave of relief through Lexie.

Well, okay, if that's what it took, she'd build every lesson around lions and fiery furnaces. After all, some of the best lessons could be learned from these stories of old. "Really. Now let's hurry and finish our chores. Then you can help me weed the garden. If we get everything done, perhaps we'll go to the creek for a picnic lunch. We can have our Bible lesson after supper tonight."

High-pitched laughter pealed across the valley. Lexie glanced over in amusement. Addy and Tuck stood ankle deep in the stream, splashing water on each other. They'd wanted to go to the river, but Lexie wasn't quite brave enough to corral the high-strung girls along the churning waters of the White River. Sweet as molasses one minute and as vindictive as a hive of interrupted bees the next, caring for these two was becoming quite an adventure.

The delicious aroma of fried chicken tantalized Lexie's senses as she spread the food out on the clean white sheet. "C'mon out of the water, girls. Time to eat."

Tuck scooped one last blast of water in Addy's face and took off running through the shallow creek.

"No fair! I'll get you for that." Addy sputtered and headed after her sister, vengeance written all over her.

"You'll have to get even next time, Addy. I want you girls to dry off so we can eat." Lexie glanced at the spread and grinned. "Look, sweet potato pie and not a bear in sight."

Tuck ducked her head and scrubbed with the dry towel. "Okay, I made up part of the story about the bear. But we really did see a bear cub once, when were playing in the woods."

"Yes, and if that cub's mama had come along, we'd have been in big trouble." Addy gave an emphatic nod, causing kinky wet strands of hair to flop into her face.

"Well, there aren't any cubs or their mamas by this creek today, so let's eat. Would one of you like to give thanks for our food?"

"Sure, I will." Addy bowed her head. "Thanks, Almighty God, for the chicken and biscuits and pickles and sweet tater pie. And please don't let no bears come try to steal our grub. Amen."

Lexie bit back a grin and cleared her throat. "That was very nice, Addy." She handed them filled plates and settled down with her own. It was time for her to find out what she could about their situation. "How long has your mother been gone? It's strange I haven't heard anything about her or you, for that matter."

Addy sent a quick look at her sister, who squinted for a moment then said,

"Oh, we weren't here but a few months. See, when our ma ran off, Pa brought us here so our uncle could take care of us while he worked on his boat. I reckon no one knew we were here on account of all the snow this year. We never went anywhere and neither did our uncle."

Okay. That made sense. After all, she and Will and Aunt Kate had been snowed in for weeks as well. And with homesteads so far apart, they didn't see their neighbors very often. Folks here in the Ozarks stayed pretty close to home once the weather turned bad. But still. . .

"Well, you must have had to tell someone when your uncle died."

Both girls stared for a moment.

"Well, you see"—Addy crimped her forehead and sniffled—"we didn't know what to do. 'Cause we were afraid they'd take us to an orphans' home. So. . ."

Tuck cleared her throat. "Just when we'd decided we'd have to chance it, a wagon pulled up and someone called out for Uncle Pat."

"Sure did." Tuck nodded at her sister. "We ran out back and hid in the root cellar for a long time. When we heard the wagon leave, we sashayed inside. Uncle Pat was gone."

Hmmm. Well, that sort of made sense. She'd heard that someone found the old man while stopping by. "You must have been very frightened."

They nodded solemnly. Silent for a change.

"And you haven't heard from your mother in all this time?"

"No, ma'am." Addy's face crumpled and she blinked rapidly. "I reckon she just don't care about us no more."

"Yep. She just quit lovin' us after that huckster doc come along." Tuck's bottom lip trembled.

"Oh, you poor little things." Lexie scooted over and enveloped both girls in her arms. "I'm so sorry I brought the subject up. You don't have to talk about it anymore."

Tuck sniffled. "Thank you, Miss Lexie. Could we go play in the creek some more before we go back to your place?"

"Of course you can. You go right along and play while I gather things up."

With sighs, the twins stood and headed for the creek. Within minutes Lexie heard them laughing again. She breathed a sigh of relief. She hadn't realized how quickly children could get over a sad moment. But she was so glad they did.

They arrived back at the farm just in time to wash up and help Aunt Kate prepare supper.

After they'd cleaned up the kitchen, Lexie got her Bible and two writing tablets and pencils from her room, and she and the girls went outside and sat on the porch swing.

The twins listened in rapt astonishment as she read the story of Daniel in the lions' den.

"Oh my." Addy's eyes were shining. "Do you mean those lions didn't even try to tear Daniel to bits?"

"That's right. The Bible says God closed the lions' mouths."

"How'd He close 'em? Did He tie their jaws together?" Tuck frowned. "And did the lions try to bite God?"

"No, Tuck. Nothing can hurt God. And the Bible doesn't say how He did it. Maybe He just wouldn't let them open their mouths." Leave it to Tuck to ask this sort of question.

"But why would God do that?"

"Because Daniel loved God and obeyed Him. He refused to bow to the king's image, even though he knew he might be killed. So God saved him from the lions."

"God must really be strong then." The words were only whispered from Addy's lips.

"Yes, God is very strong. And very powerful. There's nothing He can't do."

When neither girl spoke, Lexie smiled and stood up. "How about you girls each write what you thought about the story and what lesson you've learned. Tomorrow night, you can read them to me, and we'll talk about it some more."

Lexie stood and walked to the door. When she looked back, the girls were looking from each other to the tablets in their hands, panic on their faces. Understanding flooded Lexie, and remorse stabbed at her heart. How could she have been so stupid? "You know what? I'll just ask some questions. And how would you like to begin reading lessons?"

Relief flooded both faces, and two big grins tugged at Lexie's heart. She only hoped they'd have enough time for the lessons before their father came to get them.

Chapter 5

Jack leaned forward on the fence rail and squinted against the late afternoon sun. The roan, which should have been back at the livery a week ago, pranced around the corral while Will Rayton saddled the horse he called Jolly.

After leading the horse out the gate, Will stopped and shoved his hat back, a grin on his friendly face. "You shore look a sight better than you did two weeks ago."

"Thanks to you. If you hadn't rescued me and stayed and tended my wound, I'd have likely died."

"I'm sure you'd have done the same for me."

"And thanks for your family taking the twins." He grinned. "I hope they haven't been a lot of trouble for your aunt and sister."

"Naw. Aunt Kate loves kids. Otherwise she'd have likely thrown me in the river as ornery as I was. And the girls seemed pretty sweet to me."

"Yes." Sure they were. "They can be."

The young man swung into the saddle and reached down to shake Jack's hand. "I'll tell Lexie to get the girls ready so you can come get them. Tonight I reckon?"

Jack cleared his throat. He'd been thinking about this all day but felt a little nervous now that the time had come to broach the question.

"Uh, I was wondering. Do you think your family could possibly see clear to keep the girls until I get back?" At the surprise on Will's face, he hastened to add, "Of course I'll pay for their care, and they'll need clothes. I think all they have are two pairs of overalls each. I'd planned to try to look for a family in the area to take them in, but since I've been down so long and have to get back to my business, I don't know what to do. If my crew has done their job, we'd best be heading back downriver tonight. I don't want to put the poor things in an orphanage unless it's absolutely necessary."

"Wh–what? An orphanage? What's wrong with you, man? Can't you take them with you?"

Surprise shot through Jack as he stared at the look of shock on Will's face. Did he really expect Jack to take two children he barely knew on the river with him?

Oh, what was he thinking? "Look, it's all right. Forgive me for asking. You've done enough, and I don't blame you for not wanting to be bothered any longer. I'll try to find someone in Forsyth to take them in. It might set me back a few days, but I'll just have to try. I really don't want to take them to an orphanage except as the last option."

"W–w–wait," Will sputtered. "We'll keep them. You don't need to worry about paying anything. Enjoy your trip on the river."

Jack stared in wonder as Will kneed his horse and took off at a gallop. What in the world was stuck in the young fellow's craw? He scratched his head and frowned.

Well, at least the twins would be taken care of while he was gone. He'd find a home for them soon. Surely someone in Forsyth or maybe one of the homesteads along the river would be happy to make a home for two beautiful little girls.

Still, he couldn't help wondering at Will's behavior. Maybe he should go say good-bye to the girls and make sure the Raytons were the good folk he'd thought they were and that they wouldn't dump the girls off on someone unsuitable. But he couldn't believe Will was like that. The man'd taken care of him for two weeks and wouldn't take a thing in return. Besides, Jack had to hurry back to Forsyth and his men on the *Julia Dawn* before they decided to hire on with someone else.

But he'd make a quick stop at the general store on the way and tell Hawkins about the girls and their needs. Maybe by the time he got back, the man would have found a home for them.

⌘⌘⌘

Lexie couldn't find words. Grief shot through her. How could a father be so callous? "Will, are you sure that's what he said?"

They stood by the barn. When Will had called her out, she'd thought he was going to tell her that Mr. Sullivan wanted them to take his daughters home. The thought had saddened her; she'd grown to love them so much in just two short weeks. But oh, if only that had been the case. She could have handled her own sadness. But the thought of theirs was too much to contemplate.

Will nodded. "I couldn't believe it either. But he said it all right. Just as calm as could be."

Through her grief, a spark of anger ignited in Lexie's heart. Jack Sullivan was every bit the kind of man she'd thought him to be when she'd first set eyes on him. No, worse. He was a monster. He must be. Only a monster would think of placing his own daughters into an orphanage so that he could go about his own business. It wasn't as though he had no other means of making a living. He had the farm. But no, he must have his adventures up and down the river without a thought for his adorable twin girls.

Absently, she tapped her foot on the ground and lines furrowed her forehead. "Will, we can't let them know what he's planning. It would devastate them. And we need to make it seem as though he wanted very much to come tell them good-bye but was unable to do so."

"I hate to lie." The sins of lying and the punishment thereof were some of the first things that had been impressed on both Lexie and Will from the time they were small.

"We won't. We'll just let them know we want them to stay longer. That part is true. And if they ask questions, we'll simply have to be evasive. I won't have them heartbroken, Will!"

"Sure. You're right, Lexie. They'll be fine. After all, you did say they hardly seemed to miss their father at all."

"Well, that's probably because he's been gone most of the time. They're used to not having him around." She took a deep breath and blew back the strands of hair that had fallen over her forehead. "But if I could have one minute with that horrible man right now, I'd tell him just what I think of him." And she didn't care if his dark-brown eyes did send chills down her spine. She'd show him chills when she saw him again.

She sent up a prayer to God for help and headed for the house to tell Tuck and Addy the news that they would be staying for a while longer. She found the girls drying the breakfast dishes under the scrutiny of Aunt Kate's very particular eyes.

"Lexie! See what I can do." Tuck held a plate between two fingers and would have tried to spin it, but Aunt Kate grabbed it and placed it safely in the cupboard. "Aw, I wouldn't have dropped it."

"Umm-hmm. Well, let's not take a chance, young lady." Aunt Kate's quiet voice and calm face caused Lexie's lips to turn up at the corners. No one would guess from her aunt's composure those dishes had come over from England with Lexie's great-grandmother.

"When you girls are done, come in the parlor, please. I need to speak to you about something."

A look of dread passed between the two girls. Lexie had noticed that look every time she took them aside for a talk. What in the world were they worried about?

"They can go with you now, Lexie. I'll finish up."

"If you're sure. Thank you, Aunt Kate."

Lexie took each girl by the hand and led them into the parlor. She sat on the settee and motioned the girls to sit beside her. She stared across the room at the organ in the corner, wishing she could forget her news and have fun with the girls instead.

She took a deep breath and looked at the girls. "I have some very good news for you." She hoped the lilt in her voice was enough to convince them.

"What?" they chorused, matching expectant grins on their faces. At least the dread was gone.

"Well, it's good news for me anyway. And I hope you'll feel the same."

"Well, land's sake!" Tuck strummed her fingers against her knee. "What is it?"

"Well, your father had to leave rather suddenly. He was very late because of being incapacitated for so long."

"Inca-what?"

"I mean that he was ill and got behind."

"So he's gone?" Tuck looked too happy for a girl who'd just been told her father had left without telling her good-bye.

"What about us?" Addy's blue eyes clouded with worry.

"Why, you're going to stay with me until he returns. Is that all right?"

"All right?" Tuck jumped up and hooked her thumbs in her overalls straps. "That's great!"

Addy reached over and put her small hand over Lexie's. "Thank you, Miss Lexie, for letting us stay."

Lexie's chest tightened and she fought back tears. The girls seemed glad their father had gone away. And she intended to find out why.

But first, she'd make some dresses for Addy and Tuck. The overalls were all right for play, but there was a tent-meeting preacher coming to the area right after harvest. Maybe she'd even purchase the plaid silk. Hmmm. Probably not suitable for little girls.

A ripple went through her at the thought of the plaid silk against her skin. Then she shoved the thought away. Her blue muslin would do quite well. And her girls would be properly dressed.

⁂

Jack could hear the sweet tones of Pap Sanders' fiddle when he was still blocks away from the *Julia Dawn*. He left the horse at the livery and walked the two blocks to the boat. At least he knew Pap, his cook and old-time friend, hadn't deserted him. Pap was the closest thing to a father he'd had all these years. He had taught him everything he knew about the river and life on a steamer. And he was sure of Bull Thompson. But if the others had gotten restless, they might very well have signed on with someone else without a backward glance.

The dock was busy with activity. He reached the *Julia Dawn*, relieved to see crates swinging through the air toward the deck of his boat and noisy activity both on and off the boat. He headed up the gangplank and jumped on deck, grinning in satisfaction at the crates and barrels that covered almost every inch of the lower deck.

"There you are. I knew you'd get here in time." Relief was evident in Thompson's voice, and he hurriedly ran his hand across his mouth to hide the smile. "We've got everything about ready. Just have a few more crates to load."

"I notice the upper deck is only half-filled."

"Got a few passengers headin' to St. Louie for some meeting," Thompson said. "Wasn't sure what you'd want to do, but I figgered since their passage paid more than freight, you'd wanna take them on. They should be here any minute. Then we can batten down and shove off whenever you say the word."

"Consider the word said. I'll go to my quarters and change out of these duds." By the time Jack got back on deck, the dock was a half mile behind them. He rocked with the movement of the boat beneath his feet, a feeling that was as much a part of him as breathing air. The twins would probably love it here.

He stopped stock-still. Now why would he think something like that? The twins were much better off with Lexie Rayton. She'd teach them how to look and act like ladies.

"What are you simperin' like that for?" Pap Sanders appeared at his side. "If I didn't know better, I'd think you wuz lovesick or somethin'."

Jack looked at Pap. "Huh? You know better than that. I'm just tired."

"You sure? You didn't meet some silly woman, did you? They'll ruin a man, you know."

Jack laughed. "Of course not." But a vision of Lexie Rayton's flashing eyes and full, rosy lips caused him to catch his breath.

"Hey, Pap, I've missed your fiddling. Maybe after chow tonight you could give us a few tunes. The passengers might appreciate some entertainment."

"Sure thing, Cap'n."

Having averted Pap's curiosity and his too-near-the-truth intuition, Jack headed for the wheel. It wouldn't do for Pap to know how often his thoughts turned to the feisty beauty who had invaded his life, his thoughts, even his dreams. But if he had a say in it, she'd not get close enough to invade his heart.

Chapter 6

Jack awoke to the familiar squeal of escaping steam. A strong smell of wood smoke pouring forth from the smokestacks battled with the aroma of frying bacon. His stomach growled and he sat up and stretched.

Bounding from his cot, he yanked on his pants and stepped over to the porthole. Barrels of nails and steel bolts, headed for Springfield, lined the deck. With all the supplies needed for construction as well as goods for Forsyth, he had a full cargo. No passengers this trip.

A niggle of worry worked its way into his mind. He'd heard rumors in St. Louis that the railroad might be coming into Springfield. How much longer before trains would be running all the way to Little Rock? His business probably wouldn't last long when that happened.

A tap at the door drew his mind away from the troubling thoughts. "Come in."

The door opened and young Tod Jenkins stood, gnawing on his bottom lip. "We're coming up on the shoals, Cap'n."

"Thanks. Tell Thompson I'll be in the pilothouse shortly."

"Aye, aye, Cap'n." The door slammed behind him.

At one time, the Elbow Shoals struck fear in the hearts of boat captains and crews attempting to traverse the White River from Arkansas into Missouri. Boats had been torn apart, men lost. Nowadays, the shoals were navigable. Still, even after a number of years, it was traditional on some riverboats for the captains to take the wheels and pilot the vessels over the shoals. Jack had kept that tradition.

Coming out of the pilothouse a little while later, after an uneventful passage over the shoals, Jack headed to the galley. If he did decide to bring the twins on board, he'd need to make sure it was stocked with healthy food. Something more than beans and bacon and hardtack.

He stopped. Now why had that crazy thought popped into his mind? He wasn't about to bring those two on board.

Giving a short laugh, he headed down the stairs to the lower deck. Of course, he might not have a choice if he couldn't work something out. He knew, after several weeks of rolling it around in his mind, there was no way he could leave those girls in an orphans' home. He couldn't impose on the Raytons any longer either.

He frowned. They'd be docking at Forsyth in a couple of hours, and he'd need to scout the town for willing families. Kind, moral folks. He wouldn't leave Addy and Tuck with just anybody.

"There, I think that's everything, Mr. Hubble." Lexie smiled at the mercantile's proprietor, who stood with his arms loaded high with dress goods and school supplies.

"All right, Miss Rayton." The white-haired man headed for the counter, and she followed.

The front door flew open and a towheaded boy ran in, his sides heaving and hair dripping rivulets of water onto the floor.

Oh dear, not rain. She'd be soaked by the time she got home.

"The *Julia Dawn*'s a'dockin' right now, Mr. Hubble." The boy grinned, not seeming to notice he was wet.

"Thank you, Little Bo." He threw the boy a coin, which the child caught expertly before rushing back out the door.

The *Julia Dawn*? That was Jack Sullivan's boat. Perfect timing. Lexie knew she should count to ten. Aunt Kate would be scandalized at what she was thinking, but patience was a virtue she was still working on, and she'd waited long enough to tell that scoundrel what she thought of him. "Mr. Hubble? Would you please hold my things for a little while? I just remembered something I need to do before I leave for home."

"Sure thing. But shouldn't you wait a little while? It's pouring rain out there."

Hardly noticing what he said, Lexie headed out the door into the deluge. She ducked her head, lifted her skirts, and stomped down the muddy street toward the river, glad for the rain. It would be a lot harder to stay angry if the sun were shining.

The usually crowded sidewalks and streets were almost empty as folks darted into doorways and buildings.

Lexie adjusted her hat, thankful for the wide brim. As a gust of wind caught her hat, it tilted. A cascade of water poured over the brim, making its way past her collar and down her neck, soaking her to the skin. She squealed and shivered, stopping in the middle of the street. Maybe this wasn't such a good idea after all.

But she was only two blocks away from the dock and the *Julia Dawn* and that. . .that. . . Oh, she couldn't think of a word bad enough, and even if she did she couldn't say it. Lifting her shoulders, she started up again with new determination and headed to the other side of the street, every mud-soaked step adding to her anger.

She arrived at the landing and shielded her eyes as she glanced across the ancient double-decker boat. In typical Missouri fashion, the rain stopped suddenly and the sun came out. A roar of satisfaction exploded from the deck of the *Julia Dawn*. So this was the treasure for which Jack Sullivan left his children? This decrepit old thing? She squinted her eyes and perused it. Actually, although old, it was obviously kept up well, even sporting a fresh coat of white paint. The decks were covered end to end with crates and barrels. Apparently Mr. Sullivan's business was booming.

Now what should she do? She hadn't really thought that far ahead. She certainly couldn't go onto the dock and start shouting for the man. Lexie tightened her lips and stood, waiting for her target to show himself and hoping it would be soon.

She watched as hands lowered the plank across to the dock. Others waited, crates on their shoulders. They didn't waste any time. Well, good. Maybe Mr. River Captain would make his appearance soon.

Stevedores waited on dock for the signal to come aboard and help with the unloading. A man appeared on deck. He laughed and slapped one of the men on the shoulder then started down the plank.

Lexie straightened, her throat dry and her hands trembling. It was him. She inhaled deeply then stepped forward.

He stepped onto the dock and glanced around, starting when his glance fell upon her. Confusion clouded his eyes then worry.

Lexie bit her lip. She was probably imagining the worry. After all, what made her think she could read the emotions playing across his face?

She caught her breath as he started toward her. Her heart pounded furiously. Now why did he affect her like that? Placing her hands on her hips, she forced herself to glare at him as he drew near.

"Miss Rayton? Has something happened to one of the girls?"

Oh, what an actor he was. "And would you care?"

"What?" He moved forward and gripped her shoulders. "Tell me what's wrong."

"Let go of me." She shook herself loose. "Why would I be here if something was wrong?"

Relief crossed his face. "Well, I reckon that means they're okay, but when I saw you waiting. . ."

"Mr. Sullivan, I had no idea your boat was coming in today. I overheard it while I was shopping."

"Oh." He frowned and peered into her eyes. "Why would you think I wouldn't care if something happened to one of the twins?"

The anger that had been brewing since he'd left rose up like a tornado whirling toward her, raging and unstoppable.

"Why? Why? You dare to ask why after you said you might actually give them away? Put them in an orphanage? And then, to go off and leave them all this time?" Her mouth dropped open. "You. . .you. . . What kind of monster are you?"

❦

Jake stared at the woman before him. Her face contorted with anger, and the fists against her hips appeared quite capable of lashing out as well as her tongue lashed with senseless, angry words. Was the woman mad? Or just have a violent temper? Perhaps she resented being left with the responsibility and the financial burden. Worry made its way into his mind. Had she treated the twins like this? Or worse? Might she have struck them?

His own anger arose to match that of Alexandra Rayton. He'd thought her lovely and sweet, in spite of her unreasonable actions on the day they'd met. But apparently he'd misjudged her again. If she'd laid a hand on one of those little girls, he'd. . . "Miss Rayton, I can assure you, I won't burden you with Tuck and Addy any longer. I'll be at your farm to get them as soon as I can go home and fetch the wagon."

Her hands uncurled and something like dismay washed over her face. "Oh, but I didn't mean you should—"

"I think I know very well what you meant, ma'am. I'll be there before sundown." He tipped his hat and walked away toward the livery.

He'd planned to spend a few hours checking around Forsyth for possible foster parents, but that would have to wait. He needed to make sure the girls were all right. The *Julia Dawn* would have to leave again tomorrow to pick up another load of construction materials in St. Louis. He scrunched up his forehead as he stepped into the livery. He didn't know what he could do for the present except take the twins with him downriver.

After renting the same roan he'd had last time, he headed back to the boat. He found Pap Sanders getting ready to leave to get supplies for the galley. "Wait a minute, Pap." He knew Pap would take the news in stride. "I'm gonna have to bring those twin girls I told you about along with us on this trip."

A look of surprise crossed the old man's face and just as quickly disappeared. "Okay, I reckon we'll need a change of sorts in the galley supplies then."

"That's right. Do you need me to make a list?"

"Nah. Had two sisters of my own. I know what to buy to keep 'em healthy and happy."

Jack nodded. "Well, maybe get a little something special, just to make things pleasant for them."

"What about sleeping arrangements?"

Jack scratched his head. "I reckon we'll need to fix up a corner of my quarters for them."

"Leave it to me, Cap'n. Don't worry about a thing. Them little gals'll have a nice little place of their own by the time you get back here t'morry."

Jack heaved a sigh of relief. "Thanks, Pap. Well then, I'll see you tomorrow."

With a great deal of the weight lifted from him, Jack rode out of town and headed for his uncle's farm. Things were still too new for him to consider the farm his. Red and gold leaves rustled beneath the roan's hooves. Although he appreciated the beauty of the landscape, he knew that winter would be here soon. He hated it when he had to dock because of ice on the river. Some years he hardly lost any time at all, but there had been those times when he'd been holed up in his quarters at some harbor or another for weeks. A few times, out of boredom, he'd tried hotels, but it didn't take long for him to return to his boat.

But not this year. Unless he found a home for the girls, he'd have to find a decent boardinghouse for him and the girls if the winter got bad. He'd never had to worry about anyone but himself before. His crewmen were all independent and would have resented any attempt on his part to take care of them.

But maybe it wouldn't be so bad. Something like butterfly wings tickled his stomach. It was almost like having a family of his own. The picture he'd carried around in his mind for weeks invaded again, and he shook his head. How could anyone so beautiful be so mad-dog mean?

Chapter 7

"How could I have been so foolish?" Tears flowed from Lexie's eyes, soaking Aunt Kate's shoulder. "When will I ever learn to control my horrible temper?"

"Now dear, don't fash yourself so. Chances are he'd have come after the girls anyway."

Lexie sat up straight. "I shouldn't have let him take them. I should have hidden them."

"Lexie, don't be saying things like that." Will walked over and put his hand on her shoulder. "He's their father. There's nothing you can do."

"What if he takes them to an orphanage, the way he said he might?"

"Surely he wouldn't do that," Aunt Kate said. "That may have been worry talking."

"Do you really think so?"

"Yes, I do." But Lexie caught the hesitation in her aunt's voice.

Will picked up his hat. "I have to get out to the field. I left Old Stubborn untended."

Lexie grabbed her brother's hand. "Did he say anything to you, Will?"

"Nope. Just tipped his hat and drove off with the twins. But Lexie, if worse comes to worse and he does take them to a home, maybe then we could do something. Legally I mean. Hey, I don't want those little things in an orphanage either."

"Yes, you're right." Lexie jumped up. "But I'm not going to wait. I'm going into Forsyth tomorrow to see a lawyer just in case."

"If it'll make you feel better. But I think you should wait." The door slammed shut behind him.

"Your brother's right, you know." Aunt Kate rose from the sofa. "You may do more harm than good if you go off on a tangent before you even know what his intentions are."

"But what if he takes them to St. Louis and dumps them there?"

"Alexandra, calm down and try to think straight. Does he really seem like the sort of man who would do that?"

"But he said. . ."

"Child, people say a lot of things they don't mean when they're worried or upset. And you're forgetting something else."

"What?"

"Have you prayed and put this in God's hands?"

"Well, no." A twinge of conscience poked at Lexie. When was the last time she'd prayed? She'd been so busy taking care of the girls she had hardly given God more than a passing thought.

Aunt Kate reached over and smoothed a lock of hair that had fallen across Lexie's forehead. "The preacher will be here this weekend. Maybe you should have a talk with him."

"But what could he do?"

"Probably nothing about the situation. But perhaps he could pray with you and even give you some advice based on scripture."

"All right, Aunt Kate. If you think it will do any good, I'll talk to Brother Collins." The elderly preacher would probably just pat her on the head and tell her not to worry. That's what he'd done when she shared her concern about Will when he was behaving so strangely. Of course it turned out Will was just falling in love. So the preacher actually got it right. All her worrying hadn't helped a bit.

She followed her aunt into the kitchen to begin preparations for supper. But all she could think of were two blond-haired, blue-eyed little girls holed up at the Sullivan farm with a father who didn't seem to care much about them. And to think, she'd actually been sort of attracted to the awful man.

◦────◦

Jack threw out the burned fryer pieces. Too bad he didn't have a dog to take care of the waste. Why had he thought he knew how to fry chicken? Especially in his present state of mind. "Sorry, girls. Guess it'll have to be pancakes for supper."

"Miss Lexie makes really good fried chicken." Addy gave a mournful last look at the chicken then sighed.

Frustration boiled up in Jack's throat. "Well, you won't be eating any more of her cooking."

Tuck frowned. "Why are you so mad at Miss Lexie? She's real nice."

"Why am I. . .?" Jack took a deep breath. "Why is she mad at me? Why did she come to the docks and yell at me for going to work?"

Addy gave her sister a strange look and Tuck nodded. "I don't think that's why she's—"

"But don't worry, girls," Jack interrupted. "You're going with me on the *Julia Dawn*."

"Huh?" Tuck screeched and jumped up. "You mean it?"

Addy's screams joined Tuck's. "You mean it, Mr. Jack? You're gonna take us with you on the boat?"

"Of course. What did you think I was going to do with you?"

"Orphans' home," Tuck said.

Jack looked at the girls, and for the first time, he saw the fear in their eyes. He hunkered down and put his arms around them. "Forgive me for saying that. I don't think I ever really intended to do that. And now? Why, they'd have to tie me to a tree to get you girls into an orphanage."

Four soft arms wrapped around his neck, squeezing hard. A soft voice said, "I love you, Mr. Jack."

Something clutched at Jack's very core and his eyes misted.

"I love you, too, Addy." He knuckled Tuck's nose. "And you."

Tuck grinned. "Okay, but can we say good-bye to Miss Lexie and Miss Kate before we go?"

Jack frowned and stood. "No, you can't. And I don't want to hear any more about the subject. For the life of me, I can't imagine why you'd want to spend one minute with that foul-tempered woman."

Addy opened her mouth and then shut it as Tuck nudged her in the ribs.

Now what was that all about? Obviously Miss Lexie, as they called her, had the girls fooled. Well, they'd get over it. He'd keep them so busy with chores and sightseeing on the *Julia Dawn* they wouldn't give Alexandra Rayton a passing thought.

"Come on, let's make those pancakes and get ready for bed. We're leaving bright and early."

∽⁓◦

"He actually said he'd never leave them with me again." Lexie stabbed furiously at the weeds with her hoe, bumping the plant laden with small green tomatoes.

"Lexie, be careful before you chop down the tomatoes instead of the weeds."

At the sound of her brother's voice from the next row, Lexie looked up at the plant, relieved to see it intact. Will was right. The tomatoes were coming along nicely, and Aunt Kate wouldn't be happy if one of the heavily laden plants got demolished.

She leaned on her hoe and wiped her arm across her face. Even this early in the day, the sun bore down blistering hot.

Will had stopped at the end of the row to get a drink of water. He brought the dipper to Lexie.

She drank deeply then wiped the moisture away from her mouth. "But I don't understand why he's so angry with me. I'm not the bad person. He is."

"Lexie, will you please just drop it? They're probably already headed downriver. There's nothing you can do. And you seem to be getting a little obsessed. After all, you've only known the twins a short while."

His exasperated tone shot through her. And a niggling of doubt wormed its way into her thoughts. Why had she become so attached to Tuck and Addy in a few short weeks? Maybe Will was right. There was nothing she could do. "If you think you can manage without me, maybe I'll go to the general store and see if Mr. Hawkins hired anyone yet. Maybe he'll hire me. It's too easy to dwell on things working in this field."

"Sure, go ahead. Maybe that way the tomatoes will survive." He smiled, and she felt her lips turning up at the corner.

"Thanks, little brother. I'll see you at supper."

After helping Aunt Kate with a couple of small chores, she cleaned up and drove to Hawkins's store. She left Jolly at the hitching post, nosing around in a feed bag. "Good morning, Mr. Hawkins."

"Miss Lexie, what can I do for you today? Got a shipment of new dress goods in yesterday."

Lexie composed her face and smiled. It wouldn't do to appear nervous. "Thank you, but I'm not here to shop. I was wondering if you'd filled the employment position yet."

"No, I sure haven't. Do you know someone who is interested?" He gave her a hopeful glance.

"Yes sir, as a matter of fact I do. How about hiring me?" Her lips trembled as she smiled again.

"You? You want to work in my store?" He scratched his head. "Well, I hadn't actually considered hiring a woman. Don't they need you to help out on the farm?"

"No, sir. My brother has hired two hands to work until after harvest."

"Hmmm. Well then. I don't know. There is some lifting."

"I'm very strong, sir."

He licked his lips and, pulling out a bandana, wiped his face, obviously in deep thought. Humph. Probably trying to find a way to let her down gently.

He straightened and looked her square in the eyes. "I reckon I'm willing to give it a try. After a week, if either of us don't think it's working out, we'll part as friends. That agreeable to you?"

Light filled her heart and she felt a grin splitting her face. "That sounds very agreeable to me. You won't regret it. I promise I'll work hard."

He chuckled. "I'm sure you will. What in the world put working here in your head? I'm sure your aunt could keep you busy at home."

"That's true. And of course, I'll continue to help Aunt Kate. But to be honest, Mr. Hawkins, I need to keep my mind occupied and off some worries."

"Worries? Well, I'm a good listener if you'd like to spill them on me."

Lexie looked at the kind face. Somehow she thought it would be a lot easier to unburden on him than Brother Collins. Before she knew it she was telling him the whole story.

"Whoa, whoa, back up there a minute." He held his hand up. "Where did you get the idea Jack Sullivan was their pa?"

"What? Why, they told me, of course, when he was injured."

"And how long did they stay with you?"

"Several weeks. Why?" What in the world was he talking about?

"Miss Lexie. . ."

"Please, since I'm going to be working here, will you call me Lexie? After all, you've known me a long time."

"Very well, Lexie. I think you'd better come over here and sit down." He pulled up a stool then got her a glass of water. He stared at her a moment, and then a chuckle exploded from his lips.

"Sorry, this really isn't funny, but, honey, Sullivan found those girls holed up at his uncle's house. They're orphans. Not his kids at all. Matter of fact, I've been asking around for him to find a family that could take them in."

Lexie sat frozen, her face numb. He wasn't their father? But why had they said he was? And why all the made-up stories? A surge of horror slammed her and her stomach churned. Oh no, she'd done him a terrible injustice. He must think her a raving lunatic. She stood, swayed, and grabbed onto the counter.

"Hey, easy there. Maybe you'd better sit back down."

"I'll be all right." Her voice was little more than a whisper. She swallowed and tried again. "Do you know if they've left yet?"

"I haven't seen them go by, but I've been in the back quite a bit today, unloading crates." He gave her a sympathetic glance.

"I think I really need to try to catch them before they go." She gave him a tremulous smile. "When would you like for me to start working?"

"How about in the morning? If you'd like to come on over after breakfast, I'll show you around."

"Yes, that sounds marvelous. Thank you, Mr. Hawkins. You won't be sorry." She backed out the door and rushed to the buggy. Oh, if only she could get there in time.

She drove across country, skirting Marmoros and the cave. Why was Jolly going so slowly? They'd never get there at this rate.

When she finally pulled up at the Sullivan farm, Tom Marshall, the neighbor who'd been looking after the place, came out of the barn. "Can I help you with something, miss?" He squinted up at her from beneath the brim of his straw hat.

"Is Mr. Sullivan here?" Even as she asked, she knew she was too late.

"You mean young Jack?"

Well, of course. Did he think she'd be asking after a dead man? She had to get herself together before she lost control and started yelling. "Yes, sir. Is he here?"

"Nope, him and them ornery twins took off around daybreak."

Lexie headed back home, her palms damp and heart racing as embarrassment rose inside her. How could she bear to tell Will and Aunt Kate the news?

Chapter 8

Jack shut the door to the boiler room and took one step before he heard a scurrying noise and then Tuck's voice.

"Shh. Be quiet, Addy. If they catch us we'll be in big trouble."

She was right about that. The twins knew they weren't supposed to be down here. Now what were they up to? He stepped over in the shadows and waited.

In a moment they came into sight. "But Tuck, I don't think we should be here anyway. It's awfully hot and smelly." Addy wrinkled up her nose. "It smells like burned up old boots."

Tuck took a sniff and made a face. "I don't smell anything. And if you'd left your overalls on instead of changing into that dress, maybe you wouldn't be so hot."

"I like dresses. And anyway, Miss Lexie likes us to wear dresses."

"In a boiler room?" Tuck chortled.

"How was I supposed to know you'd drag me down here?"

"Aw c'mon, Addy. I just want to look at the boiler. Bob Shift came out of there red as a tomato the other day. I wonder how hot it gets." By now she was close enough to reach the heavy door that kept her from her prize.

As she reached forward, Jack reached out and grabbed her arm. "What do you girls think you're doing?"

Both girls whirled, their eyes big with fear. "Sorry, Mr. Jack. Just wanted to see the boiler room."

"You don't sound very sorry to me." He released her arm. "You know there's a reason you aren't allowed down here."

"That's for sure." Pap's voice echoed as he hurried toward them. His frown pierced the girls and one gnarled hand grabbed the arm Jack had released. "You want to go and get yerself boiled or somethin'?"

"Pap, we didn't mean to do anything wrong. Just wanted to see the boiler room." Addy's hand rested on Pap's. "Please don't hurt her."

"Hurt her? Why, bless yer heart, little 'un. I ain't gonna hurt her." Pap's face had gentled, like it always did when he spoke to Addy. He turned to Jack. "Sorry, Cap'n. The little critters must have slipped by me. I should have been watchin' closer."

"It's all right, Pap. I don't expect you to watch them every second. They knew better and they won't do it again." He turned a stern eye on the girls. "Right?"

Both girls nodded.

"All right. I'll hold you to that promise. Now let's go deckside."

As they stepped on deck, cool, moist drops off the river sprinkled over Jack's skin. He glanced at Tuck and noticed her close her eyes and breathe in deeply. Obviously she appreciated the difference, too. Maybe even enough to keep her promise. "Okay, you girls stay out of trouble."

"What is there to do if we can't explore?" Tuck scowled. She loved the riverboat, but once the newness had worn off the adventure, there wasn't much to do. Which was why she wanted to see the boiler. Was that too much to ask?

"How 'bout them readin' and writin' lessons?" asked Pap.

"We finished them before chow," Addy assured him. She loved saying "chow."

"Hmm, and chores?" Jack had assigned them work in the galley, and they were doing a good job. Pap had chuckled as he'd reported to Jack that Tuck could pretty near peel a potato all the way from one end to another without stopping.

"All done."

"That right?" Pap scratched his ear and glanced upward. "Well now, how'd ye like to hear a little fiddlin' music?"

Tuck grinned. "Sure would like that."

"Well then, you two set yerselves down on them crates over yonder. I'll go fetch my fiddle."

Tuck rushed to obey, with Addy climbing up beside her.

Jack leaned against a stack of crates and observed. Pap's fiddling was a treat he didn't want to pass up.

"Hey, Addy, didn't Pa used to have an old fiddle?"

"Yes, but he didn't know how to play. It belonged to Ma's grandpa."

"How do you know?"

"Because I asked Pa once where it came from. Pa said it came all the way from Ireland with our great-grandfather O'Donnell."

Tuck made a sound with her tongue as if she didn't believe her sister for a minute.

"Well, it's true, Tuck. Really it is."

Jack was pretty sure it was. Addy didn't usually make up stories unless Tuck started first.

Pap came around the corner, a big grin on his face, his fiddle tucked under his wrinkled chin. At the first sound of the bow gliding across the strings, Jack noticed Tuck's finger snapping and her feet swinging up and down to the lively music. Pretty soon she was off the crate and dancing a jig. She grabbed Addy and pulled her down, and they danced around and around the deck. The music stopped and Tuck ran over to Pap as Addy flopped down, laughing.

"That was a good one, Pap." Tuck reached her hand over and touched the smooth wood of the fiddle, then jerked her hand back and threw a guilty glance at its owner.

"No harm done, little gal. Here, you wanna hold it a minute?"

"Really? I can hold it?" Her mouth flew open and she looked at Pap with disbelief.

"Why shore ye can." He held the instrument in her direction.

She reached out both arms.

"Naw, that ain't the way. It ain't no baby. Here, hold it like this."

Tuck glanced down in awe at the wonderful object in her hands. "Do you think I could learn to play?" she whispered, gazing at the fiddle.

"Why, I don't see why not. Come 'ere and I'll give ye yer first lesson."

At a sound from Addy, Jack glanced around. Pain washed over her face, and her eyes misted as she looked at her sister. But then she smiled and nodded. "Go ahead, Tuck. It'll be fun. Maybe we can go to the cabin and fetch Great-Grandpa's fiddle for you when we get back."

Jack continued to watch her for a moment. Had that been longing in her eyes? But if she wanted to play, why didn't she say so?

There never was a more beautiful sight than the river at night. Jack stood in the bow and leaned against the rail. The sky above and all around was a black canvas filled with stars. A sliver of a moon shone down on the crystal-like surface of the White River, causing the *Julia Dawn* to appear to skim the air above the water. Almost like flying.

He turned and looked up at the pilothouse where Thompson manned the wheel. They had made three trips from St. Louis and back since they had left. All had gone fairly smooth this trip except for three crates that fell into the water when they were loading in St. Louis.

He hadn't gotten around to searching for a family for the girls. Seemed like every time he thought about it he shoved the idea into another part of his brain. He might as well admit it. The girls were becoming very important to him. He wanted to raise them himself. But he knew that was ridiculous. How could he raise two little girls on the river, even if they'd let him? As soon as some women's society found out he had them, they'd probably rake him over the coals and maybe even have him thrown in jail. They'd take the girls and then he'd never see them again.

If only Alexandra Rayton had been the woman he had thought she was. He'd known from the beginning she had a feisty, stubborn spirit. But he'd never expected she had a mean streak. Still, he knew he had some sort of feelings for her no matter if she did have some kind of problems. Come to think of it, the whole family had behaved downright strange when he picked the girls up. You'd have thought he was poison.

Pain stabbed Jack's brow just above his right eye, and he rubbed circles with his thumb. No sense trying to figure things out now. Maybe Mr. Hawkins had found a family willing to take the girls. If he couldn't keep them, at least they could live near enough for him to see them now and then.

Lexie leaned back against an ancient oak tree and gazed out over the low bluff that overlooked the river. She peered downstream, shading her eyes, hoping against hope to see the prow of the *Julia Dawn* coming around the curve. She knew Jack Sullivan and his boat had docked at Forsyth several times since they'd left. But he hadn't come home on those occasions. This time she'd catch him at the docks.

Her plan was to mount Jolly as soon as she saw the steamboat then ride like the wind home where she'd change into her blue dress—the one that brought out the ocean blue of her eyes—and her new wide-brimmed bonnet with the feathers. No, perhaps that would be too much.

She'd been thinking about the girls and their plight a lot lately. She'd come to care for them a great deal in the short time they'd stayed with her family. And now that she knew they were actually orphans her heart went out to them even more.

Her stomach jumped at the bold plan she'd concocted. If Jack cared about the girls, and she was pretty sure he did or why would he have gone to the trouble of taking them with him, then perhaps he would see that her plan had merit.

The girls needed schooling, and they also needed someone to care for them while he was away. Perhaps when he realized she'd only been concerned for the girls, he would allow her to keep them while he was gone, and then they could stay with him for the short periods of time he was home. Of course, that would mean her giving up her job, but then Addy and Tuck were more important than some old job.

In the meantime, they could still be searching for a family for the girls. Her heart lurched at the thought, but they had to think of what was best for the twins. At least if they were in the vicinity, perhaps she could still see them occasionally.

A honking sound drew her attention upward. A flock of geese flying north. This was the third flock she'd seen this week. Which wasn't unusual for the first week in September and gave strength to her plan. After all, she was certain Mr. Sullivan would see that the river was no place for Tuck and Addy with cold weather on the way.

She thought about the new dresses she'd sewn for them the past few weeks. There would be several festivities now that the harvest was about over, and she wanted them to have something pretty to wear, even if she was not allowed to be with them. They would love the pretty yellow and blue ruffled dresses. But it was with Christmas in mind that she'd created the velvet dresses, so soft one's fingers slid across the fabric like silk. One red as the cherry preserves on Aunt Kate's shelves and the other as green as the pines and cedars that grew in the woods that nearly surrounded the farm.

With one last look downriver, she stood. It would be time to help Aunt Kate start supper and afterward lay her things out for morning. The circuit preacher would be here tomorrow to hold a service. Perhaps she would find some peace in his sermon.

Chapter 9

A new preacher? Not Reverend Collins?" Lexie stared in dismay at Jane Dobson, who'd just told her the news.

"Yes, and he's young and. . ." She lowered her voice and leaned to whisper in Lexie's ear. "Not married."

Humph. So much for her little talk with Reverend Collins. She certainly couldn't bare her soul to a young bachelor. "Well, you should invite him to Sunday dinner, Jane."

The younger girl giggled, an annoying habit in Lexie's opinion. "Mama's headed that way now. She wants to get to him before Mrs. Humphrey does."

Lexie followed Jane's glance. Sure enough, Mrs. Dobson was closing in on a group of men standing by the grove of trees where the meeting would be held. Aletha Humphrey's mother wasn't far behind.

Hmm. Lexie narrowed her eyes and peered at the tall young man who stood with several of the local farmers. He was nice looking. Blond hair smoothed back from his forehead and a nice smile.

He straightened and greeted the two women who approached him at the very same instant. Poor man. He didn't stand a chance. And there were at least two more women in the neighborhood with daughters of marriageable age. Chances are they'd be pulling up in their buggies any moment. The preacher would be lucky to get away from this meeting without leaving behind a new fiancée.

"I'm going to find Aunt Kate and sit down." She smiled and waved at Jane, then made her escape, heading for the chairs and benches that had been set up.

Aunt Kate waved at her from the front bench.

Lexie groaned. She hated sitting that close. It made her neck ache trying to look up at the preacher's face. But she smiled and scooted in next to her aunt.

"There's a new preacher." Her aunt smiled and patted her hand. "He seems nice."

"Did you find out his name?"

"Reverend Hines. He hails from somewhere north of Springfield."

"That's nice."

"He's coming to dinner after the service." Aunt Kate's eyes crinkled.

Lexie groaned. "Aunt Kate, I hope you aren't trying to play matchmaker because I'm not interested." Lexie made her voice as stern as possible without sounding disrespectful.

"I've no idea why you'd think that. It was merely the Christian thing to do. Sarah Jenkins is coming, too." She glanced around and then said, "I believe Will and Sarah wish to speak to Reverend Hines about their marriage plans."

Lexie brightened. "Oh, that's good. I'm sorry I misunderstood your motives, Auntie."

Aunt Kate's eyes gleamed. "Don't worry about it."

Lexie peered at her aunt, who merely smiled and leaned back on the bench. Maybe that dinner invitation wasn't so innocent after all. Lexie shrugged and looked around. The grove was filling up, and everyone was scrambling to get choice seats before the singing began.

Horace Packard walked beside the new reverend to the platform that had been built for the occasion and waited until the rustling and whispers died down. He wiped his brow with a white handkerchief and cleared his throat. "Well, folks, I'd like to introduce the Reverend Allen Hines, who'll be replacing Reverend Collins as our preacher."

A bevy of clapping thundered through the crowd, and several people rang out with, "Amen," and, "Howdy, preacher."

Reverend Hines smiled. "I'm very pleased to be here and to meet all you good folks. I know you'll miss Reverend Collins, but he is getting up in years and the traveling was getting to be too much for him. He sent his greetings." He nodded. "I hope we shall become great friends."

He stepped back and sat on a bench behind the back of the platform.

Horace stepped forward with his guitar in hand and motioned for his brothers to join him. The Packard brothers were well known in the area for their musical abilities, and Lexie looked forward to the singing.

"Okay folks"—Horace began tapping his foot—"let's start out with something that'll put some fire in our souls."

The opening chords of "We're Marching to Zion" filled the grove, and voices arose in joyous abandon. Lexie joined in fervently. She, like most of the folks, had worked hard over the summer, plowing, planting, and all the other things that went along with living. The women had canned vegetables, fruits, and jellies until their hands were stained. People were starved for a good service and fellowship with other believers. There would be a harvest ball next month and, weather permitting, some Christmas festivities. Then the long winter would keep them isolated and lonely. Especially if the snows were heavy.

The song ended and two more were sung. Then the Packards put away their guitars, and everyone sat down.

Allen Hines stepped to the makeshift podium and glanced over the crowd. When his soft brown eyes rested on Lexie, he hesitated then smiled warmly and looked straight ahead. He cleared his throat and opened his Bible. " 'Trust in the Lord with all thine heart; and lean not unto thine own understanding. In all thy ways acknowledge him, and he shall direct thy paths.' "

Lexie inhaled sharply. Was God speaking directly to her? It seemed so. She hadn't really discussed her plans with God but had been barreling along, making one mistake after another.

I'm sorry, Lord. I bring the situation with Tuck and Addy and Mr. Sullivan to You.

She paused a moment as Jack Sullivan's handsome face and searching brown eyes invaded her mind. Then she blushed. Imagine thinking thoughts like that when she was in the middle of praying.

Forgive me, Father, for not controlling my thoughts. And please show me what to do. You are the all-knowing, all-wise God, and I'm going to trust You to direct my paths.

⌒⌒⌒

Jack sat on the deck, untangling some rope.

Tuck came and flopped down next to him. "What'cha doing that for?" She peered up at him, her blue eyes curious. "I mean, you're the boss, right?"

"Right." He worked on a particularly difficult knot, tugging until it finally came loose. "Why?"

"Well, you got all these fellows working for you. Why should you have to do this stuff?"

Jack let the long, heavy rope fall onto the deck and looked at her. "Nothing wrong with work, Tuck. And just because I happen to be the owner doesn't mean I treat my crew like slaves. This is a working boat. And even though I make most of the decisions, I still want to do my share of work."

Tuck nodded and she smiled. "Sure you should. Can I help? I'm all finished with my chores and lessons."

"Sure. Yank around on this section, and see if you can get the knots loose." He tossed the end to her and then picked up another for himself. "Always plenty of knots to work on. Where's your sister?"

"Trying to get the wrinkles out of her dress without an iron. We should've brought one along, you know."

"Didn't think about it. Never had much use for a flatiron here on the river. Guess I should have thought about it."

"Ah well, don't worry. Don't know why anyone would want to wear a dress out here on a boat. But now she's all fired up to have it on when we dock in case Miss Lexie's there waiting for us." She squinted at Jack. "You reckon she will be?"

"Maybe. But I told you you're not spending any time with her. I don't trust her mean streak."

Tuck took a deep breath with a little catch at the end.

"Miss Lexie isn't mean."

"Well, she could have fooled me."

Tuck ducked her head and swallowed. "Mr. Jack, I know why Miss Lexie is mad at you."

He looked up, surprised. "You do?"

"Yep. I mean yes, sir." She licked her lips. "First off, I want you to know it wasn't Addy's fault. I thought the whole thing up and made her go along with it."

Now this was beginning to sound important. A twinge of something like panic clutched at Jack's middle. Had he misjudged Alexandra Rayton because of something the girls had done or said to her? "What is it, Tuck?" He dropped the rope again and took Tuck's arms in both hands. "Tell me now."

"First, you got to promise if you wallop anyone it'll just be me. Because Addy's not to blame." Her lip firmed, a good sign she wouldn't be the one to give in here.

He let go of her and patted her arms. "Tuck, I'm not going to wallop anyone. I promise."

She took a deep breath. "Well, you see, it was like this. When Miss Lexie and Mr. Will brought you home shot and passed out, I was afraid Addy and me would get taken away somewhere. So. . ." She took a deep breath then let the words rush out. "I told her you were our pa."

Jack dropped her arms and sat stunned, staring at her. "You what?"

She nodded. "I'm sorry, Mr. Jack. I didn't know what else to do. I couldn't let them put Addy and me into an orphan home. But I didn't know Miss Lexie would get so all fired mad at you. Still don't know why she did."

Something like relief washed over Jack. Now at least he knew why the lovely Miss Rayton had behaved like a tigress. She'd thought he was an uncaring, neglectful father who was trying to give his daughters away.

Realizing he was grinning like a fool, he put a stern look on his face. "Well, that was a very naughty thing to do, Tuck. But I suppose I can understand your reason. You have to promise me never to lie again though."

An eager look of disbelief crossed her face. "I promise. So you're not mad at me?"

"No, I'm not mad. And guess what? I don't see any reason why you can't spend some time with your Miss Lexie after all."

"Really?" She threw herself in his arms, almost knocking him over, and wrapped her arms around his neck. "Thank you, Mr. Jack."

"But you do know that lying is a sin. And you will have to be punished."

"I know. But no walloping?"

"Not this time. But don't ever, ever do it again. And you girls will have to confess to Miss Lexie and apologize to her." He smiled. "Now go bring your sister. I need to have a talk with her, too, before we dock. We should be there before sundown. Oh, and tell her not to worry about the wrinkled dress. Maybe we can find a couple of ready-made ones at the mercantile."

Sunday afternoons were usually drowsy times when Aunt Kate napped and Will and Sarah held hands and made eyes at each other on the front porch.

Which gave Lexie free time to walk to the creek bank and daydream.

After spending two hours sitting on the front porch and trying to avoid Reverend Hines's glances in her direction, she was ready to plead a headache and go to bed. That the man was smitten, there was no doubt, and Aunt Kate's satisfied smile indicated she knew it, too.

Not that there was anything wrong with the young preacher. He was quite handsome and very well educated. His manner was kind and gentle. But for some reason, Lexie wasn't interested in the young man at all. She wished Mrs. Dobson had gotten to the preacher first.

Aunt Kate frowned in her direction, and Lexie realized Reverend Hines had just said something she'd completely missed.

"I think you're right, preacher." Will's voice held just a hint of humor, so he had probably noticed Lexie's plight. "The railroad will be a fine addition to the area."

"Yes." Realizing she'd spoken too loudly, Lexie cleared her throat. "The railroad will be a very nice change in transportation."

"I was speaking more along the lines of the transporting of merchandise." The reverend smiled gently in Lexie's direction.

Aunt Kate cleared her throat. "Lexie, why don't you bring the pitcher of lemonade and some glasses?"

"Yes, Aunt Kate." Lexie jumped up, relieved at a chance to get away for a moment.

As she prepared the tray, a thought occurred to her. What would happen to the riverboats when the train came in? She shoved the door open with her foot and set the tray on the table beside Aunt Kate. After serving everyone, she sat down. "But what about the riverboats?"

"What do you mean, dear?" Aunt Kate looked at her.

"I mean what about all the people who haul freight on the river? They make their living that way."

"Oh, I don't think trains will ever replace the riverboats." But Will's voice had a question in it. Maybe he wasn't so sure.

Reverend Hines glanced at Will. "I wouldn't be so sure about that. It may take awhile, but in some parts of the country freighting along the rivers is almost nonexistent. I'm afraid that's what happens sometimes in order to make progress. And to be honest, I won't be averse to the fact that it will limit some of the gambling that occurs on those very boats."

Lexie frowned. Not all riverboats allowed gambling. Maybe progress wasn't so wonderful after all.

Chapter 10

Lexie climbed onto a stool and rubbed her dustcloth over the top shelf. It needed to be clean before she filled it with the canned tomatoes she'd brought from the farm. Aunt Kate had been delighted when Mr. Hawkins purchased nearly her entire stock. She'd kept just enough for the family's use. And he'd promised to buy as many peaches as she could spare as soon as they were canned.

The back door slammed shut, and Mr. Hawkins came in with a smile on his face. "Well, Lexie, that boat you've been craning your neck to see just turned the bend, heading for Forsyth."

Lexie felt the stool wobble beneath her feet.

Mr. Hawkins' strong hands steadied it. "Didn't know my news would knock you over." He chuckled.

"Oh, Mr. Hawkins, don't tease. You know how I've longed to see the twins."

"Umm-hmm. Are you sure it's only the twins you're longing to see?" His smile was so kind, Lexie couldn't take offense.

"Perhaps not. But don't tell anyone I said that. Especially him. I'd be mortified if he thought I was attracted to him. I'm perfectly certain he entertains no such thoughts about me."

"I won't tell a soul. Now why don't you wait and put those tomatoes up tomorrow? You might want to go home and get the dust out of your hair before you see the. . .er. . .girls."

She laughed and stepped down from the stool.

Before she climbed into the buggy, she whispered into Jolly's ear, "Fly like the wind, Jolly girl. I need to get the dust out of my hair." Lexie hardly noticed the turning leaves as she drove hard all the way home, but she knew she'd better slow down before she reached the farm. Will and Aunt Kate would both berate her for driving the buggy so fast.

She pulled up by the barn and led Jolly inside where she unhitched her from the buggy.

"Land sakes, Alexandra." Aunt Kate frowned as she stepped into the barn. "That horse is dripping sweat and her sides are heaving. I hope you have a good reason to have worked her so hard."

Lexie wondered if the truth would be good enough but knew she couldn't lie. Her conscience had hurt her so badly over deceiving Aunt Kate about going down to the docks that she'd repented in tears and promised the Lord she wouldn't lie or break a promise again if her life depended on it. "The *Julia*

Dawn is in, Aunt Kate. I thought I'd hitch Old Stubborn up and drive into Forsyth to see how the twins are before they take off again. I would really like to explain to Mr. Sullivan about the mix-up."

Her aunt narrowed her eyes, giving Lexie a shrewd look. "Is that so?"

"Why? What's wrong?"

"So you're going to tell on the girls without giving them a chance to explain to you why they did it?"

"I hadn't really thought of that. I wonder why they did."

"Think about it, Lexie. Two little orphan girls. The man who had been taking care of them, unconscious and injured, brought home by strangers. . ."

Lexie stared at her aunt then groaned. "Tuck and Addy were afraid. As tough as they are, they were still afraid of course. They had no idea what we might do if they told the truth. But what should I do? Mr. Sullivan needs to know."

"Don't you think they'll tell him themselves sooner or later? Can you give them that chance?"

"But I'm sure he must think I'm mentally deranged."

"So it's your pride you're thinking of."

"No, of course—" Lexie stopped. Aunt Kate was right. "All right. I'll wait a while longer. But not forever. They shouldn't be allowed to get by with telling untruths, even if I do understand their reasons."

The dock was swarming with merchants, dockhands, and excited children who'd come to see the docking and unloading of the *Julia Dawn*.

Jack scanned the crowd. He had hoped Miss Rayton would be here so he could get this thing straightened out about the children, but she was nowhere in the crowd. He shouldn't wonder after the way he'd grabbed the girls and left without a word to her.

Well, she'd been kind to Tuck and Addy. She must have been since they liked her so much. He hoped, once she realized the truth, she wouldn't think so ill of him.

"Miss Lexie's not here." At Addy's forlorn voice, Jack straightened and smiled. "She wouldn't have known we'd be docking today. Don't worry. You'll see her before we leave again."

"How do you know?" Tuck, never one to beat around the bush, peered up at him.

"Because, Little Miss Tuck, we'll be going over to the Raytons' farm, so you can confess what you've done and apologize to them."

"Oh."

"Yes, oh. But for now"—he grabbed a hand of each twin and grinned—"we need to see about some ready-made dresses."

"Ugh." Tuck frowned. "I hate dresses."

"But I love them. Thank you, Mr. Jack." Addy flashed a sweet smile in his direction. "Can I have a pink one?"

"If they have pink ones, you may certainly have one."

They sauntered down the street, Tuck in her overalls and Addy in a dress that looked like it had never seen a flatiron, and headed for the Hubble's Mercantile.

An hour later, they exited the store. The girls each held a package, and Jack carried a box filled with groceries for their supper.

Their next stop was the livery stable where Jack rented horses and a wagon, hopefully for the last time. He'd instructed Tom Marshall to fetch his uncle's livestock from the neighbor who'd been caring for them and to take care of any repairs the old wagon needed.

They took the rutted path toward Marmoros, veering off past Hawkins's store then on toward Sullivan's farm.

"Look, Tuck, the leaves are starting to turn." Addy almost bounced on the seat in her excitement to be back in the familiar neighborhood.

"Yep, wait'll they start drying up and falling off. You won't like them so much then."

"Oh, Tuck, you know you think they're pretty." Addy scowled at her sister.

Tuck grinned. "I guess."

When they pulled up in front of the barn, both girls hopped down.

"How about you girls gathering up some kindling for the stove?"

"It ain't cold," Tuck said, stating the obvious.

"Well, I supposed you might want some supper." Jack grinned.

"You ain't going to fry chicken, are you?"

Jack threw his head back and laughed. "No, I promise I'll never try that again. Maybe you could fetch us a smoked ham out of the root cellar."

"Sure can."

Jack almost laughed again at how quickly both girls took off running to get the kindling and ham. He didn't blame them.

As they ate their supper of fried ham, boiled potatoes, and corn, Addy glanced at Jack. "When can we go see Miss Lexie and Aunt Kate and Mr. Will?"

"Can we go after supper?" Tuck asked eagerly.

Jack's stomach jumped and he took a deep breath. As much as he wanted to get the matter cleared up, he was a mite nervous at the thought of seeing Alexandra Rayton again. They hadn't exactly gotten off on good footing, and things had gotten worse as time progressed. "How about we clean up the supper dishes, and you girls take baths and get a good night's sleep? We'll go to the Raytons' in the morning."

"You promise?" There they went again, speaking the same thing in unison.

"I promise."

Tuck laid her fork down. "Can we help with the outside chores, too?"

"Tom Marshall seems to have taken care of everything. But you can brush down the horses if you want to. And in the morning you can help milk the goats."

"Thanks, Mr. Jack." Tuck forked a piece of ham and crammed it into her mouth.

"Could I just clean the kitchen up while you and Tuck do the milking?" Addy's nose crinkled in disgust.

"Yes, I think that's a good enough trade-off, Addy."

How in the world could twins look almost identical yet be so different in every other way?

⁓⁓⁓

"Oh, my sweet girls." The twins grabbed Aunt Kate around the waist and she hugged them hard. "I'm so happy to see you."

"I'm happy to see you, too," Addy declared, smiling up at the woman who'd been so kind to her.

"Me, too." Tuck grinned. "Where's Miss Lexie?"

"Now girls, give Miss Kate some room to breathe." Jack couldn't keep the grin off his face either and wondered if it was as broad as Tuck's.

"Why, child, Lexie is working at Mr. Hawkins's general store. And she's going to be so disappointed to have missed you." She reached a hand toward Jack and he took it gently. "And I know she wished to speak with you, Mr. Sullivan."

Jack cleared his throat. "Now girls, I believe you have something you want to say to Miss Kate. . . ."

Somber expressions appeared on each girl's face. Tuck straightened her small shoulders. "Well ma'am, it's like this. We kind of told you something that isn't true."

The old woman's eyes misted. "All right, Tuck. I'm listening."

Addy swallowed loudly. "Mr. Jack isn't really our pa."

"That's right." Tuck cleared her throat. "Our pa got killed, and we hid out at Old Mr. Sullivan's place. Mr. Jack found us there."

"And you were afraid to tell the truth? Was that it?"

"Yes, ma'am." The relief in Tuck's voice at being understood brought a lump to Jack's throat.

"You see, when we saw he was hurt, we were afraid that someone would take us away to a orphans' home. So we told an untruth."

"We lied is what we did, Addy." Tuck licked her lips and took a deep breath.

"Thank you for telling me, girls. And I forgive you. And I know if you've confessed to God, He has forgiven you, too."

"Oh we have, Miss Kate. We really have." Tears rolled from Addy's eyes.

"Ma'am, we have to be getting back to Forsyth. We have a load to take downriver tomorrow." He smiled. "Will you please explain to Miss Rayton and Will, and tell them we'll be over when we come back? I know the girls want to apologize to them, too."

"Will is in the south field, if you'd like to see him before you leave. And you're more than welcome to stop at the store and speak to Alexandra. I'm certain Mr. Hawkins wouldn't mind a bit."

"We might just do that, if you're sure she won't mind."

"I'm quite sure. In fact, I happen to know she wanted very much to speak to you."

After they'd talked to Will and he'd assured the girls he didn't hold their fib against them, the girls climbed up onto the wagon seat beside Jack.

"Do you think Miss Lexie will be mad?" Addy's voice quivered.

"I hope not," Tuck answered, chewing on her bottom lip.

When they walked into the store, the bell jingled.

"Where is she?" Tuck frowned.

Addy tapped her foot. "Where is anyone?"

Just then, Mr. Hawkins walked in from the back room. "Well, well. If it isn't Jack Sullivan and his two daughters." The man burst out laughing at the look on Jack's and the twins' faces.

"Where's Miss Rayton?"

"She headed out ten minutes ago. Heading to your place, I think. I'm surprised you didn't see her if you came from that direction."

"Oh no." Tuck leaned against a barrel of flour. "We missed her again."

"Now, Tuck, it can't be helped. We'll have to see her next time."

"Can't we go back? Please, Mr. Jack?" Addy's pleading eyes added fuel to Jack's own frustration.

He frowned then sighed as he looked at the girls' hopeful faces. "Okay, we'll go back. But we can't stay long. We'll have to get back to the *Julia Dawn* before dark. Promise you won't beg to stay."

"We promise, Mr. Jack." There went that chorus again.

"Then let's go."

The bell rang as the front door flew open. "Mr. Hawkins, I decided it wouldn't be the proper thing to—" Lexie Rayton cut her words off with a gasp, her face a picture of happy surprise.

Chapter 11

"Miss Lexie!" the twins screamed.

Lexie braced herself as two overalls-clad figures made a beeline toward her. If not for the door to lean on, she was pretty sure she'd be flat on the floor.

"Addy. Tuck." She threw her arms around them as they hugged her hard. "I'm so happy to see you. I've missed you so much."

"I missed you, too, Miss Lexie." Addy proved her words with another squeeze.

"Me, too." Tuck gave an emphatic nod. "We went to the farm, but you weren't there, and we thought we wouldn't get to see you."

"Yep, but Mr. Jack said we'd go back and try again."

"Then here you are." Tuck grinned and gave Lexie a sound pat on the shoulder.

"Now girls, I know you're happy to see Miss Lexie, but don't knock her down." At the sound of Jack Sullivan's voice, Lexie inhaled sharply. He leaned against the counter, smiling.

Oh dear, how could she tell him about the twins' deception?

He cleared his throat. "Tuck, Addy, don't you have something to say to Miss Lexie?"

Addy ducked her head and Tuck bit her lip. "Yes, sir." Tuck gave a little cough. "Well, it's like this, Miss Lexie. And before I tell you, I want you to know I'm awfully sorry and so is Addy, even though it was mostly my fault."

Lexie swallowed past the lump that formed in her throat. Should she spare them by admitting she already knew? No. Confession was good for the soul. "I'm listening, Tuck."

"Ya see. . ." Tuck took a deep breath.

"Mr. Jack isn't really our pa." Addy's hurried interruption brought relief to Tuck's eyes, and both girls rushed through the explanation then stood silently, dread mixed with hope on their upturned faces.

"I see." Lexie nodded and frowned slightly. "I do understand that you were both frightened, but lying is never the right choice. It can cause all sorts of problems. I thought terrible things about Mr. Sullivan and acted badly towards him. But I think you are very sorry and won't ever do it again. Am I correct?"

"Yes, ma'am," they chorused.

"Very well. I forgive you for deceiving my family and me. And although you need to apologize to Aunt Kate and my brother, as far as I'm concerned it's over."

While the twins smothered her with hugs, Lexie raised a shy glance to the man she had wronged and met a tender smile. "Mr. Sullivan, I wonder if I might have a word with you."

"Certainly. Shall we go onto the porch?"

"Yes." She looked at Mr. Hawkins, who was pretending to ignore them. "Mr. Hawkins, would you keep an eye on the girls for a moment?"

"Sure, maybe I'll put them to work."

With screams of assent, the twins rushed to the storekeeper while Mr. Sullivan opened the door and Lexie stepped outside. She started as he placed a hand beneath her elbow to guide her to the rocking chairs at the end of the porch.

Once seated, Lexie took a deep breath. "First of all, I would like to apologize for my atrocious behavior toward you. I thought, you see—"

"You thought I was an uncaring, rotten father." He smiled as he interrupted. "I believe anyone would have thought and acted the same under the circumstances. And your indignation proves how much you care for Addy and Tuck."

"I do, very much. Which brings me to the subject at hand."

"You want them to stay with you."

Lexie nodded. "I know you care for them, too. I thought perhaps they could stay with me while you are away, and then when you come home, they could come to your farm and spend time with you."

"You do realize they are orphans and need a real family to be part of?" He hesitated. "I mean a father and a mother."

"Yes, of course. And we should continue to search for a suitable, loving family for them." Lexie blinked back the tears that formed. "But in the meantime, they would be happy at the farm with Aunt Kate and Will and me."

"Yes, I believe they would. And I know they would be well taken care of." A shadow crossed his face.

"You want them with you, don't you?"

He sighed. "Yes, but the men that work for me are a rough bunch. It's not the best atmosphere for little girls, although the crew tried hard while the twins were on the *Julia Dawn*."

Lexie nodded. He did care. More than he was admitting. "Mr. Sullivan, I promise I'll treat them like my own, and you can come get them the moment you return."

"Yes, of course." He sat up straighter. "If you don't mind, I have to get back to my boat right away. I'll get their things from the wagon."

Lexie stood as he did. "Thank you for trusting me."

"And thank you for knowing I can be trusted as well."

After putting Addy's and Tuck's things into Lexie's buggy, Jack stepped over to her and took her hands in his. As he looked at her, tenderness filled his eyes. "You're a very special woman, Miss Rayton."

"Thank you, sir."

"I want to say good-bye to them before I leave." He seemed reluctant to let go of her hands, so she gently withdrew them from his.

Addy's and Tuck's faces lit up when they found out they could stay with Lexie, but a moment later Tuck frowned. "What about my fiddle lessons?"

"You already know a lot, Tuck," Addy said.

"That's right." Jack tugged at one of the girl's uneven braids. "And if you need more lessons, I'll try to find you a teacher when I get back from this run to St. Louis."

"Okay." She reached over and gave him a slap on the back.

Lexie shook her head. It took so little to please Tuck.

Lexie and the twins stood on the porch and waved as Jack drove away in the wagon.

A twinge of sadness clutched Lexie. Now what did she have to be sad about? This was exactly what she'd wanted, wasn't it? Then why did the sight of Jack Sullivan driving away make her want to cry?

⌒⎍⎍⌒

"Where's them girls?" Pap frowned as Jack stepped onto the deck. "You didn't leave them at no orphans' home, did ye?"

"Of course not, Pap." Jack knew his indignation at the accusation was unreasonable. After all, he had threatened to do just that. "Miss Sullivan offered to care for them while I'm away. I thought it was best for them."

Indecipherable mutterings spilled forth from Pap's lips. Then he furtively gave a swipe across his eyes. "I guess yer right. Shucks, I know ye are. A riverboat ain't no place for sweet little girls."

"That's right, Pap. I know you'll miss them. They'll miss you, too. I promise I'll bring them to see you from time to time."

"Reckon that'll do." The old man turned and headed for the galley.

"Everything's loaded and ready to go." Thompson leaned against a huge crate and gave Jack a curious look. "You're gonna miss them little gals."

"Yes, well, let's get out of here."

A few moments later, the whistle blew and the hands loosened the moorings. The *Julia Dawn* quivered slightly then slid smoothly away from the bank to start another journey up the crystal White River.

⌒⎍⎍⌒

"What? How dare she?" Lexie stood on the porch with fists clenched against her hips and stared at Will in disbelief. "What right does Sarah Jenkins think she has to make demands?"

Will twisted his hat and gave a slight kick to the railing. "Don't look at me like that. Can't you even try to be reasonable?"

"Me? You want *me* to be reasonable?"

"Yes." A thundercloud replaced her brother's usually gentle expression. "In the first place, you should have consulted me and Aunt Kate before agreeing to a plan that would affect the whole family."

"Sarah isn't family yet, Will Rayton."

"She will be in two months. And she has a right to her say in this. She's going to be my wife in case you've forgotten."

"And what if she is? Why would she object to the girls living here part of the time?"

"Part of the time? Jack Sullivan is away for weeks on end."

"I thought you liked Tuck and Addy."

"I do. You know I do. I feel almost like they're my little sisters. But they aren't, and you can't expect Sarah to feel that way. The house will be crowded as it is."

Lexie gasped, unable to speak at his words. Sarah didn't want her here either. Frustration and helpless anger rose inside until she felt like she'd explode.

Will hit the porch rail with his hat. "I'm going to the store to pick up some things for Aunt Kate before I get started in the fields. But this isn't the end of this discussion, Lexie. When Sullivan gets back, he'll have to make different arrangements."

Lexie clenched her fists against her hips and watched Will ride away. How could he take Sarah's side against his own sister? No one had ever come between them before. The girl must be utterly selfish and self-centered, only thinking about her own comforts.

Whirling, she stomped into the house. "Aunt Kate," she called out, storming into the kitchen, "can you believe that selfish girl?"

"If you are talking about your brother's bride-to-be, I don't think she's selfish at all." Aunt Kate wiped her hands on a dishcloth and poured two cups of coffee, placing them on the table. "Sit down, Lexie, and please lower your voice. I'm surprised the girls are still sleeping with your screeching."

Lexie dropped into a chair, disbelief washing over her. Was Aunt Kate turning against her, too?

"But Aunt Kate—"

"Shhh. Let me talk a minute, Alexandra." Aunt Kate scooped sugar into both cups then added cream.

"Sarah comes from a large family, you know. Before her father married Wanda, Sarah took care of her brothers and sisters for years, without a word of complaint. Now she's about to be a new bride, coming into a new family. She has never said a word about sharing her home with an old aunt and a sister-in-law. In fact, she loves us both and accepted us from the moment she and Will started going around together. But the sudden addition of two rambunctious children must have seemed overwhelming to her."

"But—"

"Let me finish, please."

Lexie sighed and leaned back.

"Becoming a new bride is a wondrous thing, but I should imagine also a little bit frightening under the best of circumstances. Perhaps if Sarah were older she could deal with the situation better. And to be fair, she never once said she wouldn't move in with the twins here. She simply expressed her doubts and fear. Will loves her and wants her to be happy. You can't fault him for that."

Lexie stirred her coffee. All right, maybe Aunt Kate had a point, but she still thought Sarah was being selfish. And after what Will had said, she knew Sarah felt Lexie was in the way, too. "I don't know what to do, Aunt Kate." Lexie bit her bottom lip and looked off into the distance. "I've committed to caring for the girls. If they can't stay here, neither can I. I've no idea what to do."

"Jesus knows. Let's try asking Him."

Anger began a slow simmer in Lexie's heart. "I'm not sure He listens."

"Alexandra Rayton, what a terrible thing to say."

"I know, I know. I'm sorry. But sometimes it seems as though He doesn't hear me. Or at least He doesn't bother to answer."

"Or perhaps you don't hear His answer because you don't take time to listen for it. Or perhaps you refuse to hear because it isn't the one you want." Aunt Kate shook her head. "One thing I know, it isn't God's fault."

Lexie jumped up. "I'm going for a walk." She slammed out the back door and headed for the creek. Why couldn't anything ever go the way she planned? This was all Sarah's fault. No matter what Aunt Kate thought, the girl was plain selfish. And not only that. . .why didn't God ever answer when she prayed?

An image of Jack Sullivan flashed through her mind. Of course, when she prayed about Tuck and Addy she was under a false understanding. God did answer her. It just took some time for her to hear the truth. Was Aunt Kate right? Did she only hear God when His answer was pleasing to her?

She sighed and bit her lip. To be truthful, Sarah had never been anything but sweet and kind before this. Was Lexie being unfair?

But God, what can I do? Where can we go?

Chapter 12

Darkness had fallen by the time Jack arrived at the farm. The run to St. Louis and back, with several side trips, had been full of problems. For the first time since he'd hired on as a boy on his first boat, Jack was glad to be on land. Maybe he was getting old. He chuckled. Pap still considered him a boy, not quite dry behind the ears.

He'd planned to go get the twins, but by the time he could make himself presentable and drive over to the Rayton farm, they'd probably be in bed. Better wait until morning.

After taking care of the horse and wagon, he started hauling water into the house to heat up for a bath.

He only hoped everything had gone well while he'd been gone. Had the twins behaved themselves? They could be a handful sometimes. But it was only orneriness. They were good kids who didn't deserve the bad breaks life had handed them. He knew it was only fair to Tuck and Addy to continue looking for a family, but he'd sure miss them. If he were a married man, he wouldn't think twice about adopting them.

A chill went through him. What if Miss Rayton had already found someone to take them? Would she have turned them over without talking to him first? He took a deep breath and forced himself to relax. She felt the same way he did about the girls. The look in her beautiful blue eyes when they rested on one of the twins was as tender as a mother's glance.

Her face had invaded his thoughts as well as his dreams nearly every night since he'd been gone. Her eyes, which had often been stormy with anger in real life, were dancing with teasing laughter in his dreams. And her hair, which in reality was usually pulled back neatly in a bun, fell in a cascade of thick, shiny, black curls.

The beautiful but volatile Miss Rayton would most likely crack him over the head with a broom handle if she could see into his thoughts and laugh out loud when she did it. She more than likely had a dozen suitors at her door. Besides, what would she want with a river rat like him, even if he was the owner of a rusty old scow?

A pang of guilt shot through him for calling the *Julia Dawn* a scow. She was a fine steamboat and had not only made a fair living for him but had given him many a moment of joy on the river.

Well, what in thunder was the matter with him? You'd think his life on the *Julia Dawn* was over the way he was thinking. He wasn't ready to turn in his sea legs yet.

With a derisive snort, he poured a final bucket of hot water into the old wooden washtub, relieved to see it wasn't leaking. He really should purchase one of the new galvanized ones on his return trip.

⁓⁓⁓

"Mr. Jack!" Tuck ran around the side of the house, yelling like an entire war party. One of her braids hung loose in curly tangles from the wind.

Jack grinned and jumped down from the wagon. "Hey there, Tuck. Miss me that much?"

She grabbed him around the waist and squeezed, then leaned back and cocked her head. "Naw, just trying to make you feel welcome."

He laughed and ruffled her hair, then looked up as the front door swung open.

Addy flew down the steps and grabbed him in almost as hard a bear hug as her sister's.

"Mr. Jack, I'm so glad you're home." Addy's eyes shone with delight.

"Mr. Sullivan, we weren't expecting you."

Jack glanced toward the porch. Alexandra Rayton stood there with a flustered look on her face, wiping her hands on a splotched apron. In spite of her disheveled appearance, a thrill went through Jack at the sight of her, and he took a deep breath. How could any woman look so enticing in a stained apron and a plain housedress?

Jack removed himself gently from the twins' arms and removed his hat as he stepped over to the porch. "I'm sorry if I've inconvenienced you. I only have today and tomorrow at home, and I wanted to take the girls right away."

"It's no inconvenience. My aunt and I are making jelly, but it will only take a moment to gather Tuck's and Addy's things."

"Thanks, I'd appreciate it." He smiled, taking in her smooth skin and the dark, curly tendrils that had come loose and hung on either side of her face. Enchanting.

She blushed and turned quickly to the girls. "Tuck, Addy, why don't you start gathering your things up? I'll be there in a minute."

After the girls had gone inside, she motioned Jack to one of the rocking chairs while she sat in the other. "Mr. Sullivan, I don't quite know how to say this. . ." She hesitated and bit her bottom lip.

Oh no, she was tired of caring for the girls. Not that he minded taking them on the boat if necessary, but he knew it wasn't the best thing for two little girls.

She cleared her throat. "You see, my brother is getting married next month, and he and his bride think it will be too crowded with all of us here."

"I see." He tried to keep the disappointment from his voice. "So of course you won't be able to keep Tuck and Addy anymore."

"Oh, I can. That is if I can find us a place to stay. Only, I'd need to work to support us and then the girls would be alone, so that wouldn't work either."

Frustration reverberated from her tone of voice.

"Wait a minute." Relief washed over Jack. "Do you mean you are still willing to care for them if we can work out the arrangements?"

"Well, yes, but—"

"Is there any reason you can't stay at my place?" At the look of horror that crossed her face, he quickly added, "I mean, of course while I'm away."

A glimmer of hope appeared on her face, and her eyes widened. "Do you mean you'd be willing for us to stay there?"

"Of course. The house is sitting there empty. I'd be happy to see it lived in, and it would be a favor to me."

"Why?"

"Because of the girls, of course."

"But the girls are as much my responsibility as yours. Even if you did find them."

He looked at her a minute. Frown lines had formed between her eyes. Was she going to be difficult? He had already seen her stubborn streak. "I guess if you don't want to stay at the farm I could rent some place in town for you and the girls."

"Oh heavens no. It isn't that I don't want to stay at your farm. I just don't want you to feel obligated." The tip of her tongue darted out and moved across her lips.

He hid a grin. "How about we consider this a joint venture? I provide the farm for living quarters, and you care for Tuck and Addy there."

She hesitated. Her mouth opened then closed then opened again. "Very well. That seems fair to me."

He drew in a breath of relief. "The farm is stocked pretty well. I'll need to show you around, and I'll leave a line of credit with the store for anything else you might need."

"That won't be necessary, Mr. Sullivan. If the farm is fairly well stocked already, then I'd prefer to pay for anything else that we should need or want." She lifted her chin. "I have money of my own."

"If you insist." He wasn't going to lock horns with her over the matter, but he'd still have a talk with Mr. Hawkins, just in case. "Then we seem to be in agreement."

She rose. "I'll help the girls. This will only take a moment."

The three of them returned shortly with two neat bundles and Tuck's hair braided neatly.

"When do you plan to leave, Mr. Sullivan?" Miss Rayton asked.

"Tomorrow after the midday meal."

"Tomorrow is Sunday and the preacher will be here this week. There will be a community picnic after the service. Perhaps you'll bring the girls to church, and I'll meet you there and ride with you to the farm after the meal."

Jack hadn't been to church in years. A pang of remorse shot through him.

"Er. . .I'm not sure I can make it to church. But I can pick you up later."

"But Mr. Jack"—Addy tugged on his sleeve—"we like church. And we want to go play with Sue and Martha afterwards."

"Yep." Tuck snorted. "Besides, Miss Kate and Miss Lexie cook a far sight better'n you."

Lexie's face flamed. "Tuck, don't be rude."

"Sorry, Miss Lexie."

Jack laughed. "I'm sure it's very true. I'm not offended at all."

"So can we go to church?" Addy turned pleading eyes up to him.

"Oh, all right. We'll go." In all honesty, the thought of all that home cooking was pretty tempting.

"Good, then I'll see you all tomorrow." She placed a hand on each girl's shoulder. "Make sure you take baths tonight, girls, and brush your hair thoroughly in the morning. Just leave it down, and I'll put ribbons in when you get to church."

"Yes, ma'am," they chorused.

"And don't forget to clean your teeth."

Jack watched her tender ministrations. She sounded like a mother. Maybe this wasn't such a good idea after all. She'd end up hurt when they found a family for the girls. His stomach clenched. He had an idea he'd be doing a little hurting himself.

⚬

Lexie put another stitch in the rip in one of Tuck's shirts. Addy had converted over to wearing dresses most of the time, but it was still a struggle to get Tuck out of the overalls except for church.

Aunt Kate and Will had gone to bed, but Lexie knew she wouldn't be able to sleep. She'd helped Aunt Kate fry chicken and bake pies for tomorrow. Fresh-picked lettuce and tomatoes were ready to make into a salad in the morning.

Excitement mixed with a smidgen of apprehension clutched at her stomach. Will had seemed relieved when she'd told them her new plans. Aunt Kate, on the other hand, wasn't so sure it was a good idea. Finally, when Will had promised to look in on Lexie and the girls every day, Aunt Kate had reluctantly agreed. Lexie didn't know what her aunt was so worried about. She and the girls would be fine. And if trouble should arise, Lexie could shoot a rifle as well as her brother.

She had packed her clothing and the rest of the twins' things, as well as the books and supplies for their lessons. She also folded up their bedding as well as her own, not knowing how well supplied the Sullivan farm would be. If they needed anything else, they could always come get it. She'd have to see if the Sullivan kitchen was equipped with the utensils she would need.

Laying the garment aside, Lexie rose and walked out onto the porch. She stood by the rail, one hand resting on the post. Moonlight flooded the yard and fields, touching the trees and shrubs. The faint smell of decaying leaves wafted across to her. The scent of early fall.

She didn't take enough time to enjoy the beauty of Aunt Kate's farm. Well, Will's farm now and soon to be Sarah's.

A twinge of jealousy bit at her. Would she ever be a new bride? A vision of Jack Sullivan's strong chin and deep-set brown eyes invaded her thoughts. She tried to brush them away, but his eyes seemed to pierce her heart, causing it to speed up.

She shook her head, aggravated at herself. Jack Sullivan was a handsome man—very handsome—and he had proven to have a good, tender heart, in spite of her first impression to the contrary. But even if she were interested in him, which she certainly was not, he had no interest whatsoever in her. Did he?

She shivered and wrapped her arms around her shoulders. Enough of this nonsense. She tossed her head and went inside.

Chapter 13

Red, brown, and gold leaves, fallen from the oaks and maples, crackled and rustled beneath the wheels of the buggy. Lexie drove into the grove where the tent was set up for services. She reined Jolly in beneath a giant cedar tree and set the brake on the buggy.

"My, it looks like everyone in the county is here." Aunt Kate peered around, more than likely looking for Maisie Turner, a friend of hers.

"I think you're right. Look, even the Maxwells are here." Lexie's voice registered the surprise she felt.

The Maxwells, a family consisting of Mr. Maxwell and three burly sons, always said they didn't cotton to preaching. Their behavior indicated they didn't cotton to much of anything else either, outside their own family and farm.

Billy Joe, the oldest of the boys, had sidled up to Lexie once at a barn-raising and taken one of her curls between his massive fingers. When she'd jerked away, he'd frowned and walked off. She shuddered at the thought of it.

Lexie's voice trembled. "I hope they aren't here to make trouble."

"Now Alexandra, is that the Christian thing to say when someone visits the Lord's house?"

"No, Aunt Kate, of course not. I'm sorry." She'd never told her aunt or Will about Billy Joe's actions that day for fear Will would confront the huge, beefy teen and get himself hurt.

"No harm done." She smiled as she stepped down from the buggy. "I, too, have to remind myself sometimes to be charitable to certain people."

As her aunt headed across the yard to join a group of women by the tent, Lexie glanced around but saw no sign of Mr. Sullivan or the twins. Concerned, she shaded her eyes with her hand and peered in the direction from which they'd be coming.

"What in the world are you gazing at?" Jane appeared at her side in a billow of blue silk ruffles and lace.

"Hello, Jane. Mr. Sullivan is bringing the girls. I was watching for them."

"Hmmm. Exactly what is that story?" Jane tapped her shoulder with the small beaded bag she held in her hand.

"What story?"

"You know. The story of how the twins came to be with Old Mr. Sullivan's nephew? And why you've been taking care of them for him?" Jane lowered her voice. "I believe the whole county is talking about it."

Anger rose in Lexie. She seriously doubted the whole county knew, much less was talking about it. More than likely it was Jane's mother and a few of her cronies. "That's strange. I haven't heard anyone talking about it. Until now. But if it will ease your mind, Jane, the twins were left in the elder Mr. Sullivan's care, I believe." A pang nipped at her conscience. But that was very close to the truth. "So naturally his nephew feels responsible for them. I'm taking care of them when he is away, until a suitable home can be found for them."

"So, you two aren't. . .you know, courting?" She grinned and nudged Lexie on the shoulder. "I wouldn't blame you a bit. He's quite handsome, in a rugged sort of way."

Lexie gasped. "Jane Dobson, what a thing to say. There is absolutely nothing going on between Jack Sullivan and me. And now, if you'll excuse me, I believe I see them coming."

It seemed to Jack the reverend's eyes turned toward Alexandra Rayton an awful lot. And she didn't seem to mind. In fact, from his place on the bench behind her, he'd seen her smile at the man a couple of times.

Jack took a deep breath. There he went again. What sort of preacher looked at a woman like that, right in the middle of his preaching? Could they be a courting couple? Seemed funny the girls hadn't mentioned it though, the way they rattled on about everything. And what was it to Jack if they were courting? He certainly had no hold on her. So why the disappointed sick feeling in the pit of his stomach?

Relief washed over him as the congregation stood to sing. By the time the second verse began, he actually heard the words.

" 'Just as I am, though tossed about, with many a conflict, many a doubt.'"

Was it really that simple? Could he go to God without fixing everything first? Would God accept him after all his years of ignoring Him? When the crowd headed outside, Jack followed and, unsure what to do, waited until he saw Miss Rayton and the twins headed his way. They stopped just outside the tent to shake hands with the preacher. Jack saw the reverend say something to Alexandra. Then as she answered, disappointment appeared on the man's face. An unexplained exultation ran through Jack as Miss Rayton and the girls turned away from the preacher and headed toward him.

"There you are, Mr. Sullivan. If you'll help me get the baskets out of our buggy, I believe tables are already set up behind the tent. If we hurry, we can be sure to find a good spot to eat our meal."

Jack followed her and grinned as the twins took off running with a gang of children of all sizes.

"Girls," she called, "don't go too near the riverbank."

"We won't," they yelled back over their shoulders.

"Here, you can carry this one with the food, and I'll get the one with our dishes and silverware." She smiled at him as she handed him one of the baskets, her eyes dancing. "Don't worry about the twins. Some of the older girls always watch out for the children while we set the food out. And some of the men are down by the river, too, choosing their fishing spots for later."

"That's good to know." He walked by her side around to the back of the tent where several tables had been thrown together and were already half loaded down with food. He set the basket on the spot she indicated and watched as she set the food around at different places on the table. He noted where she put the pan of cold fried chicken, his favorite.

When everything was ready, the children were called and the reverend gave thanks.

Soon Jack sat beside Miss Rayton and the girls on the blanket she'd brought, balancing their plates of food.

"See, Mr. Jack." Tuck grinned and held up a drumstick. "This is how chicken is supposed to be cooked."

Jack burst out laughing, but his laughter was cut off as he saw the tightening of Miss Rayton's shoulders. He glanced over in the direction she stared. A stout young man stared at her, longing in his eyes. When he noticed Jack watching, he turned and walked away.

"Who is that?" Jack jumped up, intending to go after the man, but a trembling hand on his drew his attention.

"Please, don't." Her eyes were pleading. "I don't think he means any harm. And people would be sure to think the worst if a fight broke out. Please sit back down and finish your food."

A shudder of anger rippled through him, but he sat and picked up his plate. He hoped she was right and the man meant no harm. Perhaps he'd read more into the man's expression than was there. But he'd stay close to her until they left to go home.

ᵒᵐᵐᵒ

"Really, I can have Williams continue to come over to see to the livestock, Miss Rayton."

"No, no. The girls and I can manage fine." She paused and a rosy tinge crept across her face. "I really would prefer it if you would call me Lexie, Mr. Sullivan."

His heart seemed to jump at her suggestion. He cleared his throat before he replied. "It would be an honor, but only if you will call me Jack."

She smiled. "Very well, Jack. And now, please don't concern yourself about the livestock. I promise it will be no trouble at all."

"I'll agree to that, but I'm going to have Williams stop by a couple of times a week, just in case you need wood or something needs to be fixed." He'd much rather have the man stop by every day, but Lexie seemed determined.

"That's fine. I would appreciate that."

"All right, you've seen all the outbuildings. Now I'll show you the house and where everything is."

They took a tour around the old but neat farmhouse. The rooms were spotless and Lexie smiled. Jack and the girls had been working.

"Look, Miss Lexie, this is our room." Lexie followed Addy into the small room. It was clean and neat. But she made a mental note to make some frilly things to make it more suitable for little girls.

They entered another bedroom. The bed was large and high.

Jack cleared his throat. "This is where you'll sleep. I've found it very comfortable. I trust you will also."

Warmth flowed down her face and onto her chest. She'd be sleeping in his bed? But of course she had to sleep somewhere. Ducking her head, she turned and exited the room.

From beds to chests to living room furniture, everything was lovely and handcrafted.

"The kitchen's this way." Jack headed toward the back and Lexie followed. A long table lined with two benches and a chair on each end sat in the middle of the room.

"Did your uncle have a large family at one time?" Lexie asked, puzzled.

"Actually, he never married. Perhaps he planned to at one time. I've no idea."

"Forgive me. It's none of my business." She bit her bottom lip.

"There's nothing to forgive. Will the stove be all right?"

Lexie walked over to the black stove in the corner. A woodbox at the side was full. She opened the door to the oven and found it small but adequate. "Yes, it's fine." She turned and faced him. "We'll do very well here."

"Please feel free to change anything in the house you like. I'm sure it can use a woman's touch."

Lexie nodded. She intended to do just that. Already ideas were running through her head. She and the girls would be busy indeed.

"Well, I guess that's everything but the cellar." Jack opened the door to the mudroom then went outside. Stone steps led downward. "Watch your step now."

The cellar was filled with hams, bacon, potatoes, and onions. Shelves were lined with jars of pickles, green beans, beets, and other vegetables.

"Goodness, your uncle even canned?"

"Well, he never did when I lived with him." He gave a short laugh. "Back then we lived on beans and game mostly. He must have changed some over the years."

They went back upstairs, and Jack stood looking at the three of them for a moment. "Well, if you're sure you have everything you need, I'd better get my things and be on my way before it gets dark."

Lexie nodded. "We'll be fine. Oh, I almost forgot. Will has promised Aunt Kate to check on us every day. So you see, between Mr. Williams and my brother, you have nothing to worry about."

He nodded, relief crossing his face. He brought his horse from the barn then stood looking down at her. His gaze rested on her lips, and warmth slid over her cheeks. Was he going to kiss her? Anticipation battled with indignation.

He seemed to shake himself, then grabbed his saddlebags and tied them on. He gave Addy and Tuck each a hug then mounted the horse. "I'll see you when I get back then." He put his hand to his hat, nodded at Lexie, and rode away.

She stood, her hand at her throat, and watched until he was lost from sight.

"I wish he could stay here with us." Addy flopped down on the step. "I miss him already."

Tuck dropped down beside her. "Me, too. I wish we could all be here together. Mr. Jack, Miss Lexie, you, and me."

Lexie gasped and laughed. "But we couldn't all stay here together, of course. When he comes home, I'll have to go back to Aunt Kate's."

Tuck jumped up and peered into her face. "Why can't you and Mr. Jack get married?"

"Why, why. . ." Lexie couldn't stop sputtering and her face burned. "People get married when they are in love, Tuck."

Addy got up and joined her sister. "Don't you love Mr. Jack? I do."

"Well, of course I love everyone, Addy. But that's not the kind of love married people have. Now let's go see what we can have for our supper."

But a thrill coursed through Lexie, and she couldn't prevent the smile that tipped her lips.

Chapter 14

The drone of cicadas and the chirping of crickets filled the air as Lexie drove the horses through thick woods on the way to the Flanigan cabin. Tuck, with Addy adding her appeals, had begged for the last week, since they'd been staying at the Sullivan farm, to go fetch their grandfather's violin. Finally Lexie had decided she should probably acquiesce. With the cabin deserted, it would be simple for thieves to break in and take anything they pleased. And Tuck had her heart set on that violin.

Lexie had been surprised to hear that one of Jack's boat hands had given the girl a few lessons. And it had surprised her even more that Tuck was interested. She'd have thought Addy would be more likely to take to a musical instrument. Just another example of judging someone by outward appearance and actions, she supposed.

"It's just a little ways now, Miss Lexie." Addy's eyes were bright with excitement, but at least she wasn't bouncing up and down on the seat like Tuck.

"Tuck, please sit down before you fall." That child wasn't afraid of anything.

"Sorry, Miss Lexie. Oh. Over there!" She pointed to an opening in the tree line.

The wagon rattled over some huge, exposed tree roots. Then they were out of the thick woods. A small but well-built log cabin stood in the middle of a clearing. Chickens hopped around the yard, pecking at the ground. They would need to do something about them.

"What did you do with the livestock?" She should have asked about that weeks ago. Too late now if they'd been deserted.

"Weren't any but old Buzzard Bait, and we rode him when we left. I don't know where that old stupid mule ran off to." Tuck shook her head in disgust.

"We had a milk cow," Addy piped up. "But when she went dry, Pa sold her and the calf."

At least they wouldn't be coming across dead animals. The chickens seemed to have held their own.

Tuck jumped down and tied the horses to a low branch, and she and Addy ran inside. By the time Lexie followed them, she could hear their excited voices coming from a back room.

The cabin wasn't dirty. Not the neatest she'd ever seen, but not too bad. It was merely lacking those little touches of comfort that made a house a home. Sadness washed over Lexie. What about the stepmother who'd lived there for a while? Had there been a reason she couldn't add those touches, or did she simply not care?

A squeal proceeded from the back room, and the girls came running. Tuck cradled a lovely old violin. Addy watched her sister, a wistful look on her face. The case dangled from her hand.

Tuck placed the instrument under her chin and ran the bow across the strings for a few minutes.

"That's very nice, Tuck, and the violin is beautiful. But I think it more than likely needs tuning. How about we find someone to take a look at it?"

"Okay." She handed the violin to Addy, who placed it gently into the case and covered it with a soft, faded cloth.

Lexie glanced around the room. "Is there anything else you'd like to take with you?"

They looked at each other, sending some silent message. Now what were they up to?

"Just Mama's Bible and her books. Is that all right?" Addy's eyes searched hers.

"Of course. Nothing else?" Lexie's glance rested on a carved box on top of the mantel.

Tuck's eyes followed hers. "Naw, that's just Pa's old tobacco box."

"Then let's throw some corn out for the chickens. We'll have to come back for them another day. I don't want to get caught in the woods in the dark. And they turn dark long before sundown."

With Addy carrying their mother's Bible and two worn children's books and Tuck holding the violin case close to her chest, they all got back into the wagon and left.

"When can we find someone to fix the violin?" Tuck was bouncing again.

"We can inquire of Mr. Hawkins. He may know someone nearby. Otherwise, we'll ask Walt Packard next time we have a church service. He's very good on the fiddle, and I'm sure he wouldn't mind tuning yours for you."

"Well, just so he don't ruin it." She ran her hand protectively over the old leather case.

Lexie suppressed a smile. "Doesn't ruin it. And you can stand there and watch every move he makes."

Addy giggled. "He wouldn't dare ruin your violin with you standing by his elbow glaring at him, Tuck."

Tuck laughed, but she pulled the case with the instrument close to her body, and she didn't bounce again the rest of the way.

Just as they were coming out of the woods by the Sullivan farm, Lexie thought she heard hoofbeats. She reined in the horses. "Shhh, girls. Be still and quiet."

She jumped out of the wagon and tiptoed forward until she could see the house. Nothing seemed to be amiss and there was no sign of anyone. "It's okay, girls. I thought I heard hoofbeats. But if I did, they must have been merely passing by."

Still, an uneasiness settled over her.

She stepped cautiously into the house. Nothing seemed out of order, but was that a slight odor hanging in the air?

"Something stinks in here." Leave it to Tuck to get to the point.

"Perhaps we overlooked some garbage?" Lexie peered into the kitchen. It didn't smell like garbage. It smelled like unwashed body odor.

"Nope. I threw it out to the pig after breakfast." Tuck frowned. "I don't think I missed anything."

A careful search of the kitchen revealed nothing that shouldn't be there and nothing spoiled. "Let's open the windows and air things out. It's probably nothing."

Lexie's uneasiness grew. Should she say something to Will when he came over? Maybe some drifter had come in to search for food. But in the back of her mind lay the memory of Billy Joe Maxwell's seeming fixation on her. Did he know she and the girls were staying here alone?

She shivered. If only Jack were here. Yes, she had to tell Will as soon as he came.

⌘

The *Julia Dawn* slipped into its designated berth. Jack felt a bump. Then several crewmen jumped down and secured her.

The dock here in St. Louis was noisy and crowded. Stevedores yelled up to the boats of their availability to work. But painted women with skirts pulled up and tied up above their knees called out even louder.

Jack hardly saw any of it. He just wanted to unload, reload, and then get back home as soon as possible. He sighed. That wasn't likely to be very soon though. They'd already been in and out of this port three times since he'd left the farm. Left Lexie and Tuck and Addy.

He'd almost made a complete fool of himself as he was saying good-bye. He'd made the mistake of glancing at Lexie's perfect, soft, pink lips, and for a moment the thought of pressing his own lips against hers was so strong he had to force himself to look away. She probably never would have forgiven him.

A pang of loneliness shot through him. But if there was another load going into Illinois he'd have to take it. After all, winter would be here before he knew it, and he had mouths to feed besides his own.

⌘

Bright orange pumpkins and yellow and gold winter squash lined the tables outside the store. Lexie eyed them, the taste of pumpkin pie and baked Hubbard squash almost tangible on her tongue. She realized Aunt Kate had plenty and would throw a fit if she knew Lexie had spent money on something they'd grown in the garden. But Lexie's newfound independence rose up inside her. After all, she was a grown woman and had money put away from several years of tomatoes as well as the work she'd done for Mr. Hawkins.

She chose two medium-sized pumpkins and several squash then followed the twins inside where she deposited the squash on the counter. The twins waved at Mr. Hawkins and made a beeline for the back door. Lexie didn't know why they'd bothered to come in at all.

"Morning, Lexie. I've missed seeing you." Mr. Hawkins put the vegetables in a box and set it aside.

"I've missed working here, too, Mr. Hawkins. But the girls and I keep pretty busy these days."

Tuck shot back inside and sidled up to Lexie. "Don't forget to ask," she said then hurried back out.

Lexie shook her head and laughed. "Mr. Hawkins, do you know anyone close by who can tune Tuck's violin? It has to be someone who has experience and knows what he's doing. The violin has been in their family for many years."

He grinned. "I think I know just the right person for the job. Name's Willie Van Schultz. Not sure the Van is real. He told me he added it because it sounds good. But he may've been joking. He makes his fiddle sing. I can tell you that much."

"Do you know where we can find him?"

"He lives in a shack downriver somewhere. Lives off the river and the land. But he meets a couple of other old men here every Saturday from just after sunup until sundown. They're quite a lively bunch. Squeeze-box Tanner plays an accordion. Tom Black, the banjo. They're here to have fun, but they end up entertaining my customers, so it doesn't bother me a bit. Bring the violin some Saturday, and I'm sure he'll fix it up for her."

"Thank you, Mr. Hawkins. We'll come this Saturday. Now I'd better finish my shopping."

Twenty minutes later she had everything laid out on the counter. "I think that's everything, Mr. Hawkins."

"All right then. I'll just tally these up and put it on Jack Sullivan's line of credit."

"What?" Lexie's face flamed and she glared at him. "Why would you do that?"

"Er, Jack said anything you and those girls need, I should put on his tab." A puzzled look crossed his face.

"Mr. Hawkins, I plainly told Mr. Sullivan before he left that if we needed anything that wasn't already stocked at his farm I would purchase it myself." She took a deep breath. "Now please add these up, and tell me what I owe you."

"Yes, ma'am. If that's your wish." He totaled the order and told her the amount.

"Thank you, Mr. Hawkins."

"You're welcome, Miss Lexie." He winked.

"I sort of overreacted, didn't I?" She smiled at him.

"Well. . .maybe just a little. But that's a lady's prerogative, now isn't it?"

She sighed. "I do need to learn to control my anger."

He nodded. "I don't think Jack meant any harm. He feels responsible for Tuck and Addy. Being as he found them at his house and all."

"Yes, I know. But I did tell him." And he'd ignored her wishes. But he had been so kind lately. And he was only making sure they had everything they needed. "Mr. Hawkins, I've changed my mind. I believe I will let you put my purchases on Mr. Sullivan's tab." She was surprised at the peace she'd felt once she made the decision. Being independent was fine, but a woman needed to be willing to accept help, too.

They arrived back at the farm just as Will rode up.

"Need some help?" He grinned as he vaulted off Jolly and came over to the wagon.

"Yes, I believe I do, brother dear. By the way, I want to thank you for coming over every day to make sure we're all right."

A surprised but pleased look crossed his face. "It's my honor, Lexie. You're my sister. I love you, you know."

"I know you do, Will. And I love you, too."

Chapter 15

The squeal of the violin pierced Lexie's ears, and she slammed her hands against the side of her head. Willie Schultz had been twisting and turning little knobs and running the bow across the strings over and over for at least twenty minutes. Lexie didn't know how he could get anything done with Tuck almost in his lap. Addy stood close by, but at least she didn't crowd him.

Mr. Schultz lifted his head, yelping as it slammed into Tuck's chin. Sputtering, he rubbed his head and glared at her. "Listen here, young'un. If you want this here fiddle in working order today, you'd better quit crowding me. I can jes' barely see what I'm a'doin'."

Tuck scooted backward a few inches. "Sorry, Mr. Willie. Are you almost done?"

He breathed in and out loudly. "Well, let me see here. I think I might jes' about have it."

He made another twist on the instrument then handed it to Tuck with the bow. "Let's see how she sounds now."

Almost reverently, Tuck took the violin from his hands and placed it under her chin. She licked her lips and glanced at her sister, who sent her a smile of encouragement.

Lexie listened in amazement. It was obvious the child hadn't been playing long, but still, to play that well after only a few lessons showed talent.

She finished her little song and darted a look at Mr. Schultz. Lexie only hoped he wouldn't discourage Tuck by saying something negative about her efforts.

"Well now, little gal, that ain't half bad." He nodded and narrowed his eyes at her. "If it's all right with your ma here, mebbe you could sit in with us next Saturday."

"You mean it?" Tuck's eyes were round with excitement. "I can play with you?"

Lexie stared at the old man and then at Tuck. He'd thought Lexie was the girls' mother. She needed to correct that right away. But she hated to interrupt when Tuck was so happy.

"Wal, now. You gotta promise you'll listen when I tell you something. I'll jes' be trying to help, you see." He peered at Tuck.

"Oh yes, sir." She turned to Lexie, eagerness in her eyes. "Can I, Miss Lexie? I mean, may I?"

Lexie bit her lip and thought. Coming into town every week would be an added chore to their already busy schedule. But she couldn't prevent Tuck from pursuing something she loved so much. "I think we can manage that, at least until the weather turns bad."

"Woohoooo." Tuck did an Indian dance up and down the porch.

Addy stepped forward, worry on her face. "Tuck, be careful of Great-Grandpa's violin."

Tuck handed the instrument to Addy, who placed it carefully into the case while Tuck continued to dance.

Lexie glanced at Addy. She seemed happy for Tuck, but there was pensiveness about her when she looked at the violin. Had she harbored a secret desire to play the instrument herself? A sudden idea came to Lexie. "Girls, we need to get going. I want to go by Aunt Kate's before we go home."

She turned to the old man, who was grinning at Tuck's antics. "Mr. Schultz, thank you so much. What is your fee for tuning the violin?"

A dour expression shadowed the man's countenance. "Ain't no fee, ma'am. Ain't like it's work. And that's Van Schultz."

"Then I thank you very much, Mr. Van Schultz." She reached her hand to him.

He took it and shook it gently with his calloused one. "Guess you ain't their ma after all, are you?"

"No, but it was a natural mistake. And it would be an honor for any woman to be their mother."

The smile he gave her replaced the shadow from the moment before, and good humor filled his eyes. "I reckon I'll see you'uns on Saturday then."

They found Aunt Kate outside hanging overalls and shirts on the clothesline. A fire was built beneath the large iron pot at the side of the house. Towels and other whites would boil there. Lexie and the girls joined Aunt Kate and helped to finish hanging the colored things.

"What are you three gadding about for?" Aunt Kate's words were tempered with a gentle tone and a smile.

Lexie told her aunt about the man who'd tuned the violin and his offer to help Tuck.

"That was right kind of him," Aunt Kate said. "I hope you thanked him nicely, Abigail."

"Yes, ma'am, I sure did."

"That's a good girl. Now, who wants something cold to drink?" She headed for the house, motioning for them to follow.

Lexie poured lemonade in tall glasses and placed the girls at the kitchen table while she followed her aunt into the parlor.

"What's on your mind, Alexandra?" Aunt Kate peered at her. She always seemed to know when Lexie needed to talk.

"I'm sure you've noticed how Addy gives in to Tuck about everything." She hastened to add, "Only because she loves her sister so much. And I'm not even sure Tuck is aware of it because she loves Addy, too."

"Yes, of course I've noticed how Addy never speaks up for herself. Which is good Christian character to an extent. But to be honest, I don't think it's that healthy when carried too far."

Lexie frowned. "I know. And I think the situation with Tuck getting the violin and lessons may be another example."

"Do you mean that Addy wanted to play the violin?"

"I'm not sure. It's just a feeling I get sometimes. And if it's so, this may be one of those things that you referred to as going too far."

"What do you intend to do about it?"

"I was thinking if Addy had an instrument of her own she was good at, perhaps the violin wouldn't matter so much." She looked at the organ in the corner.

"You want to teach her to play the organ?"

"I want to give her the chance to learn if she wants to. But only, of course, if it's all right with you. We will have to come here for lessons and practice."

"Not necessarily. I don't play. As you know, the organ was my mother's, your grandmother's. I always intended you to have it because you play so well. We can move it to the Sullivan farm."

"Oh, Aunt Kate, are you sure?" Lexie hadn't had any idea her grandmother's organ would ever belong to her.

"Of course I'm sure. Will can get a couple of the hands that helped him with harvest. I'm sure they'll be happy for a little extra money in their pockets."

"I suppose I need to make sure first that Addy is even interested."

Aunt Kate rose and picked up her glass. "Nonsense. The music will be nice on cold winter nights in any case."

⚬⚬⚬

Jack knew he was pushing the horse too hard, but he could only think of getting home to Lexie and the girls.

Slow down, you idiot, lest Champion drop dead from exhaustion before you've had him a full day.

Not that he would really push a horse, any horse, that far, but he pulled slightly on the reins until the horse settled into a canter. He'd purchased the golden palomino yesterday when he'd arrived back in Forsyth, but by the time his business was taken care of it was too late to start for the farm. If he got there in the middle of the night, it would create a problem.

So he'd stayed, paid for bath and shave, and bedded down in his own bunk on the *Julia Dawn* for the night. After breakfast he picked Champion up at the livery stable.

He patted his pockets to make sure the peppermint sticks he'd bought for Tuck and Addy hadn't fallen out. He wanted to buy something for Lexie but decided that was a "better not" idea. Now that he had admitted to himself that his feelings for her went deeper than casual interest, he knew he needed to be careful. First of all, she might be better off with the new reverend who was smitten with Lexie, whether she knew it or not. She could already have feelings for the man. She didn't take her eyes off his face during the sermon that Sunday. Of course, she had dinner with Jack and the girls, but maybe she was only being polite, especially since he hadn't thought to bring any food.

He passed up Hawkins's store and took the worn wagon path by the river. His mouth was dry. Would she leave as soon as he got there, or could he hope she might stay and visit for a while? They could sit on the front porch and drink lemonade or something. That would be suitable, wouldn't it? As long as they were outside. He gave a short laugh. He was pathetic, getting into a stew like this over a woman. Even if she did have hair like midnight and eyes like a stormy sea. He sighed. There he went again.

He reined Champion in and sat for a moment, taking in the sight of his home. Funny how he'd come to think of this place as home. He never had before. A terrible screeching and pounding came from the house. What in the world was that awful din?

He jumped off the horse and rushed onto the porch and pushed the front door. Locked. He pounded and heard footsteps rushing across the floor.

"Who is it?" Lexie's voice was nervous.

"It's me. Jack. Is something wrong in there?"

"No, no. Just a minute." He heard the bar slide back, and the door swung open to reveal Lexie's white face.

Wanting to kick himself, he realized he'd frightened her. "I'm sorry to have startled you," he said, stepping through the door. "I thought something was wrong. It was stupid of me."

"No, not at all, Jack." She spoke his name timidly, unaccustomed to using his first name.

"Hi, Mr. Jack." Tuck stood in the middle of the room, holding a fiddle in her hands. Addy was just rising from the chair in front of an organ he'd never seen before.

"I see I'm just in time for a musical concert."

Addy giggled, and Tuck laid the violin down and rushed over, flinging her arms around him. "You're finally home. What took you so long?"

"Lot of freight this trip, Tuck. We had to run up into Illinois several times." He felt himself relaxing. "It's good to be home."

"Oh! You must be tired and hungry. Please sit down, and let me get you something to eat." Lexie scurried toward the kitchen.

He sat in one of the rocking chairs, with Tuck and Addy on each side. He wasn't really hungry yet, but the sight of Lexie getting him something to eat was so charming he couldn't refuse. "So, Tuck, is that the famous violin that came all the way from Ireland?"

"Yes, sir. That's Great-Grandfather's fiddle all right."

"But where did the organ come from? I don't seem to recall seeing that in my parlor before." He scratched his chin.

Addy giggled. "It's Miss Lexie's. She's teaching me to play."

"Yep." Tuck grinned. "We tried to play together for the first time today, but it's not working out so well."

"Aha. That explains that awful screech and howl I heard when I rode up. I thought you were all under attack."

Both girls howled with laughter.

Lexie came back in. "I put out some cold chicken and peach pickles on the table. And there is fresh bread. Girls, you may as well come eat, too. If you get hungry again later, you'll find sliced ham and hard-boiled eggs in the pantry. I'll just gather a few things up and go to Aunt Kate's."

Jack frowned as dismay washed over him. "Please don't go yet. I'd really like to talk to you about some things."

"Oh well, all right. I'll just get my things together though. Then after we talk I'll be ready to leave."

Now what was he going to talk about? He couldn't ask to court her. It was too soon. He'd talk about the girls and ask how things had gone here on the farm. And why they'd had the house locked up tight in the middle of the day.

Chapter 16

Jack sat in a straight-backed horsehair chair on the front porch and listened to Lexie's soft voice, interspersed with the chirping of crickets and an occasional snort from Champion, who grazed a short distance away.

"Then last week, we helped Aunt Kate finish up the jelly." A laugh rippled from her throat. "You should have seen Tuck. She had juice from the strawberries from top to bottom."

She leaned back and rocked gently in Uncle Pat's oak rocker.

Addy and Tuck tossed a ball to each other in the front yard.

The peace that washed over Jack was unlike any he'd ever experienced. Was this what it was like to have a home and family? But Lexie and the girls were not his family, and he needed to remember that. "How are they doing with their lessons?" he asked.

"Very well." She clasped her hands together and her eyes shone. "Both girls are bright, and I'm so pleased with their progress. But a school will be starting in the spring. The community is planning a workday for the men to construct the building that will also be used for church services."

Jack nodded. Had it occurred to her that the girls might not be here in the spring? Should he remind her? He brushed the thought away. Not now.

"So there was no trouble of any kind while I was gone?" He had suddenly remembered the locked door in the middle of the day.

She hesitated for a moment. "No. No trouble."

He frowned. "Do you always lock the door in the middle of the day?"

She took a deep breath then bit her lip. "I—I did promise everyone I'd be careful while we were here alone."

That was true. Relief washed over him. He had cautioned her several times, and he was sure her aunt and brother had as well. She had kept her word to do so. That was all.

"I really must be going, Jack. When do you plan to leave?"

He hesitated, feeling guilty for some reason. "I'll be leaving again tomorrow afternoon."

She nodded. "Shall I take the wagon or one of the horses?"

"I'll drive you, of course." He rose and called to the girls, who came scurrying.

As the wagon bounced over the rocky terrain, he glanced time and again at Lexie. She and the girls kept a running game of who could spot the most wildlife. He suspected Lexie was using the experience as a science lesson.

They pulled up at the Rayton farm, and Jack helped Lexie down from the wagon. He continued to hold her hand for a moment, reluctant to release the softness that was enveloped in his own rough hand.

She glanced up at him and blushed, gently removing her hand from his.

"Bye, Miss Lexie." Tuck grinned. "Do we have to have lessons tomorrow?"

"No, I won't be there till early afternoon, and you'll want to spend time with Mr. Jack. But I'm going to quiz you about the wild animals you saw on the way over here today. So perhaps you could each write down the ones you can remember."

"Yes, ma'am." Addy smiled and turned to her sister. "I can remember all of them."

"So can I." Tuck frowned.

"Now, girls. This isn't a contest. It's just for fun." Lexie gave each a hug then turned to Jack. "Enjoy your time with them."

"I will. I thought maybe I'd take them to the river and try to catch some fish."

"They'll love that." With a smile and a wave, she headed for the house.

The way home wasn't nearly as much fun as the way over.

"I miss Miss Lexie," Addy said.

"Already?" Jack gave a little laugh.

"Me, too." Tuck placed her hand on his sleeve. "Do you love Miss Lexie?"

Jack coughed. "Uh, why do you ask?"

"Because I'd really like for us all to be together, but Miss Lexie says you have to be married for that to happen."

He thought of her words later as he sat in the parlor. What kind of husband or father could he be? He thought of his parents. They'd been happy together. His mother would be ashamed of him for not staying faithful to God. Moisture filled his eyes.

Lord, if I can really come to You, just as I am, then here I am. Please straighten everything out in my life.

༄

"I can't believe Will is getting married in two weeks." Lexie pushed up the sleeve that kept sliding down on her arm as she polished the furniture in her bedroom until it shone. She'd moved all her things into Will's small room, and she and Aunt Kate were determined to have it looking nice for the new bride.

"It was kind of you to give up your room." Aunt Kate smoothed the ruffle of the new curtains she finished hanging. "You don't have to, you know."

"I don't mind. It's only fair that Will and Sarah have the larger room. Especially since I'm away most of the time." She gave a final rub to the tall chest and stood back to examine her work. "There, that looks better, don't you think?"

"It's very nice, dear. And with this new coverlet you made for the bed, it looks like a brand-new room."

"The girls and I will come over next week to help with the rest of the fall cleaning. Then we can spend the following week baking."

"Mrs. Jenkins will appreciate the help, I'm sure. The whole community will more than likely turn out for the wedding and the dinner." Aunt Kate stood in the doorway and glanced around the room, satisfaction on her face. "Well, I think we've done everything we can do in here. Let's go sit a spell. I could use a glass of cold buttermilk. How about you?"

"Sounds good to me, Auntie. You go get settled and I'll bring the buttermilk." Lexie bent over and removed a speck of lint from the braided rug, then followed her aunt out of the room. She went to the well by the back porch and pulled up the crock jug of buttermilk. She carried two full glasses into the parlor and found Aunt Kate running a cloth across the mantel. "I thought you were going to sit."

The older woman laughed and eased herself into the overstuffed chair in the corner. "I thought I saw a spot of dust on the mantel. I must have imagined it."

They sipped their drinks in silence for a few minutes.

Lexie glanced over to see Aunt Kate eyeing her. Now why was she giving her that look?

"Lexie, dear, what do you think of the Reverend Hines?"

Surprised, Lexie shot a look at her aunt. "Why, I love his sermons. I know Reverend Collins was a godly man and very knowledgeable, but when Reverend Hines preaches he makes me want to get closer to God."

"That's very good, dear. But I meant what do you think of him as a man?" Her eyes danced with anticipation.

Lexie, stunned, stared at Aunt Kate. Apparently she hadn't given up her desire to find a husband for her niece. Lexie cleared her throat. "I think he's a very nice man and quite handsome. He'll make some woman a wonderful husband."

Aunt Kate frowned. "You mean you're really not interested? I thought you liked him."

"I do like him, but no, I'm not interested in him romantically."

"Oh dear." Aunt Kate placed her glass on the table beside her. "That's too bad, because I have reason to believe he's quite taken with you."

Lexie's mouth flew open. "Aunt Kate! You haven't been discussing me with him, have you?"

"Of course not. I wouldn't presume to do that. Well, not exactly."

"What do you mean by that?"

"He kept bringing your name into the conversation at the picnic. What was I supposed to do? Ignore him?" Aunt Kate frowned.

"No, no, you're right. I'll simply have to find a polite way to discourage him." Lexie sighed. Why couldn't she have fallen for the reverend instead of. . .

She tried unsuccessfully to banish Jack's handsome face from her mind where it seemed to invade at will lately. She simply must stop thinking of him in that way. He certainly wasn't interested in settling down with a wife and family. He was practically married to that *boat*.

"Yes, if you're sure you won't change your mind, I suppose it's best to let him know." Aunt Kate stood and picked up her glass, then reached for Lexie's. "I'll just go rinse these out."

"I can do it," Lexie protested, rising.

"No, no, this will only take me a minute. Why don't you wait for me on the porch and enjoy the nice fall air? Jack and the twins will be here to get you soon."

Lexie went to the small back room and gathered up her things, then walked out onto the wide front porch. Grandfather Rayton's big, old rocking chair beckoned and she slipped gratefully into it.

Red leaves floated down from the maple tree in front, and then a gust of wind caught them and they went skipping across the yard. Fall was her favorite season. A honking sound above drew her attention. A flock of geese, high in the sky, flew south in formation, indicating winter would be here soon.

Lexie shivered and pulled her shawl closer about her. Why Will and Sarah had decided on the first Sunday in November for a wedding was beyond her. She had seen snowstorms that early. Well, just once. There she went again. Finding fault with Sarah, one of the sweetest girls she knew.

So many changes had come in the past few months. She'd been so restless in the spring, longing for something to happen in her life. Well, a lot had happened, and she wasn't sure she liked the changes. The job at Hawkins's where she'd worked for a while, meeting the twins, and now, soon, Will's wedding. But those were all good things, so what was bothering her? She sighed. Or rather who? Jack Sullivan. He was bothering her. And she wasn't sure why.

He was quite handsome with his strong chin and those deep-set eyes that seemed to see right through her. The way he looked at her sometimes took her breath away. After the misunderstanding that had caused her to despise him unjustly, she'd then found out the truth and had done a complete turnaround in her opinion of him. She'd begun to see kindness then a sense of humor. His hard work had impressed her.

Of course if he had a romantic relationship with someone out there, he probably wasn't working all the time he was gone. Still, she shouldn't hold that against him. He had a perfect right to be in love with whomever he chose to.

A sudden thought crossed her mind. Maybe he would get married and adopt the girls. Pain shot through her. Another woman would be tucking them in at night and teaching them their lessons. She would receive their sweet kisses on her cheek. Lexie saw them sitting out on the porch at night—Jack, Tuck, Addy, and his new wife.

She knew her imagination was running wild again. This was ridiculous. She had Jack Sullivan married to someone who might not exist, and she had created a mother for Tuck and Addy. Would she ever stop floating away on these childish flights of fancy?

"Finally, brethren, whatsoever things are true, whatsoever things are honest,

whatsoever things are just, whatsoever things are pure, whatsoever things are lovely, whatsoever things are of good report; if there be any virtue, and if there be any praise, think on these things."

Lexie's mother used to quote that scripture from Philippians 4 to her when her imagination would run away with her. She sighed and leaned back against the wide slats. Soon the creaking of the rockers as she moved back and forth soothed her troubled heart.

Chapter 17

Excitement ran through Lexie as she pulled the wagon in front of Hawkins's. Wagons, buggies, and horses crowded the hitching post and yard. Tuck and Addy jumped down and ran to join the crowd already surrounding Willie Van Schultz and his friends.

The week had flown by and Lexie was ready for Saturday. The girls had to be, too. They'd all worked hard this week helping Aunt Kate get the house into tip-top shape for Will's new bride. Every night they'd gone home and tried to squeeze in a lesson or two. A little shopping, music, and visiting with neighbors were just what they needed.

"There's my little fiddler. C'mon, Tuck. Tune 'er up. We'll wait for you." Willie laughed and made room for Tuck on the bench where he sat.

"You girls stay right here while I do the shopping now." Lexie gave each girl a direct look.

"Yes, ma'am," Addy promised. "We won't go anywhere."

Squeezebox Tanner grinned. "Don't you worry none, ma'am. We'll keep a eye on 'em."

"Thank you, Mr. Tanner." Lexie went inside to the tune of "Old Dan Tucker." If she was any judge, Tuck was getting pretty good on the fiddle under the tutelage of Willie Van Schultz.

Jane Dobson and Aletha Humphreys bent over a fashion book, oohing and ahhing. Aletha glanced up, and when she saw Lexie, her eyes lit up and she nudged her companion.

"Lexie, come look at these gorgeous dresses. All the latest Paris fashions." Jane motioned for Lexie to join them.

Sighing because she'd rather not but didn't want to be rude to the younger girls, Lexie stepped over and looked at the open page. "That is rather lovely, isn't it?" But the lace-frilled, beaded gown was a little too fancy for Lexie's taste. "It might be better with a few less silk roses, don't you think?"

"Oh no." Aletha gave her a look of horror. "It's perfect as it is. I wouldn't want to ruin it."

"Tell me, Lexie"—Aletha gave her a curious glance—"have you seen Reverend Hines lately?"

"I saw him at church and the picnic like everyone else. Why?" And why would Aletha think Lexie would have seen him since then?

"Oh, nothing. I just noticed he seemed very interested in you." She cut a glance at Jane, who turned away.

"That's nonsense, Aletha. And I hope you haven't said such a thing to anyone else." Lexie wanted nothing more than to shake the silly girl. "That's the way rumors get started."

Jane whirled around. "Then you aren't seeing him? I mean he's not courting you or anything?"

Lexie laughed. "He came to our house to dinner the first Sunday he was here, if you want to call that courting. I assure you, I have no interest whatsoever in your handsome young preacher, Jane."

Jane's face flamed. "Oh, he's not mine. I mean, the very idea."

"So sorry to hear it." Lexie knew she was being catty. "Now if you two will excuse me, I need to get my shopping done." How many other folks thought she and Allen Hines were courting? Good gracious.

She hurried through her shopping and went back onto the porch. Addy scooted around Aletha's father, who was clapping his hand against his leg, keeping beat to the music, and slipped her hand in Lexie's.

She patted the girl's shoulder. "I'm going to sit in the wagon for a while and listen. Want to sit with me?"

They climbed up and she caught Willie's eye above the crowd. He nodded and whispered to Tuck.

The haunting strains of "Old Kentucky Home" always clutched at Lexie's heart. They always played it when Tuck had to leave. Lexie had begun to think of it as Tuck's theme song.

When the last mournful note cried out, Tuck would put her violin in the case and say good-bye to her new friends until next time.

"Miss Lexie, can we go fishing?" Tuck asked as the Sullivan farm came into view. "Or do we have to do lessons?"

"Lessons." They didn't usually do schoolwork on Saturdays, but they'd gotten behind, and the following week wouldn't be much better, with all the baking to do for the wedding.

"Awww." Tuck jumped down and kicked the wheel, then threw a contrite glance at Lexie. "Sorry."

"I should think you would be." Lexie could tell her a thing or two about letting a temper have control. She hoped and prayed Tuck would learn to overcome hers while she was still young.

"Do we have to do all of them?" Addy threw a pleading look her way.

"As a matter of fact, if you will both be diligent with your math, I think we might postpone the rest until Monday night. After all, you're both ahead in your other work."

"So we can go fishing?" Tuck's eyes shone with hope.

"To be honest, a good mess of catfish sounds really good right now. Think you can catch enough for our supper?"

"Woohoo!" Tuck took off running to the house. By the time Addy and Lexie had put the wagon away, unhitched the horses, and walked into the kitchen, Tuck had all their supplies ready and waiting.

Lexie hid a smile. "That's nice, Tuck, but aren't you hungry? We haven't eaten since breakfast and it's nearly one o'clock."

"I'm hungry," Addy declared, rubbing her stomach.

"Could we have something fast?" Tuck asked.

The girls made short work of their meal and their lessons and before long, Lexie sat on the riverbank, her fishing pole in the water.

"You know, Mr. Jack caught lots of fish when he was home last." Addy's voice was full of admiration.

"Yep. He even fried them up good," Tuck added, then yanked on her pole and tossed a medium-sized mud cat onto the ground. "I got the first one!"

Lexie leaned back against a tree and breathed in the crisp autumn air. They wouldn't be able to do this much longer. Perhaps not again until next spring. It could turn severely cold overnight in November. But for now, she reveled in the sounds and smells of fall. Woodsmoke wafted across the fields and hills. And the faint scent of spices drifted from some cookstove not too far away. Was that pumpkin pie? No...bread. She should bake some pumpkin bread tonight. It would taste good for breakfast.

"Miss Lexie." She started awake. How long had she been sleeping?

"Look, Miss Lexie. Ten of them."

Lexie sat up and stretched and looked at the catch that had caused such excitement in Tuck's voice. "Good job, girls. Those are going to taste mighty good for supper. Let's clean them here before we go home."

"I wish Mr. Jack was here to see them," Addy said, her voice wistful.

"Me, too," Tuck said.

Lexie's thoughts echoed assent. Would he make it home for Will's wedding? The thought of his glance on her lips sent a thrill through her. She had been so afraid he would try to kiss her. Was it possible he cared for her? But what about the woman he'd named his boat for? Or was that more of her imagination. Perhaps the boat had that name when he bought her.

Hope rose in Lexie. She couldn't deny to herself that she cared for him... a lot. Was it love?

⁂

"Thompson, I'm thinking about selling the *Julia Dawn*."

The hefty seaman's mouth fell open and he immediately shut it. "You don't say."

"Yes, can't bring myself to turn loose of the farm. I guess it's in my blood. My family has always farmed. Until me, that is." Jack tossed the rope he'd been repairing onto the deck.

"So when do you think you might sell?" Thompson frowned and spat over the rail.

"Like I said, I've not decided for sure. And if I do, I'll give you and the rest of the hands plenty of warning so you can find other jobs."

Thompson, who had worked for Jack for years, wasn't exactly a friend, but Jack respected the man and knew the other men felt the same about him.

"Well now. Depending on how much you'll be asking for her, I just might see my way clear to buy her meself."

Jack nodded. He knew Thompson had been saving for his own boat for a long time. He couldn't think of anyone he'd rather turn the *Julia Dawn* over to.

"If it works out that way, will you keep the hands?" Jack's main concern was for Pap, who was getting up in years. He'd even thought of hiring him to help on the farm but didn't know if the old seaman and cook would be pried away from the river.

"Most of them." Thompson nodded. "I've been meaning to talk to you about Sid Casey. Caught him with a bottle yesterday."

Jack pressed his lips together. The men agreed when they signed on with him not to bring liquor on the boat.

"Give him a warning. If it happens again, let him go." Jack believed in second chances, but if he allowed this sort of thing, it could get out of hand.

Jack went to his cabin to look through his bills of sale for this trip. Paperwork was the one thing he thoroughly disliked about owning a business.

He wasn't sure when he'd first come up with the idea of selling the *Julia Dawn*. Even six months ago he wouldn't have considered such a thing. But lately he'd been happiest on the farm. He knew he wouldn't have any trouble farming. He'd helped his father from the time he was just a little fellow, following behind him and covering the seeds and plants his father had dropped into the earth. By the time he was twelve, he knew just about everything there was to know about raising crops. They'd also had a few head of cattle for beef and a few milk cows. And, of course, a hog or two.

Lately the sight of Lexie, Tuck, and Addy waving good-bye had struck a chord inside him, and he'd begun to remember what it was like to be part of a home and family. He wasn't sure what to do about the situation. It seemed almost impossible. First of all, even though he knew he was in love with Lexie, she was more than likely being courted by the parson, which sent daggers through Jack. Of course, he might be able to keep the girls, but would it be fair to Tuck and Addy to be raised by a bachelor? He didn't know. And he didn't know who to turn to for answers.

His ma would have told him to ask God. That was always her answer. He could see her sitting in her small rocker, with the big black Bible open on her lap. He could still remember the comfort he felt at those times, like being wrapped in love and security. But even though Jack had retained the moral concepts his mother had taught him, little by little, after his parents' deaths, he'd grown far away from God. He was so thankful to be back.

The *Julia Dawn* would be docking at Forsyth by tomorrow afternoon. He'd turned down several offers and cut his trip short so he could accept the invitation to Will's wedding. Maybe that hadn't been such a good idea. The reverend would be there, and Jack didn't know if he could stand those looks the man gave Lexie. He sighed. One thing he did know. He needed to find out if they were courting or not. Because if they weren't, he would waste no time letting her know how he felt about her.

Chapter 18

Lexie sat in the second row beside Addy and tried not to shiver. Even with the large potbellied stove loaded to capacity and the wood fire roaring inside, the tent was still cold.

She knew Sarah's pa and stepma had tried to convince her to wait and be married in the spring, but the girl was determined to spend Christmas with Will this year. The first week in November was a little early for a cold snap to set in, but here it was, just as they had feared.

Lexie only hoped the Jenkins' huge barn would be warmer for the dinner. Of course, once the square dancing started, everyone would warm up pretty fast.

Tuck leaned across Addy. "Miss Lexie, my hands are so cold they're about to drop off."

"Well, put your mittens on." She'd like to put her gloves back on, too, but the sight of Will's frozen face as he stood next to his friend Hal took her mind off her chill. She hoped Will made it through the ceremony without passing out.

"Can't. I didn't bring 'em." Tuck straightened and then whispered to Jack, who sat on her other side. Lexie was pretty sure she'd told the twins to wear their mittens.

The sound of Frank Sawyer's french harp sang out, and everyone scurried to get in their seats. How in the world did he make a harmonica sound so sweet?

Sarah's sixteen-year-old sister, Betty, walked down the aisle in a pretty ruffled dress. She reached the front and stepped to the side. Mr. Sawyer hit a long note and then started playing "The Wedding March." Everyone rose as Sarah stepped in though the tent flap on her father's arm.

Lexie felt tears well up. Sarah looked so lovely and so incredibly happy as she walked down the aisle toward Will. Lexie glanced at her brother. The frozen look was gone and his face shone with joy. She breathed a sigh of relief and grinned. Apparently the sight of his bride was enough to revive him. Lexie didn't blame them for not wanting to wait.

She took her seat and her eyes met Jack's. Warmth flowed through her at the look of longing in his eyes. Quickly she averted her glance. What would it be like to walk down the aisle to Jack? She shoved the thought away and focused on Will and Sarah as they promised to love each other forever.

As soon as the rice had been thrown and Will drove away with his bride, everyone loaded into wagons and buggies and headed for the Jenkins' place. Some of the younger men and boys rode horses in hopes of getting there before Will and Sarah. Lexie wasn't sure what they were up to, but she was sure Will and Sarah would survive.

But when Lexie, with Jack and the twins, rode down the tree-lined lane and stopped among dozens of buggies and wagons at the edge of the Jenkins' yard, there was no sign of Will and Sarah. Lexie climbed down from the wagon. "Jack, will you keep an eye on Tuck and Addy? I'm going to help get the food on the tables."

"Sure, we'll find something to do, I'm sure."

"Aw, we don't have to be looked after." Tuck frowned. "Can't we go play?"

"After dinner we'll see. But I would like for you to stay with Mr. Jack for now." Lexie gave them each a questioning look.

"Yes, ma'am," Addy said.

Tuck sighed. "Oh all right."

Lexie looked at Jack and found him grinning. She laughed and shook her head, then went to join the women.

She headed across the grassy yard toward the two-story white-framed house and met Wanda Jenkins coming out the front door. "Oh good, Lexie, you're here. Your aunt Kate is taking the pies in, if you'd like to help her." People had been bringing baked items over for a couple of days.

"Sure, but I don't see Will and Sarah. Are they here yet?" Lexie asked.

Mrs. Jenkins shifted the tray of bread she carried and leaned toward Lexie's ear. "Mr. Jenkins overheard some of the boys talking about a shivaree. He warned Will to stay away for a while. I expect they went to your aunt's place." She chuckled. "By the time they get here, those boys will be too busy eating and flirting with the girls to pay any attention to them. At least, that's what I'm hoping."

"There's the happy couple." Mrs. Jenkins, beaming from ear to ear, directed Sarah and Will to the head table where a three-layer chocolate cake stood.

"Hey, don't we get anything to eat besides cake?" Will complained with a grin.

"Yes, you do, son, but someone will serve you. Sit yourself down right here beside Sarah Jane." She beamed as she bustled off to fill plates for the newlyweds.

With so many women getting things ready, it didn't take long and finally Lexie sank down gratefully beside Addy, who grinned at her between bites.

"I see you three waited for me." Lexie gave a make-believe frown in their direction.

Jack grinned. "We couldn't control ourselves. The smells were getting to us."

"Yep." Tuck swallowed. "I could smell those ribs before we even got here."

"Umm-hmmm," Addy agreed. "You should get some ribs before they're all gone."

"Yes, I can see how good they are by the sauce all over your face." Lexie smiled and handed Addy a napkin, then started to rise.

Jack touched her arm. "Wait here. I'll get your food for you."

"Oh, no," she protested. "You don't need to do that."

"But I want to. You look all done in." He placed a hand on her shoulder and she trembled.

"Well, I have been running pretty hard since I awoke this morning." She gave him a smile of gratitude. "If you're sure you don't mind. . .but I only want a little."

He nodded and headed for the food tables. Soon he was back with a refill for himself and a full plate for Lexie.

"Gracious. That certainly isn't a little. I can't possibly eat that much."

"Oh, sure you can. Try and see." He placed the plate in front of her then laid the napkin and silverware beside it.

But instead of his sitting in his former spot, on the other side of Tuck, Lexie found him next to her, their shoulders nearly touching.

∽

"Auntie, the house is spotless. Please sit down. You'll worry yourself sick." Lexie put her arm around Aunt Kate and coaxed her over to a chair by the kitchen table.

"But they'll be here soon. I want to make sure there's a bite for them to eat. They'll probably be hungry." She started to rise, but Lexie gave her a gentle shove back into the chair.

"Hungry?" Lexie laughed. "After all the food Will packed away yesterday, he shouldn't be hungry for a week."

"I wish they could afford a longer honeymoon." Aunt Kate's forehead puckered.

"Maybe they can take a longer one later. I'm sure they'll be happy right here as long as they're together."

"But it would be nice if they didn't have an old woman to get in their way."

So that's what was bothering her. "Aunt Kate, first of all you're not old. And second, you know how much Will loves you, and Sarah does, too. They would never consider you in the way."

"But I feel in the way." She placed her face in her hands.

Startled, Lexie hurried over and knelt beside her aunt's chair, gently tugging her hands from her face. "I think Will and Sarah would be heartbroken if they knew you felt that way." Lexie rubbed Aunt Kate's back in little circles. "But I can understand. I would feel in the way, too. Would you like to stay with the twins and me for a few days? It would be fun, and Tuck and Addy would love having you there."

"Oh, Lexie, I wouldn't dream of intruding on you and the girls." But hope filled her eyes.

"It wouldn't be an intrusion. I just invited you." Lexie kissed her on the forehead. "You can stay as long as you like and come home when you're ready."

"But what will Jack say? He might think it presumptuous of me. After all, you live in his house." Aunt Kate's face turned pink at the mere suggestion anyone would think she was rude.

"I'll talk to him when he and the girls come to pick me up this afternoon. Then Will can drive you over later." It would be nice to have Aunt Kate with her and the twins. Lexie hadn't realized when she left home how much she'd miss her.

"Well, perhaps in the morning would be better. That will give me a chance to finish up a few things here and to show Sarah where everything is."

"Very well, if that's what you want to do." Lexie stood. "Now I need to get my things together. Then I'll heat up some of that vegetable soup for our lunch. It's still an hour or so before they'll be here to get me."

"That will give us some time to talk." Aunt Kate smiled up at her and love filled her eyes. "I've been so busy getting things ready for Will and Sarah I feel I've lost contact with what's going on in your life, Alexandra."

Lexie gathered her things and returned to the kitchen. In a few minutes the kitchen was filled with the delicious smell of Aunt Kate's vegetable soup simmering in the iron dutch oven.

Soon Lexie and Aunt Kate were seated at the table over steaming bowls of soup and thick, crusty slices of hot toasted bread.

"I don't need to ask how you and the girls are getting along," Aunt Kate said. "I can see the happiness on your faces."

"Addy and Tuck are such a joy. Every day I discover something else wonderful about them." Lexie laughed. "Not that they are perfect. You already know that."

"Is school going well?"

"Yes, the girls are both bright and eager to learn. But it will be good when we have a real school for them to attend." Lexie glanced over at her aunt to see worry lines on her face. "What's wrong?"

"Alexandra, you don't know for sure that the girls will be here that long. What if a family is found for them?"

A chill went through Lexie. "Oh, Aunt Kate, what will I do without them?"

"I know you love the twins, Lexie." Aunt Kate sighed. "It's not easy raising children alone."

"It wouldn't be hard raising Tuck and Addy."

"You say that now, but life brings problems, and they're easier if you have someone to help solve them."

"Jack loves them, too. I think it will be as hard on him if we lose them." She felt her aunt's gaze on her and looked up. "What is it?"

"Why don't you two get married and adopt the girls?"

Lexie's mouth fell open. She couldn't deny the thought had crossed her mind. Or maybe not actually crossed it. . .perhaps teased her mind was closer. But to have it put into words was rather shocking. "But that would be a marriage of convenience, Aunt Kate." She shook her head. "I would never marry someone I didn't love."

"Are you sure you don't love him?" How did Aunt Kate know so much about what went on in her heart?

"No, I'm not sure at all. But I would also have to be loved in return." She rose as she heard the wagon pull into the yard.

Chapter 19

It seemed he'd just gotten home. How did the time go by so quickly? Jack stood in the yard holding Champion's reins. The girls were pressed to his sides, their arms intertwined around his waist.

"Do you have to go, Mr. Jack?" Addy's voice whined the words, and she followed them with a woebegone sigh.

"I'm afraid I do." But maybe for the last time. He'd made up his mind. He would sell the *Julia Dawn* as soon as possible. He could only hope Thompson meant what he'd said about buying. Otherwise Jack would have to stay with the boat until he could find a buyer. He had calculated to the penny based on his asking price. It would get them through a couple of crop seasons until the farm started producing enough to live on.

He licked his lips. "Addy, Tuck, you need to let go now. I want to talk to Miss Lexie for a few minutes before I leave."

The girls turned loose, and after giving them a final hug, he sent them to play.

Lexie stood by the steps, her shoulders stiff and her face pale.

Jack walked over, leading Champion, and tied the horse to the porch rail. "Lexie"—he took both her hands in his—"I guess it's no secret how I feel about the twins. I don't think I could give them up. And, yes, I'll admit, I've grown fond of you these past few weeks, too."

She jerked her head up and stared at him.

He cleared his throat. "What I mean to say is would you consider marrying me so we can give Tuck and Addy a home?"

Still, she stared. Then slowly, tears began to well up. She blinked them back and turned her head away. When she looked up at him, finally all traces of the tears were gone. "This is a pretty big step, Jack. I don't think I can give you an answer right now. I'll need to think and pray about it." Her voice was firm, businesslike, and she pulled her hands loose from his.

He looked at her in confusion. He'd thought she was beginning to feel the same about him that he did her. And he'd noticed she wasn't paying any more attention to the reverend, Allen Hines, than she did to anyone else, so apparently they weren't courting. Dread lay on his heart like a boulder. He must have missed something.

Had he worn his feelings on his shoulder? He didn't want to appear a pathetic figure in her eyes. But at least she was willing to consider the marriage for the sake of providing a home for Tuck and Addy. He took a deep breath. He didn't like the idea of a marriage of convenience, but if that turned out to be her terms, then he could live with the situation. He gave a short nod. "Of course. I don't have to have an answer this very minute. Think about it, and let me know when you've made your decision."

Anger cut through him as he rode away. Not anger at her but at himself. How could he have misread her so badly? And how must she feel at this moment?

⚭

Lexie's chest tightened, and her breath came in short gasps until dizziness threatened to overwhelm her. She consciously slowed her breathing and concentrated on relaxing until her breaths came normally again. Jack was out of sight now. She couldn't even hear the galloping of the horse anymore. She turned and made her way to one of the rockers and eased herself into the seat.

He'd asked her to do the very thing she'd promised herself she'd never do. She'd told herself she would rather be single than to marry without love. She shouldn't be surprised, and for that matter she couldn't really fault him. Obviously he loved the twins very much to make such a sacrifice to provide them with a home. But what about Julia Dawn? Maybe she'd died and that was why he'd named the boat after her. Well, hadn't she herself pleaded with God for a solution, any solution to the problem? If this was His answer, then she'd do it, willingly. Only, she'd never expected a loveless marriage to be part of the deal.

Oh yes, Jack had added the part about being fond of her, and maybe he had become fond of her in a friendly sort of way, but of course his real objective was the girls. She'd been foolish to believe he was falling in love with her as she was with him.

She sighed and leaned back in the rocker. Laughter drifted up from the backyard. Tuck and Addy at play. She had to pull herself together before they came back to the house. She mustn't let them see anything was amiss. And Aunt Kate would be here in the morning. She would know something was wrong unless Lexie could manage to calm herself.

She jumped as both girls landed on the step and thundered up onto the porch, giggling and laughing.

"Oh, what have you girls been doing? You're filthy." Their faces were smeared with mud, and their clothing was dirty.

"The hog got out. We had to put him back in the pen. Guess we slipped in the mud, a couple of times." Tuck glanced down at her overalls and at the mud that caked her hands.

Weariness washed over Lexie. She pulled herself up from the chair. "Come on. Let's bring water in to heat. You girls will have to wait in the mudroom until it's hot. I don't want that mess tracked into the house."

When the girls were finally in side-by-side tubs, Lexie sat on a low stool to make sure they scrubbed every inch of the mud off. The humor of the situation was beginning to sink in and had chased some of the tiredness away.

"Miss Lexie, I think Mr. Jack wants to marry you." Addy wiped soapsuds off her face.

Lexie felt the sinking in her heart again. "What makes you say that?"

" 'Cause," said Tuck, "we told him what you said about needing to get married before we could all live together. He listened real good and thought about it for a long time."

Oh no. Lexie's heart sank even more. Humiliation wrapped itself around her like a cocoon, and she fought back tears of shame. So the marriage wasn't even Jack's idea. He thought she had said she wanted to marry him. Somehow that made things even worse.

She managed to get through supper and the girls' story and prayer time without their noticing anything wrong. Afterward, she lay awake long into the night.

ᘓᘏᘎᑎᓚ

Will brought Aunt Kate over right after breakfast. The girls rushed over and grabbed her as soon as she was out of the wagon.

"Woowee, you two are about to squeeze all the air out of me." Aunt Kate squeezed back.

They all waved at Will and piled into the house, the girls carrying Aunt Kate's old brown suitcase. They led her to the extra room and helped her put her things away in a drawer they'd cleaned out for her.

"Aunt Kate, will you make ginger cookies? Miss Lexie's are always too hard." Tuck was honest to a fault. That was if honesty could be a fault. Still, Lexie planned to teach the child that a little subtlety was sometimes called for.

It was afternoon, while the children were bent over their lessons, before Lexie had a chance to talk to Aunt Kate. She'd made a decision after a long night of agonizing prayer. The two of them had gone out to the porch to have their tea. The day had warmed up some and the sun shone brightly on the chairs where they sat balancing their cups and saucers.

"So how are the bride and groom today?" Lexie smiled, determined to find joy in her brother's happiness.

"Oh, they're like a couple of lovebirds." Aunt Kate laughed. "Their happiness is making the old house sing."

"That's wonderful. I'm so very happy for them." She paused a moment then continued. "There may be another happy couple soon."

Aunt Kate perked up. "Oh. Who?"

"Hold onto your teacup." Lexie laughed. "Jack has asked me to marry him."

Aunt Kate's mouth flew open. "I knew you two were in love. You just had to find out for yourselves."

"Well, Auntie, you always seem to know." Lexie smiled.

"So when is the happy day?"

"I haven't actually given him my answer," Lexie said, pushing back the sob that wanted to explode from her throat. "So you mustn't tell anyone yet. I wasn't sure until this morning. But when I woke up today, the answer was clear. And it's yes."

Aunt Kate's smile froze on her face as she looked at Lexie. "What are you not telling me?"

Lexie laughed. "Why, Aunt Kate, why would you think that? I've told you all I know at the moment. I'm sure we'll talk about the wedding date when Jack returns from his trip." Aunt Kate opened her mouth, but Lexie rushed on. "He's planning to sell his riverboat and start farming. At the wedding dinner, he told me all about how his father was a farmer and taught Jack all about it when he was a child. Jack says it's in his blood. Won't it be wonderful to see these fields flourishing again?"

Aunt Kate took a sip of her tea then nodded. "Why, yes, it's always nice to see the land brought back. I'm sure Jack will make a very good farmer."

"Miss Lexie?" Addy stood at the door. "Could you please help me with this arithmetic problem?"

"Of course, Addy. Bring it here." Good, she needed a respite. She didn't know how much longer she could keep up the pretense.

If she was having this much trouble with Aunt Kate, how would she convince anyone else?

Could she play the part of the blushing bride? And if she could, wouldn't it be dishonest? She sighed. Surely it would get easier in time.

❧

Jack stood at the *Julia Dawn*'s bow and watched the churning of the water as they headed downriver toward Arkansas. Things sure hadn't gone the way he planned yesterday. When the girls had told him what Lexie said about getting married, his heart had soared. He realized now they must have gotten her words or the meaning of them mixed up. He should have waited a little longer before asking her to marry him. Shouldn't have told her he cared for her. It was too soon.

Well, at least good news had met him when he'd boarded the boat. Thompson was eager to take over as owner and captain of the *Julia Dawn*. Jack would tell the crew after they headed back to Forsyth. He was pretty sure most of them, if not all, would stay signed on with the new captain.

He sighed. There was no denying he'd miss the old girl. The feel of the deck under his feet, the little, almost imperceptible movements she made through different sections of the river. The smell of wet ropes and smoke from the smokestack. She'd been a good companion.

Bull would probably change her name anyway. A pang shot through him at the thought, but he pushed it away. He'd take the nameplate with his mother's name on it. He could display the sign somewhere, maybe over the mantel. Or if Lexie didn't want the memento over the mantel, he'd find another spot.

He shook his head and laughed at himself. Even after her reaction to his proposal he was still assuming her answer would be yes. Something squeezed at his insides. Who was he to think he deserved a woman like Alexandra Rayton and two great kids like Tuck and Addy?

What would he do if the answer was no? In that case, he figured the twins would be better off with her than staying with him. They hadn't had a ma in a long, long time.

Chapter 20

Not much to show for fifteen years on the river. Except for what was in his wallet. Jack grinned. He'd made a tidy profit off his investment. His needs had been slight on the river, and the belongings he'd collected, with a few articles of clothing, fit in one double saddlebag.

He'd thought he might have regrets once the deed was done and the *Julia Dawn* was gone from him forever, but instead he rode with a lightheartedness he couldn't explain. The only hitch to his good mood was the uncertainty about Lexie's answer to his proposal. But he'd be okay even if her answer was no. He knew that now.

Last night he'd been in the pit of despair over it all. Then to his own surprise, he found himself calling on God and surrendering it all to Him. The immediate peace he'd experienced had brought a joy he hadn't known since he was a small boy. Come to think of it, that must be the source of his lightheartedness. He'd always heard knowing God brought joy, but now he knew it was true.

He laughed out loud and the sound echoed across the predawn land. He pulled up beneath a flaming sugar maple for a moment to enjoy the sun rising over a tree-studded hill. Too bad he hadn't recognized the beauty of this place when he was a boy. He'd been so embittered with God and the world after his parents' deaths, he couldn't see beauty in anything.

He flicked the reins and coaxed Champion into a canter. Leaves of red, brown, orange, and gold scattered under the palomino's hooves. Soon the house came into sight.

With a start, he noticed a grizzled black mule tied to a hydrangea bush. A man was hunched over by the front porch with one foot raised to step up.

Anger in his throat, Jack jumped off Champion and landed running.

The prowler swung around at the sound of his footsteps and cringed against the porch railing. It was the young man at the picnic who'd been staring at Lexie.

Jack dove and grabbed him around the waist, dragging him to the ground.

∽⌒∾

"Girls, stop squabbling and finish your breakfast. We have a full day of studies today."

"Sorry, Miss Lexie." Addy ducked her head and took a bite from the cinnamon-topped oatmeal.

"Okay, but she started it." Tuck frowned in her sister's direction but crammed a full spoon of oatmeal into her mouth.

A crash on the porch startled Lexie, and she dropped the pan she was washing. Tuck and Addy's eyes grew wide, and Lexie clutched at her throat.

The noise continued, interspersed with yells and grunts.

Dear God, protect us. Lexie grabbed the iron skillet off the nail behind the stove and ran for the front door. She flung it open, the skillet in the air. She gasped. "Jack!"

He had someone pinned down. Lexie could only see a pair of swinging legs.

"I ain't done nothin'. Let me up. I promise. I wasn't doing anything wrong."

"Jack! It's one of the Maxwell boys. Let him up." Forgetting she'd been suspicious of the man recently, she lowered the skillet. His pleas had sounded frightened.

Jack swiveled his head and stared at her. "But he was sneaking around the porch."

"Let's at least hear what he has to say. Let him up, please."

With a snort of exasperation, Jack scrambled to his feet, then grabbed Billy Joe's arm loosely and helped him up. "Okay, let's hear it. Why were you skulking around here?"

Billy Joe darted a glance around as though looking for someone to rescue him. Finally, he met Lexie's eyes. "I'm sorry, Miss Rayton. Didn't mean to skulk. I was gonna listen before I knocked because I didn't want to wake you'uns up."

"All right, Billy Joe. I believe you." Lexie ran a hand nervously across her cheek. "Why don't we all go inside, and we'll listen to Billy Joe's story. I can use a cup of coffee about now."

They went inside, Jack's hand holding firmly to Billy Joe's arm, while the man kept his eyes to the floor.

Lexie sent the girls into the parlor with instructions to write the alphabet in cursive. Then she poured cups of coffee and put them on the table.

Jack stood grimly while Billy Joe sat at one end of the table.

Lexie sat at the other end. "All right, Billy Joe, tell us why you're here."

He swallowed, gulped, and cleared his throat. "Miss Rayton, I heered you was teaching school to these here girls."

"What does that have to do with you?" Jack lashed out before Lexie frowned him to silence.

"Wal—you see—" He took a deep breath then continued with a rush. "I figgered maybe if I ast you, you might learn me to read and write."

Lexie almost laughed in relief until she saw Billy Joe's face. Hope, shame, and challenge, all rolled into one pleading look.

She glanced at Jack, who gave her a startled look and sat down, shamefaced.

Lexie bit her lip. Was she up to it? It was one thing to jump into something in a moment of pity or charity. But on a day-to-day basis? She sighed. It would be a challenge. "Billy Joe, you do know a school will be starting in the spring?" That seemed like the best solution for him.

"Yes, ma'am. But most of the kids my age can at least read and write. I'm afraid they'll make fun of me."

Lord? Lexie looked at the boy. "All right, Billy Joe, but the girls and I will be taking a break for Christmas soon. Let's wait and start your lessons after the first of the year."

"Now wait a minute." The frown on Jack's face told more than words what he thought of the idea.

Lexie pushed her chair back and rose. "Come on, Billy Joe. I'll walk you to the door."

Motioning behind her for Jack not to follow, she walked into the parlor with the hulking boy. Lowering her voice, she looked at Billy Joe, who was giving her a worshipful look. She wondered if the look would remain after she spoke. "Billy Joe, were you here one day while I was gone?"

"Yes, ma'am. I came over one day to ask you about learning me, but no one answered my knock, so I came inside to wait. After a while I had to go, so I left."

"I see." Lexie knew the Maxwell boys hadn't had much training in manners. She'd add that to her lesson plans.

"Miss Rayton, I'm sorry I skeered you at the barn-raisin' that time. Your hair is the color that my ma's used to be 'fore she died. I jes' had to touch it to see if it felt the same."

Understanding and sympathy rushed through Lexie. "It's all right. But you mustn't ever do that again. And by the way, Billy Joe. I teach and you learn. You must learn to say it right."

"Yes, ma'am. I'll learn what you teach me real good."

Lexie watched as he climbed on the old mule and rode away.

⌒⟳

Lexie spent the morning helping the girls complete the lessons they'd begun this week. After lunch, when they went out to play, she turned to Jack. "I'll get my things together. How long will you be here this time?" She felt strange now that they were alone in the house. The subject of the proposal lay on her mind, and her whole body was numb with nerves.

"Lexie, there's something I need to talk to you about." The look he gave her was serious but tender. "Shall we sit on the porch, or would you be comfortable in the parlor? It is cold outside."

"The porch will be fine. It's a little stuffy in here." She put her hand to her collar as though to loosen it then dropped her hand into her lap.

He placed his hand on her elbow and they stepped outside. Clouds had gathered and blotted out the sun that had shone so brightly an hour ago.

"Perhaps we should call the girls in. It looks as though it might rain any moment."

"Tuck! Addy!" He called and the girls came running.

"Are you leaving, Miss Lexie?" Addy asked.

"Not yet, dear. But it looks like it might rain."

"Girls, I need to talk to Miss Lexie in private," said Jack. "Why don't you go find a puzzle, and we'll put it together in a little while."

"Aw, can't we play a little longer?" Tuck pouted.

"Abigail. . . ," Lexie said.

"Oh, all right." Tuck grabbed Addy by the hand and ran inside, dragging her sister along.

"Have you considered my proposal since I've been gone?" His deep brown eyes looked worried as he scanned her face.

She swallowed past the lump that had suddenly formed in her throat. "Yes, I have."

He took a deep breath. "And what have you decided?"

"I will marry you, Jack." Had she really gotten the words past her throat? Suddenly she felt faint. She'd just agreed to a marriage of convenience. One without love. Years and years of living with a man who didn't love her.

His face lit up. "You will? That's wonderful." He grabbed her and swung her around, then set her down and pulled her close. "I can't believe it. You won't regret it, Lexie. I promise I'll take care of you and make life as good as I can for you and the girls."

Confused, she pulled away. She could almost think he was happy to be marrying her. Well, of course he was because of the girls but— "Yes, I'm sure you will, Jack. I know you're an honorable man."

"I also wanted to tell you that I've sold the *Julia Dawn* and my freight business."

"You have? So soon?" Oh no, this was worse. She'd thought she'd have time to get used to a loveless marriage before she had to live in the same house with the man, constantly reminded that he didn't care for her that way. How could she go on seeing him every day, loving him and not letting him know?

"Yes, one of the crew offered to buy it, and since he had the money, I didn't see any sense in waiting. We should have a crop of sorts next year, but after that it'll get better. There is plenty of money until the farm starts producing enough to support us." He sounded eager, happy. Didn't he care that he was marrying a woman he didn't love?

She sighed. He was thinking of the twins. That's why he was so excited that she'd said yes. They were his priority and they needed to be hers as well. It was time to grow up and put her childish fantasies aside.

He grew silent, and she glanced up at him. His face looked strained. Had he asked her a question that she didn't hear or had he suddenly decided he was making a mistake?

"I'm sorry, Jack. I became a little distracted for a moment. Did you ask me something?"

He hesitated then smiled. "Have you considered a wedding date?"

"What did you have in mind?" Did every girl spend her young years dreaming of her wedding day? Lexie had. She blinked back the tears that started to form.

"I thought it would be best to marry soon. Then we could see an attorney about adopting Tuck and Addy."

"Yes, of course you're right. The Christmas dance is in two weeks. It's on a Saturday night, and we'll have a church service the next day. Reverend Allen will be here all weekend. We could talk to him then."

His eyes brightened. "That sounds fine. Let's plan on that."

She gave him a tremulous smile and stood. "I suppose I'd better get my things, so you can take me home and get back before the rain starts."

He stood and reached for her. She stiffened and he stepped back, a hurt look on his face. Did he expect. . . ?

"I'm sorry, Jack. I need a little time to get used to the idea."

"Of course. I should have realized. I'm the one who should apologize. I'll just go hitch up the wagon."

She stared after him, wanting to call him back. Longing to throw herself into his arms. With heaviness on her heart, she went inside.

Chapter 21

Jack scooped up another pile of straw and tossed it down to the girls.

Addy raked a portion of it into one of the stalls and began spreading it. Tuck peered up, her hand shading her eyes from the sun that burst through the open window of the loft. "Mr. Jack, you're awfully close to that edge. Maybe you should move back a little."

Jack had plenty of room, but at the worry in her eyes he stepped back a couple of inches. "I think that's enough straw for now. Help your sister spread the rest of it in Champion's stall."

Relief appeared on her face, and she grinned and went to help Addy.

A pang of sympathy shot through Jack. He knew what it felt like to lose both parents the way Tuck and Addy had. Still, since he'd been home this week, he'd noticed a concern almost bordering on fear in Tuck that something might happen to him. He planned to talk to Lexie and see if she'd noticed anything similar. Was the poor kid living in fear she'd lose the two of them, too? Funny how Tuck was usually the tough one of the twins, but Addy didn't seem to be worried at all. Or maybe she was hiding it better.

Jack sighed. Or maybe the whole thing was his imagination. In spite of the bad start they'd had with the girls lying to them both, they seemed to be doing well. He credited Lexie and her aunt with that.

He climbed down from the loft. "I'm going to do some repairs on the henhouse. After you girls finish up here, go check the woodbox."

"Checked it after lunch," Tuck said.

"Oh, all right. In that case"—he squinted one eye and appeared to be in deep thought—"I guess you'll just have to go play for a while."

Squeals of laughter exploded from both girls as Jack grabbed a hammer and a sack of nails from a shelf and ducked out the door.

Halfway to the chicken coop, he heard hoofbeats and turned to see a one-seater buggy pulling up in front of the house. He squinted against the sun as he walked toward it. A woman he'd never seen before stepped out.

At that moment, Addy flew across the yard and grabbed Jack around the waist. "Mr. Jack! That's Bella. Don't let her take us." Addy's voice verged on hysteria.

"I ain't going nowhere with her." Tuck stood with her hands on her small overalls-clad hips. She pressed her lips together and glared at the woman.

A high-pitched laugh emitted from the woman's large, painted mouth. "Oh you girls, you always were kidders."

The woman was around forty. Her bright orange hair was probably a failed attempt at dyeing it red. Her dress, tight across her stomach, bore stains across the chest.

"I ain't kidding!" Tuck stomped her foot, and Jack reached out and placed a hand on her shoulder.

Bella's eyes narrowed and cruelty darted from her eyes. But a moment later, she'd smoothed the expression off her face. "Now Abigail, you mustn't talk to your ma like that."

"You aren't our ma!" For the first time, Addy spoke directly to the woman.

Anger crossed Bella's face, but she took her eyes off the girls and looked at Jack. "I only just recently heard about their pa's death, and the first thing I thought about was those poor girls and how I must get on back and take care of them."

Jack frowned. "I'm sure you mean well, but Tuck and Addy are fine. Since you aren't their mother, you're really under no obligation."

"Obligation?" She threw her hands up. "But I love the twins. As soon as I found out where they were I went to a judge and showed them my marriage license to their pa. Here. I have papers ordering you to turn them over to me. And I insist you get their things right now."

Jack glanced over the paper she handed him, and nausea roiled inside his stomach. It was legal all right. A raised stamp was affixed at the bottom. And it ordered whoever was holding Abigail and Adeline Flanigan to release them into Isabella Flanigan's custody immediately.

He took a deep, rasping breath and licked his lips. "Addy, Tuck, I'm afraid she has a legal right to take you with her. Please pack your things."

"No, Mr. Jack," Addy pleaded, tears rolling down her cheeks. "Please don't make us go. I promise I'll be good."

Tuck took her sister's hand, her face frozen. "He can't stop her, Addy. Didn't you hear? The law gave us to her. He'll go to jail if he tries to keep us."

Addy gasped. Then with tears still streaming down her face, she followed Tuck inside.

"Where will you be taking them?" Perhaps they'd be near enough so that he could at least keep watch and make sure they were safe.

"Why, to our cabin, of course. And I do appreciate your taking care of the precious angels for me. You know their pa and I had a little squabble, and I'm such a silly old thing I just upped and left. But I always knew I'd come home." She dabbed at her eyes with a soiled handkerchief. "Oh, but to find out my poor husband was dead."

Yes, what about the huckster? Jack nearly said the words aloud. Something was wrong here. Jack felt it. This wasn't the end of it. He'd go see the judge at Forsyth. He headed for the house to change out of his soiled work clothes. If the judge couldn't be swayed, how would Jack tell Lexie?

⁕

Lexie tried to keep up a happy smile as she stood on the stool while Aunt Kate held the skirt pattern against her lower half. Her aunt had chattered with excitement ever since Lexie told her about her upcoming marriage.

"I say again, Alexandra, people might talk about you getting married on such short notice."

"I don't see why. Will and Sarah only announced theirs two months ahead of time."

"Yes, but they had been courting for over a year. That's why." She gave a short nod and stuck a pin in the paper pattern.

"Well, then they can just talk." Lexie didn't really care. If they knew the truth, they'd have a lot more to talk about.

Aunt Kate stopped pinning for a moment and looked intently at her niece. Then she nodded again. Only differently this time. "You're entirely right. Let the old gossips talk. But they'd better not let me hear them, or I'll give them a piece of my mind."

Tenderness and love rose up in Lexie. Aunt Kate might not be overly affectionate, but she loved Lexie and Will and had always stood up for them against all comers. "I'm sure once I tell them the reason, they'll understand. I don't believe even one of them would want to see Tuck and Addy have to go away."

Aunt Kate smiled and resumed her pinning. "I'm glad you can see the good in people."

"Ma and Pa taught me that. And you reinforced it." Lexie grinned down at her aunt.

"Now be still before you make me stick you." Aunt Kate fussed then stopped, her head tilted. "Is that a horse I hear? Oh my. Company's coming. I only have you half pinned. Stay right there. Don't move. Let me see who it is." Aunt Kate's heels clicked across the floor on her way to the door.

"Well hello, Jack. Wasn't expecting you this time of the day." How could Aunt Kate be so cheery when Lexie was sick inside? But of course Aunt Kate didn't know.

Jack's voice came clearly from the hallway. "Aunt Kate, I need to talk to Lexie. And is Will in the house?"

"No, he's getting wood. He decided we didn't have enough to satisfy him. Amazing the change a new bride can make in a man." She chuckled. "Sarah went along with him. She hasn't learned to let him out of her sight yet."

By now, Lexie was down from the stool, dropping pins as she went. Jack's voice didn't sound right. Was something wrong with the girls? She threw the pattern off and grabbed her robe. She headed for the hallway, tying her robe as she went.

"Now Lexie, I'll have to do that all over again," Aunt Kate protested. Couldn't she see something was wrong?

"Jack, what's wrong? Where are the girls?" She laid her hand on his arm, and he covered hers with his, gripping tightly.

Aunt Kate frowned. "Oh dear, something is wrong, isn't it, and I've been carrying on like an old hen."

"You'd both better sit down." He guided them both into the parlor.

Panic enveloped Lexie. "I don't want to sit down. Tell me, has something happened to Tuck or Addy?"

"No, no. Well, in a way. But they aren't hurt or anything like that." He tried again to lead her to a chair, but she swatted his hands away.

Finally, he sighed. "Their stepma came and got them. She had a document signed by a Forsyth judge giving her custody of Tuck and Addy."

Lexie froze. Through a haze, she heard him say they were at the cabin.

"Sweetheart, I promise I'll do what I can to get them back. I plan to see that judge tomorrow morning." He twisted his hat in his hand, agony on his face.

"Tomorrow? That might be too late. Why aren't you there now?"

"I tried. As soon as they left, I rode over to Forsyth, but the judge's office was empty, and they said he wouldn't be back until the morning. No one knew where he was, or if they did they wouldn't say."

Lexie's thoughts spun. The idea of Addy and Tuck with that woman caused Lexie's stomach to tighten. They'd never said anything about her mistreating them, but the woman had loose morals, and who was to say she hadn't taken to alcohol or something? And what if she decided to leave and take the girls with her? "We have to do something. We can't wait until tomorrow."

"I agree. I had a strange feeling about that woman. I don't know what she's up to, but I can't believe she's here because she cares about Tuck and Addy."

Aunt Kate had sat silently, her hand on her throat throughout Jack's story. Now she stood. "You're right. Something must be done. Let me call Will. He can get some of the neighbor men to go with you."

"That's a good idea, Aunt Kate," Jack said. "But not just yet. First, I want to check on the twins. Then I'm going to scout around and try to find out what her true purpose is."

"I'm going with you." Lexie narrowed her eyes. He'd better not dare try to prevent her from going.

"Lexie, I know you're worried." He took her hand again. "But I think it would be best for me to go alone. Besides, I rode Champion."

"And I think it's best for me to go with you." She placed her hands on her hips, then realizing it, let them fall to her sides. "And I can saddle up Jolly."

Aunt Kate stepped over to them and put her arm around Lexie. "You may as well let her go, Jack. She'll just follow you if you don't. But first, we need to ask God's help and place Tuck and Addy in His hands."

"Thank you, Aunt Kate." Lexie nodded. "You're exactly right."

They bowed their heads, and Lexie was surprised when Jack began to pray out loud. "Heavenly Father, we love Tuck and Addy. But we know You love them more. You know things about this situation that we don't. We want them back, Lord. But only if it is Your will. Now we place our girls in Your loving hands and ask You to give us peace. In the name of Your Son, Jesus, we pray. Amen."

"Thank you, Jack," Lexie whispered. "That was beautiful."

"All right, Lexie. You can go. But I suggest you put on heavy skirts and bring a coat. We'll need to stop at the farm for the wagon. And we'd better wait until near dark."

Lexie nodded, glad he hadn't argued any more about her going along. "Whatever you say, Jack. I'll go change and get my coat and scarf."

As she slipped out of her robe and put on a wool dress, her heart suddenly lurched. Had he called her sweetheart? Yes, she was sure he had. Maybe. . .

Oh nonsense. She was imagining what she wanted to hear. And even if he had, it was simply a name he called the girls all the time.

Chapter 22

Jack put Champion and the Raytons' Jolly in the barn and hitched his mules to the wagon. The work horses would be faster, but they had thick woods to go through and some rough ground to cover. The mules would be better. After he'd tied them to a post in front of the house, he joined Lexie on the porch.

"How long do we need to wait?" Lexie looked up at the sky.

"At least another hour. We don't want to get to the cabin before dark."

"What are your plans?" Her eyes, darkened with worry and apprehension, nevertheless showed trust.

Jack hesitated. To be honest, he wouldn't know until he arrived on the scene. If the house was quiet and peaceful, there was little they could do but go home and wait to see the judge. But if there was trouble at the cabin, he would be there to see it.

He shook his head. "Not sure at this point. So the going is rough between here and the cabin." He had planned to check out the Flanigan place, make sure no one tried to take it over. The girls might want it someday. But he hadn't made it over there yet.

"Yes, but if we take the long way around, it could take two hours, and we'd have to cross the river at one point." Lexie shivered. "And to think those little girls came all the way through the woods by themselves when their pa died."

Jack nodded. There were so many things he'd never asked the girls about. It seemed that Lexie had though.

Silence fell upon them. Jack glanced at Lexie and saw a look of sorrow on her face. The same look that had been there after she'd accepted his proposal. So it wasn't just the girls' absence causing her distress.

She didn't love him. That was obvious. She probably hated the thought of becoming his wife. He sighed. He needed to let her know he wouldn't expect her to be a wife in the physical sense. That was the only decent thing to do. Although the thought of being near her day by day and never holding her in his arms was agony. His heart sank. She probably wouldn't marry him anyway if they didn't get the girls back.

He leaned forward in his chair, and she jumped and clasped a hand at her throat. Then she gave a tremulous little laugh and sat back.

Oh God, is she afraid of me?

"Jack, hadn't we better go? By the time we get through the woods it will be good and dark."

"I guess you're right. You'd best button that coat up. It'll be colder in the

112

woods." He stood and waited for her, then took her elbow as she walked down the steps. At least she didn't pull away.

Jack lit a lantern and hung it up front. They'd need it as soon as they entered the woods. He planned to extinguish it when they got close to the Flanigan cabin. He'd have to get down and lead the mules from that point.

An owl hooted nearby, and Lexie gasped then laughed. "Only an old hoot owl."

"They can be a little startling." He scanned the woods in front and on all sides. Mountain lions sometimes came down. They didn't usually bother humans, but they might try for the mules. His rifle was in easy reach, just in case.

The wagon bumped over tree roots and rocks and rolled on. Jack felt each bump and knew Lexie must be uncomfortable. But she didn't offer one word of complaint.

After what seemed like hours but was probably only twenty minutes or so, Lexie spoke out of the darkness. "We're about halfway now. How soon should we blow out the lantern?"

"I think we can wait another ten minutes or so. The woods are too thick for a light to be seen very far away."

Lexie shivered and pulled her scarf tighter.

"I'm sorry you're cold. I never should have agreed to your coming with me."

"You couldn't have stopped me." She sighed. "I'm not trying to be stubborn or argumentative, but I need to be there in case Tuck and Addy need me."

"I understand. I know how much you love the girls. Lexie, I promise I'll do everything in my power to get them back for you."

"I know you will. And I know how much you love them, too. I trust you to do what you can. More than that, it's out of your hands. We have to trust God."

Peace washed over him. She was right. Of course. He had prayed and put the twins in God's hands. Then almost immediately he started to worry again. *Lord, grant me more faith.*

The wagon lurched and started to tip, then righted itself.

"Whew," Lexie breathed.

"Yes, whew is right," Jack said. "I thought we were going over for sure. It would have been fun trying to get the wagon turned upright in the dark."

"Jack, did you hear that?" Lexie looked around.

"Hear what?" Then he heard it, too. Voices. Children's voices.

Suddenly two small forms stumbled in front of the wagon, and the mules shied. "Whoa!" Jack pulled on the reins with all his might, and the animals stopped in their tracks.

"Mr. Jack! Miss Lexie! We knew you'd come." Tuck grinned and threw her arms around Lexie, who was already out of the wagon and holding both girls.

Jack tied the mules to a tree and joined them. "What are you girls doing in the woods all by yourselves at night?"

Tuck shrugged. "Bella and her huckster husband went to sleep early because Bella said she was beat from running after us rotten kids all afternoon. So we got ourselves out of there."

"Yes," Addy said, shivering. "But we were getting awfully cold. So we prayed that you'd come find us. And here you are."

⌘

Lexie closed her eyes and shuddered at the thought of the girls in the woods by themselves. What if something had happened to them? She breathed a "thank You" to God.

Jack turned and stared intently at Tuck. "Did you say Bella is married?"

"Yep, she even has a wedding ring. Don't know why she wasn't wearing it when she came to get us."

Lexie glanced at Jack, whose eyes met hers. Why did he have that hopeful look? What difference did it make if Bella was married? If she had a husband, the judge was even more likely to allow her to keep the twins.

"You know why she wanted us?" An indignant frown appeared on Addy's face. "She thinks our pa had a stash of treasures hidden somewhere and that we could show her where to find it."

"The very idea." Anger and disbelief rose in Lexie. "I could have understood if she wanted you girls for herself. After all, you are wonderful children. But for money?"

"Yeah, we told her we didn't know." Tuck nodded and glanced at Addy. "But she didn't believe us. She said we could think overnight about the punishment we'd get in the morning if we didn't lead her to it."

Addy shivered. "She never did say what the punishment would be, but I'll bet it would be bad. She really wants that stash."

"No one is going to punish you." Lexie's eyes swam and she blinked back the tears. "Climb into the wagon now. We need to get you girls home and warmed up."

After they were all settled in, Jack turned the wagon around and headed back toward home.

"I never knew God would answer prayer that fast." Tuck's voice held amazement.

Lexie turned and glanced at both girls, happy to have them close by once more. But for how long?

"God loves you very much. And He always answers our prayers, even if the answer sometimes isn't what we're expecting." Should she pray that God would let her and Jack keep them? But how did she know that was His will? Surely He wouldn't want the girls to live with someone like Bella, would He?

Addy darted a glance back the way they'd come. "I hope they don't wake up and follow us."

Tuck laughed. "Even if they did, they'd go the long way. They'd get lost for sure if they tried to come through the woods."

"Could you hide us, Miss Lexie?" Addy's voice trembled.

"Don't worry, sweetheart," Lexie said, her voice firm. "We won't let her take you until we've at least let the judge know the truth about her."

"That's right." Jack flicked the reins in an attempt to get the mules to go faster, but instead a groaning sound came from the axle on one of the wheels. He yanked on the reins to stop the mules then jumped down.

Lexie and the girls bent over the side, watching as he examined the wheel.

"Is it gonna come off, Mr. Jack?" Tuck leaned over until she was nearly upside down.

"Get back in the wagon before you fall, Tuck." Jack waved her back and continued to examine the wobbly wheel. He stood and looked at Lexie. "I should have brought some tools along. Don't know what I was thinking. I guess I've been on the river too long."

"What will you do?" A pang went through Lexie at the self-blame on his face.

"I think it'll hold long enough to get us back home. I'll have to lead the mules to make sure they don't take us over any large rocks or tree roots."

Slowly and carefully, they inched their way through the woods, lantern light bobbing eerily through the darkness. When they finally came out of the woods into the clearing by the farm, a cheer went up from Addy and Tuck.

"I knew you'd get us home, Mr. Jack," Tuck declared. "Didn't you, Miss Lexie?"

"Yes, I knew he'd get us home, too." A streak of mischief rose up and she grinned. "But I must admit I wasn't always sure that the wagon would make it. I felt a little nervous a time or two."

The girls howled with laughter, and Jack gave her a very fake hurt look. "And here I thought you trusted me implicitly."

"What's implicitly mean?" Tuck asked.

"I'm not sure, but it sounded good." He grinned and stopped the mules in front of the porch.

"Well," said Lexie, stepping down, "it has more than one meaning, Tuck. Why don't you look it up in the dictionary in the morning?"

"Aww, I hate dictionaries," Tuck complained.

"But do you hate cold fried chicken?" Lexie knew the answer.

"We have fried chicken?" Addy jumped up and down.

"Aunt Kate sent some with me." She glanced at Jack. "We'll get things on the table and eat when you're done with the mules. Then you can take me home."

"All right." He grinned. "That chicken sounds mighty good to me, too."

The sound of galloping hooves and squeaking wheels drew their attention. A buggy carrying Bella and the huckster flew across the yard.

"So you thought you could steal my children, did you?" Her shrill voice rang out across the barnyard. When her companion pulled the horse to a stop, she climbed out. "You'll go to jail for this."

Cold rage clutched Lexie. How dare this coarse woman come here making threats in front of Tuck and Addy?

Jack stepped forward. "Well, Mrs. Flanigan. Oh wait. I forgot you had remarried. What is your name?"

The huckster got down and darted his hand out in Jack's direction. "The name's Barker. Clyde Barker."

Jack ignored the hand. "Tell me, Clyde, when did you two get married?"

"Why, we've been married for nearly a year. Soon after we left here."

"Shut up, you idiot!" Bella's face flamed.

"Are either of you aware that bigamy is a federal offense?" Jack stood with a thoughtful look. "Let's see, I believe I heard of a recent case where a woman got seven years in jail. The law didn't take kindly to her marrying when she already had a husband."

Realizing his mistake, Clyde grabbed Bella's hand and started backing up toward the buggy. "I just remembered I have an appointment in another state in a few days."

Bella yanked her hand away from his. "You had to open your mouth, didn't you?" With a glare at the girls, she followed her husband and climbed into the buggy. "You haven't heard the end of this."

Lexie threw Jack a gleeful look as the buggy raced across the field. "Oh, I'm pretty sure we have."

Chapter 23

Laughter exploded through the Jenkins' barn. Fourteen-year-old Ted Meisner stood in the middle of the floor, encircled by more youngsters his age. The Irish jig he was attempting looked more like a toddler tripping over his feet than a dance.

"Okay, you young'uns," Lewis Packard called from the makeshift platform at the front of the barn, "you better use some of that energy and form a circle. Come on, everybody, let's shoot the owl."

Lexie laughed along with the others who were cleaning away the remains of supper. The tables had been shoved to the side, and pies, cakes, and punch would stay out for those who needed sustenance after taking part in the lively reels.

"Here comes your beau, Lexie." Mrs. Jenkins grinned. "I think he's a-lookin' for a dance partner."

Lexie looked up and saw Jack heading in her direction. She groaned. Her feet burned, and she'd hoped to avoid the stomping steps of the figures tonight. But how would it look if she refused to dance with the man she was marrying the next day?

She'd seen him and the girls nearly every day since the incident with their stepmother. The day afterward, Jack had gone to see the judge. When that good man found out about Bella and that Jack and Lexie were getting married and wanted to adopt the twins, he promised to contact the proper officials to find out the truth of the matter. Within two weeks, he had the proof, and after talking to Tuck and Addy, he had authorized the adoption when and if the wedding should take place. In the meantime, he allowed the girls to remain with Jack.

Jack's determination in the matter endeared him to Lexie more than ever. Lately she'd begun to take notice of his little kindnesses and the tender looks he cast her way. Was it possible she'd misunderstood him? His glances seemed. . .well. . .loving.

She went to meet him as he neared the table. His eyes crinkled as he took her hand. "Do you want to join the reel or would you rather find a couple of empty chairs along the wall and watch?"

"Oh, bless you, the chairs." She let him lead her around the sides of the building until they came across two chairs together. "Thank you," she breathed as she lowered herself gratefully onto the high-backed cane-bottom chair. "It's nice that the weather turned off warm, isn't it?" She waved a handkerchief in front of her face.

"You might not think so if you were out there on the floor." He chuckled and motioned toward Tuck and Addy. Perspiration ran down their faces and their wet curls were flying loose.

"Perhaps not." She waved harder. "But last year we had to cancel because of ice."

"Is that so?" He gave her a warm look and she quickly glanced away. "Lexie, are we going to speak of the weather all evening?"

"What did you wish to talk about?"

Jack glanced over at the woman next to Lexie, who was making no secret of the fact she was listening. He gave her a pointed nod, and Lexie couldn't prevent a giggle from escaping.

"Since, as you mentioned, it is a warm night, would you like to take a stroll to the river?"

Would she? She'd been so busy lately she'd had little time to spend on the riverbank, enjoying the sounds, smells, and sights. She stood and felt the vibration from the dance steps beneath her feet. "Let's ask Aunt Kate to keep an eye on the twins."

After her aunt had agreed to watch Tuck and Addy, Jack and Lexie strolled silently to the riverbank, Jack holding her hand firmly in his. She gave a gentle tug, and he just as gently refused to let go. A tingling began in her fingertips and flowed upward. She took a deep breath. He'd taken her hand before. What was different this time?

They stepped over to a huge oak tree, its branches bare and stark in the moonlight. Lexie turned to face Jack and leaned against the thick tree trunk. He loosened his grip from her hand, and disappointment washed over her. She sighed. She might as well accept it. This is how it would be, her longing for him and his pulling back. But only a few minutes ago, he'd been warm, approachable.

"Lexie, I need to talk to you about our marriage." His eyes bored into hers, dark with anxiety. Oh dear, had he changed his mind about getting married?

"Yes, Jack? What is it?"

He inhaled a ragged breath and let it out slowly. "You're probably going to think I was an idiot. But you see, when I proposed to you, I was under the impression you were starting to care for me. The way I care about you."

"But of course I care about you. You're very dear to me, Jack."

He gave an impatient little laugh. "No, Lexie. I don't mean like you care for a friend. I love you very deeply, and I thought you were beginning to feel the same."

What? He loved her? Then why hadn't he said so? A tiny spark of hope burned inside her heart then slowly fanned out into widespread joy. He loved her.

"When I realized you didn't, I knew I couldn't expect you to. . .well. . .be a wife in the full sense of the word."

She gasped. Oh no. They needn't have a loveless marriage after all. Or even the kind of marriage he was about to mention.

"So I've decided to sleep in the barn loft until I can build some sort of cabin for myself." He darted a glance at her. "I realize you want the marriage for the girls' sake, and that's all right. I wanted you to know."

She had to let him know she loved him, too. That they could have a real marriage. But how? Without sounding unseemly or wanton? Tears rolled down her cheeks, and she couldn't prevent the sob that burst from her throat.

"Lexie, honey, what's wrong? I'm sorry. I didn't mean to embarrass you. I promise I won't say another word about it. It's enough that we know."

She swallowed past another sob and wiped her eyes and cheeks with the back of her hands. She blinked past her tears and gave a little laugh. "Jack, I can't believe how foolish we've both been. I love you, too, with all my heart. I didn't know you loved me. You never really said so."

She watched joyfully as he took in what she had said. A light started deep inside his eyes and suddenly flamed with the realization that she loved him. The next thing she knew she was in his arms and he was kissing her eyes, her face, and she received his kisses with joyful abandon.

Finally he drew back and gazed at her. His eyes darkened and slowly he leaned his head toward her. She met his lips with her own.

⁂

Lexie stood outside the tent and waited for her cue. She trembled from nerves and from the cold that had come down from the north in the middle of the night. But she didn't care. Cold, warm, hot? She giggled. She experienced all those when she was with Jack anyway.

She could see the girls in their lacy white frocks. They were perfectly in step with each other and the music. She had received a few incredulous looks when she announced that Tuck and Addy would be her bridesmaids. She supposed they were a little young, and it might have been more suitable for them to be flower girls, but she'd made her choice and didn't regret it.

They were so adorable. She wished she could see Jack's face as he watched them, but from where she stood he was just out of sight.

The girls stepped to the side and turned a little. Grins split their faces.

The next to the youngest Jenkins girl, Martha, was halfway down the aisle. When she realized she was now alone, she dumped the rest of the flowers out on the floor and ran to stand beside the twins. Muted laughter reached Lexie's ears.

Oh! There it was. It was her turn. Mr. Jenkins pulled the tent flap back farther to make room for her gown.

Will stepped to her side and offered his arm with a tender smile. "I love you, sis," he whispered.

She smiled back and they stepped into the tent.

Lexie barely noticed Horace Packard, who served as Jack's best man. Her eyes saw only Jack, whose eyes adored her as she walked toward him. She forced herself to walk slowly, in time with the music, when what she really wanted to do was run down the aisle to him, like Martha had done to the twins.

In a daze, she found herself standing next to Jack, facing Reverend Hines. She barely heard his words, barely heard Jack, barely heard herself promising to love, honor, and obey.

But she heard the reverend pronounce them man and wife, and she felt Jack's kiss like she'd never felt anything before.

The reception was held in the Jenkins' barn, just as every inside get-together was. After all, they had the largest barn in the community.

Soon it was time to go. Jack and Lexie said good-bye to the girls, who were to stay with Aunt Kate, Will, and Sarah overnight.

"I don't see why we can't go home with you." Tuck frowned. "You said if you and Mr. Jack was married we could all live together."

A roar of laughter arose from the few folks who'd gathered around the bride and groom to say good-bye.

Will and Jack had hinted that the newlyweds would be going to Kansas City for a honeymoon, so Lexie was hopeful a shivaree would be avoided.

Lexie put her arms around both girls and whispered softly, so the crowd wouldn't hear, "We'll come to get you tomorrow, so we can go get you adopted, but don't tell anyone."

Tuck and Addy both gave solemn nods and hugged her, then ran to receive Jack's hugs.

Jack and Lexie walked to the buggy followed by the people. Now why was everyone grinning? Uh-oh. What had they done?

Tin cans were tied to the back of the buggy. Okay. That was usual. Jack helped her in the buggy. So far, so good.

Jack flicked the reins, then turned to Lexie and grinned. "I think we fooled them."

She breathed a sigh of relief. "I'm glad."

He put his arm around her shoulders, and she leaned against him. They headed home.

Contentment spread over Lexie like a warm quilt. *Thank You, God, for my wonderful husband and for making sure we finally knew the truth.*

They drove into the yard. Jack got down, and Lexie scooted over so he could help her out on his side.

The minute her feet touched the ground, light from dozens of lanterns flamed across the yard and a horrible din broke out. With pots, pans, anything they could bang on, dozens of their neighbors stood, laughing and grinning.

The good people of the Ozarks welcomed them home with a shivaree.

White River Song

Dedication

I'd like to dedicate this book to all the tomboys of the world and the families who wouldn't change them for anything. And to my own family. I love each of you more than I can express, and I can't imagine life without you.

Very special thanks to my Lord and Savior Jesus Christ, My All Sufficient One.

Chapter 1

Branson, Missouri, August 1901

The note hung high in the air, sweet and mournful. Kentucky Sullivan perched on the rickety bench, her bow held high. She closed her eyes, allowing the tension to build, then, with a swing of her arm, drew the bow across the strings. The note, mixed with the sounds of banjo and accordion, plunged into an ear-splitting cacophony that sounded like a passel of pigs squealing. Maybe with some chicken squawking flung in for good measure. It never failed to amaze Tuck how the four of them could make beautiful music one minute then an agony of crazy squeaks and screeches the next. But there was no denying it was fun.

She flung herself against the front wall of the feed store by the mill, wincing as the rough boards stabbed at her shoulder blades, then grinned at her fellow musicians.

"Whew! That there was some good fiddling, Tuck." Mr. Willie Van Schultz slipped his fiddle under his arm then removed his slouchy hat to wipe a hand across his bald head. "Mighty good." He grinned and plopped the hat back in place.

"Well thanks, Mr. Willie. You sounded pretty fair to middling yourself." Her shock of thick braids bobbed as she nodded, several straw-colored strands escaping their confinement.

The old man laid his fiddle on the bench next to him and cackled. He'd taught Tuck nearly everything she knew about fiddling over the last decade, and they both knew she was nowhere near his match.

With a sigh, she wrapped the silk cloth around her instrument and placed it in the case. The handmade violin had come from Ireland with her great-grandfather many years ago. A final pat, and she closed the lid with gentle pressure. "I've got to get a move on."

"Ya sure ya gotta go, Tuck?"

The cracked voice brought a smile to Kentucky's face, and she grinned at Squeezebox Tanner, the best accordion player in the entire Ozarks. Or at least as far as Tuck's knowledge went, which was just about fifteen miles on either side of Branson. "Yes, Addy will be waiting for me at the general store." She shook her head. "If I'm late, she'll throw a fit."

"You sure you're talking about your sister? Fit throwing is more up your alley, ain't it?" Tom Black's laugh came out as a wheeze, and he quickly laid his banjo on the bench and bent over until the coughing spell was over.

Tuck shrugged. He was right. Her twin never threw fits. The old man's hacking cough started up again. She winced. "Maybe you should give up that corncob pipe of yours, Mr. Tom."

"And maybe you oughta' be mindin' yore own bizness, Miss Sullivan."

Tuck covered her mouth with her hand to hide the grin she couldn't hold back. "And maybe you're right. I should at that." Tucking her fiddle under her arm, she gave a jaunty wave, leaving them laughing as she pranced off down the dusty road toward Branson's General Store.

Her twin sister stood by the wagon tapping her toe and glaring as she watched Tuck walk toward her.

Uh-oh. Tuck crossed the road and cast a side grin at her sister. "Sorry. Guess I'm a few minutes late. I got all caught up with our practice."

"A few minutes? More like twenty while I stood a gazing stock for every passerby." Her frown spoke a thousand words, and the anger in her eyes was apparently meant to cut through Tuck like a knife.

"You could have waited inside." She groaned. She'd been trying to do better with sarcastic remarks since she got baptized two months ago. Lately, it was awful hard though when her sister was around. Addy used to be the sweetest thing in the world. A little too sweet in Tuck's opinion. What in tarnation had gotten into her? "Sorry. I sort of got lost in the music."

A most unladylike snort emitted from Addy's pretty little mouth. "Music. Humph. If that's what you want to call the noise you and those old fogies squeeze out of those horrid instruments."

All right. That was it. Tuck opened her mouth to retort but stopped as her sister leaned over and hissed in her ear. "Someone is approaching. Oh my goodness, Abby, your collar is tucked inside your dress." She dug her fingers into Tuck's neckline.

"I'll fix it, and don't call me Abby!" Tuck pushed her sister's hand away. "What are you so nervous about? I always tuck my collar in when I play the fiddle."

"Hush." Addy shushed her, the frown turning into a simpering smile, as a coquettish look appeared in the previously stormy eyes.

At the *clip-clop* of a horse on the hardened road, Tuck twisted around.

The stranger sat tall and relaxed in the saddle, a hint of a smile on his lips. Dark blue eyes danced as they rested on the two sisters. When he lifted his hand and touched the brim of his hat, a lock of dark hair fell across his forehead. "Afternoon, ladies."

Her breath exploded from her open mouth with a loud *whoosh*. Had someone just kicked her in the stomach? By the time Kentucky's pounding heart settled back to normal, horse and rider had rounded a curve in the road and disappeared behind a grove of oak trees. "Who was that?" Whoever he was, she was going to marry him.

A dreamy look crossed her sister's face. "The new doctor, Sam Fields, and I think he's going to be your new brother-in-law."

Tuck returned to her senses and frowned. Obviously, Addy was as bowled over by the doctor as she was. Huh. Her sister was in for a great big surprise.

"Abby, why are you looking at me like that?" A frown crossed Addy's face.

Okay, this wouldn't be easy. First, Tuck couldn't let on that she was smitten with the doctor. "I said don't call me Abby. My name is Kentucky. Do you hear?"

"All right. Don't get so riled up. But don't you think you're a little old for such a childish nickname?"

"No, I like it." Tuck glared at her sister. Miss Bossy.

Tuck scrambled up onto the wagon seat and grabbed the reins, barely waiting long enough for her sister to scurry onto the seat before she flicked the reins. "Hiiiya, Toby, Haystack."

The mules took off at a lumbered pace. Why couldn't they go faster? If she had to be this close to Addy much longer, she might explode. She turned and grabbed the long black whip from the back of the wagon. Papa Jack had made it for one of the neighbors to use in a stunt riding show and hadn't gotten around to taking it to the man yet. She cracked the whip, and the mules took off running.

"Abigail Sullivan! What do you think you're doing?" Addy grabbed at Tuck's arm and tried to wrestle the whip away. "Let go of it. Papa Jack will kill you if you hurt his mules."

So she wants me to let go? Fine. Tuck opened her hand and Addy fell backward, teetering close to the side. Tuck grabbed her by the arm and steadied her.

She pulled hard on the reins and brought the wagon to a stop. Leaning over, she panted for breath, then finally sat up and stared at her sister. The look of horror on Addy's face struck Tuck as funny. A giggle rose from deep in her belly, exploding into great gulping, gasping laughter. "Hooo." Spent, she leaned back in the seat, her chest hurting.

"Look at me." Addy's voice was barely above a whisper.

The soft words surprised Tuck and she glanced at her sister. "What?"

"You like him, too, don't you?"

"What are you talking about? Like who?" Tuck knew the innocent tone wouldn't fool anyone, much less Addy.

"It's no use. I know you like him."

"So, what if I do?" Tuck frowned. She should have been more careful.

Addy picked up the reins and handed them to her. "Then you shall have him. Let's go home."

Tuck eyed her sister. Was she serious? Why did she always give up so easily? She flicked the reins, and the mules started up the steep hill. "Whadda you mean, I'll have him? Like a man like him would give me a second look."

A pair of lines appeared between Addy's eyes, and she pursed her lips as she examined Tuck. "It's true, you are a little rough looking, but only because of the way you dress and act."

"What's wrong with the way I dress and act?" Tuck felt the insult but wasn't about to let Addy know. "Just because I don't simper and primp?"

"Oh, never mind, sister. Let's not fight. The woods are so beautiful today. Let's enjoy the ride home."

Tuck relaxed and shifted a little on the seat. Addy was right. Oak trees, silver maple, and ash filled the woods on either side of the bumpy road, the sun glinting on their silver and green leaves. Soon the summer would be over, and gold, red, and orange would appear. Nothing was as beautiful as fall in the Ozarks. She grinned. Except maybe deep blue eyes and shiny black hair.

"So what did you mean about the way I look and act?" Tuck asked.

Addy huffed. "Really, Tuck, you're a very pretty girl if you'd let me fix you up like I'm always offering. Those braids are childish and make you look like a little girl, instead of a twenty-year-old woman. And when you're not wearing overalls, your dresses look disheveled. And...and...maybe you should use your first name."

"Well okay, maybe to the fixing up, but I'll never give up Kentucky." She gave Addy a sidewise glance. "You liked him, too. Why'd you change your mind?"

Addy laughed. "I hardly even know the man. I only met him at the store one day. I thought he was handsome. That was all. But he's the first one you've ever shown the slightest interest in, except maybe Rafe."

"Rafe?" Tuck laughed. "He's my best friend. You know that."

"Yes, but sometimes I've seen you two looking at each other with that... ummm...that look." She averted her eyes and stared at the woods.

"What look?" Tuck frowned, and indignation rose up like a cyclone inside her. "You better take that back. You know there's nothing between Rafe and me. And don't you go saying there is."

"All right, all right. Calm down. I must have been mistaken."

"I'll say you are." She gave a short laugh and flicked the reins. "Hiya. Let's go, mules."

⌒⌒⌒

Rafe chewed on a piece of green sour dock and watched as Tuck baited her hook, swung the line over the side of the boat, and then settled down on the bench seat.

She glanced at him. "Hey, aren't you gonna fish?"

"Naw, ain't in the mood." He chewed on the stalk and swallowed.

"Why'd you want to go fishing then?" She squinted. "You better quit chewing on that dock. The other day, I heard someone say it's poisonous."

Rafe stared at her. "You chew on the stuff all the time."

Tuck frowned then looked intently down at the water. "No, I don't. Not anymore. It ain't ladylike."

Rafe chuckled. "Ladylike? Since when do you care about that stuff?"

She checked her line then slung a glance his way. "Since a certain doctor moved to town. That's when."

Huh? Did she mean what it sounded like she meant? Rafe sat up. "What are you talking about?"

She bit her bottom lip, and her big blue eyes studied him for a moment. "Promise you won't tell anyone?"

"What do I look like? Some gossipy old woman?" He shrugged. "Tell me or not. It doesn't matter to me."

"Sorry. Guess I'm a little fidgety talking about it." She hesitated, and a blush washed over her face. "Truth is, I'm kind of sweet on the new doctor."

Rafe tensed and took a deep breath. He managed a sharp laugh. "I see. So is he sweet on you, too?"

"How should I know? I've never even spoken to the man." Her face softened, and tenderness filled her eyes. Something he'd only seen on Tuck when she was talking about a new baby calf or something. "But he will be. I'll see to that."

A bolt of unexplainable anger shot through him. "Oh really? And how do you mean to go about it?"

"Not sure yet." She closed her eyes and sighed. "He's just about the handsomest man I've ever laid eyes on, Rafe. Hair black as midnight and deep, stormy blue eyes."

"You mean like Lexie's?"

She glared and gave a scornful laugh. "Of course not. The doctor's hair and eyes don't look like a woman's."

"Okay. Don't get so riled up. I get it."

She sighed. "I'm going to marry him, Rafe."

Rafe's chest tightened and a knot formed in his throat. He wasn't sure why, but he'd better do something before he exploded. He took a long, slow breath and drawled, "I expect you'd better introduce yourself to him and make sure he's interested before you start planning the wedding. Besides, for all you know he may be a mad killer."

She gave him a shove, rocking the boat. "He is not, Rafe Collins. And stop making fun of me."

"Why, Tuck honey, I wouldn't think of making fun of you. Just want to make sure you're not murdered on your wedding night." He ducked, expecting a bucket full of bait in his face.

"Why you. . ."

Tuck stood, and the next thing Rafe knew he was treading water. He shook a wet cascade from his face and looked around. Several feet away, Tuck's head bobbed in the river and she grabbed for the boat. He swam over to help right it. Sputtering and gagging, they flipped it over and together dragged it to the riverbank.

Rafe hunched over, his hands on his knees, and coughed up water. Glancing over to make sure Tuck was okay, he threw himself onto the wet ground, heaving deep breaths.

Loud, guffawing laughter exploded near his ear, and Rafe flipped over on his stomach. Tuck lay on her back, slapping her legs as she howled.

What did she think was so funny? "Tuck, you know better than to stand up in a boat, you idiot."

"Sorry. I got so mad I just stood right up, didn't I?" She grinned at him, her eyes sparkling. "Bet you didn't mean to go swimming today."

Try as he would, he couldn't keep a straight face. His laughter joined hers, echoing across the valley.

Finally, she jumped up and started wringing out her shirt. His breath caught in his throat. The sun shone on her hair, giving it the appearance of gold threads. And droplets of water glistened on her skin. Rafe had never seen such a beautiful sight.

He shook his head. What in thunder was the matter with him? It was only Tuck. His best friend. The nutty tomboy who lived on the next farm.

He cleared his throat. "Look, Tuck. I'm sorry I teased you. But you aren't serious about marrying that doctor, are you?"

She stood with one boot in her hand and a faraway look crossed her face. "Dead serious. I've never been more serious about anything in my whole life."

Chapter 2

Tuck jumped off her horse, Sweet Pea, and tied the reins to the rail in front of the general store. Her stomach tossed and turned, but that was good. Maybe that meant she really was sick, instead of just faking as she'd planned. She swallowed past a lump in her throat. On the other hand, this might not be such a great idea after all.

She glanced at the store then back to her horse, envisioning herself mounting Sweet Pea and riding away. She shook her head. Nope. She'd come this far; she wasn't about to back down now. Especially since she'd gone to the trouble of donning a freshly pressed dress with rickrack around the neck. She'd even wound her braids around her head. Taking a deep breath, she headed for the store.

The bell over the door jangled loudly as she walked in. She barely noticed the blended aromas of cinnamon and cloves, leather and coffee. Probably because her face, including her nose, was numb. She took a deep breath and stepped forward.

Mr. Hawkins looked up from where he was shelving buckets of sorghum. "Good morning, Tuck. What can I get for you?"

She cleared her throat. "Is the doctor here?"

Hawkins motioned toward a door in back near the post office. "Yes, his office is back there. He has a patient though."

Disappointment wrestled with relief. "Oh. Then I'll come back another time."

"No, don't leave. They should be about finished in there. Been near onto a half hour. Sit down there and wait." He motioned to a chair by the office door then scanned Tuck's face. "You sick?"

"Why else would I want to see the doc?" Her face prickled with heat.

He grinned. "Oh, maybe the same reason half the girls in the county been showing up here. Maybe you've taken a shine to the doctor?"

She opened her mouth to retort, but a choking sound was all that came out. Whirling, she stomped toward the door.

"Now hold on, Tuck. Don't get so riled up. I was just fooling."

Tuck stopped in her tracks, torn between escape from embarrassment and her desire to see the doctor. She'd made several attempts to get his attention, but aside from being polite, he had practically ignored her.

The door to the office opened and a woman came out leading a small boy. She nodded at Tuck and Mr. Hawkins as she walked by.

Tuck's breath caught in her throat as the doctor appeared in the open doorway.

"You have another patient here, Dr. Fields." Mr. Hawkins motioned to Tuck.

Surprise crossed his face, but he smiled, his eyes quickly running down the length of her then back to focus on her face. "Ah, Miss Sullivan. I didn't expect you back again so soon."

Oh no. She was blushing again. But what did he mean, again?

Mr. Hawkins cleared his throat. "Excuse me, Doc. This is Miss Abigail Sullivan. The young lady who was here yesterday was her twin sister, Adeline."

What? Addy was here? What was she up to?

"Of course," the doctor said. "I should have noticed. Please forgive me, Miss Sullivan. Won't you come in?"

Tuck nodded and followed him into his office, her head swimming.

A new desk stood against a back wall, the new wood smell wafting across the room. He motioned to the chair in front of it. "How may I assist you, Miss Sullivan?"

She ran her tongue across her dry lips. "I'm feeling a little bit under the weather." At least she could say it now without lying.

"I see." He smiled and his eyes seemed to bore into her. Could he possibly know she was faking? "What are your symptoms?"

"Uh. . .my head and stomach hurt, and I'm a little bit dizzy." That much was true. Even if it was nerves or lovesickness.

"I see." He reached down and took her hand, giving it a squeeze before he checked her pulse rate. He gazed into her eyes and smiled. "Yes, your pulse is a little fast."

Taking the stethoscope from around his neck, he bent over and listened to her heart. "Ummhmm." He moved the instrument to her back. "Take a deep breath now."

She hadn't realized she was holding her breath until then. She let the air out of her lungs with a *whoosh* then drew it back in.

The doctor stood. "I don't think it's anything to worry about, Miss Sullivan. Maybe something you ate. I'll give you some medicine to settle your stomach."

Was that amusement in his voice? Tuck gave him a quick glance, but his face was composed, except for that heart-melting smile, as he walked to a cupboard and withdrew a large bottle of pills. He put a few into an envelope and handed them to her.

"Thank you, Doctor." She stood and extended her hand to him.

"You're very welcome, Miss Sullivan." Tingling warmth began at her fingertips and made its way up her arm as he took her hand and held it a moment longer than was necessary. "Is there anything else I can help you with?"

"Well, no—" She swallowed. "But did you know we're having a singing at the church Saturday night?"

"Yes, as a matter of fact, I did hear a thing or two about it." His eyes glittered as he looked at her.

"Uh, I thought, maybe, you being new and all, you might like to go along with me so I can introduce you to everyone." There. She'd said it. And hadn't even passed out.

"That would have been lovely, but you see, I've already arranged to attend the function with another young lady. Your sister."

Stunned, Tuck somehow managed to say good-bye and leave without passing out or screaming. Addy! So much for her sister's declaration about not caring for the doctor.

She mounted Sweet Pea and flung her knee around the horn. Last time she'd wear a dress on a horse. Wasn't anything wrong with her overalls anyway. Oh! That Addy. Just wait till she got a hold of her sister. She'd... she'd... Well, she wasn't sure, but Addy wasn't getting away with this.

Tuck set Sweet Pea into a thundering gallop down the road toward home, rushing past ancient, tall trees and herds of cattle as they raced toward home. Papa Jack would be madder than a wet hen if he saw how she was riding the horse, but who cared? He wasn't her pa anyway.

Shame shot through her, but she ignored it. It was true. He wasn't. Even if he and Lexie did raise her and Addy after their pa got killed. Okay, adopted them, too, so legally they were her parents, but so what? She was a grown-up. She'd do as she pleased. And the first thing she planned was to give that traitorous sister of hers a piece of her mind.

She found Addy in the kitchen peeling potatoes.

As Tuck stormed into the room, Addy looked up startled. "Abby, what's wrong?" Worry crossed her face.

"What's wrong?" Tuck mocked her sister then yelled, "You know what's wrong. You lied to me about the doctor then went behind my back and invited him to the singing."

Addy's face went white for a moment. Then with more spunk than Abby had ever seen from her, she stood, her lips pressed together. "Yes, I guess maybe I did fib a little. Because I knew how much you liked him." She bit her lip. "But I didn't invite him to the singing. He invited me."

Tuck gasped. "Why you little liar. You know you invited him."

"No, I didn't. I promise I didn't. " Her sudden burst of spunk gone, Addy dropped into the chair. "I'm sorry, Abby. When he asked me, I just said yes, without thinking."

"Sure, without thinking of me and your promise," Tuck yelled. She knew she was making a fool of herself but couldn't bring herself to stop.

Lexie rushed into the kitchen. "Girls. What in the world is all this bickering?"

"She's trying to steal my fellow, that's what," Tuck accused.

"I'm not either, and anyway, he's not your fellow," Addy said.

"He would be if you'd leave him alone." Tuck glared.

"That's enough, girls. Stop it, right now." Ma Lexie stood, hands on hips, her lips firm. "You can discuss this when you're calm. I won't have you fighting. The very idea. Sisters. And twins at that. Fighting over a man."

"What in tarnation has you all riled up?" Rafe frowned at Tuck, then reached beneath a hen and retrieved an egg.

"I got a right to be riled up. Addy outright lied to me. Twice." She dropped an egg into the basket she carried then held the basket out to Rafe.

Rafe couldn't help but laugh as he dropped the egg into the basket. "I can't imagine Addy lying about anything. What are you talking about?"

"Of course you can't. Because she has you fooled just like everyone else." Tuck slung her fists against her hips, her eyes widening as she realized her mistake. The egg she'd just stolen from a Rhode Island Red mother-to-be had shattered, its contents running down the side of her overalls.

Rafe howled with laughter.

She glared at him then burst out laughing. "Guess I'd better be more careful."

"Yes, if you don't want to end up with egg all over you." He grinned. "Now what did Addy do to get you so mad?"

She grabbed a handkerchief from her pocket and tried to clean off the mess. "Like I said, she lied to me. Told me she didn't care anything about the doc. Then she went behind my back and got him to invite her to the singing."

"Oh." He hesitated. He'd planned to ask Tuck to go to the singing with him, but maybe this wasn't the time. "If he likes Addy, I don't see that's her fault."

"Thanks a lot, Rafe," Tuck snapped. "That makes me feel a lot better."

"I only meant—"

She waved her hand in his direction and he stopped. In silence, they finished gathering the eggs and took them to the kitchen, then went out on the back porch.

Rafe stumbled around in his mind for a good change of subject. "Let's go fishing, Tuck."

"Don't feel like fishing." She leaned against the house and moped.

"What? Since when did you ever not feel like fishing?"

"Since Addy stole my man."

Rafe's stomach knotted at the words. If he didn't know better, he'd think he was jealous. But that was just ridiculous. Tuck was his buddy. Had been since they were little tykes. Besides, she wasn't even pretty. Was she?

The thought of her the day they'd fallen into the river invaded his mind. He sat on the step and took a long look. Blond twigs stuck out from the braids across her shoulders, and a few wisps curled around her forehead. Her blue eyes, dark with anger, sparkled as she glared at him. His palms went suddenly moist and his breath quickened.

"Why are you looking at me like that?" she asked.

Rafe came to himself with a start. How had he been looking at her? "I was just thinking about Addy," he lied.

"What about her?" A frown puckered the skin between her brows.

"Maybe it's time you give in and let her have something she wants for a change."

"What? She always gets her way." Surprise sounded in her voice and registered on her face.

"Tuck, no she doesn't. Addy gives in to you about everything. Maybe it's time you return the favor."

Tuck's mouth dropped open. "Well, I'll be. I thought you were my best friend, and here you go taking up for that—" He watched her storm into the house, slamming the screen door behind her.

Rafe sighed. He'd handled that well. As he turned away, he spotted Miz Lexie heading to the clothesline, a basket in her arms. An idea formed in his mind. He crossed the yard and took the heavy basket of wet clothes. "Let me carry this for you, ma'am."

"Thank you, Rafe. But you didn't really have to do that."

"It's okay." He set the basket on the ground by the clothesline pole. He grabbed a towel and handed it to her.

She gave him a curious look. "You and Abby fighting?"

"Sort of. She's mad because I took up for Addy."

"I see. . ." She seemed to be waiting.

Rafe cleared his throat. "Do you think she's serious about this doctor fellow?"

"Who? Addy?"

"No, I mean Tuck."

Understanding crossed her face. She placed her hand on Rafe's arm and smiled. "I wouldn't worry about it, Rafe. She hardly knows the man."

"Oh, I'm not worried. Just wondering. I mean, why should I worry? Tuck and me, we're just—" At the doubtful look on her face, he took a breath and blew it out. "This is crazy, but I think I might be falling in love with Tuck."

Lexie threw one end of a sheet over the line, motioning for Rafe to take the other end. "Have you told her?"

"No, ma'am." The horror in his voice was an exact match for what he felt. "She'd probably hit me with a hammer if I told her that."

A peal of laughter rippled from Lexie's throat. "Don't be too sure of that, Rafe. You and Abby have been very good friends for a lot of years. And that's nothing to scoff at."

"You think I have a chance against this doctor?"

"What do you think?"

He thought for a minute. The new man in town didn't know Tuck. Not like Rafe did.

"You're right. I'm not giving her up without a fight."

"Good for you." Lexie grinned. "Now how about helping me with the rest of these heavy sheets?"

Chapter 3

Tuck jerked awake and sat bolt upright. What had woken her? She glanced around. Moonlight streamed in through the window and washed a narrow swath halfway across the floor.

A muffled sob came from Addy's side of the bed.

Tuck caught her breath as guilt stabbed her conscience. She'd said some pretty mean things to Addy after they went to bed. Whispered them to her in the darkness, so Ma wouldn't hear. But surely that wouldn't cause Addy to cry like that. Shucks, if it had been the other way around and her sister had talked to her that way, she would've been mad, not sad. Still, the guilt gnawed at her. Addy wasn't like her.

She leaned back on one elbow and placed her hand on Addy's shoulder.

Addy flopped over onto her back. Tears streamed down her cheeks, and her eyes were red. She must have been crying for a long time.

"I'm so sorry I agreed to go to the singing with Dr. Fields." Her voice quivered and heart-wrenching sobs interspersed her words. "It just happened so fast, I said yes without even thinking about how much you liked him." Addy paused and blew her nose on the sodden hankie in her hand. "I'll go right into town tomorrow and tell him I've changed my mind. Will you forgive me? Please?"

Tuck stared at her twin, and shame began to work its way into her heart. She had known from the start Addy liked the doctor, regardless of her declaration to the contrary. Maybe Rafe was right.

She opened her mouth to speak and then clamped it shut. Why should she let Addy have the doc? She swallowed past the lump in her throat and managed to form a sincere expression on her face. "Are you sure, Addy? I mean. . . if you really like him—"

"Oh no, I don't like him at all. I've no idea why I agreed to go with him. But please tell me you don't hate me. I can't stand it when you're angry with me."

"Of course I don't hate you, silly." Tuck licked her lips as her conscience stabbed her again. "We're sisters, aren't we?"

Addy flung her arms around Tuck's neck and hugged her tightly. "I'm so glad you feel that way, too. Ma was right. We shouldn't let anything or anyone come between us." She jumped out of bed and padded across the floor.

The sound of a drawer sliding open was followed by a *thud* as it closed. After a scamper, her sister climbed back into bed and placed something hard into Tuck's hand. "I want you to have this."

Tuck opened her hand and made out the gold heart-shaped locket that held tiny photos of their real father and mother. When she'd claimed their grand-father's violin, a family heirloom brought all the way from Ireland, she and her sister had agreed that Addy should have their mother's locket.

Tuck shoved the necklace toward her sister. "No, it's yours. I have the fiddle. That's what we decided."

"I know, but I want you to have it. Really, I do." Her tear-filled blue eyes almost pleaded.

"Well, okay, if that's what you want." Tuck frowned. "Are you sure?"

"Yes, yes! Put it on." The eager words, a little too cheerful, rang in Tuck's ear. Addy grabbed the locket and placed the chain around her neck. "Here. Let me fasten it for you."

The chain, cold to Tuck's skin, nevertheless seemed to sear it. She shivered. Reaching up, she tucked it under the collar of her nightgown.

"There, now all is well again." Addy smiled and threw her arms around Tuck.

She accepted the hug, patting her sister on the back, stifling a sigh. A hound's ears couldn't hang any lower than she felt at that moment. Rafe *had* been right. Addy was giving up something she loved for Tuck. And Tuck was letting her.

She tossed and turned throughout the night, getting very little sleep. Between the rain that had begun in the middle of the night and her own guilt, her eyes remained wide and sleep eluded her. She'd promised to meet the oldsters for practice, so frustration clutched at her with every turn on the bed.

When she got up relief washed over her that the rain had stopped. But the still overcast skies didn't do much to improve her mood. She did her best to smile sweetly at Addy during breakfast, although every time her sister looked her way, her heart felt like it would explode right up out of her throat.

After helping with the dishes, she waved a quick good-bye, and with instruc-tions from Ma to stop at Branson's for thread, she rode to town.

Mud splattered on her overalls as Sweet Pea's hooves sloshed down the street. She was late for practice. And she didn't want to get griped at by the oldsters. The three old friends had met in front of Branson's store every week for years. In fact, that's where they were still getting together to play their music when Mr. Willie took her under his wing. The other two hadn't been thrilled about having an eight-year-old girl in their midst, but soon they declared she fit right in.

Branson's was too busy for them now though. It was hard to even hear their own music with people trudging in and out of the store so much. The young'uns screaming at the top of their lungs didn't help either. A couple of years ago, the four of them moved to the feed store down by the mill.

Maybe they'd be at the store waiting for her today, maybe not. The rain had stopped, but the clouds hung low and dark. Mr. Willie lived a good way down the river, so he might not want to chance it.

The feed store came into sight and Tuck grinned, waving at the oldsters as she pulled up in front.

"Hey, there you are." Mr. Willie grinned. "We weren't sure you were coming."

"You didn't think a little rain would keep me away, did you?" Tuck said, swinging her leg over the saddle and sliding off Sweet Pea.

"Naw," said Squeezebox. He cut a glance at Mr. Tom and Mr. Willie. A big grin split his face. "But we weren't sure if you might be spending time with the doc."

Tuck scowled. "You don't need to worry about that. I don't think he even knows I'm around."

Mr. Tom coughed. "Okay, we need to get going here. Get tuned up, Tuck."

The music practice went well, until Mr. Willie took offense at Tuck's attempt at an unplanned solo. "What in thunder do you think you're doing, going off on yore own like that? You trying to be some kind of queen bee or something?" The old man shoved his hat back and glared.

"Sorry." She knew she shouldn't have done it, but sometimes she couldn't help herself. Anyway, he didn't have to be mean about it. "Don't get so riled up. What's wrong with being a little creative?"

"Oh, so that's what you call it. How about lettin' the rest of us know next time you feel like getting creative." He stomped off without another word.

The rest of the group broke up, agreeing to meet the following week, and Tuck put her fiddle in the case and headed toward Branson's to pick up Lexie's thread before she headed out of town.

A rider on a bay mare came into view. Her breath caught in her throat. Sam Fields. And here she was in mud-spattered overalls and pigtails.

She straightened her back and forced a smile as he approached.

He tipped his hat then was past her without even a howdy-do. The very idea. . .how rude was that? He could have at least returned her smile.

She groaned. What did she expect, the way she looked. Why hadn't she worn something pretty and fixed herself up a little? She snorted. Because it was a muddy day, that was why. Mr. Stuck-up could just go butt his head against a stump for all she cared.

Sure. She didn't care. Not much, she didn't.

She sighed. As much as she hated to turn to Addy for another favor, it was time to come up with a plan to win the doc. Because she would win him, one way or another.

⁊⁊⁊

Tuck sat on a stool at the back of the stage with the oldsters and tuned her fiddle.

Horace Packard stood at the podium rifling through the songbook. His brothers joined him and began tuning their guitars. The Packard brothers were well known in the area for their singing and guitar playing, but they didn't mind sharing the stage with Tuck and her friends.

Tuck scanned the audience, keeping track of the doctor. She grinned as she saw him slip into a chair in the third row behind Ma and Pa and Addy. He'd be able to see her new blue dress perfectly from there. Addy had told her it made her eyes a deep, romantic blue. Of course, she had the same color eyes, and Tuck hadn't noticed anything special about them when Addy wore this color.

She looked down at her fiddle then, unable to resist, chanced another glance at the doctor. Was he looking at her or staring at Addy? She took a deep breath and counted to ten. She wouldn't look again. Why should she waste her time on a man that only had eyes for her sister?

And why was that? They were almost identical. Addy had dressed her hair for her, so that soft curls framed her face, with the back pulled into something called a french twist. She'd put on a very pretty dress just for him. It wasn't very comfortable either. She ran her finger under the collar and tried to loosen it, then quickly dropped her hand as Addy frowned and shook her head.

After an hour of robust singing, the Packard quartet performed two special numbers. Then Tuck and her friends delighted the crowd with a lively rendition of "Old Joe Clark."

As the audience applauded, Horace stepped up front and clapped his hands to get attention. "All right, neighbors. I know you're all about as ready for a break as I am. The ladies have loaded the tables down with all kinds of sandwiches and desserts and other delicious foods. So let's enjoy it. Then we'll come back and sing a while longer."

Laughter and small talk exploded as everyone stood and began talking to their friends.

Tuck glanced around, searching for Sam. She spotted him just as he stepped outside. She managed to avoid her family as she wove her way through the crowd to the door. Maybe she could find a way to speak to the doc alone.

Lanterns hung on trees and rails, lighting the yard. Tuck walked down the steps. Moisture clung to the brown grass and fallen leaves.

"You shouldn't be out here without a wrap, Miss Sullivan." The doctor stepped from beside the porch and smiled at her.

A ripple of pleasure coursed through her, and warmth spread across her face and neck. She bit her lip. Why must she blush every time he noticed her? "Thank you for your concern, Dr. Fields. But I'm not at all cold." That wasn't strictly true. She hoped he wouldn't see her shiver and catch her in a silly fib.

"Please call me Sam. It would please me very much." His eyes gleamed in the darkness, and she shivered again, but not from the cold.

"Very well. Sam." She'd been calling him Sam in her thoughts anyway. It was nice to have his permission. "Are you enjoying the music?" Oh dear. She hoped he wouldn't think she was fishing for compliments.

"Yes, I am." He grinned. "I especially enjoyed your part in it. You're very accomplished on the violin, or perhaps I should say fiddle."

"Thank you. Mr. Willie is the real expert. He taught me to play."

"He taught you very well." He spoke absently and glanced over her shoulder instead of in her eyes as he had before.

Tuck turned her head. Addy had stepped out onto the porch with a couple of their friends. Jealousy pinched at her. Obviously she hadn't much chance with Sam as long as her sister was around.

"I sincerely hope you enjoy the rest of the evening, Doctor. I must get inside." She whirled to go, wondering if he even saw her leave. As she passed her twin, she ignored her, pretending not to hear her when she spoke.

Tuck avoided looking in the doctor's direction the rest of the evening. And when the final song had been sung, she gathered her things and walked out to the wagon with Addy and their parents.

When she was seated in the back of the wagon, Ma turned to her with a smile. "You played beautifully tonight, Abigail." She reached back and patted Tuck on the knee. "I especially enjoyed your solo of 'Standing on the Promises.' It sounded so sweet and pure with only the violin."

"Thank you, Ma. I played it for you. I know how much you love it." And besides, she'd felt guilty about the thoughts she'd had concerning Ma and Papa Jack lately. Knowing Ma had enjoyed her performance made her feel better.

"I sort of liked 'Old Joe Clark.'" Papa Jack grinned and clicked to the horses.

"Oh you would." Ma laughed then smiled as she touched his arm. Ma preferred the slow, sweet songs. She glanced at Addy. "You're awfully quiet, dear. Are you feeling all right?"

Addy darted a glance at Tuck then smiled at Ma. "I'm fine. Just a little tired from all the excitement."

Tuck cut a glance at her sister. Addy had no idea why she was angry. How could she? She hadn't done a thing but be her own lovely self. Tuck sighed. So maybe it was time to take some lessons from Addy, the irresistible one.

Chapter 4

Tuck leaned against the counter in Branson's General Store and looked down at the notice in her hand. Mr. Hawkins had handed it to her with a grin the minute she and Addy had walked through the door. MUSICIANS WANTED. CONTACT WILLIAM LYNCH OR JIM CASTLE AT MARBLE CAVE OFFICE.

"Musicians wanted? Wahooo!" As excitement coursed through Tuck, she waved the paper almost under Mr. Hawkins's nose. "What's this all about?"

"Get it out of my face and I just might tell you." His grin softened the harsh tone of his voice.

"Sorry. Guess I got a little excited. But is this real? Are they planning some special tourist thing?"

Addy came running from the back of the store, her face pale. "Tuck, what's the matter? Did you get hurt?"

"No, no." She shoved the paper at her sister, never taking her widened eyes off the store manager. "Okay, now what's this all about?"

"That's the second time you asked me the same question." A teasing look crossed his face. "But I guess I won't keep you waiting. The Lynch sisters are going to Canada to visit family."

"Canada? How are they getting there?" Tuck couldn't even imagine how far Canada might be.

"Hmmm, I don't rightly know." He scratched behind his ear and frowned. "Train most likely. What difference does it make? The point is, they'll be gone for at least a month, maybe more. Lynch wants someone to take their place, entertaining tourists in the Cathedral Room while they're gone. I thought of you and Willie and the gang."

"A real paying job for us? Hot diggety." Tuck grabbed the notice from Addy who shot her an indignant look.

"Stop using slang, Abigail. It's vulgar and I don't like to hear it." Addy turned and headed back to finish her shopping but threw over her shoulder, "And Ma would be horrified."

"Well, don't tell her, sis. I got carried away." Tuck grinned and perused the notice again.

"Say, Mr. Hawkins. How long have you had this notice?"

"Since yesterday." He ran a cloth over the candy jar.

Tuck groaned. "They've probably hired someone by now."

"Don't worry. I stuck it under the counter. Didn't want anyone to beat you to it."

Tuck's mouth fell open and then exploded with laughter. "You're a true friend, Mr. Hawkins."

Fifteen minutes later, she and Addy headed out of town.

Tuck gave her sister a sideways glance. "I have to stop at the cave on the way home."

Addy grinned. "Like I didn't know that. All right. I'll wait in the wagon while you talk to them. Who is Jim Castle anyway?"

Tuck shrugged. "Never heard of him. Maybe a new guide or something."

Addy shivered. "I don't know how anyone can stand going down into those dark holes."

"Marble Cave isn't just a hole, silly. There are rooms down there. Do you think Miss Lynch would sit in a hole and play her piano?"

"Well, it looks like a big hole to me. And dirt everywhere. And there's no way I'd climb down from one hole to another like all those silly tourists." She stopped and gave Tuck a sideways smile. "Sorry. I know you like the place."

"That's okay. You never did care about caves and stalactites, even when we were children. But if I get a job here, you'll at least come hear me play, won't you?"

Addy bit her bottom lip. "Maybe, but I'll stand right inside the entrance."

Tuck planted her feet as the wagon rumbled and bumped down a hill. Exhilaration washed over her, and she grinned and snapped the reins. "Come on, mules. Faster."

She felt a tug on the back of her dress and looked over her shoulder to see Addy's white face.

"Mercy, Abigail. Will you please sit down before you fall off the wagon? Marble Cave isn't going anywhere."

Tuck huffed but plopped onto the seat. "I don't know why you're such a baby. Have you ever seen me fall off?"

"No, but you've come close a few times. Especially going downhill." Addy's voice was hoarse with fear and from yelling above the noise. "And I thought you were going to be more ladylike."

Tuck frowned at her sister. Why'd she have to be so picky anyway? "Land's sake, Addy. I'm wearing a dress on a weekday. What more do you want?"

"The question isn't what do I want. It's what do you want? You'll never attract Dr. Fields if you don't learn to behave like a woman instead of a back-woods mountaineer."

At mention of the doctor, Tuck's chest tightened. Her sister had a point. She pulled on the reins and the mules slowed down to their usual slow walk. "I don't think anything I do is going to matter. When you're around he doesn't even see me."

"Then make him see you." Addy's voice had softened. "You can do it."

Tuck shook her head. "I don't know how. It doesn't come natural to me as it does to you."

"You can learn how to be feminine. I learned by watching Ma. You were too busy hanging out with Papa Jack and your old mountaineers. Anyway, you weren't really interested." Addy pressed her lips together and narrowed her eyes at Tuck.

"So. . .you think I can really make him like me?" Oh, that sounded pathetic. Like groveling. How humiliating. Maybe she should forget it and concentrate on her fiddling. But Sam Fields was about the best-looking man Tuck had ever seen and the first one that had bowled her over.

"I can't guarantee it of course. But if you learn how to be a lady, there's no reason he won't. After all, you're quite beautiful."

Tuck tossed a grin at Addy. "You just called yourself beautiful."

"Oh," Addy blushed and bit her lip. "I guess that did sound sort of conceited since we look alike. But I didn't mean it that way. I see you as you. Not as me."

Tuck knew what her twin meant. She, too, seldom thought about how identical they looked until someone mentioned it.

A little tug of excitement yanked at her stomach as they approached the hill that led up to the old mine. "Okay, hang on. If we don't pick up speed, we'll never get up this next hill." Once more she stood and flicked the reins. "Yee-haw!"

Rafe stepped out of the cave entrance and wiped the dirt off his face with his bandana. He loosened his tool belt and carried it over to the shack that housed the office.

Jim Castle looked up from the desk he was bent over. "Howdy, Rafe. Platform all done?"

"Yes, snug as a bug up against the other one. Can't tell where one stops and the other starts. I'm sure glad Mr. Lynch decided to do it this way instead of moving that heavy piano to make room for the group."

Jim laughed. "Me, too. It would have taken at least four of us to move that monstrosity."

Since Rafe had begun doing some work on the cave, he and Mr. Lynch's new assistant had quickly become friends, finding they had a lot in common. They both liked farming, fishing, and hunting. They were already planning to hunt for turkey on Saturday morning.

A knock drew their attention.

Rafe's mouth fell open as he saw Tuck in the doorway, with Addy behind her. "Hi. What are you two doing here? Come on in."

Jim jumped up, knocking his chair over. His face turned red as he scrambled to pick it up. Finally, he turned toward the girls, who stood staring at him. "Forgive my clumsiness. I'm Jim Castle, the assistant manager of Marble Cave. Is there something I can do to assist you?"

Rafe grinned at the amusement on both girls' faces.

Tuck stepped forward. "My name is Abigail Sullivan, and this is my sister,

Adeline. I play the violin in a musical group and understand you have an opening for musicians."

Jim smiled past the surprised look on his face. "How many are there in the group and what instruments do you play?"

"There are four of us."

At the excitement in Tuck's voice, Rafe's heart went out to her. She'd waited a long time for an opportunity like this. She and the oldsters had been playing at social and church functions for years, but a paying position was special.

She continued. "Willie Van Schultz also plays the fiddle. Martin Tanner plays the accordion. He goes by the name Squeezebox. Tom Black is on the banjo."

Jim, who had been writing the information down, looked up and smiled. "And how can you be contacted?"

She gave him Mr. Willie's address and her own. "But the quickest way to get in touch is to leave word with Mr. Hawkins at the store."

"Thank you, Miss Sullivan. I'll pass this along to Mr. Lynch this afternoon. If he wants to interview you or have you come in for an audition, we'll be getting in touch."

Tuck grinned and offered her hand.

Jim shook it then held his out to Addy.

The girls left a few minutes later.

"You couldn't do better than to hire them," Rafe said. "They play at a lot of community things, and they're very popular. Willie and Tuck make magic on those fiddles."

"I guess you know the Sullivan girls pretty well." Jim looked down and peered at the sheet of paper on the desk.

Rafe chuckled. "I guess I do. We've been friends most of our lives."

"More than friends, maybe?" Was that more than curiosity in his voice?

Rafe shook his head, even though his friend wasn't looking. "I wish. I thought for a while we might be headed in that direction, but she's head over heels in love with someone else."

"Oh, is that right?" Disappointment tinged Jim's voice.

Rafe threw a quick glance at him. Was he interested in Tuck? But he'd only seen her this one time. Still, she was mighty pretty. Oh well. Neither of them stood a chance. She only had eyes for that new doctor.

After reminding Jim to meet him at the farm Saturday morning at the crack of dawn, Rafe mounted his dappled horse, Champ, and headed home. When he reached the turnoff to the Sullivan farm, he decided on impulse to go see what Tuck was up to. Maybe she'd want to go for a walk or something. After all, they were still friends, weren't they? And as far as he knew, she hadn't an inkling about his real feelings.

He found her seated on a stool in the parlor, with Addy behind her brushing her hair up and around some contraption.

"What's that thing you're putting in her hair? It looks like something alive."

Tuck twisted her head, and the contraption flew out and bounced on the floor. She squealed. "Now look what you did. What are you doing here?"

"What I...? All I did was walk in the door." Rafe rescued the puffy brown thing from the floor and handed it to Addy. "Looks dead, whatever it is."

A giggle escaped from Addy's lips. "It does, rather, doesn't it? Better that than alive, I suppose."

Tuck snorted. "Don't encourage him, Addy. What do you want, Rafe?"

"I thought you might want to go for a walk or something, but I can see you're occupied with something more interesting, whatever it may be."

Tuck stood. "I don't feel like sitting still any longer, anyway. And fresh air sounds good to me. Let's go."

"But Abigail, I thought you wanted to try the new coiffure."

"Sure I do. But it doesn't have to be right now. Let's wait until tomorrow." She grabbed Rafe's hand and grinned. "Come on."

"Fine," Addy called after them. "I have other things I'd rather be doing, too."

Rafe laughed, suddenly lighthearted, and followed Tuck outside. Maybe she was coming to her senses.

They walked across the field toward the creek, hand-in-hand.

"What was that thing Addy was putting in your hair? It looked downright scary."

Tuck laughed. "It did, didn't it? It's called a transformation or something of the sort. You wrap your hair in it or around it or something."

Rafe glanced at her, puzzled. "But what's the purpose?"

"It's supposed to make your hair look about four times fuller, and you perch a hat on top. I think. It's the latest style."

"I guess this has something to do with the doctor?"

"Of course. He likes ladylike girls, so Addy's going to help me be one." She peered up at him, her blue eyes dancing.

"So you're going to pretend to be something you aren't, so he'll like you better?" Rafe's mouth suddenly tasted sour.

She jerked her hand away from his and glared. "There you go again. Making fun of me."

"I didn't mean to make fun of you, Tuck. It just seems to me, if a man doesn't like you for who you are, why would you want him anyway?"

She huffed. "You don't understand. Wait until you fall in love. Then you'll know why I'm trying to change."

"I like you the way you are, Tuck." He spoke quietly and wasn't sure at first if she heard him.

After a moment, she sighed. "I know you do, Rafe. But we're not kids anymore. Things change. People change. And I have to change."

"All right, Tuck. If that's what you want, then change. But stay yourself while you're doing it."

"Stay myself?" She laughed. "I'm not likely to be anyone else. I'm still me, Rafe. And we'll still be friends."

He stopped and took her hands, looking down into her eyes. "Promise?"

"Promise. Nothing will ever change our friendship, Rafe." She looked up and her eyes blinked back tears. "Only, you have to let me do this, Rafe. I really, really love the doc."

The words echoed in Rafe's mind as he rode home and dread squeezed at his heart. Was there any hope for him and Tuck? It didn't seem likely.

Chapter 5

Huffing a sigh, Tuck lowered her fiddle again and pushed down on the top part of her sleeve in an attempt to flatten it.

A chorus of snickers sent a surge of embarrassment and anger through her. "What are you varmints cackling about?"

Tom coughed and guffawed. "Them sleeves look like legs of mutton, Tuck. Why'd you wear such a contraption to practice?"

"Laugh all you want to. Mr. Lynch said if he decides to hire us, I have to wear a fancy dress, so I'm trying it out."

"Sure you are." Squeezebox grinned. "Couldn't have a thing to do with the doc could it?"

"All right, that's enough. Leave her alone." Willie frowned at his friends and then nodded to Tuck. "Let's try again."

Tuck stood and placed her fiddle in the case. "It's no use, Mr. Willie. They're right. I can't play in these sleeves. I'll be back on Thursday."

"But what about the practice?" Tom whined and laid down his banjo. "I don't know that latest tune good enough."

"You can practice without me today," she snapped. "Mr. Willie, you'll have to play loud enough for both of us."

She turned, catching her hem on a nail sticking out from the wall. She stumbled before catching herself.

Tom and Squeezebox both burst out laughing.

Tuck reached down to loosen the fabric from the nail then glared at the two.

"Aw, we're jes' having some fun, Tuck. We don't mean nothing by it." Squeezebox grinned and nudged Tom.

"Yep. You're having fun all right. Fun at my expense. I'm getting out of here. Bye, Mr. Willie." She stepped off the porch and turned the corner, heading down to the store where Addy and the wagon waited. She kicked at a piece of wood in front of her, flinging mud from the street, then continued on.

A horse whinnied loudly behind her. As she threw a glance over her shoulder, she felt her foot catch in the hem of her dress, but not in time to keep from tripping over the full ruffle. Arms and legs flailing, she slammed facedown in a mud hole.

"Abby!" Her sister's screams set her in motion, and she pushed herself partway up, then promptly lost her balance and landed on her seat. "Jiminy!" She squinted and shook her head, causing mud to fly from her hair and face.

The sound of horse's hooves and laughter preceded a familiar voice. "I do believe it's the lovely Miss Sullivan. Fancy seeing you down there."

Disbelief and horror shot through Tuck, and she peered up at the doctor's amused face. Oh no, she must look like a wet rat.

"It's quite rude of you to laugh at my sister. You are no gentleman, Doctor."

Tuck stared. Addy's countenance reminded her of a bear protecting her cub. Wow. Who would have thought Addy could be so fierce?

The amusement left the doctor's face and he dismounted, turning to Addy. "You are absolutely correct, and I apologize."

"I think you might be apologizing to the wrong person, Doctor," Addy retorted, tapping her foot on the ground. "My sister was the recipient of your untoward humor."

"You are absolutely right." Quickly, Sam turned and extended his hand to Tuck. "Please forgive me, Miss Abigail. I don't know what came over me."

Tuck accepted his assistance and the handkerchief he offered, scrambling up from the muddy street.

He placed his hand on her back to steady her. "I truly am sorry."

She peered into his eyes. Did her mean it? He seemed sincere.

Addy shoved him aside and, retrieving her own hanky, began to wipe the mud from Tuck's face. "The very idea of him laughing at you like that," she muttered.

The doctor cleared his throat, and Tuck glanced at him then quickly turned her face away.

"Well, ladies, if I can be of no further assistance, I'll be on my way." He remounted his horse, touched his hat, and rode off.

"I hated having him see me like this." Tuck gulped and blinked back frustrated tears. "C'mon, let's go home."

Addy trailed after her. "Really, Abigail. After his rude behavior, I don't know why you'd care what he thinks."

"Oh, he probably couldn't help laughing. I'm sure I looked very peculiar." She looked at her sister. "And he did apologize and was gentle and kind when he helped me up."

"I still say he was rude and ungentlemanly."

"And I say he didn't intend to be, so stop being mean, Addy." Tuck grabbed the reins from the hitching post and climbed up on the wagon seat.

"Very well." Addy climbed up beside her. "I'm sorry if I hurt your feelings. You're probably right."

"It doesn't matter anyway. Look what happened. I let you fix my hair, I wore a new dress—"

"And forgot to lift your skirt from the ground. Which is why you tripped." Addy smiled. "I think we need to work on deportment and carriage."

"Whatever you say, sis." Tuck raked back the muddy lock of hair that had fallen across her face. "I need all the help I can get."

"How did your practice go?"

"That's something else I need to talk to you about. The puff sleeves won't work when I'm playing the fiddle." Her voice sounded forlorn even to her. But no more so than she felt. "As a matter of fact, nothing seems to be working."

Sympathy crossed Addy's face. "It'll be okay, Abigail. You just wait. You'll have the doctor knocking on the door, begging for your attention. If you're sure that's what you really want. . ."

∽✦∾

Tuck panted as she looked over her shoulder at her bulging derriere. "This isn't going to work, Addy. Aside from the fact I can hardly breathe, I have a shelf in front and a hump like a camel in back. Only lower."

Addy straightened from smoothing the dress down over Tuck's ankles. "Don't be silly. The special corset beneath your dress forms a silhouette called an S-bend. I believe it began in Europe several years ago and has been in fashion in New York City for a while now."

"So where did you get the contraption?" Tuck huffed. "And why don't you wear it yourself?"

"I sent off for it a few months ago but then decided I didn't want to stand out." She frowned and gave a little shake of her head. "The ladies around here dress more old style."

Tuck planted her hands on her hips and frowned at her sister. "Oh, but it's all right for me to be a laughingstock?"

"The doctor won't laugh." Addy grinned. "Who else matters?"

"How do you know he won't?" Tuck threw a suspicious glance at her twin. She wasn't absolutely certain she trusted her. Had she really stopped caring for the doctor?

Addy heaved a sigh. "Because, silly, he's from the city and is accustomed to the look."

Tuck puckered her forehead in thought. Addy had a point. And besides, she really didn't care what people thought.

∽✦∾

Rafe dipped the huge turkey into near boiling water, being careful not to touch the side of the big, black iron pot. He quickly pulled the bird out of the water and threw it, dripping onto the wooden plank where Jim was plucking the feathers from another bird. Rafe hunkered down across from him and started yanking feathers from the one he'd just dipped.

"Whew, wet feathers stink, don't they?" Jim said.

"Yes, but it's worth it to sit down to my ma's turkey dinner." Rafe grinned. "By the way, she told me to thank you for the turkey and to invite you to dinner after church Sunday. She'd have done it herself, but she had errands to run today."

"Tell her I gladly accept. And I was more than happy for her to take the turkey off my hands seeing as I'm living in a room at the Lynches' and they didn't want it."

They worked in silence for a few minutes, and then Jim cleared his throat.

"How's Miss Sullivan? I haven't seen her in a while."

Rafe frowned and yanked a handful of feathers. "She's too busy turning herself into something she's not."

"What do you mean?" Jim asked.

Rafe sighed and stared down at the bird in his hands. "You see, she has always been so natural. Never putting on airs. A fellow knew where he stood with her and what she meant when she said something. Now she's turned into a simpering coquette. She's acting like a different person."

"Really? In what way?"

"Well, for one thing she never wears her overalls anymore. Not that I don't like to see her in dresses, but she's not being herself. That's the part I don't like. And she hasn't been fishing or hunting with me in weeks. Says it's not ladylike." He snorted. "Like she's ever cared. I feel like I've lost my best friend. Only worse."

Jim paused, confusion crossing his face. "Miss Sullivan wore overalls and fished and hunted?"

"Sure. Tuck and me have been fishing buddies since we were old enough to bait a hook."

"Huh?" Jim stared at him. "You mean Miss Abby is the one you're in love with?"

"Sure. Who did you think I meant?" Light dawned and Rafe chuckled. "You thought I meant Addy. Now I see. She's the one you like. I thought you had a hankering for Tuck."

"What a relief. That's wonderful." Jim threw his head back and laughed, and Rafe joined him, their laughter resounding through the yard.

"We'd better get these birds cleaned up or neither of us will have a turkey dinner, much less a lady." Jim laughed and focused on the feathers.

Rafe sighed. "At least you have a chance at the lady you're interested in. As far as I know Addy isn't seeing anyone."

"Thanks for that information. Of course, I'll be leaving as soon as the cave tourism stops, so I don't suppose it can go anywhere even if the lady should be willing."

"You could always come back," Rafe said.

"Yes, I can. And will." Jim's face brightened. "Don't give up on Tuck. If, as you say, she's not behaving like herself, then maybe this infatuation with the doctor will pass."

"Maybe. I hope so. But I'm not counting on it." Rafe sighed and shook his head.

They finished plucking and cleaning the turkeys and hung them in the cellar.

While they were washing up, Jim said, "What time should I be here for supper?"

"Ma usually has it on the table at six. It's only three. I think I'll run into town and pick up some more work gloves."

"Good. We can ride together until my turnoff to the cave."

Rafe grinned. "You sure you want my great company, or do you want to find out everything I know about Addy?"

"Yes, that, too." Jim took the piece of sour dock Rafe offered him and bit down on it. His face puckered and he spat it out. "What is this nasty stuff?"

Rafe laughed. "I think you have to acquire a taste for sour dock."

They rode toward town, waving good-bye when Jim turned off toward the Lynches'.

When Rafe came out of Branson's store a little later, he spotted Tuck walking in his direction. At least he was pretty sure it was Tuck. But the strange outfit she was wearing made his mouth hang open. He shoved his hat to the back of his head and stared. Her front was thrust out like a board, and the rear end. . .well, he averted his eyes and waved.

Apparently she didn't see him. No wonder, her eyes were glued to the man on the horse coming around the corner.

Rafe scowled. Sam Fields.

Rafe watched as the man tied his horse next to his. Then with a brief nod at Rafe, the doctor sauntered down the road to meet Tuck. He extended his arm, and she rested her hand on it and simpered into the man's eyes. Tuck didn't even see Rafe as she stepped into the store with the doctor.

So that was that. Rafe mounted his horse and rode out of town. He wished he could keep riding until the sight of Tuck and the doctor was out of his mind. Trouble was he'd likely ride a long way before that happened.

Maybe it was time to leave. He'd never given much thought to leaving the farm, but there was no law that said he had to stay. Pa could afford to hire a hand to take his place. And Rafe's sister Betty and her husband Robert would help. Maybe he could find something to do in Springfield or maybe he'd hire on with the railroad. Yes, he could do that. Of course he'd need to finish the work he'd agreed to do at Marble Cave. Then, he was gone. And Tuck could marry her fine doctor.

Chapter 6

The slight pressure of the doctor's hand on her back guided Tuck to the back of the store. An unaccustomed weakness washed over her. Was this how love felt? If so, she wasn't sure she liked it.

As Sam reached to open the door to his office, a slight cough behind them caused Tuck to turn her head.

Mr. Hawkins stood with a frown on his face. "You feeling sick, Tuck?" Although the store manager's words were directed at her, his eyes pierced the doctor as he spoke.

Sam turned, switching his hand from Tuck's back to her elbow. "Miss Sullivan and I are going to have a cup of tea and visit for a while in my office."

"Think so? Mebbe you can forget the tea and do your visiting here in the store, or else take a walk down the street."

Warmth washed over Tuck's face. It hadn't occurred to her there was anything inappropriate about being in the doc's office alone with him. Slight dizziness rushed over her, and she grabbed Sam's arm to steady herself.

"Are you feeling unwell, Miss Abigail?" The doctor's voice rang with concern. Tuck's heart raced. "I'm quite all right. Perhaps we should take Mr. Hawkins's suggestion and go for a walk. A breath of fresh air would be nice."

"Very well, if you like." Annoyance had replaced the concern as Sam darted an angry glance toward Mr. Hawkins and steered Tuck toward the front door.

They stepped out onto the street and headed toward the mill. The amazing greens of summer had turned to brown patches in the grass and brown falling leaves from the heat. Tuck would be glad when autumn made its appearance and the world grew beautiful again.

"I'm very happy we met today, Miss Abigail. I've been wanting an opportunity to apologize for my manners the day you fell."

"Please forget about that, Doctor. You've already apologized and I accepted your apology." Tuck's voice sounded weak to her own ears and her chest felt suddenly tight.

"I'm so happy to hear that. By the way, I enjoyed your violin playing very much the night of the singing."

"Yes, you said that, too." Her head was starting to hurt as his voice droned on.

"Perhaps you'll let me know when you are entertaining again."

Satisfaction ran through Tuck. Perhaps the doctor truly did admire her. "Yes, I can do that. Actually we may be filling in as entertainment for the tours at Marble Cave for a while."

"Is that a fact? You be sure and let me know, so that I can be there." He squeezed her elbow, but amusement sparkled in his eyes as he gazed down into hers.

Was he making fun of her?

But the next moment his eyes darkened and his glance moved to her lips.

She trembled. What was wrong with her? She swallowed past the lump in her throat. "Are you very fond of music?"

He smiled and nodded. "Oh yes, I've been to many concerts in New York and have attended many of the finest concert halls in Europe."

"Oh, I see." No wonder he'd appeared amused about her fiddle.

A grove of oak trees, branches almost bare, stood near the mill. The mill owner's wife and two children stood on the bank of the creek watching the mules turn the water wheel.

"The wheel is splashing water pretty badly." Sam said. "Perhaps we should continue our walk in the grove so that you don't get wet."

Too late. The heavy tug of Tuck's skirts reminded her she'd forgotten to lift them. They dragged the ground, heavy with water. Besides, the thought of water droplets splattering on her skin was welcome at the moment. What was wrong with her? Had a sudden illness assaulted her?

As Sam turned Tuck toward the grove, the world began to spin around her and she felt herself falling. Arms caught and lifted her, and then she was floating in darkness.

⁂

Tuck awakened to a tugging at the back of her dress and blessed relief as her clothing loosened. Strong hands rolled her over onto her back.

She gasped, and air rushed into her lungs. What? A memory surfaced. She'd been walking with the doc and must have fainted. Surely he hadn't loosened her clothing.

Her eyes snapped open, and she sat up. A wave of nausea washed through her.

The mill owner's wife ran a damp cloth over her forehead. "Now, now, Miss Sullivan. You'd best lie back down on the cot just for a bit. That ridiculous corset was cutting your air off. You'll be fine in a moment."

"Where am I?" She glanced around at the unfamiliar room.

"The mill office. Dr. Fields brought you here, and I could see right away what the problem was." A puzzled look crossed her face. "You'd think a doctor would have thought of that."

Gratitude washed over Tuck as the kind, round-cheeked woman patted her. "Thank you, ma'am. I was getting dizzy and weak, but I didn't realize it was the corset."

"I'll bet you've never worn one before." She smiled.

"No, ma'am. And I won't ever again either." And she'd thought the strange sensations had something to do with love.

"I'd think your sister would know better." The woman prattled on. "She seems very fashion smart to me."

"It's not Addy's fault. I kept telling her to tighten it more." As she confessed, she felt foolish at the memory and changed the subject. "Is the doctor still here?"

"No, he left you in my care, dear. You needed a woman's help anyway." A knowing smile appeared on her face. "Right?"

"Yes, of course," Tuck said. "And I do appreciate everything you did for me. You may have even saved my life."

"Oh, I don't think it would have come to that, especially when you had a doctor right there with you, but you never know." She shook her head. "Dr. Fields said to tell you he was sorry to leave you, but he had a medical emergency."

"What was the emergency?" Tuck forced herself to fight off the resentment that assailed her.

"I don't know, dear. That's all he said. But it must have been serious. He was in a mighty big hurry to leave." She reached her arm behind Tuck. "Let's sit you up now and see how you feel."

Tuck complied and swung her legs from the cot. "I'm fine now. I appreciate all your help. If you could help me get laced back up, I'd best be getting home before it gets dark."

After thanking the woman again and assuring her that she needed no help walking the short distance to her wagon, Tuck left.

She'd just reached her wagon when she heard her name called. Turning, she watched Mr. Willie limp toward her. It seemed to her that his limp was worse. But then, he must be getting pretty old. The thought bothered her, and she shoved it aside and grinned. "Hey, Mr. Willie. Hadn't you best be heading home before dark?"

"Don't worry about me, miss. How about yourself?" He frowned then smiled, glancing at her dress but not saying a word about it.

"You're right. You want to ride along with me for a while?"

"It'd be my pleasure, Tuck. Got some good news for you." He loosened the reins of his grizzled horse and lifted himself slowly into the saddle.

"I could use some good news." Tuck climbed into the wagon and flicked the reins, heading out of town with Mr. Willie riding along beside her.

"Mr. Lynch sent word we've got the job. But he wants a list of the songs we're planning so he can approve them." He shook his head. "Can you believe that?"

Tuck laughed. "Yes, I can. You can't really blame him, Mr. Willie. You and Squeezebox come up with some wild ones sometimes. Remember 'Way Down Upon the Bloody River?' He wants us to entertain the tourists, not scare them to death."

The old man cackled. "Aw, that was just us a funnin'. I see what you mean though. I guess maybe we'd better get together and make him a list, then practice a couple of hours. When can you meet us?"

"I'll be in front of the feed store tomorrow at ten o'clock. That okay?"

"That's fine with me. I'll tell the others. We'll be there."

The sun was low in the west as Tuck waved good-bye to Mr. Willie as she turned off the river road and he continued downriver.

Tuck's thoughts were a jumble. She tried to focus on the numbers they should do for the entertainment. She'd been waiting a long time for a chance like this, but her thoughts kept jumping to Sam Fields.

He was a puzzle to say the least. One day he ignored her, the next he laughed at her, then again he treated her as though she were precious to him. Perhaps it was the new attire. If so, she was glad he liked her more ladylike appearance. She'd keep the hair and the ruffles, but the S-bend had to go.

⁂

"Abigail! What in the world have you done to your skirt?" Addy stared, mouth agape at the sodden fabric lying in a pile on the bedroom floor.

"The question is what did this stupid corset do to me?" Tuck retorted. "It nearly killed me. That's what."

"What do you mean?" Addy's eyes widened at her words.

Tuck proceeded to relate the happenings at the mill, embellishing the story as she went along. "I'll tell you this much. I'm not wearing it again." She nodded, shortly.

"Oh dear. I don't blame you. I'm sorry, Abby. I didn't realize what torture it would be. But that doesn't explain your skirts. Did you forget to hold them up again?"

Tuck chewed on her bottom lip while she thought. "Yes, I did forget. But I've come up with a solution."

"What's that?" Addy looked almost fearful as she waited.

Tuck hid a grin. "I'm thinking about making me some of those split skirts they wear riding."

"All right. They're fine. Better than those awful overalls. But what does that have to do with your skirts dragging the ground when you walk?"

"You misunderstand, dear sister. I plan to wear the split skirt all the time. They only come to the ankle, so I won't need to worry about them dragging the ground, will I?"

Tuck grinned as Addy's eyes widened in horror at the thought. "Oh, but Abigail. You can't wear a riding skirt on the street. Or anywhere. They're just for riding. It wouldn't be ladylike to. . ."

Tuck burst out laughing, bending at the waist and slapping her hands against her bare knee.

"Fine. Go ahead and make fun of me." Addy frowned then smiled. "All right. I did fall for that one, didn't I?"

"Sorry, sis. I couldn't resist it." Tuck wiped her eyes then pulled on a clean pair of overalls. She still wasn't ready to give them up at home.

"But you will wear dresses and style your hair?" Addy coaxed.

"Yes, if you'll help me. You know I can't fix my hair right." The last time she'd attempted to, it stuck out all over and finally came tumbling down.

"You'll get used to it. But of course I'll help." Addy smiled.

"Oh, I almost forgot. We got the job at the cave. Start in two weeks." She couldn't prevent the pride that filled her voice.

"Oh, that's wonderful, Abby. I'm so happy for you and your friends." Addy clapped her hands and her face beamed. "We'll need to get busy and fix the sleeves on your dresses then."

Tuck paused in buttoning her overall straps and peered at her sister. Why was she so nice? No wonder the doc liked her best. But now he liked Tuck, too. He had been a perfect gentleman today. Treated her like a real lady. That is until he left her passed out at the mill. But if he had an emergency, he had to leave, didn't he? Yes, but did he really have an emergency? Or did he just dump her and leave her?

"What are you frowning about? I'd think you'd be happy after your walk with Dr. Fields. It sounds like he's quite interested in you now."

"Sure. I think he is. Maybe." But a niggling bit of doubt wormed its way into her thoughts, robbing her of her joy.

"Oh, of course he is." Addy picked up the wet dress from the floor and hung it on a hook. "We'll need to get this washed tomorrow, so it doesn't stain."

Tuck glanced at her sister. Yes, Rafe had been right. Addy did give in to her and she'd always done everything she could to help Tuck get what she wanted. Why hadn't she ever realized that before?

"You don't have to help wash it, sis. I can do it." Tuck laid her hand on Addy's shoulder. "Why do you do so much for me? I hardly do anything for you."

"Now don't be silly. I enjoy doing these little things for you because I love you." She reached over and kissed Tuck on the cheek. "And of course you do things for me. Now we'd better go and help Ma get supper on the table. She's the one who really does too much. For both of us."

They found Ma Lexie in the kitchen, removing fried chicken from the skillet.

Tuck took the fork from her, and Addy poured vegetables into the serving bowl.

"Go sit down in the parlor with Pa," Addy said.

"Yes," said Tuck. "We'll call you when supper is on the table."

As they finished preparing the meal and placed everything on the table, Tuck's heart ached with sorrow and guilt. *I'm sorry, Lord. I wanted so badly to change after my baptism, but I've gotten worse. I'll do better. I promise. I'll stop being so selfish. I'll even. . .*

She paused. She'd almost promised to give Sam up. But surely God wouldn't want her to do that, would He? After all, hadn't He brought them together?

Chapter 7

Tuck climbed the ladder and peeked out the cave entrance. A crowd had gathered, and Jim stood behind a wooden booth selling tickets.

Tuck squinted against the sunlight and peered around for Sam. Not spotting him anywhere, she carefully made her way back down the wood rungs and across the vast entry cavern Mr. Lynch had dubbed the Cathedral Room. Probably because his daughter's baby grand piano stood in splendor near the back of the room. Or maybe because the ceiling was so high.

She stepped onto the makeshift platform that extended the stage. You couldn't really tell visually there'd been an addition, but it wasn't as sturdy as the original. It didn't need to be. They'd probably tear it down once the sisters took over the entertainment again.

When Squeezebox had spotted the dainty chairs placed on the stage for their use, he'd snickered. "These don't look like they'd hold a kitten. Hope I don't go crashing down."

"They're stronger than they look," Rafe had assured him, just before he'd left to help Jim with crowd control.

Anyway, the men would be standing most of the time.

Tuck perched on the edge of her chair, remembering to drape her skirts around her legs for modesty's sake. Her sleeves were now fitted instead of puffed. Not as pretty, but much more sensible for playing the violin. Narrow lace adorned the neckline instead of a collar. This was Addy's idea to prevent Tuck from folding the collar inside the neckline.

Tuck was becoming used to wearing dresses more often—and frilly ones at that. She'd never cared much about being pretty, but that was before she'd met Sam. He appeared to like her new look and demeanor, although that was mostly put on when he was around.

He'd escorted her to church the past two Sundays and taken her for drives in his carriage several times. On the last occasion, when they were on the way home, he'd grasped her hand. She'd felt uncomfortable and after a few moments managed to withdraw it from his fingers.

The men were tuning their instruments, so she bent down and took her fiddle from its case. She ran her bow across the strings and smiled, satisfied with the pure, clear sound.

Mr. Lynch came down the wooden ladder. "Jim will be bringing the first group down in one minute. You may begin now."

As instructed, the three men stood while Tuck remained seated. When the first group entered the room, strains of "I'll Take You Home Again, Kathleen" met the tourists' ears. Jim guided them around the room for a few minutes, pointing out the natural carvings and other things of interest. Afterwards, he led them through the opening into the next room of the cave.

Tuck knew from experience they'd soon hear squeals from some of the ladies as they reached the area that led in a more difficult downward path, some of the chambers accessible only by rope ladders. Most of the women would turn around and scuttle back to be entertained by the music while their men continued the tour.

Rafe stood to one side. He nodded and smiled when he caught her looking at him. He knew how much this opportunity meant to her.

She glanced toward the stairs, frowning over Sam's absence. He'd promised to be there. Perhaps he'd show up later, unless another emergency prevented him from coming at all. Her throat tightened. Sometimes she wasn't quite sure about Sam's commitment to their friendship. And Rafe's open animosity toward the doctor bothered her. Rafe was usually a good judge of character. But perhaps he was merely jealous that Tuck had a new friend. And friendship was all it was at this point.

When the first group returned, Tuck jumped to her feet. They struck up a lively rendition of "Ole Dan Tucker" as the tourists exited up the ladder.

The next group should be coming in at any moment. Mr. Willie passed around a canteen of cold water, and then they fell into another tune.

Sam came down the ladder and threw her a wave and a wink before he hurried to stand to one side. Relief coursed through her. There. He did care. She must learn to be more trusting.

She glanced at Rafe and noticed he had puckered his lips in a silent whistle. She knew that look. She really must speak to him about his attitude.

༺❀༻

Rafe's stomach coiled when Sam Fields sauntered in like he owned the place. What was it about the man that set his teeth on edge? Partly jealousy, sure. But something about the guy rubbed him the wrong way. Had been that way from the moment he laid eyes on him, even before he knew Tuck had fallen for the doctor.

It bothered Rafe that Tuck couldn't see it, too. She was the one who usually spotted a phony at first glance. Maybe the stars in her eyes were blinding her. Or maybe there wasn't really anything to see. If that was the case, Rafe should probably bow out and leave the situation to run whatever course it was meant to. As long as Tuck was happy and taken care of, he would deal with it.

After the second group of tourists came down from the sinkhole entrance, Rafe slipped outside. He had to get away before he beat the tar out of Sam Fields or did something else that would cause a ruckus. He couldn't ruin Tuck's big day.

He took Champ off his tether and mounted. The reins slashed back and forth as Rafe urged the horse to a faster pace.

He was halfway home before he made a decision and changed his course, heading toward the Sullivan farm. Maybe Jack could help him make some sense of this crazy situation.

He found Tuck's pa pitching hay in the barn.

Jack looked down and waved as Rafe came through the door. "Thought you'd stay and ride home with Tuck." He gave Rafe a questioning look.

"Sam Fields is there. I expect she'll be going somewhere with him." He climbed up to the loft and grabbed a pitchfork.

Jack stared at him in silence for a minute. "What do you make of that?"

"It's not my place to say," he muttered. But he sure felt like saying a few things.

"Since when? You've always had your say about anything concerning Tuck." Jack tossed a forkful of hay into the corner. "I haven't seen much of the man, so I'd really be beholden if you'd give me your opinion."

Rafe hesitated. But he'd planned on talking to Jack anyway, so he might as well just blurt it all out. "I don't like him. I'm not for sure just why. But something's not right. Maybe he's hiding something. Or maybe I'm imagining it, and I just don't like him because Tuck does." He paused. "I don't trust him not to hurt her."

Jack pursed his lips and nodded. "Appreciate your honesty. I'll keep an eye on him. If I see any sign you're right, I'll send the man packing."

"I don't know, Jack." Rafe shook his head. "You know how stubborn Tuck can be. If you ran him off, she'd likely take off after him."

"Maybe. But I hope she's a little more levelheaded than that." He arched his eyebrows. "What are you planning?"

Rafe shook his head. "How do you always read my thoughts?"

"If I could read your thoughts, I wouldn't need to ask what you're planning." Jack grinned. "But I can tell by that look in your eyes you've got something on your mind."

Rafe took a deep breath and leaned on the pitchfork. "I've been thinking about going to Arkansas and getting a job with the railroad. They'll be starting to lay the tracks soon between Conway and here for the White River Line."

"Hmmm. What about the farm?"

"The crops are almost all in. And it won't take long to get everything ready for winter. Pa can get Jim Shelling to help out if needed. Betty and Robert'll help, too. They only have a small crop this year." He clamped his teeth together and kicked a small pile of hay off the loft. "I can't stay around here and watch Tuck marry that man."

Jack stood silent for a moment. Rafe was thankful when he changed the subject. "Speaking of the railroad, I hear there's a fellow named Fullbright trying to buy up land. They say he represents the Missouri Pacific. You heard anything about it?"

Rafe looked up in surprise. "News to me. Why would they need more land?

They have more than enough for the new line already."

Jack shugged. "May just be a rumor. You know how folks are."

"Yes, I do." Rafe frowned. "I'd hate to see anyone sell out."

"I doubt there's anything to it. The fellow may simply want the land for himself."

"Maybe." Who cared anyway? All he cared about was Tuck. Would she marry that guy? Or worse still, would Sam Fields play her false and break her heart? The thought was enough to drive Rafe crazy. He tossed the forkful of hay into the corner and leaned the pitchfork against the wall. "Guess I'd best be getting home."

"When do you figure you'll leave for Arkansas?"

"Not for a while. I reckon I'll see you at church on Sunday." He couldn't leave. Not until he knew Tuck was safe and happy. Or at least safe. He wasn't sure he could control the happiness.

"Amen." The preacher's voice boomed throughout the church and reverberated from log wall to log wall.

Tuck fidgeted as she waited for her family to exit the pew so she could follow. She'd thought Reverend Talbot would never stop preaching. Sam was supposed to have gone home with her for Sunday dinner. But he hadn't shown up for church. She finally reached the front door and hurriedly shook hands with Brother and Sister Talbot then stepped into the yard and glanced around.

Ma Lexie walked up to her and placed her hand on her shoulder. She smiled and gave Tuck a questioning smile. "Dr. Fields isn't here, is he?"

"No," Tuck said then hastily added, "but I'm sure he has a good reason. Perhaps an emergency came up."

Unease nagged at her. Sam seemed to have a lot of emergencies. This wasn't the first time he'd missed the service after promising to meet her there.

Worry lines appeared between Ma Lexie's eyes. "He seems to miss services a lot, don't you think, dear?"

Although the same thought had just crossed Tuck's mind, resentment welled up inside her. "After all, Ma, he can't help it if someone gets sick."

"No, of course not. I didn't mean to imply anything bad about him." Nevertheless, the worry lines deepened.

Relief washed over Tuck as Sam drove up in his carriage. He would surely have a perfectly good excuse for being late. "There he is now."

Addy gasped and headed toward the wagon.

Now what had got stuck in her craw? She probably had her nose out of joint because Sam wasn't interested in her. A pang of remorse shot through her. Addy wasn't like that. She smiled as Sam ambled up to her.

His eyes flashed as he gazed at her. "I'm so sorry, Abigail. I received word that a family downriver was taken ill. There were several children, and I didn't want to take the chance of waiting."

"Oh my," Ma Lexie said. "Of course not. Was it anything serious?"

"Thank you for your concern, Mrs. Sullivan. Actually, it was a simple case of the sniffles. And only two of them were actually ill." He smiled at Ma then shifted his gaze back to Tuck. "May I drive you home?"

"Yes, of course." Butterflies tickled her stomach and she smiled back at him. "And don't forget you're having Sunday dinner with us."

"That's right. And we'd best get going." Papa Jack nodded at Sam. "Lexie has fried chicken warming in the oven, and I can't get there fast enough."

Tuck sat straight in the buggy seat, proud to be riding beside Sam. He was by far the most handsome man she knew and the most distinguished. She was quite sure even Reverend Talbot was not as cultured as Sam.

By the time Sam pulled up in front of the house, Tuck was glowing from her own thoughts. She almost floated into the house.

Soon they were all seated around the table enjoying Ma Lexie's wonderful fried chicken, mashed potatoes, gravy, and sweet peas. Tuck couldn't help but notice that although Pa and Ma were polite enough they both seemed a little reserved with Sam. But perhaps it was because they didn't know him well.

Addy, on the other hand, while not openly rude was obviously distressed and spoke only when someone addressed her specifically. Occasionally, she'd dart a glance in Tuck's direction, but when Tuck threw her a questioning look, she quickly averted her eyes and focused on her meal. Now what in thunder was wrong with her? Tuck didn't know, but she intended to find out before the day was over. She hoped her sister wasn't still holding onto a secret attraction for Sam. Because it wasn't going to get her anywhere. He belonged to Tuck, and she intended to marry him one day.

She swallowed past a sudden lump in her throat. Was she sure she wanted to marry Sam? She glanced in his direction and met his eyes. He smiled slowly, and his eyes warmed her as they seemed to send her a secret message. Heat washed over her entire body. Yes, of course she wanted to marry him. He was everything she admired in a man.

Chapter 8

Wind whipped through the entrance of Marble Cave, swooping down the opening, picking up leaves that had been tracked in, and scattering them around the Cathedral Room.

Tuck shivered, wishing she had worn something warmer. A storm had blown in within the last half hour. Overcast skies threatened a downpour, and temperatures were dropping steadily. She shivered again. It was too cold for this early in October. Well, at least now she could stop fidgeting over giving up the entertainment when the Lynch sisters returned next week. Now that a cold spell had hit, Tuck wouldn't be surprised if this turned out to be the last tour before spring.

"Think we'd better go on home?" Squeezebox turned miserable eyes on Willie. "This feels like a norther coming in. I can't imagine anyone tourin' a cave when it's this cold. My fingers are turning blue. I'm goin' to git cold blains fer sure."

"You mean chilblains don't you?" Tom snickered.

"Naw, I mean cold blains," Squeezebox snapped, frowning at his friend. "I reckon I know what I mean."

"Aw, it don't matter," Mr. Willie motioned toward the opening into the next room. "We can't go anywhere until Mr. Lynch brings them folks back out and says we can go."

Tuck blew her warm breath onto her cold hands. The tourists were due to be back in fifteen minutes or so. Were they ever in for a shock.

A wailing sound drew her attention. The four of them stared toward the opening, and soon Tuck could see the light from one of the lanterns. Mr. Lynch stepped through the opening, his face like stone, followed by a weeping woman and most of the other tourists who'd followed Lynch and Jim Castle down earlier.

Tuck's stomach lurched. What could have happened? Had someone fallen?

The distraught woman, tears streaming down her cheeks, grabbed Mr. Lynch's arm. "How long will it take them to find him? Is there any danger?"

"Mrs. Harris, please calm yourself. I assure you, we will find your son." But although his voice was positive, the uncertainty in his eyes was unmistakable.

"But we called and called. Why didn't he answer?" Her high-pitched voice warned of shock.

Tuck stared, dread filling her mind. A lost child? Oh no. *Please, God.*

Mr. Lynch sent an imploring look in Tuck's direction. She stepped from the platform and walked over.

"Miss Sullivan, this is Mrs. Harris. Her young son Tommy wandered away from the group. Mr. Harris stayed behind to help Jim search for him." His eyes spoke the danger that his words didn't as they stared into Tuck's. "I need you to get Mrs. Harris a cool drink and stay with her while I gather a search party to help."

His voice was calm, but Tuck knew the danger the boy might be in. According to legend, the Osage Indians used to call the cave Devil's Den and were afraid to enter. But that was due to their superstitions. At least there were no hostile animals inside. The main danger would be if the boy tried to walk around in the darkness. There were drop-offs and crevices he could fall into.

Tuck breathed a silent prayer that the child would sit still until they found him. If they found him. Folks had been lost in the cave before. Or so the rumors went.

As Mr. Lynch hurried toward the ladder, Tuck guided the frightened mother to a group of chairs standing near the front of the room. "Please be seated, Mrs. Harris, and try not to worry."

She was relieved to see Mr. Willie approaching with a tin cup of water. She thanked him and handed the cup to her charge.

Mrs. Harris stared vacantly at the water and then looked up at Tuck, her lips quivering. "He said I was too slow. He pulled away from me and ran up to be with his father. I thought he'd be all right. Wouldn't you think so?"

Tuck wondered if the man had even known his son had run to his side. She took the chair next to Mrs. Harris and laid her hand on hers. "Tell me about your little boy."

"Oh, Tommy is such a busy little bee. He doesn't stay still a moment. His Sunday school teacher says he's the liveliest five-year-old she's ever seen."

Five? Why would anyone take a five-year-old child into a dark cave with twists and turns and drop-offs? Even with lanterns. And why didn't the woman call out to her husband and let him know the boy had run ahead? Anger boiled in Tuck, and she took a deep breath to calm herself. Casting blame wouldn't do any good, and furthermore she didn't know all the details.

"Oh." An agonized cry tore itself from the woman's throat. "It's all my fault. I should have made him stay with me. Oh what have I done? My little boy. My sweet baby." Mrs. Harris jumped up and rushed back toward the cave. "I have to find him."

Tuck caught her and turned her gently around. "Mrs. Harris, you'll never find him in the dark. Look, you don't even have a lantern. The men will find him. Come sit back down."

"But, I—" She looked wildly around the room, swaying.

Tuck caught her just as she fell. She laid her gently on the floor and called to Mr. Willie. "See if there's someone outside with a wagon I can borrow."

"What are you planning to do with her?" Mr. Willie yelled as he half ran, half hobbled to do what she'd asked.

"I'm taking her to Ma." Ma would know what to do. She'd take care of Mrs. Harris and help her through this until Tommy was found. Tuck shuddered then, with resolve, pulled herself together. She leaned over the unconscious woman and patted her cheeks. Pulling a hanky from her skirt pocket, she dampened it in the untouched cup of water. As she patted the unresponsive woman with the damp cloth, all she received was a moan.

A man in overalls came down the ladder, followed by a huffing and puffing Mr. Willie. Within a few minutes Tuck had tied Sweet Pea to the back of the wagon and climbed up on the seat. The Good Samaritan farmer whose name was Warren Holmes, lifted the half-conscious woman off his shoulder and up onto the seat where she leaned against Tuck's shoulder. The chill in the air sent a shiver all through Tuck's body. At least it wasn't raining yet. Within minutes they were headed down the hill toward the Sullivan farm.

Before Mr. Holmes had come to a full stop, Tuck jumped down from the wagon. "Ma! Addy!" She reached the door just as it flew open and Ma and Addy ran out.

"What in the world is—?" Ma took one look and ran to show Mr. Holmes into the parlor. She motioned to the blue settee. "Lay her down here."

As her mother and sister gathered around the prostrate lady, Tuck told them what had happened, then rushed to her room and put on overalls and a warm sweater. She grabbed her coat from a nail in the closet and threw it over her arm, just in case someone needed it. She rushed back to the parlor. "I have to get back to the cave, Ma. There may be something I can do to help." Tuck fidgeted from one foot to another.

"All right." Ma had opened a bottle of smelling salts and held it beneath the woman's nose. "She seems to be coming to. We'll take care of her. Send us word as soon as you find the child."

"I'll not send word. I'll bring it myself." She kissed her mother on the cheek and grabbed Addy by the hand, pulling her with her through the door and onto the porch. "Sister, please pray for someone to find little Tommy. I'm so afraid for him."

Addy squeezed her hand. "Of course, Abby. Let's pray now."

They bowed their heads and Addy spoke quietly. "Our Father in heaven, You know all things and see all things. You know where little Tommy Harris is right now, Lord. We pray Your holy protection over him and pray that You will keep him from being afraid. Guide the men who are searching for him, and let them find him soon. In the name of Jesus. Amen."

Tuck blinked back tears. This was the closest she'd felt to her twin sister in a long time. How could she have been so mean to her? Addy never had a mean or cruel thought for anyone. Reaching out she grabbed Addy and hugged her tightly. "I love you, sis."

The joy in Addy's eyes and her warm smile were all the response Tuck needed.

She jumped on Sweet Pea and headed back to Marble Cave, her sister's prayer replaying in her mind. Surely everything would be all right.

She jumped on Sweet Pea and headed back to Marble Cave, her sister's prayer replaying in her mind. Surely everything would be all right.

Rafe removed his hand carefully from the rock slab and found another hand-hold further down. He reached with his foot and felt solid ground. The only problem was it could have been a six-inch ledge or one of the wide rock corridors that weaved throughout the cave. "Hey! Sam! I think there's a level place down here, but I need light."

"Rafe, that you?" Jim Castle's voice rang out, reverberating from the sides of the cavern.

"Yes, it's me. Dr. Fields was supposed to be holding the lantern. Where did he go?"

"Hold on. I'm coming down." A rope fell from above and then Jim slid down, holding on with one hand while the other gripped a lantern. He held it downward, and Rafe could see a huge cavernous room below.

Rafe turned loose of the rock and landed on the hard ground.

Jim slid the rest of the way down the rope. "Okay, we're down," he yelled. "Send us another lantern and mark the spot."

The rope was raised and soon was lowered again, this time with a lantern tied to the end.

Jim steadied himself against the rock wall while Rafe untied the lantern.

"Now, what happened to Fields?" Rafe asked.

Jim made an explosive sound of exasperation. "The good doctor grew faint and had to be escorted out."

"What? He was fine a few minutes ago," Rafe said. "How'd he get sick that fast?"

"Claimed there wasn't enough air, but no one else seemed to be having any problem." A wry smile twisted Jim's lips. "Anyway, I've seen cowardice enough to know it when I see it."

"So a man had to leave the search to guide him out." Rafe blew out a huff of air and hesitated. After all, this was Tuck's beau they were talking about. "I guess we really shouldn't judge the man. Anyone can panic. Maybe he has trouble with tight spaces." But all he could think of was that little boy, lost and probably scared half to death. His nephew Bobby's face popped into his head, and he swallowed hard to hold back the rising nausea. *Lord, please help someone find Tommy soon.*

"Maybe. We're more than likely better off without him. I sure wouldn't want to trust him with my life or limbs." He glanced to his right then his left. "Looks like we'll need to split up here."

Rafe lit the lamp and headed down the dark passageway. Water dripped from somewhere above. "Tommy," he called every minute or so. But no answering voice came back to him. No little boy's cry. Not even a whimper.

Tuck rushed forward as Bert Smith climbed out of the cave and half dragged Sam up after him.

"Sam," she cried out. "Are you hurt?"

His face red, Sam shook his head. "Got lightheaded and couldn't breathe. Not enough air I guess."

Surprised, Tuck glanced at Bert. His lips were pressed tightly together. He shook his head. "There's plenty of air in there. Well, I gotta head back in. They need every hand they can get."

Without even thanking Bert, Sam grabbed Tuck's arm and pulled her toward a log that lay on the ground. He dropped onto it, motioning for her to sit beside him. "That fool doesn't know what he's talking about. I tell you there's not enough air when you go deep inside the cave."

Tuck licked her lips. She'd never heard anything about thin air in the cave. And Bert had seemed upset. Had Sam panicked due to fear? She bit her lip. Everyone experienced fear, but to leave the search for a child and, to top it all off, to take someone else away, too... Wasn't that a sign of downright cowardice? She cringed inwardly at the disloyal thought. Of course Sam wasn't a coward. After all, he didn't grow up around here and maybe he looked at things differently. Besides, who could say for sure there wasn't a pocket of thin air inside the cave?

She took his hand. "Would you like for me to get you some water?"

He looked down at her hand on his and smiled, possibly remembering the time he'd attempted to hold her hand and she pulled hers away.

Heat burned her face. She removed her hand and placed it on her lap.

He stood. "Thank you, no. I really need to go home in case someone needs me."

Stunned, she stood and faced him. "But Sam, what if the Harris boy needs you?"

An impatient sound burst from his lips. "It's very unlikely they'll find the boy. And if by some miracle they do and he's alive, someone will come for me, I'm sure." He walked away and mounted his horse.

Tuck wrapped her arms around her shoulders and watched in disbelief and dismay as Sam rode away. Finally, she turned and went back to the cave, climbing slowly down the rungs of the ladder.

Chapter 9

Rafe peered through the narrow passage. He held his lantern aloft and saw another fairly large room. The oil in his lantern was low and he'd need to head back soon. As much as he hated the thought, he wouldn't be able to help the boy if he was wandering around in the dark, getting lost himself.

He took a step forward and slipped. Suddenly he began to slide down a wide crevice of some sort. He only slid a short distance before landing. He found himself in a small cavern beside a narrow opening.

He heard a sound. Holding his breath, he listened. There it was again. Was that breathing? Could Tommy be in there?

He eyed the opening, mentally measuring if he could fit through there. Only one way to find out. He squeezed through the tight opening and stopped still, his heart thumping. On the floor, next to a large, natural throne-like structure, lay a small boy, his blond hair resting on one small hand. *Please let him be alive.* Rafe stepped quietly across the way and bent over the tiny form. He breathed a sigh of relief as the child rolled over and opened his eyes.

"You found me." A smile split the small face and the boy sat up. "Will you take me to my mother now?"

Rafe heard the quiver in his voice and felt tears behind his eyelids, but he didn't care. He'd never felt the emotions he felt now at the sight of this small boy. "I'll be happy to do that, Tommy. Can you stand?"

"Sure I can." Tommy grinned and jumped up. "Isn't this a fine room? That looks like a throne over there, but it's not. My father told me all about it before we came to Marble Cave. It's a rock formation. There's a bunch of them. Father told me water and stuff formed all these thrones and posts and things, but Ma said God made them like this."

Rafe's eyes scanned the boy from his head to his feet. He appeared to be fine. "You must be a very smart boy, Tommy, to remember all that."

"Uh-huh." He held his hand out to Rafe. "I'd like to go see my mother now."

Rafe swallowed past the lump in his throat. He took the small hand and started back the way he'd come, boosting Tommy upward then pulling himself up after him. When they reached the place where he'd separated from Jim, he placed two fingers in his mouth and gave a loud whistle. The signal the child was found.

◦⁓◦

Tuck stared in admiration as Rafe handed the small boy to his father.

Tears rolled down the man's cheek. "How can I ever thank you?" Mr. Harris held his hand out and shook Rafe's.

"You don't need to thank me, sir. Any one of us could have found Tommy. I just happened to be the one at the right place."

Mr. Harris nodded and looked around at the men who had followed Rafe and Tommy into the Cathedral Room. "There are no words to express my gratitude."

Tuck gazed at Rafe, pride filling her heart. A lot of men would be taking the credit to themselves, but not Rafe. He was good through and through.

He turned and their eyes met. Tuck took a step forward, her heart racing, and then stopped at the memory of Sam's face as he'd crawled out of the cave. She blinked back sudden tears as shame washed over her. Why couldn't Sam be more like Rafe?

Through a blur, she saw Rafe coming toward her. She threw him a sad smile then turned and headed for the ladder.

"Tuck, wait. Where are you going?"

But she was halfway up to the exit. She climbed out the top and ran toward Sweet Pea, who nibbled at the browning grass around her tether. Mounting, she urged Sweet Pea into a gallop.

Halfway down the hill, Tuck heard hoofbeats. Glancing over her shoulder, she saw Champ racing after her with Rafe leaning forward in the saddle, his face tense with determination.

Tuck sighed. She might as well stop. Sweet Pea couldn't outrun Champ. She pulled slightly on the reins, and Sweet Pea slowed.

Rafe pulled up beside her. "What in the world are you doing, running off in such an all-fired hurry, Tuck Sullivan?" Rafe snapped, his voice fraught with impatience. "Is that any way to treat a friend?"

Tuck gnawed on her bottom lip and threw him an apologetic smile. "Sorry."

"Well, I guess you ought to be," he growled. "So where are you heading so fast?"

Tuck shrugged. "Home, I guess. I need to let Mrs. Harris know her son is found."

"Jim was going to take Mr. Harris and Tommy over to your place to get Mrs. Harris," Rafe said.

"Oh. All right, but I'd better get on home anyway." Any place to get away from Rafe's searching eyes. Sometimes she felt like he could read her mind.

Rafe tossed her a sideways grin. "I've got a better idea. We ain't been fishing in weeks. What do you say?"

"Are you crazy? It's getting colder by the minute, and look at those clouds. We're liable to have a gully washer any minute now."

"Oh?" His eyes danced, full of challenge. "When did that ever stop us?"

Tuck peered at her lifelong friend. There was no denying she missed him. Why not go fishing? At home, she'd just mope over Sam. Anyway, she was probably making a mountain out of a molehill and thinking the worst. She cocked her head and grinned. "Okay, but if we get drenched, Ma'll be beside herself, and I'll blame it all on you."

Rafe tossed his head back and laughed. "Sure, go ahead. She won't believe you anyway."

He was more than likely right about that. She and Rafe had gotten into so much mischief over the years. . . . "Okay, but I'll need to use one of your poles. I don't think I can get past Ma with mine on a day like this." She shook her head.

"Why, Tuck. Scared of your ma, and you a grown-up woman?"

"Oh, be quiet. I'm not half as scared of my ma as you are of yours. Race you to your place." With a "hiya" and a slight kick to Sweet Pea's sides, she took off.

They reined in winded in front of Rafe's barn, and he went inside and retrieved his fishing poles and a coat. Then they dug up worms for bait.

Rafe's old boat was tied up by the river. In no time, they'd shoved it into the edge of the water and jumped in.

"I'm sure glad your ma didn't see us. She'd have a fit if she knew we were on the river with the wind picking up like this." Tuck baited her hook and threw the line over the side.

Rafe glanced up at the sky. "I don't think it's going to amount to anything."

"Huh! That's what you said the time we almost got swept downriver," Tuck retorted.

"We made it okay, didn't we?"

"Sure, because the Maxwell brothers jumped in and grabbed the boat." Tuck laughed.

Rafe roared with laughter. "Good thing those Maxwells are all big and hefty."

"Wow, Rafe. We couldn't have been more than eight or nine. Just little tykes." Tuck leaned back and sighed. "Do you ever wish you were a kid again?"

Rafe's eyes darkened with emotion. He started to speak then stopped.

Tuck sat up. "What's wrong, Rafe?"

He exhaled and shook his head. Then gave a short laugh. "Nothing. Just thinking, I guess. But no, I like us the way we are now."

Tuck nodded and started to lean back when she felt a tug on her line. With a whoop she yanked. She grabbed the big mudcat and threw it into the bottom of the boat. "Ha, you're slipping. I got the first one."

"Yes, I see you did. Enjoy it. It's probably the last one you'll pull in. I, on the other hand, plan to catch a whole passel of them."

The first part of his prophecy came true, but to their chagrin, Tuck's mudcat was the only one either of them got. Too cold more than likely.

"Oh well. At least you were right about the storm," Tuck said as they moored the boat. "You know, this catfish would be mighty good cooked over an open fire."

"Well, I'll be. I believe you're finally right about something, Tuck. Let's cook it and eat it right here."

They made short work of cleaning the fish then cut it in half. As they sat holding their sticks over the campfire, the tantalizing aroma caused Tuck's stomach to rumble with hunger. After they'd eaten, she leaned back on her elbows, looking up at the clear sky.

The familiar camaraderie she shared with Rafe was like a warm blanket. Relaxation washed over her, and she realized she'd been tense all day. Maybe longer. Realization hit her. If she married Sam, she'd have to give up her friendship with Rafe. Sam would never stand for it. Unease prickled her skin and she shivered. Could she give up Rafe? The very thought caused an emptiness inside her.

But she loved Sam. Didn't she? A memory of his smoldering eyes burned her flesh, and excitement rushed through her. Yes, of course she loved him. And she wouldn't give him up.

Tuck ran her finger around the rim of the pan then placed it in her mouth, tasting the sweet and sour tang of the gooseberry pie filling.

Ma Lexie smiled and wagged her finger. Tuck grinned. Ma was a good sport. Always had been, since the first day she'd taken two ornery little girls into her home. It couldn't have been easy for her, caring for eight-year-old twins with minds of their own. Not that Addy gave her much trouble, but Tuck knew she herself had been a handful.

"Really, Abby, why do you do that?" With a toss of her head, her sister grabbed the pan and scraped the clinging gel-like substance into the slop bucket, then put the pan into the dishwater.

"Oh, don't pretend you never sneak a lick, Miss Priss." Tuck snapped a dishcloth at her sister's retreating back, and Addy threw her a grin then stuck her tongue out.

Ma opened the door in the front of the stove and placed the pie inside. She wiped her hands on the dish towel Tuck had proffered and smiled. "Is Sam coming to supper, dear?"

Tuck frowned and shook her head. "He had a political meeting in Forsyth. I don't know when he'll be back. Tomorrow I guess."

"He's away an awful lot, isn't he?" Addy blurted then bit her lip.

"What's that supposed to mean?" Tuck felt anger soaring up from somewhere deep inside. "He's a busy man with his medical practice, and he's involved in a lot of political stuff. What's wrong with that?"

"Nothing." Addy turned back to the dishpan. "I was just asking. Sorry."

Tuck grabbed a clean dishcloth and started drying the dishes. "Okay. Sorry I snapped. To be honest, I'm a little put off that he's gone so much. But I know he's a very busy man."

"Of course he is." Ma Lexie took a small pot off the hook and some potatoes out of the bin. With a sigh she sat at the table and started to peel the small brown globes.

Addy tossed the dishwater out the back door and wiped the pan. "Here, Ma. Let me do that for you."

"Oh no. It feels good to be off my feet for a while." She smiled and patted a chair. "Sit down. You, too, Abigail. I have something to tell you."

Dread clutched at Tuck. Ma had looked a little peaked lately. What would she do if something happened to Ma? She stared at the woman who had raised her as her own child.

"Is something wrong, Ma? You're not ill, are you?" Leave it to Addy to voice what Tuck was feeling.

Tuck leaned forward, her eyes glued to Ma.

Ma gave a little laugh. "Heavens, no. I couldn't be better. I have good news, not bad."

Impatient now that her fear was absolved, Tuck waited.

"You girls are going to have a brother or sister soon." Pink washed over Ma's face. And something else. Joy. That was it. But surely she didn't mean. . . Ma was nearly forty and had never had a child. Tuck had just assumed she never would.

"Do you mean—?" Addy had a grin from ear to ear.

Ma nodded.

"When, Ma?" The joy had somehow jumped onto Tuck as well, and excitement welled up inside her.

"The early part of March, I believe." So that was the reason Ma's clothes were looking a little tighter. She must be around four months along.

Addy jumped up and threw her arms around Ma. "What does Pa think about it? I'll bet he's hoping for a boy."

Ma laughed, a tinkling little joyful sound that rippled across the air. "He says he doesn't care, but I think he's secretly hoping for a son."

"Who can blame him?" Tuck grinned. "After being surrounded by females all these years."

"Blame me for what?" Papa Jack stepped into the room and planted a kiss on Ma's cheek, a lock of hair falling across his forehead. Sandy colored hair without a speck of gray. "Ummm. Is that gooseberry pie I smell?"

"Yes." Ma's eyes sparkled. "And don't you go getting any ideas. It's for after supper."

"Shucks." Pa shook his head. "But I reckon I can wait."

Tuck watched her parents. It was obvious to anyone they were still very much in love. Pa was always so tender with Ma, even while being playful.

Tuck sighed. Would Sam ever look that way at her? Would he ever touch her softly on the cheek the way Pa was touching Ma. She swallowed past the lump in her throat. Would she ever have with Sam the deep devoted love Pa and Ma had together?

Chapter 10

H ow in the world had she let herself get roped into this? Tuck shoved a stack of baskets aside and kicked at a tied-up bunch of cornstalks. "I don't know why people just bring things and dump them off. It wouldn't hurt them to stay and help."

"Now Abby, don't be like that," Addy said. "You enjoy the harvest festival as much as anyone. No one forced you to volunteer."

"Maybe they didn't force me, but I sure feel like I've been hornswoggled into it." She snorted. "Do we have to spend every spare minute we have in this place?"

"We do if we want to get everything done. And don't act like no one else is helping." She motioned to several women who scurried around sweeping straw from the floor of the Jenkinses' old barn. Since they'd built a new one, the old barn was used pretty much to store anything and everything. And of course to hold community parties and such.

"Who'd believe we had a dance here in the spring." Tuck shook her head. "Maybe they should do some barn cleaning in between times."

"Abby!"

At the distress in her sister's voice, Tuck looked up and caught sight of Mrs. Jenkins standing just inside the door. She couldn't tell if the kind woman had heard her or not. Why couldn't she learn to keep her lips buttoned up? She whirled around and lined a basket with straw, then placed small pumpkins inside.

Addy leaned over. "I don't think she heard you," she whispered.

Tuck sighed with relief. "I didn't mean it. I don't know why I blurt things out like that."

"Remember that time you called Mrs. Batson an old sow, and she overheard you?" A giggle rippled from Addy's throat.

"Yes, and the seat of my pants remembers, too. That had to be the hardest spanking Pa ever gave me." Tuck recalled the pain only too well, and she had to restrain herself from reaching back to rub her backside.

Addy giggled. "If you'd called her an old bear you'd have been closer to the truth. I never saw anyone so grumpy."

Tuck grinned. "She was grumpy. But I guess I gave her good reason to be."

"Yes, you did," Addy said, grinning. "Many good reasons."

"Sam was supposed to help today, but at the last minute he had to go to Forsyth on business." Tuck bit her lip and frowned. He seemed to have a lot of business lately. He was always going somewhere.

170

"Hmmm." Addy ducked her head and focused intently on an engraved walking stick that someone had dropped off for the festival.

"What's that supposed to mean?" Addy hadn't said two words to Sam lately, and it wasn't like her to be that rude.

"Nothing. Nothing at all." Addy glanced around. "I think I need to help them get those corn shocks up. They seem to be having trouble getting them to stand."

Tuck watched her sister scurry away. Addy wasn't fooling her a bit. She had something against Sam, and Tuck meant to find out what. Surely she wasn't still upset because Sam had chosen Tuck over her. She shrugged and got back to work.

"Abigail, what a pretty dress." Anne Lofting, a seventeen-year-old who thought she was God's gift to the male population, smiled at her. But the smile looked more like a smirk to Tuck. Anne had made fun of her more than once.

Maybe she was being overly suspicious and Anne really was sincere this time. After all, Tuck had thought Sam would be here, so she'd taken extra care with her hair and dress today. She knew she looked nice. "Thank you. They say blue is my color."

"Oh definitely." Anne giggled and sauntered away.

Tuck shook her head and continued filling a basket with apples and oranges, the aroma tantalizing her nose. The festival was only a couple of weeks away. She and the oldsters would be playing for the crowd. Their first time to play in public since the Lynch sisters got back last week.

There was a loud gasp behind her and she whirled around. Her twin stared at her with wide eyes, her hand over her mouth. "Abby," she choked out, rushing forward.

"What's wrong?"

"Turn around," Addy whispered through her teeth.

Tuck did as instructed and felt a tugging at her back.

"Your dress was tucked up. You must have caught it on something. Your bloomers were showing."

"Oh." Tuck blushed. "Must have happened when I went to the necessary earlier."

"You really must be more careful, Abigail."

"Oh, don't get your drawers twisted. Nobody saw them but Anne Lofting." But Tuck inwardly seethed. Her bloomers were pale blue.

"Abby! Don't you care that she probably told everyone?"

Addy's scandalized whisper tickled Tuck's ear and she grinned. "Nope, not a bit." That wasn't strictly true, but Addy was such a prude, it was fun to shake her up sometimes.

Addy clicked her tongue. "We need to finish up what we're doing and leave. Ma will be expecting us home soon."

Tuck glanced around. Baskets and tables stood neatly against the walls.

Festoons of autumn colors were draped across the rafters and over tables. All they'd need to do was set up food tables the day of the festival. Then toward the close of the day, everything would go back against the walls to make room for the auction. Hal Swanson was the best auctioneer in three counties. Tuck could almost hear the rhythm of his voice and words now.

"Why, Abby, your face is flushed and you look so excited." Addy's eyes twinkled. "Are you looking forward to the festival?"

"I am excited. It'll be fun to have a party again." And to stroll around outside on Sam's arm, watching the shooting gallery and the ring toss. Or maybe she'd even allow him to hold her hand. She hoped he wouldn't have something to do at the last minute to prevent his coming to the shindig.

◦~◦

Rafe stood beside the wagon and waited for his mother to come out of the Jenkinses' barn. His breath caught as Addy stepped out followed by Tuck. When she saw him she waved, said something to Addy, and then headed his way. His heart thumped so loudly he could almost hear it. He sure hoped she couldn't.

"Hi there, Rafe. Haven't seen you in a couple of weeks." She gave him an accusing glance.

Now why would she accuse him? "Not my fault. Every time I go to your place, you're off somewhere with Sam Fields." He hadn't seen her except at church since the day they'd gone fishing. He'd been hopeful after the good time they'd had together, but the very next day, he'd seen her making simpering eyes at the doctor.

"Well, after all, Rafe, he's practically my fiancé." She turned her head, and a hank of kinky blond hair escaped from the bone pin holding it in a knot at the back of her neck.

"Practically?" That sounded hopeful. "So, is he or isn't he?"

"He hasn't actually asked me yet." She tossed her head. "Not that it's any of your business."

He slumped against the wagon as she stomped off after her sister. He'd done it again. She'd looked happy until he had to go and spoil it by being sarcastic. He straightened and forced a smile as his mother stepped out of the barn and moseyed across the yard. She must be tired. Her usual stride was lively as a young'un's.

After his ma was seated and he'd climbed up beside her, she reached over and patted his hand. "What's wrong, dear? Why do you look so sad?"

Rafe sighed. Why did he even try to fool her? "Sorry, Ma. It's nothing."

She jiggled her fingers at Tuck and Addy as they drove past their wagon. "Rayford. Abby is a sweet girl, and I know you care for her. But she seems to have made her choice. I can't bear to see you suffering so. Especially when there are half a dozen girls standing in line for your attention."

He sighed. "Ma, I'm fine. You don't need to worry about me."

"I know and I won't, but I was just thinking about Carrie Sue Anderson. She's a very nice girl and pretty, too." She gave him a teasing smile and tapped him on the leg with her reticule. "And I know she's sweet on you."

"Ma, no matchmaking. Please." He knew he might as well be talking to the side of a barn. Ma thought he felt rejected and so she had to fix it for him.

She was dead right about his feeling rejected. He couldn't deny that. But he was pretty sure no one could fix it for him. Not even pretty, blond Carrie Sue with her enormous blue eyes and a dimple beside her mouth that just begged to be kissed. Tuck had ruined him for every other woman; no one else was like her. Whoever else he'd marry would always play second fiddle to Tuck.

He shook his head and flicked the reins to speed up the horses. He wouldn't coat his hurt ego by wooing another girl. Wouldn't be fair to her. . .whoever she might be. No, his original plan was better. He'd head down to Arkansas and join the railroad crew that was laying ties for the White River Line. By the time he worked his way back to these parts, Tuck would have married Sam Fields and it would be over and done with.

Pain knifed his heart. He stopped at the front step and helped Ma out of the wagon, then headed for the barn to do evening chores before supper.

❧

Tuck had always made fun of girls who swooned over a man. She'd scoffed and accused them of pretending. Now she wasn't so sure.

The feathery touch of Sam's lips brushing across her hand sent shivers through her body. She was pretty sure she was close to swooning herself.

"You're looking lovely today, my dear." Sam smiled, making no move to release her hand.

"Th–thank. . ." She cleared her throat. "Thank you."

He'd driven over to the farm in his new carriage, and now that supper was over, the two of them stood on the front porch watching the sunset.

"I thought perhaps you'd like to go for a drive." He squeezed her hand.

With a little tug, she gently removed it from his. After all, they weren't engaged yet. "I don't know. It will be dark soon." And Ma wouldn't approve at all.

"Just a short drive then. We have plenty of time before it's actually dark." He gazed down at her, his eyes almost piercing her.

Fire shot through her body. How could he have such an effect on her? She shuddered. And how could he be so charming one moment and so disturbing the next? "I don't know, Sam."

A shadow crossed his face. "I've barely seen you at all lately, with my trips and medical practice. I would think you'd want to spend time with me."

Tuck bit her lip. She wasn't easily intimidated but felt almost powerless against his aggressive personality. She wanted to break free, and then again, she didn't. A part of her wanted to follow him wherever he wished to lead her.

"All right. Let me tell Ma and Pa we're leaving."

"Nonsense. We'll be back in a flash. They'll never even know we were gone."

Tuck sighed and surrendered. "All right. If you promise to bring me home in just a few minutes."

His face smoothed, and once more he flashed a bright smile. "Of course." He placed his hand beneath her elbow and helped her down the steps, as though she hadn't been running up and down them since she was a little girl.

She was pretty sure she could manage them without help. She was just about to step up into the carriage, when the front door opened and Pa stalked out onto the porch.

"What's going on here?" He glanced at Tuck then turned thunderous eyes on Sam.

Sam gave a nervous laugh. "We were only going for a short drive in my new carriage. I thought she would enjoy it."

Pa studied Sam for a moment. "I think you'd better wait for another time. It will be dark shortly."

Oh dear, this hadn't been a good idea at all. Pa looked like he was ready to knock Sam off the porch. She'd better do something. "Thank you so much, Sam, for coming to supper. I'd better get inside now. See you at church Sunday?" She made her voice as cheerful as she could and smiled brightly.

Sam nodded and bowed, then climbed into the carriage. Another shadow eclipsed his face, making her shudder.

With a troubled countenance, Papa Jack watched him drive away then turned and smiled at Tuck. "Let's go inside. Your ma wanted to ask your opinion about something."

She found Ma and Addy bent over the kitchen table peering at some fabric samples.

"Oh, there you are, Tuck." Ma looked up. "Come help us decide on dress colors for the Christmas ball. Would you like this evergreen shade? Or perhaps this cranberry color?"

Tuck laughed. Ma always had such a delightful way of describing things. Never just red or green. "Isn't it a little early to decide? It's only October. We haven't had the harvest festival yet."

"But Christmastime will be here before we know it." Ma smiled, her eyes sparkling. Tuck wasn't sure if it was because of the baby or because Christmas was so near. Probably both.

Ma loved everything about Christmas. So did Rafe. Every year Ma and Mrs. Collins filled baskets for some of the neighbors, especially the older folks, and Tuck and Rafe delivered them. Her heart fluttered at the thought. Then she sighed. Another tradition she'd have to give up if she married Sam.

Perhaps Sam liked Christmas, too. If not, if he brooded, or worse still, made fun of their traditions, it would ruin it for her. But why wouldn't he like Christmas? She was being silly again. She didn't know why she allowed so many negative thoughts about Sam to enter her head lately.

Chapter 11

B ut Sam, you just got back from a week in St. Louis and now you're leaving again? You'll miss the festival." Tears threatened to spill over, and Tuck blinked hard, anger rising within her. She never cried. Well, hardly ever. She'd cried on Rafe's shoulder a few times, but that was different. And she cried sometimes when she got mad. Like now.

She'd ridden into town to pick up some sugar for Ma, and Sam had asked her to come to his office. Happy for his attention, she'd complied, only to be greeted with the news he had to go to Kansas City for two weeks.

"I know, sweetheart." He sounded as dejected as she felt, and her heart quickened at his use of the endearment. "But it can't be helped. My mother isn't as strong as she used to be and needs help with some business matters. I can't ignore her needs, now can I?"

Oh, he'd never mentioned his mother. Guilt bit at her. Hadn't she only recently promised God she wouldn't be so selfish? Here Sam was, trying to be a dutiful son, and she could only think about going to the festival without him. "Oh, of course not. Please forgive me. Certainly you must go to your mother's assistance."

Relief washed over his face. He took a step toward her, then darted a glance at the open door and stepped back. "I knew you would understand, my dear."

Amusement cut through Tuck's disappointment. Sam knew Mr. Hawkins would be watching and listening as long as Tuck was in the office.

"When will you leave?" Ma had given permission to invite him for supper. At the time, Tuck hadn't even been sure she wanted to invite him, but now, disappointment washed over her. What was wrong with her anyway? She was turning into a double-minded simpleton where Sam was concerned.

"This afternoon, I'm afraid. I need to visit a family on the Forsyth road this morning. But I'll have to leave right afterwards." He smiled. "I can't wait to tell Mother about you. And when I return we'll do something special. I promise."

Her heart fluttered. She loved it when he was sweet like this. It didn't happen often enough to suit her. Quickly she pushed the thought away. After all, he was busy and had the care of most of the county on his shoulders. Perhaps she expected too much of him.

She returned Sam's smile. "That sounds wonderful. And don't worry about the festival. I'll go with my family and spend time with Addy and Rafe."

His eyes flashed with irritation. "I don't know why you have to hang around Rafe. How do you think that makes me feel? After all, you and I practically have an understanding."

That was news to her, but good news nevertheless. Satisfaction rippled through her. He really did care for her. She hadn't been sure before.

"Oh, Sam." She laughed. "Rafe and I have been best friends since we were children. There's never been anything more than that between us."

"Then I'm very sorry I allowed my jealousy to show. I know I can trust you. Now, my dear, I do need to make my rounds, so you need to run along." He took her hand and squeezed. "The two weeks will pass quickly. You'll see."

Being summarily dismissed, Tuck left his office and did her shopping, then stood outside the store and glanced around. This was practice day, and Tuck had missed her last two sessions with the oldsters. She always dropped whatever she was doing when Sam wanted her to do something with him. The troubling thought hit her unexpectedly. But he had so little free time and naturally they wanted to spend it together. She frowned. Still, he never seemed to mind that she would give up something important to her every time he showed up.

She retrieved her fiddle from beneath the wagon seat and headed over to the feed store. Mr. Willie and the rest were tuning up.

"Hey. Would you look here at what the cat drug in." Squeezebox slapped his leg and grinned good-naturedly in Tuck's direction.

" 'Bout time, too." Tom tried to look stern, but his sudden coughing spasm ruined the effect.

"I guess I could turn around and leave if you all don't want me here." Oh, there she went again. Snapping at them when she knew very well they were just teasing.

"Naw, don't leave," Mr. Willie soothed. He was always afraid someone would hurt her feelings. "They're jest foolin', Tuck."

Tuck looked up at the sky for a moment. "Well, all right. I reckon I'll stay then."

Squeezebox cackled. "All righty then, get her tuned up, girl. We ain't got all day."

Tom snorted. "Why not? You don't do anything else but lay around your shack snoring all day. You and that hound of yours."

"Hank don't snore." At the sound of his name, a flop-eared hound dog raised his head about an inch from the floor and then plopped it back down. Squeezebox scratched him behind one ear and then picked up his accordion.

Tuck removed her violin from the case and tuned up. "Okay, did we decide which one we're doing first?"

"I thought we'd start with 'Frog Went A-Courtin'" and then 'Old Joe Clark.' Get everyone good and stirred up for the fun," Mr. Willie said. "That way, they'll likely buy more stuff and the ladies will have more money for the Christmas dance."

"Good thinking, Mr. Willie." Tuck grinned as she placed a soft cloth on her shoulder and her violin beneath her chin.

They ran through the two songs then went into a few more numbers they planned to play at the festival. Right in the middle of a soft rendition of "Sweet Adeline," a thunderous snore roared from Hank's direction, followed by the dog jumping up and howling loud and long.

The roar of laughter that followed nearly drowned out the dog.

⁓

Rafe swung the ax down hard, splitting the short logs for Ma's cookstove. Some of the neighbors were using oil stoves to cook on, but Ma said absolutely not. They'd have to be a sight better than they were now before she'd give up her woodstove. Rafe chuckled. Fine with him. The smell of bacon and eggs frying on that old stove was about the most tantalizing thing he'd ever had a sniff of. Except maybe Ma's fried chicken.

Horse's hooves sounded on the lane leading to the house. Rafe looked up. Tuck was almost lying down on Sweet Pea's neck as she urged her forward. That girl was going to break her neck one of these days if she didn't stop riding so hard. She'd gone flying a few times before, luckily escaping with scrapes and bruises.

"You trying to kill yourself or something?" He frowned as Tuck jumped down and sauntered toward him, a big grin on her face.

"You should talk. Who's the one who broke his collarbone twice and his arm three times, and what caused it?"

"Hey, one of those broken arms was from falling out of a tree. You know that." But he grinned.

"Of course, I remember." She cocked her head and grinned. "But you were practicing jumping into the saddle from the branch of the old oak in the middle of our pasture. So it still involved a reckless act with a horse."

She had a point. "Okay, we're both lucky to be alive with all the shenanigans we pulled."

Laughing, she punched him on the arm. "Yep. You can say that again."

"Where's your fancy dress and hair geegaws?"

She shrugged. "No sense in torturing myself when Sam's not around to see me, is there?"

"Oh, the fancy doctor's gone again?"

"What's that supposed to mean?" She planted her hands on her hips and glared. "He has a perfectly good reason for being gone. Just like he always does."

Rafe snorted. "Listen to yourself, Tuck. Like he *always* does?"

"If you're going to make insinuations about Sam, I'm leaving." She spun around and stomped back to her horse.

Rafe exhaled loudly. Lately, all he seemed to do when they were together was to rile her up. "Come on, Tuck. Don't leave. I'm sorry, okay?"

She jumped on her horse. "Sure you are. I can see it all over you. I guess you forgot I told you I'm going to marry him. If you dislike him that much,

I guess we can't be friends." She wheeled Sweet Pea around then yelled back over her shoulder, "And for your information, he's in Kansas City helping out his mother."

Rafe loaded up his arms with logs and stalked toward the house. Fine. If she could sling their friendship away that easily, so could he. There was no way he could pretend to like Sam Fields. He dumped the logs in the wooden box by the stove.

His mother looked up from the pan of potatoes she was slicing. "I thought I heard Abby. Didn't you invite her in?"

"She had to leave, Ma. I'm going over to the cave. I'll finish up the chores when I get back." He gave her a peck on the cheek.

As Champ's hooves thundered down the road, Rafe attempted to get his thoughts under control. He reckoned, somewhere in the back of his mind, he'd always figured he'd marry Tuck. There was no one else he'd rather be around. No one else who could make him laugh those roaring side-splitting howls of joy. No one who could calm him down with a word and melt his heart.

But that was then. Tuck had made her choice, and there was no use making himself miserable by thinking about it.

Anger roiled inside him. Who needed her? There were dozens of girls he could have. Carrie Sue's sweet smile crossed his thoughts. She had curls as yellow as a sunflower and eyes as blue as a spring sky. Also a sweet disposition. She wouldn't drive a man crazy with her wild and willful ways the way Tuck did. No sir. Carrie Sue would be there for her man and treat him the way a man wanted to be treated by his woman.

He turned his horse and headed for the Anderson farm. It was time for him to stop mooning over Tuck and get on with his life, and he intended to start right now. He hoped Carrie Sue didn't have an escort to the festival, because he'd like nothing better than to stroll past Tuck with Carrie on his arm.

Just before he reached the farm, he reined his horse in. What kind of idiot was he anyway? Planning on taking Carrie to the festival to get even with Tuck? That was the sort of thing a kid would do. He sighed. And Tuck probably wouldn't give a hoot anyway. With a heavy heart, he turned back toward home.

⁂

Tuck laid her fiddle on a chair and stepped off the platform. Her stomach rumbled as she headed for the barn where tables were laden with food. The auction was winding up. She glanced at Rafe as he held up fingers to indicate a bid. Curious she peered at the auction stage to see what he was bidding on. A saddle. Looked like a good one, too. She looked back at him and he grinned.

They'd made their peace the day after their squabble. Both of them apologized. Rafe hadn't made any more comments about Sam. Tuck, on the other hand, was being careful not to mention him when she was with Rafe. Not an ideal compromise, but better than losing their friendship.

"Sold! To Carter Foster." The auctioneer's voice boomed across the barn, and Rafe shrugged and went to help move the benches and make room for tables.

Tuck waited until he was finished and grabbed his hand. "C'mon, I'm starving." She dragged him across to a table holding platters of fried chicken and bowls filled with potato salad and corn on the cob. With plates piled high, they found two empty spots at a table.

"Hello, Rafe. You must be hungry, judging by that plate of yours."

At the sound of the lilting voice, Tuck peered around Rafe and saw Carrie Sue Anderson sitting on the other side of him.

"I sure am." Rafe smiled at the pretty blond. "I'm hungry enough to eat a horse."

Her rippling laughter grated on Tuck's nerves. "Oh no, you won't need to do that. My mama and I brought plenty of fried chicken. And we're mighty good cooks, if I do say so myself." Tuck glared at her, and she tossed her head and added, "I notice you have rather a hearty appetite as well, Abigail."

"The name is Tuck. And what's wrong with an appetite?"

"Why, nothing at all, if you want to blow up and look like the side of a barn." She smiled sweetly, and Tuck felt sick. "A lady must be careful you know."

"A good thing I don't care about being a lady then," Tuck retorted.

The gasp from behind her had to be Addy. No one else could gasp like that. "Abby, of course you don't mean that. You're very much a lady. Just a high-spirited one." She glanced around for a place at their table.

Rafe stood. "Here, take my place, Addy. Jim just came in and I need to talk to him about something."

Tuck stared as he bolted across to the door where Jim had stopped to talk to some of the men. Now why did he take off so fast? She turned and saw Carrie gazing after him, with the expression of a sick cow.

Oh. So that's what was going on. Carrie was after Rafe, and he was well aware of it.

Chapter 12

H ere, let me wrap this blanket around you, my dear." Tuck blushed as
Sam spread the thick gray blanket across her legs and tucked it a little
too closely for her comfort.

"Sam, the blanket is fine. Please. Leave it alone." Tuck scooted away and
tugged the blanket loose. Didn't he understand propriety at all?

"Sorry, I simply don't want you to be cold. I didn't mean to embarrass you."
Sam's eyes darkened, a warning he was irritated. Well, so was she.

"Where are we going? It's too cold for a buggy ride, anyway. We should
have stayed home and played games with Ma and Pa and Addy." Tuck's heart
thumped hard and fast. What was wrong with her? This was Sam and he
loved her. Of course he didn't mean to be inappropriate.

"Must you spend all your time with your family, Abigail?" he snapped. "Can't
we ever have time to ourselves? Even for a simple ride in the countryside?"

She stared at him. Was she being unreasonable or was he? She enjoyed
doing things with her family. But if she was going to be Sam's wife, she would
need to put his wishes first. And he had made it plain he didn't like being
around them a lot. What if he refused to let her spend time with them after
they were married? Of course, he hadn't actually asked her to marry him, but
she was certain he would soon. Maybe that's why he wanted to be alone now.

She brightened and sat up straight, placing a hand on his forearm. "I'm
sorry. I'm being selfish. Of course I want to spend time with you."

"Well, that's more like it." He placed his hand over hers and smiled. His
glance intensified as he looked deep into her eyes, but the expression that used
to send thrills through her only made her uneasy.

Sam flicked the reins and drove to the river, following the old horse path
that rumor said was an old Indian trail.

"Where will the White River Line tracks be, Sam? Will we still have access
to the river?" Tuck shivered. She couldn't imagine not going fishing with Rafe.
Confusion washed over her. She wouldn't be allowed to fish or float on the
river with Rafe much longer. Or do anything with him for that matter. Not
when she was Sam's wife.

"I know absolutely nothing about the railroad except it's a lot more comfortable riding in trains than on horseback or in coaches clear across the country."
He softened his tone and smiled. "You would love the train. They even have
dining cars where they serve the finest cuisine."

She laughed as she tried to visualize eating on the train. "How good can
food be cooked in a moving car? I'll bet it's not nearly as good as Ma's chicken.

And Sam, have you ever eaten trout cooked over an open fire? There's absolutely nothing like it."

His face wrinkled with distaste. "No, I haven't and have no intention of trying it. Really, Abigail. Have you no desire at all for the finer things of life?"

She sighed. For the first time she admitted to herself that she and Sam had little in common. But they loved each other. That was all that mattered. "It's getting dark. We really need to get back to the house before Ma and Pa start to worry."

"All right. All right. Soon. I promise. Let's just stop and look at the river for a moment." His voice sounded distracted and strange as he pulled off the path.

"But Sam, it's cold, and my hands are like ice." She shivered, not sure if it was entirely from the cold.

But Sam had already stopped the horses and set the carriage brake. He turned and smiled. "Here, let me see those hands."

"No, they're all right. Let's just look at the river for a moment. Did you have something you wanted to talk about?" She waited, expecting him to bring up the subject of their future.

He reached over and brushed a curl from her forehead. "You're so beautiful, Abigail. I didn't realize it the first time I saw you, with you in those awful overalls. What a pleasant surprise it was when you appeared in my office that day, transformed into a stunning lady."

"I'm happy you are pleased with my appearance. But I'm the same person as I was in the overalls." For some reason, it was important for her to make that clear. She'd been pretending with him for too long.

"Nonsense. Not at all, my dear. Now you're a woman. A very alluring woman." He moved over closer to her on the seat and placed an arm around her shoulders, pulling her close.

"Sam, what are you doing?" She pulled back, but the side of the carriage stopped her retreat.

"Don't be shy, my dear. After all, we've been seeing each other for some time. A kiss would be quite appropriate. Don't you think?"

His lips were almost touching hers now. Without another thought, she gave him a shove backward then slapped him hard.

"Why, you little—" Venomous rage filled his voice and his eyes blazed with anger. He made a move as if to lift his arm.

Tuck gasped. He was going to hit her. She balled up her hand into a fist, and a rush of anger exploded within her. Let him just dare.

He drew his hand back and swiped it across his face as though wiping away the sting of her slap. His breath came in angry spurts, and his eyes knifed through her, furious and threatening. Grabbing the reins, he tore off down the road, not slowing until he jerked the team to a halt at her front porch. As soon as Tuck had jumped out of the carriage, he laid the whip across the backs of his horses.

Tuck, with her heart racing, ran up the steps and into the house. She leaned against the door, letting her pulse and breathing calm down. It wouldn't do to let anyone see her like that.

The house was silent, but a dim light shone from the parlor.

Forcing a smile upon her stiff face, she paused at the parlor door long enough to say good night to Ma and Pa. She scurried away and up the stairs before they could speak.

Could she fool Addy? They'd always shared a room, enjoying the late night talks, but at this moment, Tuck wished one of them had taken over the guest room.

As Tuck walked into the bedroom, Addy, lying in bed, glanced up and smiled, laying aside the magazine she was reading. "How was your ride? I was beginning to worry a little."

"Oh, it was fine. There was no reason for you to be concerned. It's only just now getting dark." She hung her cloak on a hook and sat in the rocking chair by the window. The memory of the rage on Sam's face when she slapped him sent her heart racing again. If he'd made a move, she'd have socked him a good one.

"Abby, what's wrong?" Her sister threw her legs over the side of the bed and slipped her feet into a pair of crocheted slippers.

"Nothing is wrong. What makes you think something is wrong?" Her voice sounded frantic even to her own ears, and her heartbeat pounded in her ears.

"Oh, maybe because you're rocking so furiously. If you go much faster, that chair is going to fly out the window."

Chagrined, Tuck stopped rocking. Okay, she could do this. She took a long, slow breath and then threw a grin at her sister. "The window is closed. I do believe the rocking chair is quite safe."

Addy pressed her lips together. "You can't fool me. I know something happened to upset you."

"Well, you're wrong." She yawned and stood so fast she set the chair to rocking back and forth again. "I'm sleepy. That's all. Don't worry about me so much." Without another word, she changed into her nightgown and crawled beneath the pile of quilts. "Good night, Addy."

She lay still, and slowly, moment by moment, her anger dissipated. What if Sam's attempt to kiss her wasn't as awful as she had built it up to be? After all, he mentioned an understanding, so obviously he intended to marry her. Then why did she have this sinking feeling inside her?

Until he actually declared his intentions, a kiss was out of the question and inappropriate as well as disrespectful to her. If Sam treated her with disrespect now, how could she expect him to treat her if they should marry? She wished she could talk this over with someone. Ordinarily, Addy was her confidant, but telling her about this was out of the question.

Rafe's face, safe and friendly, popped into her mind. Immediately she pushed the thought away. Rafe would likely tell her she was a fool to even consider forgiving Sam. And then he'd go beat the tar out of him.

⁐

Rafe shivered as the wind whipped around the house and nearly knocked him over. He grabbed Addy and steadied her. He'd invited her inside, but she'd insisted she needed to talk to him in private. His mother might think it strange that Addy was here to see Rafe without her sister.

"Let's at least go stand by the barn where we'll be shielded. You're not even wearing a coat." He frowned as he glanced at the shawl wrapped loosely around Addy's shoulders. If it was Tuck, he'd just go inside the barn, but Addy would think it was inappropriate.

"It wasn't this cold when I left the house. How was I supposed to know a norther was going to hit?" She followed him across the yard to the shielded side of the big, weathered structure.

"Before you leave, I'm going to find a cloak or something for you to wear on the way home." He didn't need anything else on his conscience, like Tuck's sister catching pneumonia.

"There's a blanket in the wagon. I can use that." Addy stomped her small foot, and wrinkles puckered the skin between her eyes. "Stop fussing, Rafe. I need to talk to you."

"I'm sorry." Rafe frowned. He should've noticed how nervous Addy seemed. Maybe someone was ill. Dread washed over him. "Is Tuck all right?"

She took a deep breath. "I'm not sure. She says she's fine, but she's been behaving strangely ever since she went for a carriage ride with Sam a few days ago."

Rafe's stomach twisted and knotted, and he tightened his lips. "Have you questioned her?"

"Of course I've questioned her. She just laughs or gets angry and tells me to stop fussing over her. She insists everything is fine." Addy twisted the hand-kerchief in her hand. "Rafe, I don't trust that man."

Worry niggled its way inside Rafe's mind. Addy knew Tuck better than anyone, except maybe him. If she thought something was wrong, she was likely right. Of course, this was the first time Tuck had taken up with some man. That might change things. There could be some things she just didn't want to share with her sister, and maybe some of those things weren't so good. He licked his dry lips.

He'd always thought Tuck pretty levelheaded, but she'd fallen pretty hard for Fields. His chest tightened. He didn't trust him either. He never had since he'd first laid eyes on him. He wasn't sure why, couldn't quite put his finger on anything really wrong. He'd finally decided it was jealousy on his part. But now, with Addy saying the same thing, he wasn't so certain. Surely the man hadn't taken liberties with her. Naw, she'd have come straight to Rafe and told him. Wouldn't she?

"Look, Addy. I don't know what I can do. Tuck's not talking to me the way she used to. Why don't you talk to your pa?" Yes, that would be the sensible thing. Jack would check it out.

"Because, I don't know what Pa would do. Probably go straight to Abby and confront her. Then she'd never speak to me again." She bit her lip and blinked back tears. It was obvious this wasn't just a small concern to her.

"All right. Let me think about this. I'm not sure what I can do, but I'll figure out something. If anything is wrong, I promise I'll find out. Trust me?" He laid his hand on her shoulder, and it felt so much like Tuck's he jerked his hand away.

Addy smiled. "Of course I trust you. Why would I have come here otherwise? I know how much you care about Abby. I wish she would open her eyes, because I know she cares about you, too, Rafe."

He smiled. "I know she does. Like a brother or something."

"I think you're wrong, Rafe. You mean a great deal more than that to her. She just doesn't realize it yet." She placed her hand, so much like Tuck's, on his arm. "Don't give up on her."

He sighed. "I don't know, Addy. Sometimes it seems hopeless, and I think I'm an idiot to keep hoping she could ever love me."

"Well, if anyone is an idiot, it's Abby, not you. I hope she finds out before it's too late."

"Me, too. But the important thing now is to figure out what's going on. Don't worry. If anything is wrong, I'll take care of it."

As he watched her drive away, Rafe sent up a silent prayer that he could keep his promise.

Chapter 13

The store was dark in spite of the oil lamps placed around the big room. Tuck hated these cloudy days when she didn't know if it was going to pour down rain or not. Especially when she and the oldsters had a practice. She walked to the post office at the rear of the store. She needed to mail Pa's letter before she did Ma's shopping. Otherwise she'd probably forget.

There was no sign of the manager in the store or behind the post office window. He must be in the storage room. She laid the letter on the counter in front of the window where he would find it. She'd pay for the stamp after she finished shopping.

As she walked over to the dry goods section, the front door opened and Sam walked in. She caught her breath. She hadn't seen him since the attempted kiss and what followed.

He saw her and started toward her.

She stiffened, not knowing what to expect or even what she wanted him to do or say as he stopped in front of her.

"I'm so sorry, Abigail. I don't know what came over me. Maybe it was the moonlight shining on your hair. I guess I lost control for a moment." Sam gave her a contrite and pleading glance. Like she'd fall for that.

She stared, not sure what to say. She didn't want to assume he was lying, but she couldn't forget his cold rage and her suspicion he wanted to hit her.

"Say something, please. Tell me you forgive me." He smiled sadly. And the expression on his face seemed sincere.

"What about the fit you threw?"

He looked away then back. "I was shocked when you slapped me, although you had every right to do so. I think that, combined with the realization of what I'd done, caused me to lose control."

"For a moment, I thought you would hit me." Again, anger began to boil inside her. He would have been in for a surprise if he had. She took a deep breath. Who was she kidding? He was a lot stronger than she was.

"Oh no, Abby, please don't think I would ever harm a hair of your head, my dear. You're much too precious to me." She avoided the hand he reached out for hers. "And of course, I wouldn't strike any woman on any account."

She swallowed. Should she believe him? Trust him? As he looked at her with those deep, searching eyes, her resolve began to melt. Perhaps she should give him a second chance. He deserved that, didn't he? After all, everyone needed a second chance now and then. "All right, Sam. I forgive you. But if anything similar should ever happen again, don't come near me or even attempt to speak to me."

This time when he reached for her hand, she made no move to avoid it.

The smile on his face seemed real enough. Although there was a possibility he was manipulating her, she needed to give him a chance. The Bible did say something about forgiving others when they asked you to.

"Let's celebrate. Come on back to the office. Mrs. Carey brought me a delicious apple cobbler yesterday, and it hasn't been touched yet." He flashed her a grin. "We'll leave the door open of course."

"I'm sorry, I need to do my mother's shopping and go practice with the group." A thrill of victory ran through her for not changing her plans. There. Let him chew on that.

Disappointment washed over his face. "Very well. Another time then. May I drive you to church on Sunday?"

"Yes, I suppose that would be all right." She nodded then turned to the dry goods on the shelf.

"Good day, then." She listened as his footsteps crossed the floor and the door opened and closed.

Anxious to get to the feed store before the group started practicing without her, she hurried through her shopping then paid Mr. Hawkins for the stamp. A little twinge of excitement ran through her as she thought of the Christmas ball which was only a few weeks away. They'd be playing again for this one, but she meant to stop in plenty of time to have some fun herself. After all, the oldsters had been playing music for a long time before she came into the group, and she had a right to have some fun, too.

As she walked out the door, Rafe rode up. He grinned and waved as he dismounted.

"Tuck, what are you up to?"

The sound of his voice rippled through her entire body. She felt laughter well up inside.

"Rafe! Getting ready to go practice with the gang. It's good to see you. Why haven't you been by?"

"Well, I figure you're busy now that the doc is courting you." He grinned, but it didn't quite reach his eyes.

"I'm never too busy for old friends. I thought maybe Carrie Sue had you all roped and tied."

He chuckled. "Nope. Don't know why you'd think that."

"Huh! The way she was hanging all over you at the festival could be one reason." She peered at him closely to see his reaction. Maybe he liked having Carrie crazy over him. "It's obvious she's after you."

His eyes glinted, and he laughed again. "Tell you what. If she ever catches me, you'll be the first to know." He gave her a wave and went inside.

She loaded her things into the wagon and covered them with a tarp in case it rained. Then she headed down to the feed store. Her thoughts turned to Sam, but they were different than they were a few weeks ago. Oh, he was still handsome and he could be charming, but she no longer felt weak-kneed when she saw him.

When had her feelings begun to change? It was before the incident by the river. She sighed. Of course feelings would change when the new wore off a relationship. She still loved Sam. It just felt different.

She'd always thought love would be a happy feeling, but being with Rafe just now was the happiest she'd been in a long time. Why couldn't Sam make her feel like that?

⚬⚬⚬⚬

"Hello there, Rafe. Forget something when you were in here yesterday?" Mr. Hawkins came out from behind the post office cubicle and held out his hand.

Rafe shook his hand, silently gloating over Tuck's first sign of jealousy. If he wasn't imagining it. "No, sir. Don't need a thing. Is the doc in?"

"You're in luck. He just came in from a house call a few minutes ago, and as far as I know he doesn't have a patient in there with him." Mr. Hawkins motioned toward the doctor's office. "You ailing with something?"

"Just a sore neck and shoulder." He felt a slight pang at the lie. Actually, he'd had a sore neck the week before, but it was fine now except for a twinge now and then. It gave him a good excuse to go see Fields though. He went back to the doctor's office and knocked, then opened the door.

Fields appeared cautious when he saw Rafe step through the door.

Suspicion wrapped itself around Rafe's mind. Why would the doc be concerned about him? Except that he knew Rafe was Tuck's friend as well as a friend of the family.

"What can I do for you, Collins?" Fields stepped forward, a questioning look on his face.

"My neck and shoulder have been giving me fits. May have strained something hauling wood to Forsyth." That much was true. He didn't have to tell the man it was pretty much healed up. "Thought maybe I should have you check it out."

The doctor motioned to a wooden stool. "Why don't you sit over there and take your shirt off? I'll take a look."

Rafe obliged and sat while the doctor probed his shoulder and examined his neck. He refused to flinch, even when Fields's fingers dug into a tender spot.

"Hmmm. I can't find anything out of place. You're probably right about the strain." He stood back and looked at Rafe. His mouth twisted and his eyes bore into Rafe's.

Was that a knowing look on his face? Probably just Rafe's imagination. Why would Fields suspect anything? Rafe was another patient, and a paying one at that. That was all.

While Rafe put his shirt on, the doctor walked over to a cabinet and took out a bottle of liniment. "Here, rub this on the sore spots a couple of times a day. It'll help a little. Mainly you just have to wait it out though. It'll get better."

Rafe nodded. "Thanks, what do I owe you?"

He handed the amount Sam mentioned over to the doctor, then took the bottle and headed out the door. What a waste. He hadn't learned a thing. Although he had no idea what he'd expected to find out from a doctor's visit.

He went outside and glanced at the liniment in his hand. This was silly. They had jugs of the stuff at home. He might as well leave it here for someone else. He turned and walked back into the office.

Fields, his back to the door, stood by his phone and laughed softly into the mouthpiece. "I love you, my dear. You do know that, don't you?"

Rafe inhaled sharply then held his breath. Now who was the doctor professing his love to? Maybe this visit wouldn't be such a waste after all.

Fields spoke into the phone again. "Yes, of course. I'll see you soon. Very soon. Yes. Good-bye, my sweet."

Rafe turned and slipped out the door before the doctor turned around.

Was the conversation what it sounded like? If so, he felt like giving the guy a good trouncing for the hurt Tuck was going to feel when she found out.

He waved at Hawkins and left the store again, a thunder roaring in his brain. How did he think she was going to find out? He sure couldn't tell her. She'd probably think he was making it up, although there was no reason why she'd think that when she didn't know how he felt about her.

Champ whinnied when he stepped over to untie him. He patted the horse and slipped him a lump of sugar before mounting.

Bothered by the conversation, he rode toward home. How could he handle this? The doctor could be totally innocent. Rafe'd only heard a couple of sentences. Maybe it was the man's mother he was talking to. But his voice when he said I love you wasn't the tone a man used when he spoke to his ma or his sister. It had been downright seductive. No, he was talking to a sweetheart.

Which brought Rafe back to his problem. How could he handle this in a way where Tuck wouldn't get hurt? Even if his suspicions were true, it wasn't his place to reveal it to her. He should probably talk to Addy. But he hated to give her more to worry about.

He turned toward the Sullivan farm, urging Champ forward. He needed to speak to Jack about this. Tuck's pa would know how to handle it. He didn't know how long Tuck would be in town. From the look of the sky, probably not too long. He needed to hurry and talk to Jack and leave before she got home.

Reining his horse in, he jumped off and tied him to the front porch rail. He knocked on the door and after a minute heard footsteps.

Lexie opened the door and smiled. "Come in, Rafe. How nice to see you."

Lexie was the happiest person he knew. And she always acted as if she hadn't seen him in weeks, even if it had been the day before.

"Thanks, it sure smells good in here." Grinning, he sniffed in appreciation of the sweet, fruity aroma.

The corners of her eyes crinkled with pleasure. "That's my apple cobbler you smell. And it'll be cool enough to dish up in a few minutes."

Rafe shook his head. "Wish I could, but I need to talk to Jack then hurry home. It looks like it might storm, and I'll have to help Pa get the animals into the barn."

"You'll find him in the barn. I have no idea what he's doing, but I'm sure he'll be happy to see you." She patted him on the arm. "I'll save you some cobbler to take home for you and your folks. There's plenty."

"Thank you, ma'am. I'm obliged. I'll just go on out there now." With one more breath of longing for the cobbler, he crossed the yard to the barn.

The sound of "Amazing Grace" greeted him as he walked into the barn. Jack sat on a bale of hay, singing at the top of his lungs, while he polished an old saddle.

"Hey, Jack."

Jack Sullivan glanced up and grinned when he saw Rafe. "Come on in, boy. I'm glad for some male company. All those women talk about is dresses and geegaws for the Christmas dance. I had to escape to the barn for my sanity."

Rafe laughed. "Yes, I can imagine. I think all the ladies in the county have gone a little bit Christmas crazy. And it's still only the middle of November."

"What brings you out on a day like this? It's likely going to storm within the hour." He frowned. "I hope Tuck makes it back before it hits."

"I saw her in town about an hour ago. She was going over to practice but didn't plan to stay long." Rafe looked at the ground then back at Jack. "I really need to talk to you about something. And it just might concern Tuck, sir."

Chapter 14

A lilting feeling tickled Tuck's stomach, and laughter bubbled up inside her as she noticed Champ tied up by the barn. Rafe was here. Apparently he'd come to see Papa Jack, but maybe he'd stay for supper and they could have a long talk afterward.

She stopped in front of the house to make it quicker and easier to unload the wagon. Jumping down, she headed across the yard. Rafe would help her carry things inside.

The barn door was open a crack, and Rafe's voice drifted out. "At first I sort of gave him the benefit of the doubt, thinking maybe he was talking to his mother or sister. But believe me, that tone of voice wasn't the way a man speaks to his ma. I wanted to drag him outside and teach him a lesson he wouldn't forget. The idea of him toying with Tuck like that while all the time he's got a sweetheart somewhere. . ."

Tuck's breath caught in her chest, and pain shot though her. Rafe could only be talking about Sam. But. . .what did he mean? Sam loved another woman? Surely it was a misunderstanding.

"Tell me again what Fields said. Maybe it wasn't as bad as you think." Pa's voice of reason fell like a healing balm on her ears.

She listened as Rafe, his voice tight with anger, repeated word for word what he said he'd heard.

"Now calm down, Rafe." Pa still spoke with quiet reason, but an underlying hint of suppressed anger revealed his real feelings. "I know you're angry, the way you care about Tuck. I am, too. But you need to be sure before you say anything to her."

"Say something to Tuck? You should know I can't be the one to tell her. Not with me being in love with her. It would just seem like jealousy on my part." Rafe's voice shook with emotion. "Anyway, she's changed so much, I hardly know her anymore."

Shock hit her. Fire centered in her forehead and spread outward and down her entire body. Shame and delight battled within her. How could she have fallen for Sam's lies when all the time he was courting someone else? But Rafe. . .Rafe loved her? Confusion swirled in her mind, twisting and inter-twining with the other emotions.

She spun around and ran to the house. She couldn't let Rafe see her like this. He would know she'd overheard him. She stopped at the porch, her breath coming in gulps. She had to calm down before she went inside.

She began unloading the wagon and placing things on the porch. That would calm her down. Besides, it would seem odd if she left a wagon with supplies standing in front of the porch. Ma must not suspect anything was amiss. With a smile on her face, she carried some of the household supplies inside.

Ma and Addy were in the kitchen preparing the evening meal. "Abigail, I was beginning to worry that you'd be caught in a thunderstorm." Ma glanced at her and smiled.

Addy hurried over. "Here, let me take one of those baskets. Your arms are piled high."

"Just set them on the pantry floor, girls. We'll put them away after supper," Ma directed.

Just as Tuck was about to return to the wagon to get the remaining basket and the sack of flour, Pa came in the front door, carrying everything.

"Why didn't you call me to help, Tuck? I was right in the barn."

"Oh, I saw Rafe's horse and figured you two were talking. I didn't want to disturb you." A poor excuse, as her pa's puzzled expression confirmed. Ordinarily she'd have simply barged into the barn and dragged Rafe out to help.

"Abigail, get that covered bowl off the dough table and take it out to Rafe. I told him I'd send apple cobbler home with him."

Panic rose in Tuck. She groped around in her mind for an excuse.

Pa shook his head. "He's already gone. Wanted to beat the storm home. I guess he forgot about the cobbler."

Relief washed over Tuck. She'd have to see him sooner or later, but there was no way she could face Rafe now. How could she? Knowing he loved her and that he didn't know she knew. It was an impossible situation.

She frowned. Why did he have to go and ruin their friendship by falling in love with her? And why'd he have to spy on Sam? He'd probably got it all wrong anyway.

But something stirred deep inside her. A warmth unlike any she'd felt before.

After they'd eaten and the dishes were washed, Ma and Pa settled in the parlor. Ma with her sewing and Pa with a rifle that needed to be cleaned. Addy and Abby put the supplies away in the pantry.

"You're awfully quiet, Abby. Is something wrong?" Addy threw her a glance filled with curiosity.

Tuck leaned against the wall. She and Addy had always stuck together. As far as she knew, they'd never kept secrets from each other until recently, and that was Tuck's doing. She knew that Addy loved her, and although she loved her sister, too, Tuck also knew that her twin had been kinder to her through the years than she'd been in return.

Suddenly, she missed the talks they used to have, the laughter they'd shared. When had they lost it? Tuck sighed. She knew she was the one to blame. She'd pulled back from Addy out of jealousy. Addy had a sweet disposition that drew people to her. Tuck, on the other hand, knew she'd always been selfish. "I'd like to talk to you about something later."

"All right," Addy said, a question in her voice. "Let's finish up here and go to our room."

They finished putting the supplies away then went to the parlor to say good night to their parents.

Pa and Ma looked up when they came in. They both had worried expressions on their faces.

"Tuck, your mother and I would like to talk to you about something in private," Pa said.

Tuck took a deep breath. Here it was. It had to be about Rafe's accusation against Sam.

"All right, Pa." Tuck sat on the stool in front of her mother's rocking chair and waited while Addy said good night and went to their room.

Papa Jack cleared his throat. "Abigail, your mother and I know you are a young woman and old enough to make your own decisions, but we think your relationship with Dr. Fields is moving too fast."

Tuck licked her lips. How could she handle this? She couldn't let Pa know she'd overheard the part about Sam without also revealing she'd overheard Rafe's declaration of love. She swallowed. "What do you mean, Pa?"

Pa took a deep breath and looked at Ma. She placed her hand on his arm and nodded.

Tuck sat, frozen, and listened to the story once more. How should she respond? She hadn't yet had the time to think it over. She'd hoped her talk with Addy would help. She cleared her throat. "I'm not sure I believe it to be true."

"Abigail," Ma said, "surely you don't think Rafe would make up a story like that."

"No, of course not," Tuck said, frowning. "But he may have misunderstood. I think Sam at least deserves a chance to explain. Don't you?"

"Yes, certainly," Pa said quickly. "But how will you know if he's being honest?"

"I don't know, Pa. I guess I'll have to trust God to show me, won't I?"

The misery on her parents' faces stabbed her like a knife. Sharp and cruel. And suddenly she knew. They felt her pain.

"I promise I won't marry Sam Fields unless I can do so with your blessing and your assurance that all is well." They could count on that. Tuck wasn't sure if the pain she felt was grief or anger, but she knew she had to find out the truth about Sam.

⁂

When Tuck walked into her bedroom, she found Addy seated in front of the stove in one of their twin rockers. She glanced up from the hem she was mending and smiled. "You still rip more hems than anyone I know, in spite of your new ladylike ways."

"You shouldn't be doing my mending for me, Addy. It's time I started doing things for myself."

"I needed something to do while I waited for you." She bit the thread and tied a knot, then handed the dress to Tuck with a smile.

Tuck tossed it on the bed and sat in the rocker beside her sister. She held her hands toward the stove, enjoying the warmth that enveloped them. "Sis, I don't know if I'll ever really be ladylike. I pretend really well when it suits me then go right back to my old ways."

"You're doing better," Addy said. "Don't put yourself down."

"But to tell the truth, I miss being me. Oh, I know I need to work on some things, but in doing so I'm not sure who I am anymore."

"You're our own precious Abigail Kentucky Sullivan, that's who. And I think you're just fine the way you are." She wrinkled her brow and bit her lip. "I know I nagged at you about changing, but I would never want you to stop being yourself."

"Well, obviously Sam doesn't feel that way." She leaned her head back.

Addy frowned. "What do you mean? What did he say?"

"Nothing. Not to me, that is." Pain ripped through her, and she thought she'd be sick. "It seems Rafe overheard him talking to someone on the phone. A woman. He told her he loved her."

Addy's mouth dropped opened, and then she pressed her lips together. Her face crumpled.

Tuck frowned. "What? What were you going to say?"

"Nothing," Addy hastened to say. "Perhaps Rafe misunderstood. Tell me exactly what he said."

She repeated everything she'd overheard. "Do you think it's possible Rafe misunderstood?"

"Well, it's possible." Addy's face was washed with misery.

"But you don't think so."

"Well, no." She licked her lips.

Tuck stood and looked down at Addy, peering into her eyes. She knew her sister well enough to know she was hiding something. She'd suspected as much for some time but had shoved the suspicion aside. "Addy, you know something you aren't telling me."

Addy's face crumpled, and she placed her hands over her face. "I should have told you before."

Tuck reached down and pulled them away. Addy's eyes were full of tears. "Just tell me, Addy. Tell me now."

"I've been so miserable." Addy jumped up and clutched Tuck's shoulders. "At first I thought it was my imagination telling me Sam was making advances toward me. A wink here, a suggestive smile there. But it didn't stop. Then one day when I was leaving the store, he approached me and asked me to go for a drive with him. I told him in no uncertain terms what I thought of him for that. And, Abby, he behaved the same way on different occasions to Phyllis Carter and Jane White."

Tuck stood frozen. A roaring in her ears drowned out the rest of what Addy was saying. *Please, God. Help me.* Suddenly clarity returned, and she heard her sister's voice loud and clear.

"Abby, are you all right? Should I get Ma?"

"No, no. Don't get Ma." She sat in her rocker. "But why didn't you tell me? Why would you keep such a thing from me?"

Addy dropped her hands and shook her head. "I'm so sorry. I don't know why I didn't tell you. Except, I didn't want to hurt you and I wasn't even sure you'd believe me."

Tuck closed her eyes for a moment. Would she have believed her? Sam had shown more interest in Addy than her at the beginning. She'd been jealous, and even after he started courting her, she still felt unkindly to Addy. Her jealousy must have shown through. No wonder her sister had been afraid to tell her about Sam's advances.

She stood and pulled Addy to her, wrapping her in her arms. "I'm so sorry. I should never have let anyone come between us. Can you forgive me?"

"Oh, Abby." Addy squeezed her tightly. "I've missed you so much."

They talked long into the night. And between tears and laughter, the bond that had always been between them grew stronger.

But there was one more question that Tuck knew she needed an answer for. "Addy, I know you had feelings for Sam in the beginning. And he was interested in you. I shouldn't have gone after him the way I did." She paused before continuing. "Do you still have those feelings?"

Addy drew back in horror. "Heavens, no! When I noticed how he treated you and how rude he could be, any feelings I had for him dissipated. I don't want to hurt you, Abby, but quite frankly, I can barely tolerate the man, and I know he's not good enough for you."

After Addy had fallen asleep, Tuck lay awake, her thoughts twisting inside her mind. What now? Although she never wanted to see Sam again, she knew she needed to confront him. He had a right to answer the accusations, although she doubted he could defend himself against them. Neither Rafe nor Addy would have lied about it. And she couldn't think of any plausible explanation that could make him innocent.

Finally, although she tried hard to keep it at bay, the memory of Rafe's declaration of love for her filled her thoughts. She had no idea how she felt about that or what to do about it, but it filled her heart with awe.

Chapter 15

After a restless night, Tuck got up early and slipped out to the barn to saddle Sweet Pea. The storm had ended, but light rain continued to fall. Ma would have been sure to protest Tuck's riding off to town.

A cold drizzle fell on Tuck and Sweet Pea as she rode fast and hard toward Branson's. She pulled up in front and, after taking care of Sweet Pea, went inside.

Only one customer browsed the aisles of the store. Tuck glanced around and saw Mr. Hawkins stocking the top shelves. Tuck walked quietly to Sam's office and tapped on the door.

Sam started when he saw her. Scorn twisted his face as his eyes took in her overalls. "Abby. What a surprise. Please come in."

Tuck kicked the door closed behind her and slipped past him, avoiding his hand that he held out toward her.

"Whatever will Mr. Hawkins say, my dear?" He flashed her a nervous smile. When she didn't return it, a thoughtful look crossed his face.

"I understand I'm not your only dear." The calmness of her voice surprised her. It certainly didn't match her desire to scratch his eyes out.

"Why would you say such a thing? Have you seen me with anyone else?" He frowned. The hurt expression on his face would have fooled her a few weeks ago.

"I have my reasons, Sam. I know you've made advances toward other women." She took a deep breath. "Did you really think you could get away with it, when I know most of the girls in the county?"

"Abigail, I don't know who has been telling these tales, but I assure you they are nothing but lies. I've hardly looked at another woman since I met you."

She shook her head. "You are pathetic. And how dare you call my sister a liar."

"Ah. Well, there you have it. She always was attracted to me." He chuckled. "Just a little case of jealousy."

She planted her hands on her hips and glared. "It's no use, Sam. Stop lying. Besides, someone heard you on the phone yesterday when you were professing your love to someone in quite a provocative voice."

A trapped look crossed his face. Then understanding dawned, and he laughed. A very unpleasant laugh. "Ah, I see. Caught by your devoted Rafe Collins. I don't suppose I could convince you he's making a mountain out of a molehill."

"No, you can't." *Thank You, God, for this peace.*

"Well then, I suppose I must confess. I like pretty women. Never could resist them." He smiled. "I actually was quite taken with your sister at first, I will admit."

"Then why did you turn your attentions to me?" The weasel. How could she have thought he had charm?

"Why, you were very entertaining, dear Abigail. It fascinated me that you were so enamored of me. You actually managed to turn yourself from a backwoods hillbilly into a lovely young lady. Of course, you still have rough spots, but perhaps someday those will smooth out."

"I see. So you were simply playing with my affections, leading me to believe that you were an honorable man who wanted to marry me." She stomped her foot. "Not that I'd marry a snake like you."

"Marry you?" Laughter exploded from his mouth. "Let me tell you a little secret, my dear. I couldn't marry you if I wished to, which I don't. You see, I'm already wed to the daughter of a very famous surgeon in Kansas City. In fact, we worked out some of our little problems when I was there recently, and I'm sure we'll be reuniting very soon."

She gasped. "You vile man. My pa will tar and feather you when he hears about this. And so will every other man in the neighborhood. You'll be run out of town faster than you can say, 'my dear' anything."

"Hmmm, you may have a point there. And I'm sure your Rafe will lead the pack. Well then, I was bored with this place at any rate, so perhaps I'd best say adieu. There are plenty of other communities in need of a doctor."

Tuck gave a short laugh. "Why don't you go on back to Kansas City to your wife? I suppose she's the one you were talking to on the phone?"

"You suppose wrong." He smiled a mocking smile. "That happened to be a sweet young lady I met in Wichita last year. Perhaps it's time to head that way until my wife makes the right decision."

Tuck laughed. "I thought you were getting back together."

"Unfortunately, her father isn't quite ready to forgive me, and he controls the purse strings and his daughter." He bowed.

"Serves you right, you womanizing four-flusher." She spun and headed for the door.

His mocking laugh hit her like a sack of potatoes.

Boiling, seething anger roiled up inside her. Her hand clutched into a tight fist. Spinning around, she slammed her fist into his face.

He yelled and hit the floor.

With a tight smile, she rubbed her hands together. "Enjoy your trip."

She made it outside before her anger deflated, and she leaned against the front of the store, weak and trembling. How could she have been such a fool? He'd cared nothing for her. He had played with her affections and humiliated her. What kind of woman did he think she was that he would show disrespect to her so?

Batting tears from her eyes, she stalked over to the hitching rail. She mounted Sweet Pea and rode away toward the Collinses' farm. She had to talk to someone. She needed Rafe. He was the only one who could always help her think straight.

A pang shot through her, and she yanked on the reins, bringing Sweet Pea to a stop. How could she have forgotten? Things were different between her and Rafe now. He wasn't just her best friend anymore.

Shame washed over her at the very thought of revealing to him the things Sam had admitted to her. Oh, how could she have thought she was in love with such a vile man? If only she could go back and do things differently. But she couldn't. All she could do now was try to salvage some of her dignity and get on with her life.

At least she had Ma and Pa and Addy. She'd never tell her parents the truth about Sam. If he was really leaving, they wouldn't have to know how bad it really was. But she could talk to her sister. Addy would help her through this.

Suddenly she thought of Ma's favorite scripture verse. *"Commit thy works unto the Lord, and thy thoughts shall be established."* She'd never even consulted with God about Sam. She'd wanted her own way, and it had never crossed her mind to ask God if Sam was His will for her life.

"Father, forgive me for being so willful. From now on I only want to do things Your way. And Lord, I can't imagine my life without Rafe in it. But I know I'm the one who messed everything up. Really, I only need You. Please don't let Rafe be hurt because of me. Have Your way, Lord. In Jesus' name. Amen."

Peace flowed over her as she headed for home.

⁓♡

"I tell you, Jim, if that guy hurts her, I don't know what I'll do."

Jim gave him a commiserating look and nodded. He'd come over to say good-bye before he left for Arkansas and had stayed for lunch.

Rafe leaned back in the chair and glanced out over the yard. The rain had picked up again, and there wouldn't likely be a leaf left on a tree if it kept up. They'd held on pretty long as it was, considering this was the third week in November. He threw the piece of wood he'd been chewing on into the yard. "Oh well, enough of my whining. I'm sorry to see you go, Jim."

"Thanks, Rafe, but now that Marble Cave is shut down for the winter, I need to go where the work is," Jim said.

"Too bad you won't be around for Thanksgiving. My ma's pumpkin pies are the best in the county." His mouth nearly watered just thinking about them.

"I hear you. She makes a real good turkey, too." He grinned. "Rafe, I wouldn't worry about Tuck if I were you. She's a smart girl and independent. She'll catch on to Fields sooner or later."

"Sooner I hope." Some women never found out their men were rotten, until they were wed and expecting babies. His stomach tightened at the thought of Tuck in a situation like that.

"Don't give up on her. She might care more about you than you think." Jim's voice held hope, and Rafe knew he was probably wishing the same about Addy, although he'd barely spoken ten words to her since the first time he laid eyes on her.

He sighed. "I don't know, Jim. When I came out of the barn last night after talking to her pa, she'd gone in the house. My horse was in plain sight, so she knew I was there. Didn't say hello or even ask me to help her carry the supplies in."

"Did you go in and say hello to her?" Jim gave him a knowing look.

"Nope. She'd have known something was wrong, and she has a way of wringing the truth out of me. I couldn't be the one to tell her, so I left."

"Well, she may have had her reasons for not coming to tell you hello." Jim didn't sound too convinced, much less convincing.

Rafe nodded. "Maybe."

"You sure you don't want to go with me to Arkansas? They're still needing hands. Maybe a change in scenery is what you need. It could help you think clearly." He snapped his fingers. "I almost forgot to tell you. I found out why they're buying up land all around the store and mill."

"Why?" Rafe turned his attention fully on what Jim was saying. Nearly everyone he'd talked to lately had wondered about that.

"Seems the Missouri Pacific plans on building a township. They'll keep the name of Branson, since that's what most people call the community already."

"Is that right? That's interesting," Rafe said. "Old man Berry might have something to say about that. You know he owns the land the store and post office are on. He's the one who wants the mail to be postmarked Lucia instead of Branson. I'd hate for that to happen, but who knows?"

Jim shook his head and stood. "The railroad will more than likely buy that property, too, so that'll take care of that."

"Yes. If Berry will sell. He's a hardworking, God-fearing man, but a stubborn old coot as well. If he decides not to sell, his sons will stand behind him. They're a close-knit bunch." Rafe stretched and stood up, reaching out to shake Jim's hand.

"Well, I'll be back this way in a few months, if not sooner. It'll depend on when Lynch wants to reopen." He mounted his horse. "Good-bye, Rafe."

"Good-bye and take care. Depending on what happens here, I may follow you." He waved and headed for the barn as Jim rode away.

His pa was currying Paintbrush, the Indian pony they'd had since Rafe was a boy. Pa treated all his animals well, but Paintbrush was special. He got the finest care of any horse they'd ever owned.

"Pa, I found out why the railroad's buying up so much land. They plan on building a town over by Branson's."

"You don't say. What do they want with a town? Must be up to something." Pa scratched his ear and frowned, two deep lines appearing between his eyes.

"Or maybe they plan to bring some businesses in here." Excitement rose in Rafe, almost making him forget his worry about Tuck.

"Hmm. Well, I sure ain't selling. They'll get my farm over my dead body." Pa gave an emphatic nod and patted Paintbrush on the rump. "There you go, old feller. Pretty as can be and not a burr in sight."

"Well, I thought you'd want to know," Rafe said. "Is there anything I can do?"

"Yes, you can tell me why you been in such a bad mood all day. Your ma's right worried about you, boy."

Rafe cleared his throat before answering. "Sorry, Pa. I know I've been sort of moping around lately. I'm a little worried about Tuck and that doctor. I don't trust him to treat her right."

"Ain't no use worrying. When a gal takes a shine to a fellow, ain't nothing can get him out of her head unless something opens her eyes and she sees for herself." He turned slowly, rubbing his lower back. "But I don't blame you for not trusting that Fields fellow. I've thought he was a bad one ever since I laid eyes on him."

Rafe nodded. Maybe he needed to have a talk with Tuck after all. She couldn't do much more than bite his head off. He took a deep breath. He couldn't do it. Not yet. Maybe Jack had spoken to her about it.

Pain stabbed at his heart as he walked to the house with his pa. He had to do something. If he couldn't talk to Tuck about it, there wasn't a thing to prevent him from talking to Sam Fields. Tomorrow he'd see the doctor again. This time he'd have a few questions for the man. If he didn't like the answers, he would talk to Tuck, even if she hated him for it.

Chapter 16

Tuck emitted a growl of frustration as Tom hit the wrong note on his banjo for about the tenth time since they'd started practicing, followed by an apologetic look at Mr. Willie. She frowned at all three of the men. "What's wrong with all of you today? Mr. Willie, your fiddle sounds like a dying cow and Squeezebox's accordion sounds like a dying bull. I can't even think of anything that sounds like Tom's banjo. Someone want to tell me what's going on?"

She was exaggerating, but so what? She knew what their problem was. And it was time to bring it to an end. "Look. It's not that I don't appreciate your concern, but I've told you over and over I'm all right. I don't care a hoot about Sam Fields hotfooting it out of here last night. I'd already ended things with him. The only thing I'm sorry about is that we won't have a doctor close by."

Tom gave her a look that wasn't quite disbelief but pretty close. "You sure, Tuck? Because every man in this town is willin' and ready to go after him and give him a trouncing if he just run off and left you, so to speak."

Tuck rolled her eyes and looked upward. "Mercy. What do I have to do to get it through your thick skulls?"

"How about you'uns leaves the girl alone?"

Bless Mr. Willie's heart. He always looked after her feelings. Tuck glanced around at her three friends. They'd known her since she was a little girl, and she had no doubt that each loved her in his own way. Why not tell them the truth?

She swallowed and sighed. "Well, I guess you might as well know what's going on. But you have to promise you won't breathe a word of this to anyone because I'd be downright humiliated if it got around."

Squeezebox frowned. "You know we ain't loose lipped, young lady. Tell us or not, don't make no never mind to me."

Tuck gave him a lopsided grin. "I know that. I'm just trying to get up the courage to tell you."

"Wal, just say it, gal." Tom's tone was much more gentle than usual.

"Sam Fields didn't just turn out to be a no-good skunk. He's a married, no-good skunk." She inhaled deeply and let the air out with a *whoosh*. There. She'd told. No one but Addy knew that bit of information. She hadn't even revealed it to Ma and Pa.

"Well, I'll be." Squeezebox's eyes widened. "Do you mean that so-called respectable doctor was a bigamist?"

Tom gave him a disgusted look. "He'd have to have married two women for him to be a bigamist. He's just a four-flushing womanizer. And I'd like to get my hands on him for deceiving our little gal here."

Tuck glanced at Mr. Willie, surprised that he hadn't said a word. Lips pressed tightly together and brow wrinkled, his eyes blazed. If she'd ever seen murder in anyone's eyes, she was seeing it now, in the countenance of the gentle, tenderhearted Willie Van Schultz. "Mr. Willie?" She laid a hand on his shoulder. "Please. I'm all right. I promise."

"He never laid nary a hand on you, did he?" The words were like bullets. She shuddered, wondering what he'd do if he knew about the night by the river.

"He never did." Mr. Willie didn't need to know how close that came to being a lie.

Mr. Willie nodded, and his face relaxed a little, but his eyes still smoldered.

Another shiver ran over Tuck. She knew little to nothing about Mr. Willie's past, but she had a feeling it was very different from his present peaceful existence.

He sat up and positioned his fiddle. "Wal, we best quit dillydallyin' and get busy if we're going to be ready for the Christmas dance."

Tuck, relieved to have the subject over and hopefully done with, tucked her collar inside her dress and got ready to play. Maybe her life would get back to normal now. Her heart seemed to tilt. Except for her and Rafe. She shook her head to expel the thought. No time for that now.

After the practice, Tuck rode home to find the parlor filled with chattering ladies. She slapped herself on the forehead. She'd completely forgotten the ladies involved in the Christmas bazaar would be here for a final meeting. The bazaar was being held the first week in December, and there were always last-minute plans to cover.

Besides the bazaar, Tuck had to get music ready for the Christmas dance, and she had a dress to finish. She'd also need to help with baking for the holidays. Maybe she was spreading herself too thin. How could she be expected to remember everything? On the other hand, staying busy was probably good for her. At least it would help keep her mind off Rafe.

"Sorry, everyone." She smiled apologetically as she stepped into the parlor. "I was with the oldsters, practicing. I forgot all about the meeting."

"Abigail." Ma smiled a welcome. "How did your practice go?"

She walked over and kissed her ma on the cheek. "It was a good practice. Never fear, ladies. Our music will be ready for the dance."

Ma's Aunt Kate waved from across the room. "We're very grateful for your talent, Abigail, as well as the oldsters as you call them."

"Hummph." Mrs. Humphrey's eyes darted disapproval. "Yes, and that sounds very disrespectful to me. Besides, in my opinion, she's much too familiar with those old men. Men being what they are."

"Mother!" Aletha Humphrey's whisper was loud enough to reach Tuck's ears. "Please don't start."

"Start? Start what? I guess I have a right to express my opinion."

"Well, I think Abby and the *oldsters* are perfectly delightful, and the friendship they all share is lovely." Mrs. Dobson, a friend of Aunt Kate's, smiled at Tuck. "And by the way, Abby, you worked very hard for the fall festival and dance. And now you're going to be playing for the Christmas dance as well. It's time you had some fun. I think you should leave this bazaar to us older women so you can enjoy it with the rest of the young folks."

Murmurs of assent greeted Mrs. Dobson's suggestion.

"Thank you, Mrs. Dobson. I believe I'll take you up on that." Tuck grinned. "Now may I serve you ladies tea or something?"

"We're about to finish up here, dear." Ma said. "We had our refreshments earlier."

"Then I think I'll go find my sister." She gave a wave and headed for the kitchen.

The bazaar was only a few days away. She and Addy and Rafe had always hung out together at these gatherings. Except when Addy sometimes deserted them to visit with the other girls. Could she get up the courage to talk to Rafe before then? She sighed. Probably not. It would very likely do her good to spend more time with the other girls her age anyway. Maybe she could learn something useful.

Of course, Rafe had indicated to her pa that he didn't like the change in her. But she was through trying to please men. She'd be herself. And there was nothing wrong with continuing to cultivate ladylike manners, even if she did still wear overalls.

∽⁓∾

Rafe hung onto the plow as the mules pulled the blades through Ma's depleted house garden. As soon as this plot was turned under, he'd be done with plowing until spring planting time. Then the long winter would drag on forever. Or so it seemed.

Ordinarily he'd be looking forward to the Christmas bazaar. Not because he liked it but because he and Tuck always had a lot of fun together. Not this year though. Tuck wasn't speaking to him.

He'd seen her over by the mill yesterday, and she'd turned and headed down to the river, pretending not to see him. Maybe she was embarrassed because the doc took off without a by-your-leave. Or maybe his company just wasn't to her liking any more.

Anger flashed through him. Who needed her anyway? She didn't even act like a girl half the time. Maybe he wasn't really in love with her but was just used to her. Like an old shoe. It was hard to let go.

He kicked at a clod of hard dirt then yelled across the field, "I don't need you, Tuck Sullivan. You're not the only fish in the ocean."

That's right. Lots of pretty little fish. Like Carrie Sue who wanted nothing better than to bat her pretty blue eyes at him. Maybe it was time to pay some close attention to those eyes. Of course no one had blue eyes like Tuck's. He kicked another dirt clod. He could forget her and he'd start right now.

After he'd eaten supper and done his evening chores, Rafe tidied up then saddled Champ. He belted out "Old Dan Tucker" at the top of his voice while he rode. By the time the Andersons' farm came into view, he was feeling a lot better. Maybe life had something to offer him after all.

He jumped off Champ and sauntered to the front door. After knocking, he stood, hat in hand, a big smile on his face.

Mrs. Anderson opened the door to his knock, and when she saw him, her eyes sparkled. "Good evening, Rafe. Won't you come in?"

Rafe wiped his feet on the pile of old rags outside the door and stepped inside. "Thank you, ma'am. Is Carrie Sue home by any chance?"

"She certainly is. Here, make yourself at home in the parlor and I'll go get her." She nearly skipped down the hall.

Rafe sat on an overstuffed sofa, twisting his hat in his hands, and waited what must have been at least thirty minutes. Fidgeting, his exuberance wore off little by little. This had been a mistake, a big mistake. Should he make an excuse and leave? He stood then plopped back down. Nope. The gossip would be all over the county, and when Ma heard it, she'd be humiliated and probably take a broom to him.

"Hello, Rafe." Carrie Sue stood in the doorway dressed for company. His company. Her blond tresses were swept back from her face, and her blue eyes shone.

Rafe stood. "Hello, Carrie."

"You wanted to see me?" Her voice cracked, and she blushed as she seated herself in a chair across from the sofa.

The blush and nervousness of her voice were his undoing. He couldn't back out now. She'd be hurt and insulted. On the other hand, he couldn't make small talk for an hour either. Smiling, he reclaimed his seat on the sofa. "I know it's rather late for an invitation to the bazaar, but if you haven't made other plans, would you like to go with me?"

Her face brightened, and a pretty pink blush washed over her smooth cheeks. "Why yes, I'd love to accompany you to the bazaar. Thank you for asking me."

"It's my pleasure." He stood and smiled down at her. "Well then, I'll come by around eleven. That way we can eat lunch before we look through the booths."

"That sounds wonderful. But. . .what about Tuck?" She dropped her lashes then raised them slowly.

"What do you mean?" He raised an eyebrow.

"Oh, now that Dr. Fields is gone, I thought you two—" She broke off in apparent confusion.

Rafe tensed against the stab of pain but managed a laugh. "Tuck and I are just friends. I thought everyone knew that."

"Oh, that's wonderful. I mean. . .you and Tuck were always together before the doctor started courting her, so I assumed that you were in love with her." She lifted her chin, gazed at him with eyes that might have bowled him over if she hadn't just mentioned Tuck and fluttered her long lashes.

"In love with Tuck? Not at all." He gave a short laugh, but a sick feeling tugged at his stomach. "Well, I'll see you Saturday then."

A coquettish smile tipped her lips, and she nodded. "I'll look forward to it, Rafe."

He took the tiny hand she offered him and shook it gently, then swallowed past the lump in his throat.

She shut the door, and before he made it off the porch, he heard her scream of excitement. He grinned. She must like him more than he'd thought.

He whistled as he rode away on Champ. He patted the horse on the neck and crooned. "Yes, I think the girl was happy to see me, old boy."

He laughed. What would Tuck think when he showed up with Carrie Sue at his side? His stomach lurched. What if Tuck had been hiding away because she was hurting? He'd been so happy when he heard Fields had left, it hadn't occurred to him that Tuck might suffer. Maybe that's why she'd avoided him. She couldn't face anyone. She probably felt humiliated, too. He groaned. What had he done? He should have given her more time. Instead he'd just kept company with another woman and had even pretty well denied being in love with Tuck.

He pulled up on the reins. Champ gave an impatient whinny, then bent his head and munched at the brown grass. Maybe he should just go back and make some excuse to Carrie Sue. But it was too late for that. If word got around, which it would, he'd be branded as heartless, and some of the other females would laugh behind Carrie's back. He couldn't be the cause of that. That would be one step toward becoming a worthless sidewinder like Sam Fields.

Chapter 17

Tuck tapped her foot to a boisterous rendition of "Up on the House Top." In order to give Tuck and the oldsters a break, the Packard brothers, famous over the years for their leading of music at church socials and community parties, had come out of retirement for the occasion. She grinned as Horace, the eldest of the brothers, grabbed for the red stocking cap that had slipped from his balding head.

Wood smoke from the tall iron stove in the corner blended together with the fragrance of gigantic pine boughs that hung from the rafters of the Jenkinses' barn and the fronts of individual booths. Kettles emitted smells of cinnamon and clove.

Tuck inhaled deeply in appreciation. She smiled at the festive touch of holly berries and bright red bows trimmed in lace.

Addy smiled and waved at their friends, Phyllis and Jolene. "Let's go talk to them, Abby."

Tuck would just as soon not, but reminding herself she'd promised to spend more time with the other girls, she followed her sister without complaint. They stopped at one of the booths and purchased hot apple cider, then continued across the room.

"Oh, that cider smells delicious. I think I'll get a cup, too." Phyllis, her plump cheeks glowing, turned to Jolene. "Would you like me to bring something back to you?"

"I think I'll have cider, too. I can't resist it," Jolene said, her brown eyes sparkling. "Go to Thompson's booth. Mr. Thompson makes the best cider in the whole state."

Tuck grinned. Thompson's cider was good, but she suspected Jolene's love affair with it resulted from her crush on Ralph, the oldest Thompson son. The funny thing was Ralph had been moping after Addy and Tuck for years. He didn't seem to care which one.

Tuck glanced around for Rafe, having no idea what she'd do if she saw him. Memories of last year's bazaar assailed her mind, and longing washed over her. She missed him. There was no denying that. Would he seek her out when he got here? She didn't want that, did she?

"Why, look." Exaggerated surprise filled Jolene's voice. "There's my cousin, Carrie Sue. Isn't that Rafe beside her?"

With controlled calm, Tuck slowly turned her head. Rafe strolled past a quilt display, his attention on the girl at his side. Tuck clenched her teeth. Carrie Sue clung to his arm as though she was afraid he might get away. Which he would do, if he knew what was good for him. Carrie Sue certainly wasn't.

Phyllis gave Jolene a wry grin and tapped her on the arm. "As though you didn't know he was bringing her. You told me yesterday, silly."

Jolene had the grace to blush, accompanying it with a slight laugh. "Oh that's right. I forgot for a moment."

Tuck's breathing sped up then hitched when she tried to control it. *Oh God, please don't let me faint. I do want Rafe to be happy. If it was anyone but Carrie Sue...*

She started as her sister's breath warmed the skin by her ear. "Abby," Addy whispered, "pull yourself together. Don't give Jolene and Carrie Sue the satisfaction of knowing you care."

Tuck took a deep breath and gushed. "It *is* Rafe and Carrie Sue. How nice to finally see her with someone. She's been hunting for so long."

Oh, Rafe. It had only been a few days since she'd overheard him declare to Pa that he loved her. Had she misunderstood? She'd told herself at the time she wished only to be Rafe's friend. But seeing another woman at his side made a mockery of her words.

Jolene tossed her dark curls. "That was quite a rude thing to say, Abby. A number of young men have asked to court Carrie. I believe she's been saving herself for Rafe. I hope you have no problem with that."

Problem? She'd show her problems. Tuck opened her lips to lambaste the girl who was supposed to be a friend, but a jerk on her arm brought her to her senses.

Addy smiled with warning in her eyes. "Come, Abby. Let's go look at the wood carvings. I believe some of Pa's are being presented." With another tug on Tuck's arm, she dragged her away.

They walked a few feet and stopped at a booth that featured a variety of Christmas-themed linens.

"What did you do that for?" Tuck glared at her twin. "I didn't do anything."

"Abby," Addy spoke through clenched teeth, "you can't just fly off the handle at people whenever you feel like it."

"What? I didn't say a word." Tuck frowned.

"No, but you were about to, and don't deny it," Addy snapped.

"Well, talk about two peas in a pod. You girls even have twin frowns."

At the sound of Carrie Sue's voice, Tuck stiffened then whirled around. The simpering blond held onto Rafe's arm as though her life depended on it.

"Carrie Sue. Did anyone ever tell you your voice sounds like a screeching parrot?" Tuck inwardly cringed. Oh no. Did she really say that?

Addy gasped and glared at Tuck, then walked away, her face flaming.

Now she'd embarrassed Addy, and she probably wouldn't ever speak to her again.

Tuck glanced at Rafe and caught his mouth twisting and pressing together to hold back a grin. Whew. At least he wasn't mad at her for her unkind words. "Hi, Rafe."

"Hi, Tuck. Enjoying the bazaar?" His gaze bore into hers, and for once she couldn't read his eyes.

"Not much. You?" She deliberately ignored Carrie Sue, who stared daggers at her.

"Not re—" He glanced at Carrie and cleared his throat. "Sure. It's a great bazaar. We're just headed over to Thompson's booth to get some cider. Join us?"

Tuck almost laughed aloud at the exasperated sound that exploded from Carrie Sue. Rafe wasn't piling up a lot of points in his favor. He'd better watch it.

"Really, Rafe, I'm sure Abby has other things to do than tag along with us. Let's go."

Tuck toyed with the idea of hanging onto Rafe's other arm and going along just to aggravate Carrie Sue. But on second thought, she'd been rude enough for one encounter. Besides, Addy was furious enough with her already. If Rafe wanted to keep company with a silly thing like Carrie, he was welcome to her. She forced herself to smile. "No, thank you. I think I'll head outside for some fresh air. It's getting too stuffy in here for me."

Carrie Sue tossed her head and, with a pull on Rafe's arm, guided him away. He threw an unreadable glance over his shoulder at Tuck as he went, but with heaviness in her heart, she turned away.

She couldn't believe he would actually fall for Carrie Sue's silliness. Carrie was actually a nice girl, and she was very pretty with her shiny blond curls and enormous blue eyes. She'd always had a crush on Rafe. Furthermore, Tuck sighed as truth slammed into her thoughts. She'd probably make him a wonderful wife.

Pain shot through her gut and tightened her lips together. Rafe was hers. And she was his. That was the way it had always been. She just hadn't realized what it meant. Over her dead body would Carrie Sue or anyone else take him from her.

⁙

Every time Rafe glanced at Tuck, his heart jumped like crazy and he couldn't stop smiling. Several times he'd caught her glancing at him and Carrie with jealousy all over her face. He'd always been able to read her like a book until Sam Fields came along. What better time for that ability to return?

A bubble of glee rose in him. Maybe she cared more about him than he realized. She might not even know it herself because she'd allowed infatuation for that doctor to cloud her reasoning. He didn't want to get his hopes up, but nevertheless, the possibility that he and Tuck had a chance seemed more certain than ever.

Carrie Sue returned his smile, her eyes shining with delight. It was obvious she believed she was the source of his happiness. Guilt wormed its way into his conscience. Carrie would be furious when she learned today was not only their first date but also their last. He didn't blame her. He should have never asked her to accompany him. Carrie was very nice and extremely pretty and would more than likely make some man a good wife. Just not him.

No other woman was as beautiful in his eyes as Tuck, with her wild curls and dancing eyes. And with the way she threatened to knock the tar out of him when he teased her.

A laugh escaped from his lips. Carrie glanced at him, and her joyous expression faded. She'd caught him staring at Tuck. Her face puckered, and she blinked back tears. She didn't deserve this. Guilt riddling him, Rafe reached out his hand to her. Shaking her head, she blinked back tears then composed her face. Relief mixed with his guilt. At least she wouldn't make a scene. Not in public at any rate.

Determined to avoid hurting Carrie as much as possible, he devoted himself to her for the rest of the afternoon, making a valiant, although not completely successful, attempt to keep his eyes off Tuck.

The bazaar shut down at six, and Rafe sighed a breath of relief as he helped Carrie Sue into the buggy. She appeared exhausted, perhaps from trying to keep up appearances. She'd done a good job so far. He just hoped she didn't tear into him on the way home, although it would serve him right if she did. She stiffened as he wrapped the carriage blanket around her to shield her from the cold night air.

The silence as they drove home only deepened Rafe's guilt. Carrie Sue deserved some sort of explanation or at least an apology. If he'd left her alone, she'd probably have spent this afternoon with someone who would have given her the admiration she deserved.

He cleared his throat, searching for the right words. "Carrie. . ."

"Never mind, Rafe. I know you love Abby. I've always known it. I guess when she started going out with the doctor, I hoped you would turn to me." She bit her lip then smiled. "It's all right. Don't worry, I won't go into seclusion. Several young men are waiting in line for my attention."

"I don't doubt that. You're a nice girl and very lovely, by the way." He smiled. "I thought you'd hit me over the head. Wouldn't blame you a bit if you did."

A sad smile tipped one side of her rosebud mouth. "You can't help who you love."

Rafe shook his head. That was another thing that puzzled him. He must really wear his heart on his sleeve. "How did you know I'm in love with Tuck? I didn't know myself until recently."

She laughed. "You two are so funny. Everyone knows you love each other. It's so obvious. How could we not know?"

"So you think Tuck loves me and doesn't know it?" He probably shouldn't be talking about loving Tuck with Carrie Sue, but he couldn't stop himself.

"I think she knows it now, Rafe. And if she doesn't realize you love her, she's blind as a bat."

Rafe turned into the Andersons' cedar-lined drive. When he stopped in front of the house, he took her hand. "Carrie Sue, if I wasn't so much in love with Tuck, I can't think of another girl I'd rather fall in love with than you."

"Pity's sake, Rafe. Stop trying to make me feel better. I'm quite all right. You're not the only eligible man in the county, you know." She laughed and tapped him on the arm. "You're not even the best-looking one."

Heat rose up his neck and singed his cheeks. Had he been assuming she cared more about him than she did? He must have sounded like an idiot.

"Oh, now I've embarrassed you." She patted his arm. "Sorry. Now help me down and go say sweet things to Abby. I'd say she's the one who'll hit you."

He wouldn't mind a pounding from Tuck about now. It wouldn't be the first time. Always in fun, of course. He chuckled. "You're more than likely right about that." He stepped out of the carriage and went around to help her out, then walked her to the door where she stopped.

"I wish I could say it was a wonderful afternoon, Rafe, but that wouldn't be exactly the truth, so I'll just say good-bye. I hope everything works out for you and Abby." She smiled and, with a little wave, opened the door and went inside.

Rafe breathed a sigh of relief that Carrie had been such a good sport and that he hadn't had to face her mother.

Night came early in Missouri this time of the year. The dark canopy above him as he drove away from the Anderson farm was studded with diamonds. Never had he seen such a night sky. He breathed in the clean night air then shivered from the coldness in his lungs. Tuck should be here with him. They'd always loved to go riding at night. Usually on horseback.

A picture of her astride Sweet Pea, her head thrown back in laughter, filled his thoughts, and his heart raced. What should he do now? He didn't want to make a wrong move and mess things up.

He'd see her at church in the morning. Maybe he could manage an invitation to dinner. Nah. He might have before, but things were different now. Maybe he'd invite her to dinner.

He sighed. The best thing would be to pray and leave it in God's hands. God would show him what to do. And Rafe would sure keep his eyes open so he wouldn't miss it.

Chapter 18

"Move over, Bessie. You're going to knock the bucket over." Tuck gave the cow's rump a shove then returned to the milking. Streams of milk dinging against the galvanized bucket combined with her daydreaming had almost caused her to doze off. Ma wouldn't have been happy, to say the least, if she'd lost all the milk due to carelessness. Nevertheless, Tuck couldn't keep the daydreaming at bay.

The memory of Carrie Sue hanging all over Rafe had tormented her ever since the bazaar, nearly a week ago. Every time the picture crossed her thoughts, a fresh pang sliced through her. She'd just begun to get used to the idea that Rafe was in love with her. Now he'd apparently forgotten his own feelings. Or, more likely, she had misunderstood what he said. If so, that was good. She and Rafe could go back to the way things used to be. Yes, that was good. But why didn't she feel like it was good?

"Abby, are you about done? It's getting colder." A gust of wind followed her twin through the barn door. Addy carried the egg basket in the crook of her arm. "Hurry and we can walk back to the house together."

That meant Addy wanted to question her again about how she felt about Rafe and Carrie Sue. The nosy thing. She'd been trying to get her to talk about it all week. Tuck didn't intend to utter one word about it.

"I'm not done with the milking yet. You go on. I'll be there in a few minutes." Maybe after she strained the milk she'd slip away and saddle Sweet Pea up for a ride.

"Oh, I'm in no hurry." Addy sat on a bale of hay with her basket on her knees. "Wasn't the bazaar fun? We should have them more often. I loved the little wooden stars I bought for the Christmas tree."

"They are pretty. Did you show them to Ma?" Ma and Pa both loved Christmas. Tuck loved seeing Ma's childlike enthusiasm for the holiday.

"No, I want to keep them a secret until we get the tree." Addy loved decorating, but it fell to Pa and Tuck to fetch the evergreen every year.

"I can't believe it's only two weeks until Christmas." She supposed Rafe would spend the day with Carrie Sue. She took a deep breath and shoved the thought away. This was getting ridiculous.

Bessie mooed. Tuck started and stared at the bucket of milk.

"Abby, you haven't gotten a drop of milk in the past two minutes. What's wrong with you?"

Tuck sighed and stood, shoving the stool away with her foot. "Nothing. I guess I'm just still half asleep."

Addy stood. "Well, hurry and get Bessie back into her stall. I'm getting cold. Besides, we promised Ma we'd finish sewing our Christmas dresses today. The Christmas dance is only one week away."

"And one day." Tuck led Bessie back to her stall and forked some hay into her trough. Then, carrying the bucket of milk, she followed her sister out the door. Addy was right. The air felt a lot colder than when they'd come outside to do their morning chores.

Tuck washed her hands and strained the milk, then went to join Addy and Ma in the parlor for a long day of sewing. She wrinkled her nose at the thought. If she could afford it, she'd buy all her dresses ready-made.

Ma's smile didn't quite meet her eyes as she held out Tuck's gown with both hands. "Yours is all finished except for hemming."

"What? How?" She took the silky blue gown and held it up. Sure enough. The lace was even sewn on. "I haven't worked on it at all this week." Oops. She really needed to watch her words.

She cut a glance at Ma who was already busy arranging the piles of fabric in her lap.

"Addy did it for you." Ma glanced up and her eyebrows rose slightly. "In spite of her own work load."

Tuck flashed a quick glance of gratitude at Addy but wished her sister had been a little more secretive about the good deed. "Thanks, sis."

"It was no problem. You know I love to sew, and you've been busy practicing your music for the dance."

Tuck nodded. Addy was always taking care of her. She guessed it was a good thing.

Ma glanced up. "Yes, you do make beautiful music, Tuck. It was a blessing that Mr. Van Schultz was willing to take you under his wing."

"And Pap Sanders," Tuck said. "Don't forget Pap. If not for him, I might never have known I loved the fiddle."

She often thought back with nostalgia to those days when Papa Jack had been a riverboat captain. It was on the *Julia Dawn*, his boat, that Tuck and Addy had become fast friends with Pap Sanders, his fiddle-playing cook. When the old man had noticed Tuck's interest in the fiddle, he had taken her under his wing and taught her the basics. She'd done so well that Addy had insisted she take possession of their grandfather's violin. She sighed and stabbed her needle at the hem in her hand. The locket that lay beneath her shirt felt cold and heavy.

"Of course, Abigail," Ma's voice was tender. "I know Mr. Sanders played a large part in getting you started."

Tuck swallowed past a lump that had suddenly formed in her throat. Addy was always doing things on impulse to make Tuck feel better. She should never have allowed her sister to give her their mother's locket. It was precious to her, in a deep way it had never been to Tuck. Tuck had chosen the violin and would have done the same today.

Ma cleared her throat. "I wonder how Rafe is. I haven't seen him since the bazaar. The Anderson girl seems quite taken with him."

At the sudden turn in the conversation, Tuck jerked her head up and looked at Ma. She sat looking intently at her sewing, but Tuck wasn't fooled. Ma had always had a soft spot for Rafe and had even tried matchmaking a few times over the years. Huh. If she was trying to get a reaction out of Tuck, she was doomed to failure.

Still, it wouldn't hurt to take a ride over to Rafe's just to check out his intentions toward Carrie Sue. That is if she ever got this fool hem done.

⌒⤙⤚⌒

Rafe mentally patted himself on the back for coming up with the perfect Christmas present for his nephew, Bobby. Every time Rafe dropped by his sister Betty's house, the four-year-old plied him with questions about the White River Line. Just last week, Bobby had informed him that he wanted to be a train engineer when he grew up.

Rafe leaned back on the crate where he was sitting and examined the wooden train engine on the floor in front of him. It was shaping up nicely. All Rafe had to do now was attach the wheels and slap on a coat or two of paint. He could envision Bobby scooting around the house on it on Christmas day making train sounds.

At the sound of horse's hooves in the yard, Rafe got up and walked to the barn door. His heart jumped as Tuck slid off Sweet Pea and stepped up onto the porch. "Hey, Tuck," he yelled. "I'm out here."

She turned and waved, grinning as she walked toward him. "Maybe I came to see your ma." She stopped in front of him. "Ever think of that?"

"Oh well, in that case, you'll find Ma in the house." He turned as though to walk away, then turned back around and grinned. "It's good to see you."

"You just saw me at the bazaar a few days ago," she retorted.

"You know what I mean."

"I know." She paused then shrugged. "I've missed you, too."

That sounded promising. If she meant it the way he hoped she did. He squinted at her. "I'm not the one that made myself scarce."

She stiffened, then relaxed and took a deep breath. "I know. Sorry about that, Rafe. I guess I went a little crazy over that no-good doctor."

He wouldn't exactly say she sounded hangdog, but accompanied by the regret in her voice, he knew she was beating herself up. "Hey, let's go fishing tomorrow." He cringed inwardly. That was brilliant.

She laughed. "If it keeps getting colder, the river will be iced over by then. At least part of it. What do you plan? Ice fishing?"

"Okay, okay. Bad idea. I have another one. That railroad guy is holding a meeting at the church house tomorrow. Want to go?" Not as good as fishing, but it could be interesting. At least he'd be spending time with Tuck.

She frowned. "What's going on with them? Do you know? I heard they're trying to buy up everyone's land."

"I'm not sure. Jim said they just want the area around Branson's and the mill."

Her eyes brightened. "Okay, we might as well go find out what they're up to. What time?"

"Ten o'clock, I think. If I hear differently, I'll ride over and let you know." He didn't really care what they did, so long as he could be with her. "Maybe you should mention it to your folks. My pa's going."

"I was thinking the same thing. They might want to attend the meeting." She glanced toward Bobby's train. "That's a nice train engine."

"Thanks. I'm making it for Bobby for Christmas." He eyed it. "Think he'll like it?"

"Will he be able to ride on it?" she asked.

"Yes, I'm getting ready to put the wheels on. It'll roll with a push of his feet, I hope. It's supposed to anyway."

Rafe had missed hearing her laughter, which rippled out now. "I'm sure it will. And yes, I think he'll love it. What little boy wouldn't?"

"I would've," he said.

"Sure, you'd have loved taking it apart." She cut a sarcastic glance his way.

"Now what makes you say that?" he asked with a chuckle.

"As if you didn't know. Remember the time you took Hank's desk apart?"

"Well, a screw was in crooked. How was I to know the whole thing would fall apart?"

"Ha. Only after you removed about a dozen more of them." She bent over with laughter.

The next thing he knew they were both howling.

Tuck wiped her sleeve across her eyes. Was she crying? If so, he understood. Even if she never loved him the way he wanted her to, at least they hadn't lost what they had before. He hadn't lost his best friend.

Emotion welled up in him, and he swallowed hard. "You want to help me paint this thing, after I get the wheels on?" He immediately regretted the invitation. The first, last, and only time they'd painted anything together, she'd made such a mess he'd had to do the whole job over.

She laughed. "You should see your face. Don't worry. I'm not taking you up on that."

He blew out an exaggerated sigh of relief. "Well then, we can go inside and beg Ma for some of those Christmas cookies she's been hiding for the last week."

"I'd love to, but I need to get home. I sort of sneaked out when no one was looking, and we're baking today, too." She smiled. "I'll see you in the morning then."

"Okay. . .uh. . .don't saddle Sweet Pea. I'll bring the buggy." Warmth spread across his face.

She blinked, and pink washed over her face. Was that a blush or a flush or anger? She blinked again. Her lips tipped at one corner. Was she going to yell? "Okay, that would be nice. See you then." She mounted Sweet Pea and rode away without a glance back.

Delight rushed over Rafe, and he couldn't keep from grinning. Tuck cared. He knew she did. The question was did she know it?

"Waaaaahooooo." His cry of victory resounded across the yard. The hound jumped up and bayed. Rafe threw his head back and laughed.

He'd have to go slowly. But not too slowly. He wasn't about to take any chances on losing Tuck when he was this close to winning her.

Chapter 19

A nervous murmur rippled throughout the packed church. Tuck sat with Rafe on the bench beside his parents. His brother-in-law, Robert, sat at the other end. Ma, Pa, Addy, and Aunt Kate were in front of them.

Fullbright, the railroad representative, stepped up on the platform and stood behind the pulpit. He cleared his throat and glanced down at some papers before him on the pulpit. "Ladies and gentlemen, thank you for coming." His voice boomed across the room. At least they'd be able to hear him.

Tuck forced herself to sit straight while Rafe leaned forward, his arms crossed on the back of the bench in front of them, his eyes focused on the railroad man.

"First of all, let me introduce myself. My name is Charles Fullbright. As most of you probably know, I'm an employee of the Missouri Pacific Railroad, and yes, I'm here to obtain land."

"You're not getting mine." Howard Thompson, who owned a small farm a few miles away, stood and shook a fist toward Fullbright. Another, then another, joined him, their angry voices added to his.

Fullbright raised his hand and shouted. "We don't want your farmland."

The men sat down, but uncertainty, if not downright disbelief, remained on their faces.

"Let me explain. I'm sure every one of you is aware of the Missouri Pacific's plans to build a line following the White River, from Helena, Arkansas, to Carthage, Missouri. The White River Line will not only benefit the railroad but everyone who lives along the line."

Heads bobbed in agreement, but Thompson shouted, "What does that have to do with your buying land around here?"

"That's a legitimate question. One I'm happy to answer. The White River Line, although beneficial to all, will be very expensive to construct." He paused, but now he had their attention and no one spoke.

"My assignment here is to purchase land around and near the post office. This land will, in turn, be sold for businesses. In this way, the White River Line will be funded, and the Branson Town Company will create opportunities for progress in the community. We hope to plant orchards along the line as well, and encourage new mining ventures. All our plans will be beneficial to you. As many of you know, we have already obtained a great deal of land uphill from the river, but we need more."

As Fullbright paused, excited chatter broke out.

Rafe sat back and grinned at Tuck. "Looks like we're going to have a real town. Branson, Missouri."

"Just a minute." The loud voice cut through the noise. Tuck turned to see Thomas Berry, the old man who owned the land on which the store and post office were built. He swayed as he stood. Tuck thought for a moment he might fall. "There's one problem with your plan. I'm not selling my land to you or anyone else. In fact, I have plans to plat a town of my own, the town of Lucia, Missouri. From now on all mail leaving from the post office on my land will be marked Lucia, not Branson. So you may as well take your men and find another post office to build your town around." He turned and stomped out, followed by his son.

"I had a feeling." Pa muttered with a sigh. "I thought Berry would put the brakes on this."

"Well, that was interesting." With a little laugh, Mr. Fullbright took charge of the meeting once more. "I can assure you, Branson Town will be platted. With or without Mr. Berry's land. Now I'll open the meeting to questions and discussion."

The meeting lasted for another hour as Fullbright attempted to avert any concerns the people had. Rafe listened closely and even asked a couple of questions. Tuck's concentration had shifted from Fullbright. She couldn't get Mr. Berry off her mind.

By the time they came out of the stuffy church building, Tuck was more than ready to breathe some fresh air. Even cold air. After waving good-bye to Ma, Pa, and Addy, she let Rafe help her into his buggy.

They drove away from the church, and Rafe headed down the river road. He glanced at Tuck with a grin. "Branson, Missouri. Has a nice sound, doesn't it?"

"Yes, it does. I like it a lot better than Lucia. But what if Mr. Berry won't sell?"

"I don't think you need to worry about that." Rafe chuckled. "This is the railroad, remember? They usually get what they want."

Tuck bit her lip. "Why can't they start a town without the post office?"

He shook his head. "It wouldn't work."

"It doesn't seem quite right, does it?" She chewed on her bottom lip.

"What doesn't sound right, honey?" He looked at her with interest.

Tuck's stomach leaped at the endearment, and for a moment she couldn't speak. She took a deep breath. "Well, shouldn't a man be able to keep his land if he wants to?"

Rafe frowned. "Well yes, but sometimes there are exceptions. By holding out like he wants to do, he's preventing us from having a town."

"He says he wants to plant a town himself," Tuck snapped. "What's wrong with that? Why shouldn't he? What gives the railroad any right to come in and take over?"

Rafe was quiet for a moment. "Tuck, we need the railroad. Without it, our progress is pretty much at a standstill."

She nodded but didn't reply. She could see both sides, but Mr. Berry had fought in the Civil War. He'd worked hard farming and doing blacksmith work for the community. He had a very large family. Why shouldn't he be able to leave them the land they'd been born on?

"Hey, Tuck. Let's go grab something to eat at my house then go hunting. You haven't gone with me a single time this season," His eyes sparkled as he smiled at her.

Oh, how she'd missed his smile, the fun in his eyes. "I'll have to go change. I can't go hunting in a dress."

"We're almost to my place. Why go all the way back? You can wear something of mine. Ma won't care."

Scandalized, Tuck stared at him with wide eyes. Although they really weren't any different than her own overalls, still, the idea of wearing a pair of pants that Rafe had worn sent heat rushing over her face and down her chest. "Why, Rafe Collins, shame on you. I can't wear your clothes."

His face turned red. "Okay, okay, we'll go back. Don't get so upset." He turned the horse and they headed back.

Surprised, she stared at him. She'd never seen Rafe give in so easily before.

⟿

Rafe stuck his tongue in his cheek as he crept through the trees. He didn't expect to kill anything with all the noise he and Tuck were making from their laughter and cutting up, but who cared?

They'd spent the whole morning and half the afternoon together. After his initial embarrassment at Tuck's reaction to his offer had worn off, he was just plain tickled. It was the first sign he'd had that she was thinking of him as a man instead of a childhood friend.

That wasn't the only thing different. Although it had bothered him to see her changing for Sam Fields, he had to admit, now that she had discarded the silliness, he didn't mind some of the more feminine characteristics she'd picked up from Addy. Obviously they were already a part of her and had just needed to be brought out. Otherwise, they'd have dropped away like some of the silly stuff had done as soon as Fields was out of the picture. Not that he wouldn't have been just as happy if she'd gone completely back to her old ways. She was Tuck. His Tuck. He loved the person she was.

He'd kept up a continuous line of humor going for hours just so he could hear her laugh.

Now, she walked close beside him, her rifle lying casually in the crook of her arm. "Rafe, we haven't spotted anything, and I'm tired of walking through these woods. We've been off your property for the last two hours. Maybe we'd better start back."

"I've got a better idea. Let's start a fire and talk some more. It won't be dark for a while yet."

"Sounds good. Lead the way."

After another half-hour's hike, they forged their way from the thick wooded area into a clearing. A cedar-grown hill rose on one side.

"Willie's cabin is around here somewhere. Maybe we could search for it and surprise him."

"Nah. We could wander around for two days before we found it." Besides, Rafe wanted to be alone with Tuck. He planned to let her know how he felt about her before the day was over.

"Is the wind picking up?" She shivered as she helped Rafe gather small pieces of wood to get a fire started.

"Maybe a little. You'll warm up as soon as that wood catches good." He grabbed a bigger piece of wood and threw it on with the others.

As the fire caught, they continued to pile on branches and fallen logs until they had a small-sized but roaring bonfire.

Tuck sat on the ground and leaned back on her elbows, her legs stretched toward the fire.

Rafe dropped down beside her. Her half-closed eyes caused Rafe's breath to catch in his throat. He let it out with a *whoosh*. He'd never thought of Tuck as sultry before. His hand trembled as he put another dead log on the fire. "That fire feels good, doesn't it?"

"Hmmm." She sat up and rubbed her arms. "Not really. Is it getting colder? I'm freezing."

"You really are cold, aren't you?" He put his arm around her and pulled her close, tucking her head beneath his chin. "Let's warm up some then head back toward the house so I can take you home."

"Carrie Sue might not like it if she saw you hugging me like this, you know. She might not understand that we're just friends."

He grinned, trying not to laugh. He'd been waiting for her to bring up Carrie Sue, as he knew she would, sooner or later, if she really cared about him. "I imagine she'd think I was in love with you."

Tuck emitted a not very convincing chuckle. "The silly girl."

"Actually, she's a very nice girl. Not nearly as silly as she seems." He hugged her a little closer. Warmth wrapped him in a pleasant cocoon, and he doubted the fire had much to do with it.

"That's nice. She's very pretty, too." Her voice tensed.

"Oh yes, very pretty." Laughter threatened to spring up from the joy in his heart.

She lifted her head and took a deep breath. "I suppose she'll make a good wife."

He shoved her head back down. "Yes, I'm sure she will."

She grew very still. He could barely make out her words, she spoke so quietly. "So when are you getting married?"

"Just as soon as I can." He wondered how long it would take her to catch on.

"Well, have you set a date yet?" She shot the words through clenched teeth.

"No." He grinned. "I thought I'd leave that up to you."

"What?" She sat up and stared at him.

"Hey, what's going on down there?" The yell came from up the hill.

Tuck shoved away from Rafe and jumped up.

Rafe groaned. Things had been going so well, too. In another moment he'd have asked her to marry him. Served him right for teasing her. He stood and peered up the hill.

Willie Van Schultz was making his way down the brushy path. "Well, I'll be. You two don't have any sense at all. Can't you see a storm's on the way?"

Rafe glanced up at the sky. Why hadn't he noticed the heavy gray clouds? "Looks like we're in for some snow."

"A lot of it, from the look of that sky. The way the wind's blowing, it may turn into a blizzard, too." He eyed them and their rifles. "Don't reckon you rode your horses. Come on. My cabin's just over the hill. I'll take you home."

Tuck mumbled something about not realizing his cabin was that close. Rafe sent her a worried look. Her face was ashen.

After they'd extinguished the fire, Tuck followed Willie up the hill with Rafe trailing behind. Ever since Willie had shown up, she'd avoided Rafe's eyes and hadn't spoken a word directly to him.

He had to find a way to talk with her privately. She had no idea that he'd been teasing her, and from the conversation they'd had, she must think he was in love with Carrie Sue and planned to marry her. Now how was he going to get out of this crazy situation?

Chapter 20

Mr. Willie, usually quiet, sang Christmas carols nearly all the way. After church last Sunday, Ma had invited him, along with Tom and Squeezebox, to share their Christmas dinner, since none of the old-sters had family nearby. This had become a tradition the last few years, and Mr. Willie looked forward to it. Tuck was relieved she didn't have to talk.

For some reason, Rafe had lost the good mood he'd been in earlier. Probably wishing he was with Carrie Sue instead of Tuck and Mr. Willie.

Sleet began to fall as Mr. Willie turned off the river road and headed toward the Sulllivan farm. "I reckon this here is one of the nicest pieces of land in the county. Yore pa's done a right good job of improving it, too."

Tuck forced a smile on her numb lips. She'd been strangely numb since Rafe had dropped his news on her. Of course, he couldn't know how it affected her. To Rafe, she was a pal, nothing more.

When they stopped at her front steps, she jumped out and waved at them both. Rafe gave her a strangely desperate look as Mr. Willie drove away. Tuck slunk inside, wishing there was some way to avoid the family. They'd know something was wrong, and she'd have to tell them. Their sympathy would make the pain worse.

The house was silent. A note from Addy lay on the kitchen table stating that Pa was driving her and Ma to town to get some more baking supplies. Tuck breathed a sigh of relief and went to her bedroom.

She threw a log on the smoldering fire and dropped into one of the rocking chairs. How could she have been so foolish? She'd wasted months running after a no-good man, and in the process, she'd lost Rafe, her best friend, and she now admitted to herself, much more than a friend. If there was such a thing as soul mates, she and Rafe fit the picture.

She must have misunderstood when she thought he'd told Pa he loved her. He couldn't have fallen out of love with her and in love with someone else that quickly. But even so, the old camaraderie was still there. Being with Rafe today had been like coming home. That was until he told her he was going to wed Carrie Sue. A surge of pain shot through her, and she jumped up and paced the floor, finally stopping at the wardrobe that held the new dresses.

Her blue gown hung next to Addy's rose-colored one. She brushed a finger across the delicate lace on the scooped collar. Would Rafe think it was pretty? He probably wouldn't even notice. He'd be too busy looking at Carrie.

She spun around and paced to the window then back. A picture of Carrie floating across the dance floor in Rafe's arms assaulted her imagination. A sob tore at her throat. She hated Carrie. She wished she'd die. Tuck groaned. She fell into her chair and let the tears flow.

God, I'm so sorry. I don't really hate her. It just hurts so much. Help me to bear it.

The door opened and closed, and then Addy's soft hand brushed Tuck's hair back. "Abby, what's wrong?"

Oh no. She hadn't heard the wagon drive up. But it was Addy, and Addy always made everything better.

Tuck flung herself around and into her sister's arms. "Rafe's going to marry Carrie Sue."

"What? No, he isn't," Addy said. She drew back and lifted Tuck's chin. "Where did you get an idea like that?"

"He told me so himself. It's true. I've lost him, and it's all my fault." She broke out in a fresh barrage of tears.

"What? But Tuck, it can't be true." Addy held Tuck and patted her while she continued to cry.

"Why can't it be true?" Tuck sat up and fisted her eyes, gulping back tears. "People fall in love every day and get married. Why shouldn't Rafe?"

"Of course Rafe should get married. But not to Carrie Sue." Confusion crossed her face, and bewilderment filled her voice.

"Why not to Carrie Sue? She doesn't exactly look like a horse, you know."

Addy pulled back and stared at her. "No, but—"

Tuck should do something for Carrie. She gasped. Was that thought from God? It must be. But could she bring herself to do anything for Carrie Sue? Maybe not, but she could do it for Rafe. Yes, she'd do it for Rafe. Then no one would know her heart was breaking.

"Addy, I'm going to ask Carrie what I can do to help her plan the wedding. I can do that much for Rafe. If I'm a friend to Carrie Sue, maybe she at least won't make him hate me." She choked back a sob. "Maybe I can even see him now and then."

Addy's hands grabbed her shoulders and shook. "Abby, listen to me. It's not true. I saw Carrie at the store today, and she was prattling along all excited about the dance. She's going with Frank Cade."

"Huh?" She tried to make sense of her sister's words.

"Yes. She said Rafe is obviously head over heels in love with you. Then she said if you have any sense, you'll grab him before he finds out what you're really like." Addy paused and, obviously realizing she shouldn't have revealed that, blushed a bright pink. "I told her that wasn't very nice, and she just laughed and said she doesn't care a bit and intends to get on with her life."

"But. . ." Tuck let her mind wander back over her conversation with Rafe while they sat by the bonfire. What exactly had he said? He said Carrie was nice. Then he agreed that she was pretty. Then when Tuck said she'd make a good wife, he said he was sure she would. Then Tuck had asked when they. . .no, when he was getting married. And he said—

She gasped. A smile tried to peek out from her tear-ravaged face. Joy and anger battled.

"That dirty dog! I'm going to kill him."

"Now, calm down, Abby. You know Rafe can't resist a good joke. And you've really raked him over the coals these last few months because of your infatuation with Sam."

"Well, that's not my fault!" She stopped. Of course it was her fault. "Oh, I don't care. He flat deceived me, and he did it on purpose. And here I've been bawling like a three-year-old. You just wait until I see him."

❦

The ax blade whizzed the air and hit the short log, splitting it down the middle. Rafe kicked the two halves aside and grabbed another log. Splitting wood was the best thing he knew to get rid of a case of nerves. And he had a bad one.

The sleet had changed to snow, and wind howled and beat against the house and against Rafe. It promised to be a bad storm, so even with the woodpile stacked high, the storm gave him an excuse.

He'd had no chance to explain to Tuck that he'd been teasing her about Carrie. Rafe had suggested that Mr. Willie take him and Tuck to his house and he'd drive her home, but Tuck had said no, she'd rather be dropped off first. If he could talk to her and get the Carrie Sue thing straightened out, all would be fine. He was 99 percent sure Tuck would accept his proposal and they could set a wedding date.

He figured after that everything would sort of work itself out. Pa'd already promised to deed enough land to him for a house and a little acreage. They'd need room for a garden and space for kids to run and play. Hope rose in him as his thoughts progressed.

He propped the ax upright on the ground and grinned, hardly noticing the flakes that pummeled him from all sides. He'd bet his and Tuck's kids would be a sight. He hoped they all had shocks of wild blond hair like Tuck. He picked up the ax and swung. Of course, he'd have to wait until after the winter to build, but they could live here with Ma and Pa until then. Tuck was already like one of their own.

Yep, he had it all figured out. The only problem was he couldn't leave the farm. Pa was down with flu, and Rafe had to take care of all the night chores as well as preparing the house and animals for a possible blizzard. The milking and feeding were already done, but by the time supper was over, it would be too late to go calling on anyone, even if the storm slacked up.

In the meantime, with Tuck thinking he was going to marry Carrie Sue, there was no telling what could go wrong. He'd just have to get over there first thing in the morning if the storm had died down and the snow wasn't too deep. Tuck'd be madder than an old wet hen when she found out he'd been teasing her, but she'd calm down after a bit. Just so she didn't run into Carrie Sue or one of her friends before Rafe could talk to her.

"Rafe!" He turned at his ma's call. She stood in the doorway, a shawl pulled tightly around her head and shoulders, her apron flapping in the wind. "You're scattering wood all over the yard. You'd best get it picked up and stacked on the woodpile before the snowstorm gets any worse. Supper'll be ready by the time you get it done."

"All right, Ma. I can taste those beans and fried potatoes now." He flashed her a smile.

At his words, her face brightened. "I've got biscuits in the oven, too. Your pa had a hankering for them." She smiled and slipped back inside.

Rafe's stomach rumbled. Some folks liked corn bread best, but Rafe didn't think anything was better with pinto beans than hot buttered biscuits. The tantalizing smell of beans simmering and potatoes frying in the old iron skillet lingered even with the door closed.

He wondered if Tuck made good biscuits. He was pretty sure she did. After all, Lexie was one of the best cooks around Branson, and she would have taught the girls.

His thoughts went to Addy. How would she feel about Tuck getting married and leaving home? For that matter, how would Tuck handle being away from her twin? They'd never been apart. Not even for one whole day and night. Rafe frowned. Well, if they got to missing each other too much, Addy could come live with her sister and him.

He chuckled as he placed the fresh split wood on the woodpile. He already had their lives worked out, and Tuck still thought he was marrying Carrie Sue.

After supper, Rafe looked in on his pa. He was sitting up in bed drinking a cup of coffee. Pa didn't drink much of the bitter liquid, but he had to have his hot, black coffee at breakfast and another right after the supper meal.

"Got the cows in the barn, son?" Pa wasn't used to being still, and Rafe had a feeling Ma wouldn't be able to keep him down for long.

"Yes, sir. Milking's done, all the stock's fed, and the chickens are shut up in the shed."

Pa nodded. "Good. Sorry you had it all to do by yourself."

Rafe shrugged. "No problem. How are you feeling?"

"Fit as a fiddle. I'll be up and about tomorrow." He peered at Rafe. "You got something on your mind, son?"

Rafe grinned. "I was wondering, as soon as you're up to it, if we could go check out my land. I thought maybe you could help me decide on the best spot for a house and barn."

"I reckon so. Any special reason you're in such a hurry?"

Rafe nodded. "I plan to ask Tuck to marry me."

"Is that right? Well that don't surprise me. I've always sort of expected it. Then that doctor showed up." He shook his head. "Guess she's over that."

"She was only infatuated. Nothing serious. Maybe it took something like that to wake me up to my true feelings," Rafe said. "You think it'll be all right for Tuck and me to move in here until I get a house built next spring?"

"Fine with me. But your ma's going to have a fit if you don't give her time to fix things up for your bride." He grinned. "You seem pretty all-fired sure Tuck's going to say yes."

Rafe stared at his pa. His mouth went dry and he licked his lips. Pa was right. He'd been living in a dream world for the past few hours, making all these plans, never once thinking Tuck might say no. And even if she said yes, she'd want time to make plans.

His expectancy deflated. What had he been thinking? He hadn't even asked to court her yet. He'd just taken it for granted because she acted a little jealous that she felt the same way he did. Maybe she was jealous because she didn't want to share his friendship. Carrie Sue's thinking Tuck was in love with him didn't make it so. Neither did his own wishful thinking.

He sighed. Maybe he'd better hold off on his plans for a while. He'd feel an awful fool if she laughed in his face.

Chapter 21

A bby, the dough is kneaded more than enough."

Tuck frowned at her sister and pounded her fist into the pillowy mass twice more. "Fine. You finish."

"Abby, come back here."

Ignoring Addy's imploring voice, Tuck headed to the parlor and looked out the window again. Would it ever stop? Drifts piled up high on the porch, and a vast carpet of snow stretched out as far as her eye could see. Four days of almost continuous snow was bad enough, but the howling wind made it impossible to even think clearly.

Pa made the arduous trip to the barn twice a day to tend to the animals, and Ma paced the floor each time until he was safely back inside. Tuck had pleaded with him to let her help, but he wouldn't hear of it.

At least the enforced confinement had calmed her temper down. She wasn't sure what kind of scene she'd have thrown if she'd seen Rafe anytime soon after hearing about his little joke on her. She still inwardly seethed over it, but at least she didn't want to tear his hair out by the roots.

She'd made Addy repeat Carrie Sue's words over and over until she had them memorized. If the girl was correct and Rafe truly was in love with Tuck, then he may have been trying to find out her feelings for him, and she could easily forgive him. Although, she might let him suffer a little bit, as he deserved. But—and this was very possible—if Carrie was mistaken, then Rafe had just been making mischief. Tuck would have to be careful. Otherwise, she could make a fool of herself and perhaps ruin their friendship, and she didn't think she could bear that.

She sighed. If only the snow would let up soon. Otherwise, the Christmas dance would be canceled, and there would go her dreams. Dreams of dancing, lightly and romantically, across the dance floor, in Rafe's arms, her dress billowing like a cloud and his eyes staring into hers adoringly.

She gave a chuckle. This confinement must be doing things to her mind. She returned to the kitchen to see Addy making loaves and placing them in the pans to rise again. They needed to get them all baked before Ma woke up from her nap. Otherwise she'd insist on doing it herself, and she tired so easily nowadays.

Addy gave her a sideways glance, and Tuck grinned. "Sorry. Guess I'm a little fidgety."

"I'll say," Addy said. "I don't blame you though. I'm getting cabin fever myself."

"I hope we won't have a bad winter. I don't think I could stand months of this." They'd had winters they'd been cooped up for weeks on end, with maybe a day here or there when they could escape the confines of the house.

"Remember the year we were snowed in with Great-Aunt Kate for a whole week?" Addy rolled her eyes and made a face.

Tuck chuckled. They'd been nine at the time and still getting used to being part of the Sullivan and Rayton families. "How could I forget? Uncle Will threatened to tan our hides, and Ma told him if there was any hide tanning to be done Papa Jack was more than capable of doing it."

"Yes, then Aunt Sarah got all over Ma for daring to be so mean." Addy giggled. "Those two boys of theirs are worse than we ever were."

"Hmm. I'm not sure of that. We were pretty ornery."

Addy nodded. "So, what would you rather have? A little sister or brother?"

"I'm not sure if it matters. All babies look like little toads for the first few months anyway." At least all of them she'd ever seen.

"Abby. That's terrible." Addy's mouth twisted, and a laugh exploded from her mouth. "They do look funny at first. But they're sweet. I plan to have at least three someday."

"You do?" She'd never thought of Addy as a mother. She picked up the dishrag and started wiping the table down.

"Of course. Don't you?" Addy raised an eyebrow in her direction. She opened the oven door and placed a pan of bread inside, then reached for another.

Tuck stood and stared at her sister. "I've never thought about it."

"Really? I think about it all the time." She wiped her hands on her apron. "Do you think four loaves will be enough?"

"Huh? Oh. Yes." She eyed her sister. "Who do you think of as the father?"

"Well, when we were in eighth grade, I used to think about marrying Joe Smith, but then he moved away. Since then, no one. I just think about my children." She gazed at Tuck. "You should think about it, Abby."

"I don't know if I'd be a good mother."

"Sure you will." Addy grinned. "And Rafe'll be a wonderful father."

Heat washed over Tuck's head and ran all the way down to her toes. "What if I don't marry Rafe?"

Addy's eyes held hers, and she smiled. "You will. You know you will."

She thought she would. Yes, she knew she would. Or was it just wishful thinking?

❦

Rafe dug the long-handled shovel down into the drifted snow and scooped the last of the piled-up snow to the side of the path. The heavy winds had lasted for nearly three days. Snow had fallen steadily for four, finally dwindling down to next to nothing this morning. He'd breathed a sigh of relief and wasted no time clearing a path from the side porch to the barn. He'd been trudging through the cold, wet depths every day to take care of the animals. Pa was up and around now and couldn't wait to get busy again.

Rafe stepped inside and looked around at the contented animals. Must be nice. He chuckled at the ridiculous thought. They'd all been fed earlier and the cows milked. His sight drifted up to the rafters and rested on the pair of sleigh runners. He and Pa had repaired and oiled them at the end of winter last year. They never knew when they'd have to use them to get around. Either that or wait until the snow melted to get needed supplies.

However, Rafe had another purpose in mind. He'd removed the buggy wheels a couple of days ago. Now all he'd have to do is attach the runners. He climbed up in the loft and reached for the sharp runners, lifting them down carefully, one by one.

He had them fitted on the buggy, when the door opened and Pa stepped in, bundled up from head to feet. Ma's doing, more than likely. "I figured that's what you were up to out here," Pa cackled, his voice still a little hoarse. "So this is the big day I take it?"

Rafe nodded. "If I can get Tuck to go with me for a ride, I intend to ask her, Pa."

Pa squeezed Rafe's shoulder. "God go with you, son. I'll be praying. If Tuck loves you, she'll say yes."

Rafe swallowed past the lump that had suddenly formed. "And if she doesn't?"

"Then it's best you find out now, so you can quit pining and wait for the right one." He turned. "You'd best get some blankets to take along. Don't want the girl to freeze while you're popping the question."

"No, that wouldn't be good." Rafe laughed then sobered. "Thank you for your prayers, Pa. I don't know if I've ever told you, but knowing you and Ma pray for me has always given me comfort."

"You haven't told me, but I knew. I had a praying ma myself. No telling where I'd be today if it wasn't for her prayers." He reached a hand up and wiped at his eyes. "Guess I got something in my eye."

Soon Rafe was gliding across the rolling farmland. His mouth was dry and his face numb. From the cold? Or the uncertainty of what was to come?

He stopped the horses alongside the front porch, and before he was out of the transformed buggy, the door was flung open and Jack stepped outside, holding the door open for him. Good sign. At least Jack was still friendly.

A moment later, he stood in the parlor greeting Lexie and the girls. Addy grinned and said hello.

After looking at everything in the room but him, Tuck finally looked him in the eye. "Hi, Rafe."

"Abigail, why don't you get Rafe something hot to drink? He looks half frozen." Lexie sat in a rocker with a blanket over her lap. She pursed her lips and smiled.

"No thank you, ma'am. I don't want anything to drink. I really came to see if Tuck wants to go for a sleigh ride."

"Oh, but it's terribly cold out there." Lexie frowned and glanced at Tuck.

"I didn't get cold at all, ma'am. There are plenty of blankets, and Ma sent hot water bottles for our feet. . ." He darted a glance at Tuck. "That is, if she wants to."

Her eyes widened as she stared at him. Then she jumped up. "I'd like to go for a sleigh ride. That is, if you won't worry, Ma. I'll be fine."

Lexie reluctantly agreed, and soon Rafe drove down the lane, with Tuck swaddled in coats and blankets and her small feet placed on the hot water bottles.

"Thanks for coming with me, Tuck. I really need to talk to you about something." How to begin?

"Uh-huh. It wouldn't by any chance have something to do with Carrie Sue, would it?"

"Err. . .sort of. That is. . .I was teasing about her." He cleared his throat. "She's a nice girl, but not for me."

"Yes, so I discovered." She turned and glared at him.

His stomach roiled. She knew. How? Who could have gotten to her in this weather and blabbed before he had a chance to talk to her? "I'm sorry, Tuck. I don't know what got into me." Pure orneriness? And a little bit of revenge?

"I felt like a fool when I found out the truth. I was going to offer to help her plan the wedding." Her teeth chattered. "What if I had? It's a good thing Addy saw her in town that day."

"You were going to help her plan the wedding? When you thought she was marrying me?"

"It was all I could think of to do for you, Rafe." Her face was like stone. "For all I knew, Carrie wouldn't want us to be friends anymore. I thought if I became her friend, too, she wouldn't mind."

His heart sank. "So you want things to go on like they've always been between us?"

She turned her head and looked away. Her breath rose and fell in gasps.

"Tuck? Is that what you want?"

"It's what you want, isn't it?" The sob in her voice was unmistakable.

Why couldn't he breathe? He took a deep, slow breath. "Look at me, Tuck."

She shook her head, and her shoulders shook.

He put his hand on her shoulder and turned her around. Her eyes swam with tears, and he took one finger and wiped them away. "No." He could barely get the words out. "It's not what I want."

The hope in her eyes met the hope in his heart. "What do you want, Rafe?" she whispered.

"I want you to be my wife," he croaked out.

She let out a *whoosh* of air and glared. "Just like that? I don't get to be courted first? Even Carrie gets to be courted. You almost courted her yourself."

"Tuck, calm down. Of course I'll come courting. We can't possibly get married before spring anyways. Our mas wouldn't hear of it. Do you always have to argue about everything?"

She turned her face up and looked him full in the face, her eyes dancing with mischief. "Not always."

His breath caught, and then he laughed. "I'm so glad."

He lowered his head and met her waiting lips.

Epilogue

May 10, 1902

Tuck stood in the small Sunday school room at the front of the church. Ma adjusted Tuck's lacy veil and tucked in a straying lock of hair. A baby cried in the sanctuary. Ma smiled and kissed Tuck on the cheek. "I love you, Abigail."

Tuck grinned. "I love you, too, Ma, but I think you'd better go take care of my baby sister."

Ma laughed, a bubbling, joy-filled laugh, and headed for the door. "I think you're right. Princess Elizabeth calls."

Finally, Tuck was alone with Addy, whose face was joyful and forlorn all at once.

The piano signaled it was time for Addy to precede Tuck down the aisle. Addy smiled. "That's for me. The next time we speak, you'll be Mrs. Rafe Collins."

Tuck leaned forward and gave her a hug, then turned her around. She slipped a gold chain around Addy's neck and fastened the clasp, letting the locket drop down across the bodice of her soft blue dress. "This is yours, sis. It's always been yours. I just borrowed it for a while."

Addy gasped and clutched the locket. "Oh, Abby. Are you sure?"

"Very sure. Remember? We agreed. Grandfather's violin was mine and mother's locket was yours. I've always loved my fiddle more."

"But it's the only picture we have of our mother."

"I can still see it, silly. We'll always be close together."

A moment later, her twin stepped from the room and walked down the aisle.

Mrs. Jenkins struck a chord. Tuck breathed deeply then stepped out and took Papa Jack's arm.

Her heart raced as she took the first step then calmed as she focused on Rafe standing next to Jim, his best man. As she walked toward him, he smiled and his eyes adored her, just as they did in the dream. They weren't dancing this time, but she wore a beautiful dress that billowed like a cloud.

Papa Jack kissed her cheek and placed her hand in Rafe's, then went to sit down.

"Dearly beloved, we are gathered together, to join this man and this woman in holy matrimony. . ."

Tuck turned to Rafe and found his waiting eyes filled with love. Her Rafe. Her darling best friend.

White River Sunrise

Dedication

I dedicate this book to Eldon and Angie Shivers who helped me find my love for Silver Dollar City. Thank you for taking me there at Christmastime and for all the fun times thereafter. To Torey Shivers, another SDC buddy, thanks for sharing your family fun days with me. And to all of you who love not only Silver Dollar City, but the scenery, the atmosphere, and the soul of the area, I hope I've captured just a tiny bit of the wonder of it all. May God bless you with many more years of enjoyment at Silver Dollar City.

Prologue

S he stood on the bottom step of the train for a moment and looked at the old depot. Nostalgia rushed over her. Hard to believe it had been fifty-five years since the first train had pulled into this station.

Ignoring Paul's hand, Addy stepped down from the train unassisted onto Branson's busy platform. Her grandson had offered to fly her here, but at seventy-nine, she didn't welcome new adventures. Her stomach jumped. Except for this one. This was one adventure she would not miss.

Paul's hand cupped her elbow. "Grams, they're waiting."

A long, black limousine stood at the curb. Tomas, his salt-and-pepper hair slicked back, stood by the door attempting to hide a grin.

Why everyone thought it was amusing for her to be here was beyond her comprehension.

"Hello, Tomas. How is your arthritis these days?" There. That should take him down a peg or two.

Instead his grin widened. "I think it's some better, ma'am." He opened the door with a flourish, and she slid onto the deep leather seat.

She tried not to gawk as the car slid smoothly and noiselessly down the street, past building after unfamiliar building. Was nothing the same? Her heart fluttered at the sign that said Mercantile. She shook her head at her foolishness. Of course it wasn't the same one. Why had she imagined it would be?

They stopped at a light, and Addy stared at a building under construction. A sign said Skaggs Hospital. "I thought Skaggs Hospital had been here awhile."

"Yes, ma'am." Tomas's hat bobbed. "They're adding on to it. Going to be a fine medical facility when it's all done."

"Are we going to the hotel first?" She had freshened up on the train and was eager to see the downtown area.

"No, ma'am. Not enough time," Tomas said. "They told me to bring you right on over. They don't want you to miss the grand opening."

She pushed down a tinge of disappointment. She hadn't been back since her beloved sister Abby passed away back in '51. The familiar tug of grief tightened her chest, and she took a deep breath. Abby wouldn't want her to be sad today.

Even in the fifties, there had been changes. A lot of them. Ah well, she could see the town later. And maybe visit the old farm.

Addy perked up as they turned onto a familiar dirt road. The way to Marble Cave. Or Marvel Cave as they called it now. Excitement stabbed at her. Of course she couldn't miss the opening. A new craft park. But more than a park. Or so they'd told her. Built on the land where the old mining town of Marmoros used to stand, just above Marble Cave. And her husband would be waiting to escort her through the frontier-style town. Silver Dollar City they called it, although she had no idea why. She chuckled. There was about as much chance of finding silver here as there'd been of finding marble in the cave. Still, it was a nice name.

"What's so funny, Grams?" Paul smiled and laid his hand on hers.

Her heart squeezed. She loved this boy so much. Just twenty. Youngest son of her eldest son, Jack, who they'd named after her pa. That is, her second pa. How sad she seldom thought of the first one. "I was thinking how some things change so much and others are always the same."

"Look. There's Grandpa and Dad and Uncle Rafe." He leaned forward, eager as always to join the men of the family. "Oh, Great-Aunt Betty's standing right behind them."

She squinted against the brightness of the sun until she made out the form of her husband. The car pulled up in front of the big wooden gate. He stepped forward and opened the door. They reached for each other at the same moment, and their hands touched. His eyes crinkled, and creases deepened in his wrinkled face. Wrinkled, but still handsome after all these years.

As she stepped out of the car, he leaned over and brushed a kiss across her lips. He whispered in her ear, "You're going to love it, sweetheart. And I have a surprise for you."

A jolt of excitement thrilled her. Her darling knew how she loved surprises.

Betty shoved her way in and threw her arms around Addy. "I'm so glad you're here, sister. It's been too long."

Addy laughed. Her younger sister had just visited them at Christmas. "Yes, it has been. And I'm glad I'm here, too."

Her husband placed a protective arm around her shoulders and guided her toward the gate.

"Hello, Mom." Jack planted a kiss on her cheek and smiled. "How was your train ride?"

"Fun. It was fun." She grinned. "I still love trains."

"Hi, Addy."

Tears filled her eyes as she hugged her brother-in-law, Rafe. The sight of him brought back a vision of her twin sister.

"Tuck would have loved this," he said.

Addy nodded and turned away. Rafe was right. Abby should be walking by her side, her head thrown back in joyous laughter. The thought was almost more than Addy could bear.

She glanced around. Oak trees stood on all sides, just like they had when Marmoros still stood. Addy could almost imagine the charred smell of the burned-out town. But of course, that was silly. She shivered, and her husband pulled her closer as they walked through the gate.

Chapter 1

Branson Town, May 1905

Sam Thornton! I see you back there. Turn loose of Amanda's hair right now." Addy Sullivan frowned at the nine-year-old culprit who dropped the braid and tried to look innocent. Another few seconds and the blond strands would have been saturated with ink.

Amanda's screech reverberated through the room, piercing Addy's temples. The girl glared at Sam. "You leave me alone."

"Aw, I wasn't really gonna do it." Sam's face flamed as giggles and guffaws burst out across the room.

"Children, that's enough." Addy walked to Amanda's desk and examined the long, neat braid just to make sure damage hadn't already been done. She patted the girl on the shoulder and then returned to her own desk.

Lifting the small filigreed watch that hung from a black ribbon around her neck, she breathed a sigh of relief. Ten more minutes and it would be time to ring the bell. "Children, make sure you have copied all the homework assignments that are on the blackboard. And don't forget, your essays are due on Monday."

A corporate groan rolled across the room, and Addy hid a smile. Smug expressions on several faces revealed the ones who had not procrastinated. The others would have to scurry to get them done over the weekend.

A memory popped into her mind, the picture of her sister Abby, her face pale, hand stretched out, waiting for a ruler to descend. The sound of the ruler slapping against her sister's tender palm remained with Addy to this day. After that incident, Addy had always made sure her sister's assignments were on time, even if she had to do them herself.

"On second thought, I'm going to extend the date to Wednesday. I expect every essay to be complete at that time."

Probably not fair to the ones who'd done their work on schedule and maybe it sent the wrong message to those who hadn't. She took a deep breath. Everyone needed a little mercy now and then.

She rang the bell, and the students filed quietly out. Seconds later, hoots of joy sailed back through the door. Addy grinned as she straightened the room and gathered her things together. She couldn't say she loved teaching, but the children made her heart sing when they weren't making her head pound. She locked the door behind her and went outside.

Twelve-year-old Bobby had just arrived from the livery stable with her horse and buggy. He petted the dappled mare, a gift from Rafe and Abby when she'd started teaching.

"Thank you, Bobby." She took the reins and gave him a coin.

"It warn't nothin', Miss Addy." He tossed the coin up and caught it then headed back toward the livery.

Addy bit her lip as Bobby walked away. He'd been faithful and eager to attend school last year and made wonderful progress but hadn't come back when school started. The child had to help his mother keep food on the table. Everyone knew his father had deserted the family over the summer. She blinked back angry tears. How could anyone walk out on a family?

Longing washed over her. She'd been lonely when Abby got married and left home. A part of her was missing, and she had no idea what to do about it.

Ma, sensing her discontent, had suggested she get her teaching certificate and be ready to accept a teaching position when one came available. This past year she'd been fairly content. But lately, whenever her eyes would rest on Abby's twin toddler boys, David and Dawson, the old empty feeling returned.

The sound of footsteps drew her attention. A tall man walked briskly toward the schoolyard from the direction of the stable. A lock of dark hair fell across his forehead, and gold-flecked brown eyes sparkled when his glance fell upon her. He stopped a few steps before he reached her and gave her a slow smile.

She gasped, then with a toss of her head, turned her back on him and climbed into her buggy. When she looked up, he gave her a puzzled look, tipped his hat, and walked away toward the new Branson Hotel.

Her heart pounded as she urged her horse toward home. The very idea. What impudence from a total stranger. If she hadn't turned away, he would doubtless have spoken to her. She really should talk to the school board about fencing the schoolyard, so people wouldn't use it as a shortcut to the main part of town.

But the man's handsome face—and there was no denying he was handsome—remained with her as she turned onto the lane leading to the Sullivan farm. A niggling worry pinched at her. Now that she thought about it, that face seemed rather familiar. Oh dear, what if he was one of Papa's acquaintances? Or perhaps he was connected with the new school board in some way. Now that Branson had an official school district, things weren't as casual as they had been when she was hired for the teaching position. She racked her brain for a clue to his identity. She must be mistaken. There were so many new men in town connected with the railroad. She'd probably seen him around town. That must be it.

She drove to the barn, and after she'd unhitched the horse, she went to the house. The smell of fried chicken permeated the air. Her stomach growled in anticipation as she headed to the kitchen.

"Addy, Addy." Her three-year-old sister grabbed her around the legs and hugged.

She bent down and kissed the plump cheek.

Betty's blue eyes twinkled, and she whispered, "Mama made fried chicken."

"Oh I know. My tummy is rumbling just from the smell." She grinned. She'd enjoyed that fried chicken since Ma Lexie and Papa Jack had adopted her and Abby when they were eight years old.

Betty giggled and skipped off.

Ma was placing a pan of biscuits in the oven. She straightened and turned. "Addy, you're home. How was your day?"

"Tiring. How was yours, Ma?" She gave Ma a kiss on the cheek. "I'll go change and set the table."

"All right. Don't forget to set extras. Abigail and Rafe and the twins are coming for supper, remember?" A dreamy look crossed her face, as it always did when she spoke of her grandsons.

Addy could understand that. Every time she saw her little nephews she wanted to squeeze them tightly.

"Oh by the way, did you happen to run into Jim Castle today? He's back in town, you know."

Addy stopped short on her way to her room. Her mouth flew open. Jim Castle? No wonder he'd looked familiar. He must either think she was a total idiot or very ill mannered. Embarrassment washed over her. How could she not have recognized her brother-in-law's good friend and best man?

<hr/>

Addy Sullivan! Still as beautiful as ever, and no ring that Jim could see. Of course, he could have missed it, during the short minute before she turned her back on him. He could kick himself for gawking. No wonder she took off so fast. Still, he'd have thought she'd at least have said hello. After all, he and Rafe were good friends.

He sat in the conference room of the Branson Hotel and let his thoughts wander as Charles Fullbright, the representative for Branson Town Company, discussed the benefits of the new hotel with potential future businessmen.

Tourism in the area was already starting to flourish, with Marble Cave and the float trips every summer. Now with plans for the Maine Exhibition Building from the World's Fair to be moved here and reconstructed as a hunting and fishing lodge, adventure-seeking men would flock to the area. And this new luxury hotel would draw their families.

Jim predicted that once the White River Line began passenger service next month, tourism would triple. He calculated Fullbright would need his services here in Branson Town for at least a year. Twelve months to get better acquainted with a certain blond beauty. Maybe he could finagle a meeting at Rafe's house.

He grinned. As much as the girls looked alike, when he'd first seen them that day at Marble Cave more than three years ago, he'd been instantly drawn to Addy rather than her outgoing twin. But for some reason, he and Rafe had gotten their wires crossed, Jim thinking Rafe was in love with Addy while Rafe thought Jim was interested in Abby. When they'd finally figured it out, they both felt foolish but mostly relieved that they wouldn't be competing for the same girl's affections.

Well, Rafe got his girl. They'd been happily married for three years and were the proud parents of eighteen-month-old boys. Jim heaved a deep breath. Rafe was a local farmer and doing well. He'd built a home on land his pa had given him. Steady and reliable, that was Rafe.

Jim, on the other hand, was never in one place for long. How could he ask a woman to share his life? What woman in her right mind would agree to travel all over the country? Not Addy, he was sure, as close as she was to her twin. Not even if, by some miracle, she fell in love with him.

A burst of laughter invaded his thoughts, and one of the prospective hunting lodge owners boomed out. "At least we don't have to do business in a town called Lucia."

One of his partners laughed. "I would never have opened a hunting lodge in Lucia."

Fullbright smiled. "Well then, men, it's a good thing that Branson Town Company managed to purchase the Lucia post office and land and choose the name we preferred for the town."

"And what the people of the area preferred from what I hear," another booming voice input.

Irritation bit at Jim. "That's right, they did. But the original owner was a good man. I'm sure he had his reasons for choosing the name of Lucia and for not wanting to sell. After his death, his sons honored his wishes as long as they could."

The room quieted, and some of the men threw curious looks his way.

"Well, gentlemen"—Fullbright stood—"I believe we've covered everything on the agenda for the present. Castle and I will be available for consultation if any problems or concerns should occur to you."

The men filed out, leaving Jim and Charles Fullbright in the room. Fullbright peered at him through narrowed eyes. "What was that all about?'

Jim shrugged. "Nothing really. Thomas Berry was a veteran and a good man. He and his entire family were hard workers. I guess I'd just like him remembered that way."

"So you knew him personally?" Fullbright peered at him, his eyes scanning his face.

"No, but his neighbors thought a lot of him. They got a little edgy when he balked about selling the post office to the railroad, but they didn't seem to lose their respect for the man. I guess they figured he had a right to do what he liked with his own property." Jim put his hat on and nodded. "Guess I'll be on my way if you don't need me."

"No, no, that's fine. But Castle, don't be riling up these businessmen. We plan to start selling off lots to the locals for businesses in the next few months. That's how Branson Town will be built up, you know."

"I know. I'll keep that in mind. Don't worry, I won't upset the applecart." He nodded again and left then stood outside the hotel.

A boardwalk lined the dusty street. Not much, but an improvement over three years ago. Two saloons stood opposite each other as though squaring off for a duel. And a small hotel stood around the corner, overrun with the railroad workers who had been pouring in. Plenty of business for both hotels. And as more and more workers filled the town, it wouldn't be long before the Branson Hotel would be full as well, even though its prices were higher.

He envisioned a town with respectable businesses lining the street. Businesses that could service not only the tourists that flocked to see the sights but also the many families moving to the area. Cafés, barber shops, maybe a ladies' boutique or two, and a hardware store.

He shook his head. Why should it matter to him what sort of town grew from this small beginning? Rafe and Abby mattered of course, but as long as the tourism drew people, there would be revenue for the railroad, and it would also benefit the locals. It always did.

A vision of Addy's thick blond curls hit him like a locomotive. She'd marry and have a family some day. Who would the lucky man be? For a moment he entertained a picture of Addy by his side as they walked hand in hand down a street of neat businesses and homes with picket fences encasing neat lawns and shrubs standing like sentinels in front of wide porches.

Realizing he'd been holding his breath, he let it out with a loud *whoosh*. He had to stop this foolish daydreaming. He was behaving like some lovestruck girl instead of a man with a purpose in life.

Chapter 2

Perspiration poured down Reverend Smith's face as he pounded the pulpit. A giggle, followed by a sharp slap, resounded from somewhere off to the side of the building.

Addy winced. Why couldn't people correct their children in private? She sighed. At least they had children to correct.

No, she wouldn't go there. Most of the eligible bachelors had been snapped up, and she'd turned several of them down anyway, including Reverend Smith, who'd married Carrie Sue Anderson six months later. But that was fine with Addy. None of them had moved her heart, and she wasn't about to marry unless she was in love. And with a man who loved her, too.

A picture of deep-brown eyes and dark, wavy hair crossed her mind, and she drew in a sharp breath. She darted a glance around to see if anyone had heard. Now why had she thought of Jim Castle? Especially in the house of God. Drawing herself up, she focused on the preacher, who now spoke calmly about accepting God's will for one's life and avoiding the temptation to do things one's own way.

Lord, are You telling me it's not Your will for me to marry? I want Your will for my life more than I want anything else, but— A pang of guilt shot through her. If it really was God's will for her to remain single, there could be no "buts."

A few minutes later, the reverend closed in prayer, and one of the deacons led the congregation in a final song.

Addy headed for the door, and after she shook hands with Reverend Smith and Carrie Sue, she glanced around for Ma and Pa. She spotted Abby motioning from her and Rafe's wagon and walked over.

"Addy, come to dinner. I have a humongous pan of fried chicken warming in the oven, and we need someone to help us eat it."

"I don't know. I have papers to grade." She reached over and tickled little Dawson under the chin and was rewarded with a giggle. She'd much rather spend the afternoon with her sister and nephews than grade papers.

Abby waved her hand in the air and grabbed for Dawson, who nearly slid off her lap. "Oh, do it later. I promise we'll get you home early."

"Well, all right. Let me tell Ma and Pa to go on without me."

"I already did. They left five minutes ago." Abby grinned, patting the seat beside her. "C'mon, I'm driving."

Laughing, Addy climbed up next to her then took Dawson onto her lap. "So that's why Rafe and Davy are in the back. You knew I'd have to say yes or walk home."

"Tuck always has a plan," Rafe said with a laugh. He was the only one who still called her sister by the nickname she loved. Short for Kentucky, where they'd lived until they were four. Shortly after their mother died, their pa had moved them to the Ozarks—lock, stock, and barrel as he called it. A few years later, he was gone, too.

Addy shoved the memories away and bounced Dawson on her knees while she and Abby laughed and talked all the way to the Collins' farm.

The first view of her sister's home always took Addy's breath away. The small frame house nestled at the foot of a flower-covered hill. A myriad of red, purple, white, and blue blossoms spread like a giant bouquet from the top of the gentle slope down to the edge of Abby's backyard. A fence peeked out from behind the house. It protected Abby's vegetable garden from critters. A henhouse stood beside the barn. Guineas waddled around freely, occasionally taking off in flight and perching on tree branches. A short distance away, a tiny stream danced over rocks as it rippled its way to the nearby White River. She wondered if the trains from the new railway would interrupt the tranquility that reigned here.

Abby climbed down and came around to take Dawson from Addy's arms. She set him down, and he wobbled over to his brother.

"I love your home." Addy hoped she didn't sound as wistful as she felt.

"Thanks, sis. So do I. Every day I thank God that Rafe's father and mother were generous enough to deed this section of land over to Rafe. A lot of young couples aren't as blessed."

She took little David's tiny hand in hers and helped him toddle along, while Rafe did the same for Dawson.

Addy caught her breath at the tender smile that passed between her sister and brother-in-law. It never ceased to amaze her how her independent, tomboy sister had taken to marriage like a duck on a June bug. Not that she had changed that much. But she'd mellowed. Addy grinned. That was an expression they used when people got older, and Abby most definitely was not old in any way.

She followed them inside and, as soon as she stepped through the door, felt a tug on her skirt. David gazed up at her, a sweet smile on his face, then lifted his arms. Laughing, she picked him up. "All right, Davy boy. You know Auntie Addy will do anything you ask."

The words were hardly out of her mouth before he squirmed to get down. She set him gently on the floor and followed her sister to the large, comfortable kitchen. Wonderful aromas tantalized her senses.

"Let me wash my hands, and I'll set the table for you." She went to the washbasin that sat on a table in the corner. A moment later, she took dishes out of the cupboard and began to place them on the long table.

"Thanks, sis." Abby fluttered around the kitchen, getting things ready. "Oh, set an extra plate. We have another guest coming."

"Who?" Her stomach jumped. She knew exactly who.

Abby threw an innocent look her way. "Do you remember Rafe's friend, Jim Castle?"

"Yes, of course I remember Mr. Castle. He was Rafe's best man, wasn't he?" Oh dear. Had he mentioned to Rafe that she hadn't recognized him when he'd approached her in town? Or worse still, did he think she'd just been flat-out rude?

"There's a horse coming up the lane. That must be him now." Abby grabbed a thick cloth and opened the oven door then pulled out the pan of fried chicken.

A tap on the door was followed by Rafe's voice welcoming his guest.

Addy groaned. How was she going to face him?

Jim lifted a drumstick and bit into its salty, crunchy goodness. His glance drifted across the table where Addy sat staring intently at her plate. He put the chicken leg down and cleared his throat.

She jerked her head up and met his glance then quickly brought a forkful of potatoes to her lips.

Okay, now he'd embarrassed her. He wasn't sure how, but he'd try to rectify it. "Mrs. Collins, I believe this is the best fried chicken I've ever had."

"Thanks, Jim, but why are you calling me Mrs. Collins? Did you all of a sudden forget my first name?"

"Okay then, Abby, I believe this is the best fried chicken I've ever had."

"Thanks, but you should taste Addy's." She sent an amused smile in her sister's direction. Jim wasn't sure what was so amusing, but she was obviously having fun at Addy's expense.

Rafe made a choking sound, and Addy frowned at him then shrugged and smiled at Jim. "They're teasing me, Mr. Castle. No matter how often I try, my fried chicken always ends up burned on the outside or half raw on the inside." She paused, as though for effect. "Sometimes both."

As Rafe and Abby both laughed, admiration for Addy's spunk rose in Jim.

"It's not that bad, sis," Abby said. "And your chocolate cake is the best in the county."

Rafe nodded. "And your catfish is second only to Tuck's."

"Ha. A good thing you said that, Rafe Collins." Abby's smile rested on Rafe, showing affection laced with familiarity.

The lucky cuss. Jim hoped his friend appreciated what he had. He pushed his empty plate aside and leaned back in his chair.

"Don't get too comfortable," Rafe said. "I happen to know there's blackberry cobbler for dessert."

After the meal was finished and Jim and Rafe had been shooed out of the kitchen by Abby, they sat on the front porch.

"I'm really glad to see you back. I've missed our talks." Rafe leaned his hide-bottomed chair back on two legs and stuck a piece of sour dock in his mouth.

Jim chuckled. "Still chewing on that dock I see."

Rafe grinned and shook his head. "Tuck used to try to break me of the habit, but now she says I could be chewing on something a lot worse, like Squeezebox and his tobacco."

"Is the group still together?"

Rafe shook his head. "Mr. Willie passed away last year, and the heart sort of went out of the rest as far as their music goes."

"You mean Abby isn't playing her fiddle anymore? It used to pretty much be the love of her life."

"Oh yes, Tuck still plays for church socials every now and then, and of course we can't have a family get-together without someone begging her for a tune. But Squeezebox Tanner and Tom Black bowed out completely." Rafe winked. "And I'm the love of her life now."

"Sorry to hear about Squeezebox and Tom."

"It's sad. Tuck tries to get Addy to join her on the piano, but she won't play for anyone but family, and not very often." He flashed a grin. "And speaking of Addy, I think our plan may be working."

Jim shook his head. "I don't know, Rafe. She didn't seem to be that interested in seeing me again."

"That's what you think." Rafe chuckled. "Why do you think she was so nervous? It took a little teasing to get her to loosen up."

The door opened, and Addy stepped out. "Rafe, Abby would like for you to help her get the boys down for a nap if you're not busy."

Rafe cut a glance at Jim then back to his sister-in-law. "Sure I will, if you'll stay out here and talk to Jim. Can't leave company alone, now can we?"

Addy bit her bottom lip. "Of course, I'd be happy to keep Mr. Castle company until you get back."

Jim stood as she stepped out onto the porch. When she eased into a rocking chair, perching on the edge of the seat, he sat back down. "Miss Sullivan. . ."

"I'm so. . ."

They both stopped and laughed.

"Please, Miss Sullivan, you first." He was so happy to see a sparkle in her eye that he could have simply sat in silence and watched her.

"I only wished to apologize for not recognizing you the other day." A pink blush washed over her cheeks. "I knew you looked familiar, but I was rather distracted. When it came to me who you were, I was already at home, so I couldn't very well go back and apologize."

"Of course not." Jim leaned forward. "If anyone should apologize, it's I. I should have identified myself. Instead, I startled you. It's no wonder you bolted." He cringed. That probably wasn't the best word to use.

A smile tipped her lips, causing a tiny dimple to flash. "I did rather bolt, didn't I?"

He couldn't keep from grinning. This wasn't going so badly after all. "So now that we've both apologized, could we put the incident behind us and start over?"

"I would like that very much, Mr. Castle."

"So would I. And if it's not too presumptuous of me, do you think you could bring yourself to call me Jim? After all, we've known each other long enough, it seems."

"That's quite true. We met at Rafe and Abby's wedding. Very well, Jim, and since we're such old friends, you may call me Addy."

Her rippling laughter floated on the air like music, and he absorbed it into his heart and memory. Funny she didn't remember they'd met before the wedding.

Chapter 3

"Miss Sullivan, did you hear about the train coming in next week?" The gap between Eugene's two front teeth yawned as he flashed a grin at Addy.

"Yes, I did hear that, Gene." She smiled at the little boy standing beside her desk. "That's exciting, isn't it?"

Within seconds the entire class had crowded around her desk, voices raised in excitement and wonder.

Petite Margaret could barely be seen among the taller children, but her voice rang out loud and clear. "I wish I could ride on it. I think I'll ask my mama to let me."

"Aw, you dumb girl. It's a freight train. You can't ride in it."

"Johnny Carroll, shame on you." Addy frowned at the freckled-faced red-head, who was actually one of her favorites. "You apologize to Margaret right this instant."

He mumbled an apology then stood with his hands in his pockets, waiting to see if he'd get more than a reprimand.

"That's better. Please see that there's no more name calling. Now, please take your seats, children." She turned to the blackboard to finish writing the arithmetic problems. When she faced her students again, everyone was seated, anticipation on each face. She smiled. They knew her too well.

"Before we begin our arithmetic, perhaps we'll have a short discussion of current events." As murmurs began, she held up her hand. "In an orderly fashion, please."

A hand popped up from one of the rear seats, followed by several others. "Yes, Eugene?"

"Pa says the train can't go any farther south 'cause the tracks aren't laid yet."

"That's right, Eugene. The White River Line from the north has reached us, but nothing can go farther south until the teams of workers from both directions meet. Then the line will be complete. Yes, Ronald?"

The boy jumped up, eagerness flushing his face. "They're bringing supplies for the town and the railroad."

"Thank you, Ronald." She motioned to Annie Bolton, a tall girl in the front row. "Annie?"

"It's not just supplies. My pa said they're bringing more railroad men to help finish the tracks." She nodded and sat back down.

More railroad workers? Addy frowned. Most of the men were respectful, but some of the newer employees were of a rougher sort. She hated to contemplate the two saloons with more patrons. Occasionally fights spilled out onto the boardwalks. So far, the ones participating in these brawls had been quickly and speedily escorted to the town's improvised jail. But if the town became overrun?

"Well, thank you, Annie." She gave the girl what she hoped was a bright smile. "More citizens for Branson Town. That's very exciting."

"Not as exciting as the train, though," Eugene said.

Johnny Carroll raised his hand.

"All right, Johnny, you're the last one for the day. We need to get on to our regular subjects."

"I was just wonderin', Miss Sullivan. Do you think we could take the day off school to see the train come in?"

Now that wasn't a bad idea. "Perhaps. I'd have to check with the school board. They might agree if we make it a school project."

A groan resounded across the room.

"You mean we'll have to do a report about it?" The woebegone expression on Johnny's face was so comical Addy had to press her lips together to keep from grinning.

"Yes, but perhaps we'll make it a group report. You can all write down a few things that impress you, and then we'll put them all together." She included the class in her smile.

Annie's hand shot up once more. "Like a story?"

"Exactly. We'll even illustrate it and put it up on the bulletin board for parents' day." As their faces brightened, she hastened to add, "But remember, we have to get permission from the school board first."

One good thing about the formation of the new Branson School District was that it relieved her of certain responsibilities. Such as disappointing her students if the answer was no.

The children were on extra-good behavior the rest of the day, not wanting to risk the possibility of missing the grand, history-making event. Addy didn't blame them. Bolts of excitement charged through her as well.

Of course, to be honest, the near certainty that Jim Castle would be there when the train chugged into the station might have been responsible for a good deal of her eagerness. She frowned and attempted to push the thought away. . .without success.

She'd been surprised at the depth of her attraction toward him that Sunday at her sister's. She'd anticipated seeing him again, believing he felt the same, but nearly three weeks had passed, and she'd seen him only in fleeting moments around town. Usually he tipped his hat and went on his way. Twice he'd paused long enough to exchange civilities.

More than likely she'd only imagined his interest. Embarrassment washed over her. Had her interest in him been obvious? How humiliating if he'd noticed. She'd make sure to be polite but cool the next time she saw him.

That afternoon, when she'd dismissed the class and closed up, she headed for Dr. Gregory Stephens's office. As chairman of the school board, he'd be the one to which she should broach the subject of a field trip to see the train come in.

At the sight of Jim Castle's tall form striding toward her, she almost turned around and went back to the school, but he'd already spotted her and smiled as he came near. "Addy, how nice to see you." He reached for her hand, and the next thing she knew it was enveloped in his.

Warmth flowed through her fingers, all the way up to her shoulder. She cleared her throat. "Hello, Jim." Oh no, her voice shook. So much for being cool and distant.

Her hand trembled in his. She must get away before he noticed. She spotted the doctor coming out of Brown's Mercantile, an honest excuse to escape. "I'm sorry, I have an appointment. It was nice to see you again as well." Slipping her hand from his, she hurried across the street and approached the doctor.

Well, she would have an appointment if Dr. Stephens wasn't busy. It was only a little fib. Still a pang of guilt shot through her. A lie was a lie.

❦

Disappointment tugged at Jim as he saw the tall, broad-shouldered doctor take Addy's hand and smile down at her. Were they a courting couple? The expression on the doctor's face sure indicated it.

Of course, it was probably for the best. Jim had known from the beginning there was no chance for him with the lovely Addy. Which was why he'd avoided her since the Sunday dinner at Rafe's house. Rafe must not know about the doctor or surely he'd have mentioned it.

Some other man would be standing by that white picket fence with her, just as he'd thought. Someone who had a stable life right here in Branson Town. Like the doctor. Jim was happy for her. He was. So why the sick feeling inside his gut?

He sauntered down the sidewalk and attempted to focus his thoughts on his upcoming meeting later in the week with Fullbright and the owners of the Maine Exhibition Building. He'd advise them to change the name of the establishment to something that would reflect a local flair. Since it would be constructed on a bluff overlooking the river, he thought Mountain Lodge or White River Lodge would be a good choice. He doubted they'd go for it though. They were pretty stuck on Maine Hunting and Fishing Lodge.

Arriving at the livery stable, he retrieved his horse, Finch, and mounted. A quick ride to Forsyth might help clear his head of Addy and the doctor. He had a couple of telegrams he needed to send anyway. A new park in Virginia had requested his services, but he'd have to let them know it would be at least ten more months before he could leave Branson Town. He'd more than likely lose the job, but there were always more tourism projects to take on.

As he rode down the narrow road, hemmed in by giant oaks and black walnut trees, he whistled a tune. He'd disliked enclosed places since he was a child. The job he'd held at Marvel Cave had helped him overcome that, but he still preferred wide-open spaces.

Relieved, he came out of the woods and into a clearing. He took a deep breath, inhaling the scent of honeysuckle carried by the soft breeze. The fragrance reminded him of Addy, who always smelled like flowers.

He emitted a short laugh. It seemed everything reminded him of Addy lately. And it was hopeless because nothing had changed since he was here before. Even if she cared for him, which she obviously didn't, he'd never ask a woman like her to leave the stability of home and hop from one town to another. His job even took him out of the country at times.

Why couldn't he get the woman out of his mind? She was extremely attractive, but he'd met his share of pretty women, some as pretty as or even prettier than she. So why did he carry her face in his head just about everywhere he went? What was it about her? She wasn't even that nice to him most of the time. And likely she was in love with the doc. A sharp pain stabbed through him.

He urged Finch forward and didn't slow down until he rode into Forsyth. He sent his telegraph messages then wandered down to the docks to watch the steamboats battening down for the night. There were only two docked. Thanks to the railroad, they were a dying breed. The price of progress.

He turned away and went to a local café to grab some supper. The special was corned beef and cabbage, which he despised. Not wanting to take the time to have anything cooked from scratch, he ordered coffee and a ham sandwich.

Someone had left a newspaper on the counter, so he opened it. It was a weekly, and all the news was old, so he busied himself reading the ads. Anything to fill his mind so that thoughts of Addy wouldn't torment him.

By the time Jim got back to Branson Town, everything was shut down except for the hotels and the two saloons. He sat for a moment, tapping his fingers on his leg. He sure didn't need to be alone with his thoughts. Maybe he should ride out to Rafe's and find out what he knew about Addy and the doctor.

After a moment of gnawing at his lip, he thought better of that idea. Abby probably wouldn't take too kindly to his showing up this time of night. Farmers went to bed early.

He rode to the livery stable and saw that his black stallion, Finch, was taken care of and then headed to the hotel on foot.

Cigar smoke hung over a small group of men in the lobby. A heated discussion seemed to be going on. He knew most of them casually. Businessmen or potential businessmen who knew the possibilities of investing in the fledgling town and were willing and able to cash in on it.

One of the men waved a hand. "Castle. Maybe you can clear this debate up for us."

Jim smiled and shook his head. "Another time perhaps. I have a stack of ledgers waiting for my attention." Making his escape, he headed for the stairs only to stop short when he passed the dining room.

Seated at a table across the room, Addy smiled at the doctor, who leaned forward, his eyes intent on hers.

Jim's face tightened, and his body tensed. So that was that. Apparently they were courting. With a heavy heart, he turned away and headed up the stairs to his suite.

Chapter 4

Two straight lines of eager students filed out of the classroom and lined up behind Mrs. Carroll and Mrs. Bright, who had volunteered to help with the field trip.

Addy and fourteen-year-old Annie Brown made up the rear guard to make sure no overly adventurous children decided to head out on their own.

Annie darted a nervous glance at the girls, standing tallest to shortest in her line. "Miss Sullivan," she whispered, "the boys' line isn't in order." She motioned toward the front.

Sure enough, a curly mop of red hair poked out from behind Thomas Carter, a tall thirteen-year-old at the head of the line.

Addy pressed her lips together to hold back a smile. Johnny. She walked up the line and stopped beside him then tapped her foot as she looked down at the culprit.

Johnny glanced up, and his eyes widened. "Oops. Guess I must have lost my bearings, teacher."

"Yes, I believe you did," Addy said. "Shall I hold your hand and lead you to your place?"

Thomas guffawed, and Johnny's face flamed. "No, ma'am. I reckon I can find it all right."

Addy shot a look of reprimand at Thomas then motioned for Johnny to precede her to the end of the line, where he scooted in between Harry and Eugene. She patted him on the shoulder then blew a small whistle to get everyone's attention. "Children, we have a place reserved for us at the depot where everyone should be able to see just fine. So please stay in your places. Otherwise we won't be able to keep track of everyone."

Johnny ducked his head then looked up at her. "Sorry, Miss Sullivan."

"It's all right, Johnny. I'm sure you won't do it again."

Addy couldn't help a surge of pride as the two lines filed across the school-yard then down the boardwalk, the boys marching like soldiers, the girls with perfect deportment. She only hoped it would last.

A crowd thronged the road by the depot.

Addy covered her nose and mouth with her plain white handkerchief to keep the flying dust from her throat.

Several of the children began to cough.

"Children, cover your mouths until we get to the station." Someone bumped into her, and bodies rushed by, obscuring her view. Panic rose as she searched ahead for the children.

"Make way, there. Can't you see there are women and young children trying to get through?" Dr. Stephens's booming voice sounded angelic to Addy at the moment.

With mixed feelings of relief and dread, she allowed him to take her arm and guide her and the rest of the group across the road and onto the depot's wooden platform.

"Now, boys and girls, stand still and don't move until your teacher says the word," the doctor said.

She smiled and held out her hand. "Thank you, doctor. Now I really must count heads and make sure we're all here before we go to find our place."

"I'd be more than happy to assist you. In fact, I thought you might need my help with the children today."

"Oh, that's kind of you, but..." Addy tried to protest, but his hand grasped her elbow, and before she knew it she, the children, and the two mothers had been herded to the spot designated for them.

She managed to retrieve her elbow and turned to check on her young charges. "Move back a little more, children. You're too near the edge of the platform. Mrs. Bright, if you can stay there at the end, and Mrs. Carroll, will you please stand at the center of this row?"

She soon had them all settled, the older children behind the younger ones with the adults and older children dispersed evenly among them.

A shadow of disappointment crossed the doctor's face as he saw they were separated by an entire row of children. She silently congratulated herself.

The week before when she'd accepted his dinner invitation, she'd regretted it almost immediately. What she'd thought was merely a dinner meeting to discuss the field trip had turned out to be an evening of revelation by the doctor of his need for a wife and hints that she was his number-one choice for the position. She'd managed to avoid him since then. Until now.

A roar of excited voices surrounded her, and the crowd surged forward. She stepped in closer to her students and glanced down the rows, then on down the platform.

Through an opening in the throng, she spotted Jim. Their eyes locked. An electric charge ran through her, and she stared, helpless to look away.

The sound of the train's steam whistle broke the spell, and she whirled around. The engine wasn't in sight yet, but the chugging sound as it slowed could be heard clearly, and once more the shrill whistle rent the air.

A collective sigh made its way through the crowd. Then the engine came around the bend, and a roar exploded from the enthusiastic men, women, and children. Hats flew into the air.

Addy couldn't make a sound. Excitement and unexplainable joy surged through her. Her eyes took in first the engine and then the boxcars that followed.

She'd seen trains before, even ridden on one once when her family had taken a trip to Kansas City. But to actually see it, shining and black, smoke pouring forth, right here in Branson Town was enough to render her speechless. A whole new world was opening. As soon as the southern tracks were completed, the passenger trains would run.

Addy's breathing quickened, and in her mind's eye she saw herself climbing aboard and rolling away from the station. Away from Branson Town. Maybe even away from Missouri.

Would she dare? But how could she? Leave Pa and Ma and Abby? Whatever had gotten into her?

The engine slowed to a crawl, and its loud squeal seemed to go on forever as it came to a stop in front of the depot.

The roar of the crowd finally faded to a murmur as a man in a dark-blue suit stepped down and onto the platform.

Mr. Fullbright stepped forward and extended his hand. "I'd like to welcome the White River Line to Branson Town, Missouri."

⁓

Jim's gaze drifted from the welcoming speech and down the platform to rest upon Addy. Her face glowed with excitement, and even from several yards away, he could see the sparkle in her eyes. A grin split his face. He'd never seen her this animated.

Instead of following Fullbright and the newly arrived White River Line representative across to the waiting carriage, he began to push his way through the crowd toward Addy.

Spotting the doctor in the midst of the children, he hesitated, and then taking a deep breath, he stepped resolutely forward once more. He had to at least speak to her and share her excitement for a moment.

"Jim!" He turned to see Fullbright motioning to him from the street, an expression of impatience on his usually placid face.

He turned to look at Addy once more, but the crowd was so thick he could no longer see her.

Stalking across the platform, he stepped onto the street and climbed into the carriage after Fullbright.

⁓

Addy scanned the area where only a moment before Jim had appeared to be coming toward her. Now he was nowhere to be seen.

Disappointed, she motioned to her assistants. Time to go back to the classroom for another two hours.

"Miss Sullivan, I'd be happy to escort you and the children back to the school." Dr. Stephens had once more appeared at her side.

"Thank you, doctor, but that really isn't necessary." She smiled and motioned to Annie and the ladies. "As you can see, I have plenty of helpers."

"Oh, well, if you're certain." He hesitated. "I wonder if you've thought any more about the matter we discussed at dinner last week."

"Well, no. I'm afraid I haven't. I've been dreadfully busy." If only he would drop the subject. Addy didn't want to hurt the man's feelings. He was very kind and quite good looking, if one liked the large, ruddy type. Addy wished she were interested in him. He'd probably be a fine husband. Unfortunately, she wasn't the slightest bit attracted to him, and he rather bored her.

"Then perhaps you'd care to join me on a picnic this weekend, and we could discuss the subject more thoroughly."

Panicking, she grasped around in her mind for a reasonable excuse to refuse. Taking her silence for acceptance, he smiled. "I'll be at your home Saturday morning at eleven then. Please don't worry about the food. I'll have my landlady pack us a lunch."

Addy watched in helpless consternation as he walked away.

A laugh drew her attention. Johnny's mother looked at her with kind amusement on her face. "Apparently, the good doctor is smitten enough he can't tell when he's refused."

A short laugh escaped Addy's throat. "Is it that obvious?"

"Well, it was to me. Apparently not to him, though." Mrs. Carroll grinned and turned aside to help get the children lined up.

The trek to the school was uneventful. After Mrs. Bright and Mrs. Carroll said good-bye, Addy turned to the excited class and held up her hand to quiet them. "I thought this important event called for a celebration, so I brought cookies from home this morning."

Cheers rang out, and once more Addy held up her hand. "Before we have our party, I have a short assignment for you, so please take out your tablets and pencils."

She waited until the rustle stopped before continuing. "I'd like for you to write down as many things about today's event as you can think of in the next ten minutes. Afterward we shall have our cookies."

"Do we turn our papers in, teacher?" Eugene asked.

"Not today. You can finish them over the weekend and bring them with you on Monday. Then we'll see how much combined information we have for our group report."

While the class concentrated on their assignment, Addy's thoughts drifted back over the afternoon. She couldn't think of a time she'd been this excited. At least, not since Papa Jack took her and Abby on his riverboat, the *Julia Dawn*.

She'd never shared with anyone how much she'd loved that experience. Drops of moisture from the river spraying across her skin. The smell of lumber and other supplies Pa had transported up and down the river. The train's whistle had reminded her of the escaping steam from the *Julia Dawn*'s smokestack.

She sighed. It had broken her heart when Pa sold the boat, and she could tell it was hard for him, too. But he'd needed the money that first year of farming, and if he'd kept the boat, maybe he and Ma couldn't have married and adopted her and Abby.

Would she ever find a love like Pa and Ma's? She sighed again. Probably not.

Jim's cool demeanor and warm eyes filled her thoughts. She'd truly thought he returned her admiration, but she must have been wrong. She knew so little about men. What a silly goose she was. She'd even believed he was coming over to speak to her at the depot this afternoon. Then the next moment he'd totally disappeared.

She simply had to stop thinking about him. He'd be leaving in a few months anyway. Maybe it would be easier to get him out of her mind once he was gone.

"Miss Sullivan?" The stage whisper from the front row snapped her out of her reverie.

"Yes, Margaret?" She shook her head to dispel unwanted thoughts.

"We've been writing an awful long time."

Addy lifted the chain and looked at her watch. She smiled. It had been twelve minutes. "Mercy, you're right, Margaret."

The day ended on a high note for the children, with the cookies being a success and their excitement about the coming weekend.

For Addy, however, the day, which had begun with such high expectations, now seemed dismal. She simply had to make herself snap out of it. Perhaps a picnic with the doctor wasn't such a bad idea after all. Why should she let Jim Castle affect her emotions like this?

Chapter 5

Addy shivered as a thrill of excitement ran through her, and she stared as Pa slapped a huge spoon of mashed potatoes onto his plate then passed the bowl to Ma.

"Pa, are you sure? The State of Maine's exhibition building? The big log building we saw at the World's Fair?" After the gloom of her afternoon, she welcomed this bit of good news. Even if it seemed impossible.

"That's right, daughter." Pa nodded as he spooned green beans from the rose-printed serving bowl. "Jim Castle told Rafe they've already disassembled it in St. Louis."

"And it's for sure going to be a hunting lodge? Right here in Branson?"

He nodded and passed the vegetable bowl to Ma. "They're bringing the sections by train, and when it's reassembled we'll have a hunting lodge overlooking the White River."

How exciting. They would probably hire local folks to cook and wait tables and clean. Maybe she could get a job there.

A shock jolted her. What in the world was wrong with her? She couldn't give up her teaching position to work at a hunting lodge. The very idea.

"I thought Abby, Rafe, and the boys were coming for supper tonight." She'd actually been looking forward to a nice long talk with her sister.

Ma placed a small piece of roast on Betty's plate and began cutting it up. "Change of plans. We're having a picnic tomorrow. If you don't have school work tonight, maybe you could help me cook?"

"As long as you don't make me fry chicken." Addy made a face at Pa, who chuckled.

Ma cast a slight frown at her. "Now Addy, you just need more practice and you'll do fine. Perhaps you should fry the chicken, after all."

A choking sound from Pa drew their attention. He shook his head.

"Fine, Pa. It had crossed my mind to make your favorite pineapple upside-down cake." She smiled. "Maybe I will anyway."

It would be nice to spend the day with the whole family and would give her a chance for that talk with Abby. They hadn't had an outing by the river in quite a while.

Suddenly she gasped. Oh no. She'd promised to go on a picnic with the doctor. She bit her lip. "Ma, would it be all right if Dr. Stephens joined us?"

Surprise filled Ma's eyes, and creases appeared between her brows, but she quickly smiled. "Of course."

Addy frowned. She knew that look. "Now Ma, don't get any ideas. He invited me to go on a picnic with him, and before I could think up an excuse, he presumed the answer was yes."

"Why, I had no ideas at all. You have a perfect right to have friends. Even gentlemen friends."

Pa cleared his throat. "Do I have a right to an opinion?"

Addy stared at her pa, half hoping he'd forbid her to see the doctor.

"Dr. Stephens is a fine man. You could do worse."

"Trying to marry me off, Pa?" Addy was only half joking. After all, she wasn't getting any younger. Maybe her parents were tired of having her around. The familiar pang of loneliness ran through her, and she caught her breath.

"Nope. I'd keep all my daughters single at home forever if it was up to me." Pa shook his head. "Of course Abby had other ideas, and I'm sure you will, too, someday."

Betty's sweet voice rang out. "I'll never get married and leave you, Pa."

"That's my girl." Pa lifted her onto his lap and kissed her cheek.

Addy smiled. She had to stop imagining things. Pa and Ma loved her, and she'd be welcome here as long as she wanted to stay. "Maybe I'll stay home, too. You and I can be old maids together, Betty girl."

A little frown crossed Betty's face. "I thought I'd be a teacher like you. I don't want to be a maid."

Addy laughed. "Me either." Unless she could be one at the new lodge. Oh. There she went again. She must get these ideas out of her head.

After the table was cleared and the dishes washed and put away, Addy joined her family on the wide front porch. She leaned back in her chair and shut her eyes for a moment. She loved the sound of night birds and didn't even mind the chirping of insects.

Mosquitoes buzzed and flitted. Her eyes shot open, and she slapped one away from her ear. Mosquitoes she could do without.

"Is Aunt Kate coming to the picnic? I noticed she wasn't at church last Sunday." Addy loved Ma's Aunt Kate. In spite of her strict ideas, she was gentle and loving. Always had been with Addy and Abby.

"I don't think so, dear." Worry shadowed Ma's eyes. "She's not feeling well lately. You and Abby really need to visit her more often. She misses you."

Guilt pricked her. "I'm sorry. I'll stop by Uncle Will's after school on Monday."

"That would be nice." Ma leaned back on the swing, resting her head against Pa's shoulder.

Addy gave them a wistful glance. Even after all these years, they were still sweethearts. Jim's face flashed across her mind, and exasperated, she jumped up. "I think I'll go inside and work on an assignment for Monday since we'll be busy tomorrow."

Betty clapped her hands, and her eyes danced. "I can't wait for the picnic tomorrow."

Ma smiled at her youngest. "It'll be so much fun, won't it?"

Addy bid good night to all. She usually looked forward to family get-togethers, but knowing the doctor would be there spoiled it for her. Why hadn't she simply made an excuse and told him no?

⚭

Addy couldn't help being amused at the look of disappointment that crossed the doctor's countenance. For a moment she'd thought he would protest the new arrangement.

"But. . .but. . .I'd hoped. . ." Slowly resignation crossed his face, and his shoulders drooped. "Of course, if your family is also having a picnic, we'll join them. Yes, that's only right."

"Thank you for understanding, doctor." She smiled as he took the basket full of food from her then helped her into the buggy.

As they led the way to the picnic site near the river, he turned to her and smiled. "We'll have a nice day in spite of. . . That is, we'll have a nice day I'm sure with your family."

"Yes, doctor, we will."

He cleared his throat. "Miss Sullivan, I was wondering if you would mind calling me Gregory."

Panic gripped Addy, and her chest tightened. How to get out of this one? If she agreed to call him by his Christian name, he'd be sure to take it as a sign that she wanted him to court her. Which she most certainly did not.

"Well, Dr. Stephens, don't you think that would be a little premature? After all, we haven't known each other very long."

"No, no, of course you're right," he said. "Please forgive me for making the suggestion."

"That's quite all right. No offense taken, I assure you." Addy breathed a sigh of relief to have gotten out of it so easily. "Look, there's the picnic spot."

The doctor turned the horses into the clearing and stopped beneath a towering oak tree. Abby and Rafe's wagon was already there, and Rafe had thrown together some boards for makeshift tables.

David and Dawson sat on a quilt in the sunshine, tumbling over each other in an attempt to reach the tall blades of grass.

Abby threw her hands up in the air. "Yay! You're here. Betty, will you please watch your nephews and keep them from getting too far from the quilt?"

Betty giggled, and a smile creased her face. "Sure, Aunt Tuck." She ran for the boys, who let out screams of rapture when they saw her.

Ma shook her head. "Abby, I wish you would discourage her calling you Aunt Tuck."

"Aw, Ma. She hears Rafe call me Tuck, and I don't mind. I think it's kind of cute."

Addy laughed and nodded at the three children tumbling about on the blanket. "I think we've got a three-member mutual admiration society."

"I know. Isn't it adorable?" Abby nodded at the doctor. "I'm glad you could join us, Dr. Stephens." But the look she threw Addy warned that a question-and-answer session between them was coming up soon.

The chance came a few minutes later, when the doctor reluctantly followed Pa and Rafe to the river to fish.

While Ma was occupied taking food out of one of the baskets, Abby sidled up to Addy as she set out silver on another table. "Okay, what's going on with the doc, sister dear?"

Addy shook her head. "Not a thing on my part. I think he's got his heart set on marrying me."

Abby laughed. "Well, don't you think bringing him to a picnic might encourage that idea just a little bit?"

"Well, I guess. I think I got snookered into it. One minute he was asking, and the next he was telling me when he'd pick me up." Addy frowned. "I didn't know how to get out of it."

Abby snorted. "You always were too nice."

"Yes, well, don't forget your own experience with a certain doctor."

"Eww, you're right. Sometimes we get ourselves in a pickle jar with no way to reach the top."

"Well, this is one pickle that's floating to the top. I'm going to tell him later that I'm not a bit interested." Addy gave an emphatic nod.

"Too bad he's here. Jim Castle will be here any second. And I don't think he's coming to spend time with Rafe and me."

Addy couldn't stop the gasp from escaping. "Oh, Abby. Did you invite him?"

"He sort of invited himself. I think he's falling hard for you, sis."

Addy's heart raced. "You're imagining things, Abby. Stop teasing."

"Okay, suit yourself." At the sound of wheels and horses' hooves, Abby grinned. "Here he is now."

Sure enough, Jim's buggy pulled into the clearing. He jumped down and threw his reins over a branch. He doffed his hat and flashed that devastating, mind-numbing smile of his. "Good afternoon, ladies. I hope I haven't missed the picnic."

Abby laughed, and glee shone all over her face. "Not at all, Jim. We're just now setting things out. The men are fishing if you'd like to join them."

"Maybe later." He turned to Addy, and his eyes seemed to blaze into hers. "I'm sorry I missed you at the depot yesterday. I was unavoidably detained for a moment, and then you had disappeared."

"Oh, did you wish to speak with me about something, Mr. Castle?"

"I thought we'd dispensed with formalities, Addy."

Heat washed over her face. Oh dear. He was right. That had probably been a mistake made in a moment of romantic foolishness. Anyway, what would the doctor think if she called Jim by his given name after refusing to do the same for him? Oh, so what? She didn't care what the doctor thought. Jim had been a friend of Rafe's for a long time, and that made the difference.

"Yes, I believe we did. Jim, then." She smiled.

"Oh, look who's coming." Abby chortled. "Why I do believe it's your date, Addy."

Jim scowled as the doctor came into sight, followed by Rafe and Jack Sullivan.

The doctor's glance went to Jim then to Addy.

Jim watched in surprise as Dr. Stephens stepped over to Addy and put his hand on her arm. That was overly familiar unless there was an understanding between them.

"Is there anything I can do to help?" Dr. Stephens asked.

Addy frowned and moved away from the doctor's hand. "No, I think we have everything under control."

Jim glanced from Addy to the doctor and narrowed his eyes. Was she interested in the man or not? If so, he'd bow out. But the look in her eyes when she'd spotted Jim yesterday and then again today told him she had feelings not for the doctor but for him. And he wasn't giving up until he knew for sure.

Suddenly she stepped over to him. "Jim, have you met Dr. Stephens? Doctor, this is Jim Castle."

The doctor looked as though he might choke.

Jim almost laughed. Had Addy made a statement by calling him Jim? Maybe he was making too much of that, but it was something to grab ahold of anyway.

Mrs. Sullivan cast a startled glance at Addy and both men. She stepped over to her husband and laid her hand on his. "Everything is ready, Jack. Will you ask the blessing, please?"

They bowed their heads.

"Dear gracious heavenly Father," Jack said, "we thank You for this food You've supplied from Your bounty. Please bless it, bless those who prepared it and all who've come together to partake of it."

As Jack continued praying, Jim sent up a special request of his own. *God, this woman is mine. Please see that she knows that.*

Hmm. Maybe that prayer wasn't exactly reverent. He'd have to talk to the Lord about it later.

Chapter 6

Dr. Stephens stood with his plate and Addy's in hand and nodded toward a spot beneath an apple tree, some distance from the rest of their group. "That apple tree is a nice place for us."

Addy frowned. "Oh, but don't you think that would be rather impolite? I think I'd prefer to sit near my family."

A grimace passed over the doctor's face. "Really, Adeline. How will we ever plan our future if we're never alone?"

Addy's jaw dropped, and she snapped it firmly shut. Her nostrils flared, and her throat constricted while drawing in a deep breath. This had gone on long enough. "Dr. Stephens, I don't know where you got the idea you and I have a future. I'm sure I haven't encouraged that thought in any way."

He gave her an astonished look. "But I told you that you were my choice for a wife."

She planted her hands on her hips and glared at him. "Yes, you did hint at that possibility, but did I at any time indicate I was interested in marrying you?"

He closed his eyes for a moment and took a deep breath, letting it seep out while throwing her a look he'd give a child. "I can see I've been too hasty, rushing you like this. Please forgive me. I'll take things more slowly."

"You will not take things any way at all concerning me. I'm more than happy to be your friend, but I can assure you that is all we shall ever be."

His face flamed red. "Then perhaps I'd better leave." He placed both dishes on the table.

"Nonsense. You are quite welcome to stay and enjoy the picnic with us." Not exactly true, but it would be the height of rudeness to tell him what she really thought.

"I don't think so. Of course, I will be happy to drive you home if you wish to leave now." He gave her a look that was almost comical in its hopefulness.

"No, I don't wish to leave. I'm very sorry for the misunderstanding, doctor. I hope we can remain friends."

He gave a short nod and stalked off to his buggy.

The tightness in Addy's neck and jaw eased as the doctor departed. But a surge of guilt mixed in with the relief as he drove away. She could have avoided the incident if she'd had the wisdom and courage to tell him how she felt from the beginning.

"The good doctor had to leave?" She spun around at the sound of Jim's voice.

"Yes, I suppose he did."

He raised his eyebrow, but she didn't speak, so he turned to the table and glanced at the two filled plates. "I assume one of these is yours."

She smiled and picked up the doctor's plate, raking the food back into the serving dishes. She then picked up her own plate and smiled at Jim. "Let's join the family. We're missing all the fun."

Jim placed his hand beneath her elbow, but she gently moved her arm. She wasn't giving him ideas either. As much as she liked him and enjoyed his company, there were obstacles to any type of relationship between them other than friendship. The main one being that his job would take him away before long.

"You two slowpokes hurry, or we'll eat without you." Rafe winked. "Don't worry, Jim. Addy didn't fry the chicken."

"Be careful"—Addy threw a mock frown at her brother-in-law—"or I might not let you have any of my chocolate cake that you like so much."

The meal and banter went on for nearly an hour before the men headed back to the river to fish while the women put the children down for naps. With that accomplished, they sat on the ground beneath a wide spreading oak.

"What was that with the doctor, Adeline?" Ma waved a mosquito away from Betty then glanced at her daughter.

"What do you mean, Ma?" Addy blushed. She knew very well what her mother spoke of.

"He left rather suddenly. Did he have medical duties to attend?"

"No, I don't think so." Addy bit her lip. She may as well tell Ma the truth. "He somehow imagined that I was willing to enter into a long-term relationship with him."

"He wanted to marry you?" No beating around the bush with Ma.

"Yes, ma'am. When I told him we could only be friends, he decided to leave."

"I see." Ma nodded, and Addy held her breath waiting for what her mother would have to say next. "Well dear, I don't think he quite suited you. I hope you told him kindly."

"Well, perhaps I might have been a little more gentle." At the thought of the doctor's presumption, her teeth clenched. "But he made me so mad. He rather took things for granted."

"Besides, she has a hankering for someone else." Abby laughed and slapped her overalled knee. Addy's twin took any chance that came along to wear her favorite clothing.

"Behave yourself, Abby. I do not."

"Oh no? I think you do. I think you're falling hard for Jim. But that's okay. He's already fallen for you." Her blue eyes sparkled.

Addy blushed. "I guess I am rather falling for him, as you say. But it can't go anywhere."

"Why not? Jim's a great fellow." Abby frowned.

"Do you want me to move away?" Addy gave her sister an intent look.

Abby gasped. "No, of course not. Oh sister, I hadn't thought ahead that far. Well, Jim will just have to stay in Branson. Plenty of jobs. Mr. Fullbright will have to find something for him to do around here."

A glimmer of hope shimmered inside Addy. Would Jim even consider staying in Branson? With all the new businesses and the tourism, there should be work for him here, shouldn't there? But why should he? He wasn't that interested in her. A bee buzzed by her face, and she swatted it away then laughed. "Don't be silly, Abby. And stop imagining things. Jim Castle and I are only friends.

Jim couldn't believe his luck. He'd offered to take Addy home, fully expecting a resounding no after the lambasting she'd given the doctor.

Instead, she'd lowered those beautiful blue eyes for a moment then lifted them and murmured a soft, "Thank you. That's very kind of you."

Now as the horse trotted down the road toward the Sullivan farm, the sway of the buggy created a lazy rocking-chair effect. Jim glanced toward Addy on the seat next to him. Her eyelashes rested on her cheek, and a half smile tilted one corner of her mouth.

"Oh!" She sat up, a startled expression on her face. "I almost fell asleep. Please excuse my lack of manners."

Jim grinned. "Not at all. I came close to nodding off myself."

She smiled. "It's been a lovely day."

"It has. Too bad it has to end." Perhaps he could stretch it out a little longer.

She slipped her hand into her pocket and retrieved a lacy handkerchief. Fanning it in front of her face, she said, "I hope it cools off a little soon. Rain would be nice."

Okay, small talk was fine, but they'd be at her home in a few minutes, and he'd like to talk about something besides the weather. "Did your class enjoy their outing to see the train come in?" There, that was better than the weather.

Animation brightened her face. "Oh yes. They were so excited. We're doing a class project on the historical event with pictures and stories. We may also have a play of sorts. It will be a nice end-of-school program for the parents, don't you think?"

"I should think so, yes," he said.

"I can hardly believe the change in Branson Town. The new hotels and other buildings make it seem like a completely different place." Suddenly she turned toward him, her eyes bright with excitement. "Speaking of historical events, would you mind telling me about the new hunting lodge?"

Surprised, he stared at her for a moment. Now why would a lovely young woman be interested in a hunting lodge? "I'd be happy to tell you anything you'd like to know. Within the limits of my knowledge of it, of course."

"Is it true that the State of Maine is being reassembled here?" Her eyes were wide and her lips slightly open.

Jim resisted the impulse to catch his breath. Her beauty was almost too much to bear. He wanted nothing more at the moment than to lean over and kiss those luscious lips. If she only knew how inviting they were, he was certain she'd be horrified.

Pulling himself together, he licked his own lips. If she knew what he was thinking, she'd slap the tar out of him and send him packing. "Er. . .yes, yes, the State of Maine Exhibition has been disassembled and is on its way here. Are you interested in the building?"

"Oh yes. Pa took us to the World's Fair in St. Louis. The State of Maine exhibition was my favorite. The World's Fair was the most exciting thing. Actually, the only exciting thing that I've ever done, except for when Pa took Abby and me with him on the *Julia Dawn*."

Delight ran through Jim from his head to his toes just watching her excitement. "The *Julia Dawn*?"

She laughed. "That was Pa's steamboat. He used to haul cargo up and down the White River and even the Mississippi."

"I had no idea. I thought your father had always been a farmer." Yet he could imagine Jack Sullivan as a riverboat captain. There was something in the man's demeanor, as though he was comfortable issuing orders.

"Yes, when Addy and I were eight years old our real father died. Our ma had died years before, so we had no one. Papa Jack gave up his business and married Ma Lexie. Then they adopted us."

Jack pulled up alongside her front porch just as the sun sank below the horizon. "It sounds as though they must have loved you very much."

"Yes, they do. And I love them." Suddenly she stopped talking and furrowed her brow at him. "Why, we're here already. Oh dear, I've been talking nonstop. And such frivolous talk at that. Please do forgive me." Before Jim had a chance to say a word or to get down to help her from the buggy, she murmured a hasty thank you, jumped down, and hurried into the house.

He sat there for a while, his heart pounding. So, sweet Addy Sullivan had an adventurous streak. Who would have guessed it? He turned his buggy and headed back to town, barely able to keep his feet from tapping a reel on the buggy's floor.

❦

Stupid, stupid, stupid. How could she have gone on like that? She must have sounded like a schoolgirl.

Addy yanked off the ribbon that held back her curls and tossed it on the washstand. She dipped her hand in the washbasin's cold water and splashed it on her heated face. After dabbing it with a dry towel, she dropped into the rocking chair by the window and closed her eyes.

What exactly had she said to Jim? She forced herself to go over every word of their mostly one-sided conversation. As far as she could remember, she'd never bared her soul to anyone the way she had to Jim Castle in those few short minutes. If they hadn't arrived home when they did, she would have gone on to tell him about her secret dreams of traveling the world. Things she'd never revealed to anyone. Even Abby. What must he think of her?

She groaned. At best he'd think her a foolish, childish woman. At worst? Her face flamed. At worst he'd think she was in love with him and trying to impress him. He must be terribly amused. Probably laughing his head off.

She sat up straight and took a deep breath. Well, she'd simply have to correct that misassumption. But how? Avoid him? Probably not possible. Well, then failing that, she would ignore him except, of course, for common courtesy. He might wonder why she'd suddenly changed, but better that than the other. Better that than for him to feel sorry for her for making a big fool of herself.

Chapter 7

The whistle announced the train's arrival just as school let out.

Addy smiled and shook her head as several of the older boys took off in the direction of the depot. A flash of red tried to get past her, but she grabbed the collar of Johnny's plaid shirt before he could accomplish his mission.

"Hey!" He broke off his yell as he saw who held him captive. "Aw, Miss Sullivan. Can't I go?"

Addy turned loose of the shirt and smoothed it. "Your mother will be expecting you at home, Johnny. You wouldn't want her to worry, would you?"

Resignation crossed his face, and a loud sigh whooshed from his throat. "No, ma'am."

"That's a good boy. Now run along home." She smiled as he tromped slowly across the schoolyard and down the street. Then she glanced around. Now where was her horse and buggy? She bit her lip. It wasn't like Bobby to be late. She tapped her booted foot and looked up and down the street. No sign of the boy.

With a sigh, she started across the school yard in the direction of the livery stable. Several men and boys ran past, stirring up dust. Addy covered her mouth and nose, resisting a sneeze.

Mrs. Clancy, who cooked lunch at one of the cafés, trudged past.

"Where's everyone going?" Addy asked.

"Depot I reckon." Mrs. Clancy didn't bother to stop.

"What's going on?" Addy called after her.

She shrugged and walked on.

Probably just checking out the train. Addy supposed it would be a novelty for some time. She couldn't imagine the uproar once the passenger cars began running.

Laughter and shouts reached her ears, and she hesitated and glanced toward the depot where a crowd was forming. She turned toward the livery then stopped, glancing back to the depot. She really should get her buggy and go. She'd promised to visit her great-aunt Kate today. Still, it wouldn't hurt to just find out what all the excitement was about. If it was anything Uncle Will needed to know, she could pass the information on to him. Yes, she'd better check it out.

The depot wasn't as crowded as it had been when the first train had pulled into the station, but excitement buzzed through the small crowd. One of the cars had been unhitched and stood by the loading dock while a second was unhooked.

Addy shaded her eyes with one hand and peered across, trying to see what the cars contained.

"What do you think it is?"

Addy glanced around and saw a woman tugging on her husband's arm.

"Could be all the parts and supplies for the hunting lodge," the man said.

"Huh!" his wife said. "Well, don't you go getting any ideas about that."

He laughed. "Like I could afford to go there anyway."

The engine began to chug slowly down the track, leaving the two cars behind.

A group of men headed for the loading dock. The doors on the side of the car slid open with a screech.

Addy held her hands over her ears until the doors were completely open. Curiosity overtaking her, she walked down the platform toward the car.

"Addy!" She'd know that voice anywhere. Whirling around, she spied Jim rushing toward her.

She couldn't prevent the rapid thumping of her heart at the sight of him. She clenched her fists at her side and composed herself. She must be polite but aloof. "Yes?"

"It could be dangerous once they start unloading. You need to move to the other end of the platform."

She stared at him. How dare he tell her what she needed to do? "I'm not a child, Mr. Castle. I believe I can take care of myself, thank you."

He took a step backward, his eyes dark with confusion. "I'm sure you can. I simply don't want you to get hurt. Will you please step back out of harm's way?"

"Castle! Get that woman out of the way and make sure no one else gets too close."

Addy's face flamed at the burly man's commands. She should have moved when Jim asked her to. "Excuse me, Mr. Castle." She slipped past him and hurried away.

"Addy!"

Her heart jumped at the sound of his voice, but she hurried down the steps and onto the street.

Jim scratched his head and watched Addy stomp off. What had he done to rile her up? He'd been so pleased at the way things went at the picnic. Why was she angry? Well, he didn't have time to go after her, even if that would do any good. Women.

"Castle, I need you to help me check these items off."

Jim lifted his hand in acknowledgment and went to assist the new owners of the State of Maine Exhibition Building.

"Miss Sullivan." Bobby pulled the buggy up alongside her and stopped.

"Bobby, where in the world have you been?" Her voice sounded harsh even to her own ears.

"Looking for you, ma'am." He jumped down. "I had to run an errand for Mr. Jacobs before I could bring your rig to you. Then when I got to the school, you weren't there. Sorry I was late."

"All right, Bobby. It wasn't your fault. I'm sorry I snapped at you." She climbed into the buggy and took the reins. "Get in and I'll take you back to the stable."

"That's okay. I'm going to find out what's going on at the depot. Do you know what the train brought in?"

Addy bit her lip. She supposed it was the supplies for the lodge but wasn't sure. If only she hadn't gotten so flustered she'd still be there watching them unload. Oh well, why should she care anyway? "No, I don't. Sorry."

She was halfway home before she remembered she was supposed to go to her great-aunt Kate's house. Turning the horse, she headed cross-country to the road that led to the Rayton farm. She had to pull herself together before she got there. Aunt Kate didn't miss anything.

A sigh escaped her lips. What was wrong with her lately? She'd always been the calm, levelheaded twin. Now she was as flighty as Abby used to be. Worse even. Of course, she'd always had that secret desire for adventure, but she'd managed to keep it under control. In two days she'd been incredibly rude to two men. And she was pretty sure she was in love with one of them. What if someone besides family had witnessed her berating the doctor? Even if he was presuming and controlling. And what would people think of her if she did something foolish? Such as quit her job and work for a hunting lodge? Or jump on a train and travel across America?

She pulled to a stop alongside Aunt Kate's porch and sat unmoving. She took several deep breaths in an attempt to control her rambling thoughts. Aunt Kate deserved her full attention.

The door flew open, and Uncle Will's wife, Aunt Sarah, stepped onto the porch. "Land's sake, Addy. What are you sitting out here for? Come on inside."

Ma's younger brother, Will, married Sarah Jenkins the same year Ma and Pa got married. At first Addy had felt a little bit strange calling her Aunt Sarah. She was only nine or ten years older than Addy and Abby. But Ma would have whipped her good if she'd ever called an adult by her first name only.

"Is Aunt Kate at home?" Addy climbed down from the buggy and walked up the steps of the weathered old log cabin. Uncle Will really needed to paint or whitewash the place.

"Of course. She seldom goes anywhere these days except church." She darted a glance at the door then turned to Addy. "I'm a little worried about her. I know she's getting older, but it's like her energy just drained out of her all of a sudden."

"Maybe she should see the doctor." In spite of Addy's anger towards Dr. Stephens, she had confidence in his medical knowledge.

"She refuses to go. I'd hoped Lexie could talk some sense into her. Or one of you girls. She never takes me seriously." The worry lines in her face showed her concern.

Addy nodded. "I'll talk to her, but Ma's the one who can influence her better than anyone."

Aunt Kate sat on the settee in the parlor, a box of mending beside her. Her eyes brightened when they rested on Addy. She laid down the shirt she was mending and started to stand. "Addy." Her voice sounded weak.

"Please don't stand up, Auntie." Addy rushed over to her and, bending down, planted a kiss on her cheek.

Aunt Kate grabbed her hand and squeezed it. "I'm so glad you came. Sit across from me there so I can see you while we talk."

Addy obediently sat on the little rocking chair. As she got a better look at her aunt, she had to force herself not to react. In the three weeks since she'd seen her, something had taken its toll on Aunt Kate.

"Auntie, I hear you haven't been feeling well lately." *Lord, please help me convince her she needs to see a doctor.*

"Oh, everyone fusses over me too much." She shot a fiery look at Sarah. "It's only indigestion. I'm fine."

"Hmmm." Addy nodded. "You're probably right, Auntie. But you know there has been a lot of sickness going around."

Aunt Kate pressed her lips together and frowned. "I said I'm fine."

"I know, I know. I was just thinking of Sam and Larry."

At the mention of Will and Sarah's boys, Aunt Kate's head shot up. "What about Sam and Larry?"

"Well, nothing." Addy smiled at her aunt. "Except I know you wouldn't want to take a chance on passing something along to them. I mean, just in case you have something contagious."

Aunt Kate pierced Addy with her glare. "Don't try to trick me, young woman." She grabbed the shirt and began stabbing the needle through it. "Fine. All right. I'll go to the doctor. Tomorrow. Now is anyone going to bring me some tea?"

"I will, Aunt Kate." No one could have missed the relief in Sarah's voice. She smiled at Addy and left the room, returning a few minutes later with cups and a pot full of tea.

An hour later, Addy relayed the events to Ma as they put dinner on the table.

"So she is for certain going to see Dr. Stephens tomorrow?" Ma asked.

"Yes, ma'am. She gave her word before I left."

"I wonder if I should go with her." The slight quake in Ma's voice revealed her concern.

"It might not hurt. At least you could talk to the doctor and find out exactly what's wrong." It would be like Aunt Kate to keep any news to herself that she didn't want anyone to know.

Addy was in bed with the light out before she realized she hadn't thought any more about Jim Castle or working at the hunting lodge or running away on a train. She gave a low chuckle. Everything she needed was right here at home.

But Jim Castle's beguiling smile invaded her thoughts. In her fantasy world, she watched breathlessly as he rode up on his black stallion, moonlight streaming down on his jet-black hair. He gazed down at her, an inviting smile on his lips and a dangerous light in his eyes. Then the light darkened and his eyes smoldered. Slowly she nodded, and he reached down and swung her up behind him. She threw her arms around his waist and laid her head on his broad back, feeling the muscles ripple beneath his shirt. They rode away into the night.

She gasped. What was she thinking? Besides, she couldn't even get her fantasies right. His hair was more dark brown than black.

Groaning, she flopped over onto her stomach and pulled her pillow over her head. But just before sleep claimed her, a thought drifted through her mind. What would it be like to ride away with Jim and see the world?

Chapter 8

Nineteen heads bowed over books or tablets as Addy cleaned the blackboard and then began writing the assignments for the next day. Thankfully the children were behaving extra well today. With thoughts of riding off in the moonlight with Jim Castle continuing to rattle her, interspersed with worry about Aunt Kate, she wasn't sure how she'd handle an unruly classroom.

When she'd finished, she turned and sat at her desk. One by one, the children closed their books or laid pencils on the desk and looked at her expectantly. She placed a finger to her lips as a reminder that some were still busy with their lessons.

When little Charlotte Greene took a deep breath and laid her pencil down, Addy smiled at the class. "Everyone finished?"

Heads bobbed in the affirmative; eyes shone with expectation.

"I'm so proud of how well you've all done on our class project. With the end-of-school program just a week away, I'm sure you'll all work hard to do your part to make it special for your families." She smiled at the serious expressions of the younger children as they nodded.

From the back of the room, Tom Schuyler, one of the older boys, raised his hand.

"Yes, Tom?"

"My pa says if you don't let us out of school soon, he's gonna take me out anyway. He needs me on the farm."

"I know, Tommy. Your father spoke to me yesterday, and I explained to him that we were running a little longer this year because of the heavy snows last winter." She sent him a reassuring smile. "He said another week would be fine."

Several hands shot up.

"Class, I've talked to each of your parents about the delay, and they all agreed they could manage without your help for another week." She wished they'd chosen to inform their children of that fact.

All the hands went down except one.

"Yes, Johnny?"

"Teacher, guess what the train brung in yesterday?" His grin just about split his face, and his freckles seemed to stand out against his face.

A cacophony of voices roared across the room.

"Children, children, please be quiet." She stood until all the voices had ceased. "Brought, Johnny."

"Yes, ma'am. You know what the train brought?" He stressed the last word, his eyes sparkling.

"Why don't you tell us?" She was pretty sure she knew but wouldn't mind confirmation.

"All the parts of a broken-down old building. They brung. . .brought it all the way from St. Louis." He took a deep breath. "Guess what they're gonna do with the stuff?"

Once more hands waved in the air.

"Philip, do you know the answer to Johnny's question?" It wouldn't do to let the boy be the center of attention every moment.

"Yes, ma'am." Philip, who walked with a limp due to a birth defect, smiled. "A group of businessmen bought the State of Maine Exhibition Building that was at the World's Fair. They took it apart and brought it here. When they reassemble it, they'll turn it into a hunting lodge."

So, it was true. The butterflies in Addy's stomach flitted and zoomed.

"Can we all go there?" Annie hadn't bothered to raise her hand, but Addy couldn't blame her. The news was exciting.

Carl twisted in his seat and frowned. "No, dummy, I mean, sorry, Miss Sullivan, no, Annie. Only rich people will be allowed in."

"How did you manage to get that bit of information, Carl?" Addy could well imagine it would have come from his father.

"My pa said so. He said only rich folks could afford to go there."

"I see. Well, we'll have to wait and find out if your father is correct, won't we?" she said. "And now, I think we have just enough time to go over your lines for the program. If you'll all come to the front of the room we'll go through the play from beginning to end."

With help from several of the older students, Addy had written a short play for some of the children to perform that told the story of transportation and shipping in the area, beginning with horses, oxen, wagons, ferries, and riverboats, then ending with several students playing the parts of the officials of the White River Line. At the end of the play, the entire class would sing a lively rendition of "The Levee Song," also called "I've Been Working on the Railroad." Afterward the parents would view the illustrated essay the class had put together about the first train to arrive at the Branson Depot.

Addy's heart raced as the children rehearsed their parts. She chuckled. If she was this proud and nervous for them, she could only imagine how their parents would feel. A few of them stumbled over their lines, but Addy felt sure all would go well for the actual program the following week.

"That's wonderful, children. Please line up at the door."

After dismissing the children, Addy stepped outside and locked the door. Bobby was waiting beside her horse and buggy. She smiled and gave him his money, then waved as he walked away beaming.

She patted the dappled horse on the nose, climbed into her buggy, and sat for a moment, indecision coursing through her. She should hurry home to find out what the doctor had said about Aunt Kate. But would it hurt to swing by the bluff on which the new lodge would be built? Not for long, just to see if any activity was going on yet?

She licked her lips. It would only take a few extra minutes, fifteen or twenty at the most, to drive over that way, take a quick look, and drive back. Addy picked up the reins. With a flick of her wrist and a click of her tongue, she turned her buggy toward the river bluff.

Rough shouts of laughter reached her ears as she drew near her destination. She pulled on the reins and stopped in the middle of the narrow, rocky road. Perhaps this wasn't such a good idea, but she'd stay out of sight and just take a quick look.

Taking a deep breath, she urged her horse on. She stopped at the edge of a large clearing. Someone must have been working here for some time. The last time she'd been in this part of Branson thick woods reached almost to the bluff overlooking the river.

Several brawny men hauled beams on their shoulders; others pounded huge nails into what looked like parts of walls. Addy gasped as one man yanked his shirt off and threw it on the ground. Backing up, she turned the buggy and hurried the horse back toward town, her heart thumping wildly.

What had possessed her to come up here? She should have known there would be a lot of rough men working. She should have waited until the lodge was constructed, and then she could have made inquiries. She groaned. Inquiries about what? There she went again. She absolutely would never go to work in a hunting lodge.

As she neared a bend in the road, a horse and rider appeared. She pulled up. Jim Castle. She glanced around to see if there was anywhere she could hide her horse and buggy before he spotted her.

But his horse quickened its pace, and Jim stopped beside her, bewilderment on his face.

⚬⚬⚬⚬

Jim stared at Addy. What in the world was she doing up here?

Her face was flaming red and her hands trembled.

He tightened his lips. There was no telling what she'd seen or heard. The construction crew on this job was a pretty rowdy bunch. He should have warned her, but how was he to imagine she'd have a reason to come up here? Dismounting, he hurried over to her side. "My dear, are you all right?"

She glared at him for a moment. Then suddenly the red washed from her face, and she paled. Her face crumpled and tears pooled in her blue eyes.

Jim patted her hand, his heart pounding. Had someone accosted her? He rushed to the other side of the buggy and climbed up. Reaching over, he pulled her into his arms and patted her shoulder while she cried.

Suddenly she jerked her head up, almost slamming into his chin.

"Someone needs to tell those ruffians not to. . .not to. . .disrobe in public."

"Disrobe?" Jim stared at her, horrified at what she might have seen.

"Yes. He took his shirt off and threw it on the ground, right there in front of everyone."

Relief washed over him. The men often got overheated and tossed their shirts aside, working in their undershirts. Still, to an innocent young lady it may have seemed scandalous. "I am so sorry, Addy. I'll speak to the foreman immediately."

"Thank you, Jim," she whispered. She swabbed her eyes with her frilly white handkerchief then blew her nose daintily. She breathed in a little sigh and smiled. "I'm perfectly all right, Jim."

"You're sure?"

"Yes, I am. I'm going home now."

"I wanted to let you know how much I enjoyed the picnic with your family. I'd like to repay you by taking you out to dinner, but there isn't really a nice eating establishment in town other than the Branson Hotel. Would you do me the honor some evening soon?"

"No, no. Not the hotel," she said.

A surge of disappointment shot through him.

"I have a better idea. Why don't you come to church Sunday then join us for dinner?"

Jim couldn't keep the grin off his face. "Are you sure it'll be all right with your folks?"

"Of course. Ma always cooks extra just in case."

"In that case, I'd be delighted."

A gust of wind swirled around them, and the sky suddenly clouded. Addy shivered.

"Perhaps I should put the top up on your buggy in case it should rain."

"Thank you. That would be nice." She smiled, lowering her lashes. "I'll expect to see you at church on Sunday then."

⁓⁓⁓

Addy smiled all the way home, the memory of the bare-chested man lost in the memory of Jim's concern and care for her. He must not have minded that she'd talked so much when he drove her home from the picnic. She was so silly to have worried so.

She drove into the barn to put the horse and buggy away. The wagon was gone. Pa must have gone into town.

When she stepped into the house, she was met with an unnatural quiet, and no delicious aromas greeted her. Ma must not have started supper yet. She walked into the kitchen and saw a note propped up on the table.

She scanned it quickly, her heart fluttering. Aunt Kate. Not taking time to change from her school clothing, she rushed back out to the barn and once more harnessed the horse to the buggy.

She fought the urge to run the horse all the way to Aunt Kate's house. By the time she reached the Rayton farm, her bottom lip was cut from her teeth clamping down on it. Jumping down, she flung the reins over the porch rail and ran inside.

Aunt Sarah, seated on the sofa in the parlor, looked up, her face white.

Betty jumped up from the floor where she'd been playing with her dolls. She threw her arms around Addy's legs. "Addy, Mama and Papa had to go away with Uncle Will and Aunt Kate to the hospital."

Addy reached down and lifted her little sister. "I know, sweetheart. It's okay. They'll be home as soon as they can. And we'll wait here for them. Betty dear, I'm going to help Aunt Sarah cook some supper. If you'll stay here and play for a while, I'll let you help set the table."

"Okay." She returned to her dolls, holding them on her lap and speaking softly to them.

Sarah got up and followed Addy into the kitchen.

Addy placed her hands on Sarah's shoulders. "What's wrong with Aunt Kate?"

Sarah burst out crying. "They think it's her heart."

Heaviness sat on Addy's heart as they fixed supper and fed the children.

"Addy, if they aren't back by bedtime, could you and Betty sleep here?"

"Of course. I doubt I'll be able to sleep anyway until we know something."

Chapter 9

After tossing and turning for hours, Addy sat on the side of the bed, her head in her hands. Her skin and nightgown were damp, from either her nervousness or the warm night. She had to get some rest. Otherwise, how would she be able to teach, much less keep order in her classroom, the next day?

Betty whimpered and kicked at her covers, which had become twisted around her legs.

Addy got up and walked around to her sister's side of the bed and rearranged the light covers, tucking them up around Betty's chest.

Addy stood for a moment, trying to decide whether to give the elusive sleep another chance. Maybe a glass of water would help.

She tiptoed into the kitchen so as not to awaken Sarah and the children. Moonlight streamed into the room from the window over the washstand, lighting her way. She stood for a moment, looking across the backyard. The leaves on the oak trees moved slightly, and a trace of a breeze sifted through the open window, touching her damp skin. She shivered.

After she'd filled a glass, she walked toward the front of the house. She grabbed a light shawl from the stand by the door and stepped onto the front porch. Aunt Kate's wicker rocking chair seemed to send an invitation and she sat. Leaning her head back, she shivered as the breeze brushed across her damp skin.

The rattle of harness and the *clip-clop* of hooves startled her, and she jerked awake, confused. She twisted her neck to loosen the tight muscles. Suddenly aware of the sound that had awakened her, she jumped to her feet, wrapping the shawl around her shoulders for modesty.

Uncle Will's two-seater open carriage came into view, the horses' coats shining in the moonlight. Addy peered anxiously. Then relief washed over her. Aunt Kate sat beside Ma in the backseat. Uncle Will pulled alongside the steps and got out then reached to help Aunt Kate. She stumbled a little as her foot touched the ground, but Uncle Will quickly steadied her. Addy took her great-aunt's other arm as Pa helped Ma down from the buggy.

Addy bit her lip as Aunt Kate wobbled a little. "Are you all right, Aunt Kate?"

"I'm fine, as I told everyone I was. Just tired."

"Aunt Kate." Sarah appeared in the doorway, her wrapper pulled snug around her waist and her hair hanging loose around her shoulders. "Are you all right?"

"Yes, yes, child. I'm fine. I need a nice cup of hot tea. Then I'm going to bed."

"Yes, ma'am. I'll get it right away." She rushed toward the kitchen.

When Aunt Kate was ensconced on the settee in the parlor, Addy seated herself next to her and took her hand, throwing Ma a questioning look.

Ma gave an imperceptible shake of her head.

Soon Sarah was back with the laden tray. Addy helped her hand out the cups, and Sarah poured. Pa made a face as he quickly drained his cup. He always preferred a strong cup of black coffee.

Uncle Will, Ma, and Pa talked quietly of their trip to Springfield for a few minutes, and then Ma helped Aunt Kate to bed. Addy slipped away to get dressed.

When she returned to the parlor, Ma smiled. "She fell asleep almost as soon as she laid down."

"I'll hitch up the wagon and pull it around, then come in and get Betty so we can go home," Pa said and left the room.

"Ma."

"Wait, Addy." Ma turned to Sarah. "I'll let Will tell you what the doctor said, but I'll be over in the morning after I stop by Rafe and Abby's to let them know what's going on. We'll talk then."

Sarah nodded, concern in her eyes. "I'll have a pot of coffee ready."

A few minutes later, Addy climbed into the back of the wagon, seating herself on a pile of quilts and stretching her legs out. Pa laid Betty beside her, gently placing her head in Addy's lap.

As soon as they started down the lane, Addy blurted out, "Please tell me about Aunt Kate. Is it her heart?"

Ma turned on her seat, and the sadness in her eyes answered the question even before she spoke. "Yes, dear. Her heart is giving out. The doctors said she needs to slow down. They don't want her even doing housework for now or outside chores."

"But. . .is she dying?" Addy's mind could hardly wrap itself around the thought. Aunt Kate had been so full of life for as long as she'd known her.

Pain crossed Ma's face. "The doctor didn't say how long she has, Addy. I think a lot of it depends on how well she follows orders."

Addy sighed. Aunt Kate wasn't likely to voluntarily sit back and do nothing. "Well, we'll just have to make her follow them."

Ma's brow wrinkled as she gave a little nod. "Honey, you need to remember she's not a young woman anymore."

"I know, Ma." Addy's voice broke, and she fought back the tears she'd been holding in for hours. Aunt Kate had been in her fifties when Ma and Uncle Will had come to live with their father's older sister. That was more than thirty years ago. "I'm so sorry, Ma. I know how much you love her."

Ma nodded, her eyes swimming, and turned back around on the wagon seat.

"Ma, would you like for me to ride over to Abby and Rafe's before I go to school in the morning?" That not only would save her mother time but would also keep her from having to tell the sad news once more.

"Yes, if you're sure you have time. I wouldn't want you to be late." The relief in Ma's voice was obvious.

"I could take Betty over there if you want me to. I know Abby wouldn't mind watching her while you go over to Uncle Will's."

"That might be a good idea, Lexie," Pa said. "That way she won't have to go out to the field with me."

Addy leaned back against the side of the wagon and let her silent tears flow.

⁌

Jim laughed as one of the twin boys grabbed Rafe around the knees.

"Take me, Papa. Take me." The toddler chortled, holding tight.

"Now, Dawson"—Rafe leaned over and gently removed the child's arms from his leg—"I told you, you can't go to the field with me today. I have too much work to do."

Dawson's chin quivered as he attempted to hold back tears. "But I help."

As Rafe spoke softly to the child, Jim couldn't help but grin at the change in his friend over the last few years. He turned at the sound of horses approaching. His heart thundered inside his chest at the sight of Addy.

Rafe stood, holding Dawson in his arms while Jim lifted tiny Betty from the buggy then helped Addy to alight.

"Betty honey, why don't you take Dawson and Davie to their room and tell them a story while I talk to Rafe and Abby."

"Okay, but her name's really Tuck, you know." Betty took the hand of the little boy whom Rafe had deposited on the porch, and they went inside.

"What's wrong, sis?"

Jim glanced at his friend. He'd never heard Rafe speak so tenderly to Addy before. Usually he just teased her.

"Oh Rafe, it's Aunt Kate." Her face crumpled, and she fought back tears.

Jim took a step toward her but stopped when Rafe put an arm around her and led her toward the door. Jim wanted nothing but to go with them, to wrap his arms around Addy and shield her from whatever was causing her grief. But he hadn't the right. He took a deep breath.

"I'll wait out here," he said.

Rafe nodded, but Addy stopped and gave him an almost pleading look. "No, please come inside with us."

"Of course." Mixed feelings battled within him. Sorrow and fear at whatever was causing Addy's pain but joy that she wanted him with her.

When they stepped inside, Abby came from the kitchen, wiping her hands on her apron. "Addy, what are you doing here this time of day?"

"It's Aunt Kate. There's something wrong with her heart." She reached both arms out to her sister, and they held each other tightly.

"Come into the parlor and sit down. Tell me everything."

Jim frowned as Addy told them the news about her great-aunt.

Abby jumped up, her face white. "I'm going over there right now. Maybe she'll listen to me. I'm not ready to let her go."

Rafe took his wife's hand and pulled her gently back down beside him. "Sweetheart, calm down. You can't go over there in this state."

Addy took her sister's other hand. "I don't know yet just how bad it is. Ma was too upset to talk much. But she needs to go over and check on Aunt Kate and talk to Sarah and Will, probably about Aunt Kate's care. I really need you to stay here and keep Betty while I'm at school. Would you mind?"

Abby let out a long, slow breath. "All right, I will. But as soon as you pick her up, I'm going."

Addy stood and placed a hand on her sister's shoulder. "Try not to worry too much. Ma didn't say she was going to die, just that she had to slow down. Remember last year, when Mr. Wilkins started having heart problems? His daughters all thought he was dying, but he's doing fine."

"That's right." Abby perked up. "He played three games of horseshoes at the last church picnic."

Jim watched in amazement at the composure on Addy's face. She'd calmed down not only her sister but herself as well. Jim followed her out onto the porch. "I'm heading into town, too. Would you mind if I ride along beside you?"

Relief crossed her face. "I'd be grateful. To be honest, I'd just as soon not be alone with my thoughts."

He mounted Finch and kept his pace with Addy's. They rode in silence for a few moments, and then Addy sighed.

Jim groped in his mind for something to say to get her mind off her aunt's condition.

"I don't believe I've ever seen so much honeysuckle growing in one area." Great, talk about flowers.

"I know." She threw him a pensive smile. "I've always loved the aroma. Even better than lilacs, I believe."

Well, if talking about flowers would make her feel better, that's what he'd do. "Have you ever smelled magnolia blossoms?"

"No, I don't believe I have." She glanced up, her blue eyes wide. "They grow on trees, don't they?"

"Yes, and mostly down south. The blossoms have a sweet, lemony smell."

She giggled. "Sweet? Lemony? Lemons don't smell sweet."

He laughed. "Maybe I should have said lemonade."

"Or lemon pie," she said with a teasing grin.

"Or lemon soda," he said, picking up the game.

"Do magnolia trees grow very big?"

"Some of them are very large. And the leaves are deep velvety, satiny green."

"Now there you go again. How can they be satin and velvet at the same time?" Her lips puckered in an amused smile, and he wanted nothing more than to bend over and press his own against their softness.

"You're absolutely right." He wondered if his voice sounded as shaky to her as it did to him. "I need to get my facts straight before attempting to teach a teacher."

They arrived in front of the school laughing. Jim dismounted and held his hand out to her. As she placed her soft hand into his rough paw, his throat constricted, and he swallowed past what felt like a lump.

She looked up into his eyes and smiled. "Thank you for getting my mind off Aunt Kate for a while. It wouldn't do for me to be in tears all day while I'm trying to teach."

"It was my pleasure, Addy." He lifted her hand and brushed his lips across their softness.

"Have a pleasant day, my dear." He stood and watched as she entered the building. Then he mounted his horse and headed toward the hunting lodge construction site.

Chapter 10

Would the man ever get to the point? Addy cringed at her disrespect as Reverend Smith's voice droned on and on. But really. If her nerves hadn't been on edge from being sandwiched between her mother and Jim, she was sure she'd have nodded off to sleep by now. She fanned her fingers in front of her face. It didn't do anything for the hot air, but at least it kept her from yawning.

The sermon was on mutual respect in the family and should have been interesting and helpful, but Addy was hard put not to squirm.

Wait. What was he saying? *No, oh please, God, don't let him read from Song of Solomon. Not with Jim Castle seated next to me.*

" 'Behold, thou art fair, my love; behold, thou art fair; thou hast doves' eyes within thy locks: thy hair is as a flock of goats. . . .' "

Chapter four. He was reading from chapter four. Addy's mind tore through the chapter she had thought so beautiful in her private Bible readings. Oh no. Surely he wouldn't continue. She gasped as he continued through verse four.

A movement beside her drew her attention. Jim was shaking. Was he laughing at her?

In spite of her embarrassment, she threw him a look that she hoped would show him what she thought of his inappropriate amusement.

"Well, I won't go on because I don't want to offend any of our ladies, but the Song of Solomon reveals Christ's love for the church, and as we are told in Ephesians 5:25, 'Husbands, love your wives, even as Christ also loved the church, and gave himself for it.' "

Addy let out a breath she hadn't realized she was holding and focused on Reverend Smith's face in an attempt to avoid Jim's.

As soon as the final benediction had been said, Addy stood and followed Ma out, conscious of Jim crowding her from behind.

When she stepped outside the old log building into the sunshine, she inhaled deeply of the fresh air.

Jim stepped up beside her. She glared at him but nevertheless took his proffered arm.

Ma turned to Jim with a huge smile. "We're so pleased you are coming to dinner, Mr. Castle."

"Thank you, ma'am. And I'm honored to have been invited, but I assure you, I'll understand if you want to make it another time. I realize Miss Rayton's illness is a worry for you." He returned her smile.

"Actually Aunt Kate is doing very well. She's even following doctor's orders and is feeling much better." Ma's voice rang with relief.

They'd all been surprised when Aunt Kate rallied a couple of days after her visit to the doctor. Addy wondered if the doctor had given them a false diagnosis. She couldn't help the hope that rose in her at the thought.

"I'm very happy to hear that. And since that is the case, I will be delighted to accept that invitation." He hesitated before adding, "I hope you don't mind if I offer Addy a ride to your home."

"I don't mind at all. You two run right along. We'll see you there." She climbed into the carriage beside Pa and Betty, and the next thing Addy knew she was standing beside Jim, quite alone.

"Addy, I'm so sorry that I offended you when I laughed. I don't know what came over me."

She narrowed her eyes at him. He seemed sincere. Perhaps he really hadn't intended to laugh, although what he could have possibly thought was funny was beyond her. "Very well, Mr. Castle. I think I can overlook your indiscretion just this once."

"I'm deeply grateful, but it's Jim, remember?"

She took a deep breath and blew it out with a gush. "Oh, all right, Jim."

As they rode down the lane toward the farm, Jim glanced at her. "How about going for a drive this afternoon?"

"A drive where, in particular?"

"Oh, I haven't been to Marble Cave since I've been back in town."

She wrinkled her nose. "Why do you want to go there? I've always hated that dirty cave."

"We wouldn't need to go inside the cave. I'd sort of like to say hello to the Lynch family."

"I suppose that would be all right. I haven't visited with the Lynch sisters in ages." She threw him a teasing glance. "But don't think you'll change my mind about going inside that cave. Because you won't."

"I wouldn't dream of it. He grinned and clicked to the horse that'd slowed to a walk. Within a few minutes they were pulling alongside the Sullivans' porch.

Addy turned toward the door, and Jim placed his hand on her arm. "You're really going to have to stop jumping down by yourself. How will I ever convince you I'm a gentleman if you won't even allow me to help you from a carriage?"

She blushed but remained in her seat until he came around to help her down.

After leaving Jim in the parlor with Pa, Addy went to the kitchen to help her ma, who was dishing up summer squash and stewed tomatoes into serving bowls. A platter filled with slices of sizzling fried ham stood on the kitchen table.

Addy washed her hands and donned an apron. "I'll set the table."

"Ma already set the table," Betty announced. "And I helped. And I took the preserves and pickled peaches in, too."

Addy gave her little sister a smile and planted a kiss on her head. "You're getting to be such a big girl, Bets, and a real help to Ma."

Betty nodded, a proud grin on her face. "That's what Pa said, too."

Addy wondered, not for the first time, why Ma and Pa waited so long to have a child. Addy and her sister were nearly twenty-one when Betty was born. So Ma Lexie would have been close to forty. Of course, it couldn't have been easy, starting their married life with two nine-year-old orphan girls. She wondered if that was why they'd waited. She'd never had the nerve to ask the personal question. "Well then, I'll start carrying the food into the dining room, Ma."

"Oh, thank you, dear. The bread will be nice and warm in just a moment."

A few minutes later, Addy surveyed the laden table. She straightened a napkin or two then went to the parlor to call Pa and Jim to dinner.

Jim looked up as she entered the room, and as their eyes met, butterflies did a flip-flop in Addy's stomach. He stood and offered his arm.

When she placed her hand on his forearm, a tingle began in her fingers, and by the time they arrived at the table, it had reached her heart.

⁂

She felt it, too. He could tell by the look on her face. It wasn't his imagination. On the other hand, her obvious embarrassment that had begun with the minister's sermon seemed to be growing worse, and his heart ached for her. He simply must do something to get her mind off it.

"Jack, it's come to my attention you were a riverboat captain at one time." Oops. That might not be the best topic since she was the one who told him about her father's previous occupation.

A light came into Jack's eyes. "Yes, as a matter of fact, I was. I captained the *Julia Dawn* for a number of years."

"That must have been exciting. Ever come across river pirates?" Of course not. The man wasn't that old. River piracy had pretty much come to an end before the mid-1800s.

Jack gave him a curious look, and then his glance flitted to Addy. He turned his attention back to Jim, understanding in his eyes. "No, the river pirates' day had ended before my first cabin boy job. But I knew an old galley cook who could tell some hair-raising stories about when he was a lad on the river."

Addy's eyes came alive with excitement. "Do you mean Pap Sanders?"

"That's right. Pap was getting up there in years by the time I signed on as a cabin boy. He almost made me wish I'd been born back in the days of the river pirates." A hearty chuckle exploded from his lips. "Of course, youngsters don't have a lot of sense."

"He didn't tell Tuck and me about any river pirates. I mean Abby and me."

"Because I threatened him within an inch of his life if he so much as mentioned the word in your presence." Jack smiled at her then looked at Betty, who stared at him, wide eyed. He gave her a wink then turned to Jim. "Which reminds me there is a child at the table. We'd best continue this conversation later."

"Of course," Jim said. "Did you grow up around here, sir?"

Jack didn't answer for a moment. Then he nodded. "I lived in this house with my uncle for four years after my parents died. I didn't have much use for it then. Or anything else for that matter. I took off when I was sixteen. Signed on with the first steamboat I came across that would hire me."

His eyes rested on his wife, and they exchanged warm smiles. "It was years before I learned to love this place. I miss the river now and then, but I've never regretted selling out. Farming is in my blood now, and I love it as much as or more than I ever loved my life up and down the river."

Jim was almost embarrassed to be witnessing the love between Jim and Lexie. What would it be like to come home to a wife and children who loved him? He swallowed past the lump that suddenly clogged his throat. What was the matter with him? It wasn't like him to be sentimental. But he couldn't deny the longing that had sprung up inside.

He cleared his throat and took a bite of squash, relishing the buttery taste. It was good to get some home cooking. And the fried ham slices were about the best he'd ever tasted. Almost as good as the fried chicken at the picnic. He wondered if Addy would ever learn to fry chicken like that.

Realizing the direction his thoughts were headed, he scrambled around for something to say to get his mind off marriage to Addy. "Mrs. Sullivan, you're a wonderful cook. I can't remember ever eating ham that tasted this good."

A pleased blush washed over her cheeks. "Why thank you, Mr. Castle. I do believe you said the same thing about my fried chicken at the picnic. I'm very pleased that you like my cooking."

After the meal, Addy and her mother began clearing the table.

"Jim, let's go sit on the front porch and let our food settle," Jack suggested.

"Sounds good to me." Jim followed him outside where they sat on cane-bottomed chairs. "Did you make these?"

Jack grinned. "Wish I could take credit, but I never had the patience to learn the craft. Rafe's pa makes them. His pa taught him, and I guess his pa's pa and on up the line. I also have a couple of horsehair chairs he made."

Jim shook his head. "I think I saw a couple of those at Rafe's house."

"Yes, it's going to be a lost art before long. The younger folks want fancy store-bought furniture and don't appreciate the beauty and the love that goes into these."

"Or the time."

"Or the time," Jack echoed.

The door opened and Addy stepped onto the porch. "Oh, blessed relief," she said. "It feels nice out here."

Jack stood and stretched. "Well, I think I'll take my Sunday afternoon snooze. I guess you two can keep each other company."

"I guess we can, Pa," Addy said. "Enjoy your rest. We might go over to Marble Cave. Let Ma know so she won't worry about where I am." She gazed after him with a fond smile then sat in the chair he'd vacated.

"We don't have to go there if you don't want to, Addy. We could go for a ride by the river. It's probably cooler there."

"No, I don't mind. I'm sort of looking forward to seeing the Lynch girls." She giggled. "Although I don't think they could rightly be called girls, and neither one of them is a Lynch anymore."

He grinned but not at her words. What an enchanting little giggle. A ride by the river was sounding more and more pleasant. Too bad he'd mentioned the cave. Ah well, he wondered if the sight of the place would remind her of their first meeting.

Chapter 11

Addy leaned back in the buggy seat, enjoying the summer greenery as they passed through the narrow tree-lined road. Addy was surprised to see at least a dozen buggies in the clearing by the cave in addition to a number of saddle horses. She hadn't realized the Lynches were this busy.

As they pulled up in front of the Marble Cave office, a sense of familiarity surged through her. She didn't think she'd come here since Abby married. And she'd only been here a couple of times before that. Once to hear her sister and the old men in her band.

Did Abby miss playing the violin in public? She said she didn't, but she sure didn't turn down any chance to play for the family or church programs. There was no denying Abby had talent. With the proper training, there was no telling how far she could have gone.

As they got out of the buggy, Mr. Lynch came forward, a huge grin on his face. He grabbed Addy's hand in both of his huge ones. "Tuck Collins! It's about time you came to see me."

Addy laughed. "Sorry, sir. I'm not Tuck. I'm her twin sister, Addy Sullivan."

Consternation crossed his face. "Oh. Miss Sullivan, forgive me. I never could tell you two apart. Except when Tuck was wearing her overalls." His jovial voice boomed.

She retrieved her hand, which was growing numb in his tight clasp. "That's quite all right, Mr. Lynch," she said. "It's a common mistake." Though not as often since Addy had been teaching school in town.

The two men shook hands, and Mr. Lynch said, "What brings you today, Jim?"

"I mainly wanted to see the place for old time's sake." As organ music bellowed from the cave, Jim darted a glance in that direction. "What's going on in the cave?"

"Ah, a wedding today. A young couple from Forsyth thought it would be romantic to get married in the Cathedral Room. After the ceremony, you should take a look at how well my girls decorated the cavern." He spoke with pride, and Addy knew it was well deserved. The Lynch sisters were known for their talents in music and decorating. "They're also providing the music. My youngest is playing the organ, and the oldest sang a special song. I wish you could've heard her sing." He kissed his lips to his fingers in appreciation.

"I've heard her sing many times, Mr. Lynch, at community socials," Addy said. "It's something I always look forward to. She has such a lovely voice."

"Ah yes, Miss Sullivan, and your sister is very talented, too. Tell her I miss her fiddle very much."

"I will." Addy smiled and glanced at Jim. He held out his arm, and she laid her hand on it, relieved he was ready to go.

"If you don't mind, sir, I'd like to take Addy for a stroll."

She groaned inwardly. The sooner she got away from the cave, the happier she'd be.

They strolled through a wooded area then walked up a path until they stood on a bluff overlooking the cave.

"Isn't this the site of the old mining town?"

"Yes, Marmoros." He shook his head. "I've heard it was a fairly wild place before it burned down."

Addy nodded. "It didn't just burn down. The Baldknobbers did it deliberately, or so they say."

"Yes, I heard that, too." He frowned. "I wonder why they did it."

She shrugged. "Who knows? From what I've heard, they wanted to control everything. They didn't want the town here for some reason. And it seems they got their way." Sudden nostalgia gripped her. "Actually that was the night I first met Ma Lexie."

"Really?"

"Yes. You see, Papa Jack had taken Abby and me in a few days before." She gave him a side grin. "Well, actually, we were camping out in his house when he came home from a trip down the river. He found us and didn't know what to do with us."

Interest washed over his face, and he laughed. "I'd like to hear all of that story."

"Maybe someday," she said with a smile. "But to go on with this story, Papa Jack smelled smoke and finally saw flames coming from Marmoros. He told us to stay in the house and took off on his horse. About an hour later, we were just about to go looking for him when Ma and Uncle Will showed up with Pa all wounded. At first we thought he was dead."

"That must have been frightening."

"It was. When we saw he was alive but unconscious, we figured they might take us to an orphanage, so we pretended Jack was our Pa. Boy did that lie cause a lot of trouble for everyone." She still felt guilt over that every now and then.

"So your parents met here by Marble Cave," he said with an odd look on his face.

"Well, so to speak. They actually saw each other once before in Forsyth."

"You and I met here, too, you know," he said. "I think you've forgotten."

"Here?" She searched her memories. "No, Jim. We met at Abby and Rafe's wedding, remember?"

"Think back, Addy. Remember the day Abby came to apply for the temporary job for her band? Because the Lynch girls were going away on vacation?"

Suddenly light broke through the darkness. She remembered following Abby into the little office. Rafe had been there and. . .Jim! He was the one who took Abby's application. "Yes, I do remember now. I was in such a hurry to get away from the place, I couldn't think of anything else. I just knew Abby would try to talk me into entering the cave."

"You were wearing a blue dress with lace on the sleeves and collar," he said. "And you had a blue ribbon in your hair."

"Fancy you remembering that." How could he have carried around such a momentary memory for all this time? Even to remembering what she was wearing?

"It was easy for me to remember, Addy. You were and still are the most beautiful girl I've ever seen."

✤

Jim watched as varying emotions washed over Addy's face. Had he said too much? Would she think he was foolish? Or worse still, could he have been wrong to think she was beginning to return his feelings? That would make him as pathetic as the doctor.

He held his breath as a blush washed over her cheeks. She didn't appear to be angry or disgusted. If anything, she looked pleased. He took a deep breath as relief surged through him.

She cleared her throat. "Thank you. That's a very nice thing to say, although I'm sure you're only teasing me."

"My dear"—he took her hands, and she lowered her eyes—"I mean every word of it."

"Thank you," she whispered then gently removed her hands from his. "But perhaps we should go now."

"Of course." He led her down the steep pathway toward the cave, where the wedding party was ascending from the enormous Cathedral Room below. He hoped the stairs had been replaced with something a little more fitting for formal clothing.

The bride and groom stood to one side shaking hands with their guests. Apparently they had no plans to run away from the crowd, at least not for the present.

Addy had paused, and when Jim looked at her, her eyes were focused on the bride. Her hand resting on his arm trembled. She darted a look up at him, and when she realized he was watching her, she blushed once more.

He helped her into the buggy and started down the road toward her home. Wanting to put her at ease, he smiled. "If you have no objection and no other plans, I'd like to take you to dinner at the Branson Hotel next week. After all, I've accepted your family's hospitality several times."

Suddenly she looked straight into his eyes. "I have no objections at all."

He grinned at her sudden transformation from shyness to honesty. "In that case, will you marry me?"

"Oh, you. Don't be silly." She cast a captivating smile his way. "Don't get too sure of yourself. I've only agreed to dinner. I haven't said I'd marry you."

"Are you by any chance telling me to slow down?" He felt giddy as a girl from her new attitude toward him.

"Yes, indeed, Mr. Jim Castle." Suddenly the laughter slid from her face. "I would love to be your friend. Rafe and Abby have been best friends nearly all their lives. I believe friendship is very important in any relationship. Don't you agree?"

"I do agree. And since we're now discussing Rafe and Abby, does that mean you might marry me after all?"

"Oh! There you go teasing me." She pressed her lips together in an unsuccessful attempt to hide the smile that was teasing her lips. "Let's talk about something else."

"Very well. Your wish is my wish. What would you like to talk about?"

"I don't know." She was silent for a moment. "Oh, yes I do. Tell me about the new hunting lodge."

This girl never ceased to surprise him. "What do you want to know about it?"

"What sort of staff will they need? And will they be hiring local people?"

"Partly. They'll bring a management team from St. Louis. But they'll be hiring locals for bellboys and other serving and cleaning staff."

"Will they hire any women?"

"I'm sure they'll hire women for housekeeping."

"But not for the desk or serving?" Disappointment filled her eyes. Now what had she been thinking?

"Very unlikely. Since this will be a gentleman's lodge, they'll hire mostly male staff." He cut a glance at her, curious about the types of questions she was asking. "Why? Do you know someone who needs employment?"

"Oh, no, no. I was just curious, that's all." She frowned and looked away. "My, the honeysuckle does smell sweet."

Back to flowers again. "Yes, they do. Quite a heady smell, I'd say."

When they arrived at the farm, the family was sitting down to supper. Lexie insisted that Jim join them for ham sandwiches and potato salad left over from dinner.

Betty kept up a continuous round of questions directed at Jim, until finally her Pa told her that was quite enough and to stop being rude. With a pout, she said, "I'm sorry, Mr. Jim."

"That's quite all right, Miss Betty. I always enjoy the conversation of beautiful young ladies." He threw her a grin and a wink, and she giggled.

When he'd taken his last delicious bite of blackberry cobbler, Jim asked Jack if he could speak to him in private.

With a knowing look, Jack agreed, and they went onto the front porch.

As Jim drove toward town later, he couldn't help laughing at himself. He'd been as nervous as a gangling boy as he asked Jack for permission to court his daughter. And the nervousness didn't end there. Jack had shot question after question at Jim for at least a half hour.

The hard question he'd saved for last. "What are your plans for the future?"

"Sir, I wish I could say we'd settle down here, but you know my job takes me all over the country. Sometimes out of the country."

"Does Addy know you intend to stay with your present job?"

Jim shook his head. "We haven't actually discussed that yet. But I promise I'll speak to her about it soon."

Jack nodded. "Make it very soon. Before you talk to her about courting. I won't have you courting her under false pretenses."

"I'm leaving for Kansas City tomorrow, but I promise I'll talk to her as soon as I get back. In fact, we're having dinner together next Sunday." He hastened to add, "Just as friends of course."

Finally Jack offered his hand and said he had no objection at all as long as Addy was agreeable as well.

As Jim rode into town, worry and a niggling doubt wormed their way into his thoughts. He'd finally settled it for himself that things could work out well, even if he was on the road a lot. She could travel with him most of the time.

But now he wasn't so sure. What if she wasn't willing? Maybe he shouldn't have been in such a hurry to talk to Jack.

Chapter 12

Addy couldn't believe how much she missed seeing Jim around town. When she drove in each morning, her eyes automatically wandered to the Branson Hotel, although she knew he wouldn't be back until later in the week. When she left school in the afternoon, her vision roamed the area, searching for a sight of his tall form and broad shoulders.

He'd said good-bye Sunday night and told her he'd be gone most of the week but would try to be back in time for the children's program on Friday.

She wondered what he'd spoken to Pa about after dinner Sunday night. Could he have been asking to court her? But then, wouldn't he have said something? Or wouldn't Pa have? Unless Pa said no, but that wasn't likely. After all, this wasn't the Dark Ages, and a girl had a right to choose her own beau these days. If Pa had disapproved for some reason, he'd have still left the choice to her.

"Miss Sullivan, Johnny pulled my hair!" A screech from across the room drew Addy's attention back to her class.

She focused her gaze on the small culprit. "Johnny, go sit on the stool in the corner."

"Aw, Miss Sullivan, I'm sorry."

"I certainly hope you are sorry. Perhaps while you're in the corner you will consider how it feels to have someone yank on your hair. Then perhaps you will be truly sorry and can honestly apologize to Alice."

"Yes, ma'am." Johnny trudged to the punishing corner and perched on the stool, his back to the classroom.

"All right, class." She motioned to the class project hanging on the front wall. "Our project looks wonderful, and it's very informative. All the individual pictures and essays will go on the wall tomorrow. We only have today and tomorrow to practice for our program. Friday, we'll have to get the classroom ready. No homework tonight. Is everybody happy?"

A chorus of "uh huhs" and "yes, ma'ams" thundered across the room.

Addy grinned and lifted her hand. "All right. Put your things away and line up."

"What about me?" Johnny wailed from his stool.

"You, too, Johnny. But I'd like for you to apologize to Alice for pulling her hair. And I'm not sure you've learned your lesson in ten minutes. So you will have to clean the blackboard the rest of this week."

Ten minutes later, she dismissed the children and gathered her own things together. She locked the door behind her and stood on the step for a moment, glancing toward the business section of town, finally resting her eyes on the luxury hotel down the street. Her heart raced, and she pictured herself seated across a cloth-covered table in a corner of the room. The lights would be turned down low.

Oh stop it, Addy. You'll be dining on Sunday afternoon in broad daylight.

With a shake of her head, she stepped into the dusty street. She spoke a few words to Bobby before handing him his coin then climbed into her buggy.

She sat for a moment, undecided about whether to ride over to see Aunt Kate or go straight home. Finally she drove to the Rayton farm and spent time with her great-aunt. She was pleased and relieved to see some color back in Aunt Kate's face.

"Mercy, child, don't you be worrying about me. I'm taking things slow just like the doctor said, and I'm feeling a lot better." Aunt Kate rocked back and forth slowly in her chair. "See? I'm even rocking slowly."

Addy laughed as she drove away an hour later. Restless and on a sudden whim, she took the river road and drove to the family's favorite picnic spot. She got out and sat on a low bank, her feet almost touching the water.

Her thoughts went back to gliding past here on the deck of the *Julia Dawn*. She could almost hear the tinkling laughter of her and her sister as they ran and played above and below deck.

And good old Pap with his fiddle and his wild stories. It was true she'd never heard about the pirates from him, but she could remember shivering with fright as she and Abby huddled together on one of their bunks after a ghost story told on deck as the moon drifted behind the clouds. Of course Papa Jack never knew about it. He'd have raked Pap over the coals, but the girls would beg, and finally Pap would give in. She could still get goose bumps thinking about some of those old stories.

Her favorite times on the *Julia Dawn* were those mornings when they were allowed to get up early and watch the sun rise, its colorful rays peeping through the trees and reflecting on the water. The most beautiful sight she'd ever seen.

Someday she was going to board a steamboat and go down the river again. Of course, they were few and far between these days, and now that the White River Line was almost completed, they might disappear altogether. Anyway, it wouldn't be the same without Abby.

She scampered to her feet and climbed into the buggy. She was being silly. After all, she was a grown woman. It was time to put away childish thoughts of adventure.

She arrived home just in time to help Ma get supper on the table.

"How many days until the school program, sister?" Betty asked her this every day. The little girl was beside herself with excitement.

Addy smiled. "Just three more, Bets."

Betty jumped up and down, and Addy grabbed the plate her sister was carrying just as it slipped from her hands. "Oh, Sorry, Addy. I'm so excited. I can't wait."

Addy laughed, "Me either. It's going to be a lot of fun, and you'll hear about adventures galore."

She looked fondly at her little sister's glowing face. Thank goodness Betty had years before she'd have to put aside her dreams of adventure.

⌘

Jim opened the oversized menu with the star on the front. He'd had two invitations to dinner tonight but didn't feel like being around a lot of people. All he wanted to do was brood over Addy.

Dinner invitations weren't the only things he'd bowed out of. He'd turned down two more job offers this week. One group needed him next month, so that one had been easy to say no to, but the other, an exclusive New Orleans restaurant that had been losing its clientele, offered to wait until September in order to obtain his services. Jim knew he'd be finished here in Branson by then, but he didn't know if his situation with Addy would be settled. Would she be willing to leave Branson? He'd refused the offer. He could kick himself for not getting it settled before he'd left for Kansas City. He was afraid. That was the problem.

Maybe he should look around in Kansas City or St. Louis for a job. There wasn't any rule that said he had to keep doing what he was doing. Then they'd be close enough to visit Addy's family often. Not traveling all over the country. What had he been thinking? What kind of life was that for a woman?

The waiter came and took his order.

Jim took a long drink from his glass of ice water. Could he do it? Give up the career he'd built up over the past couple of years?

His steak arrived, but he'd lost his appetite. The porterhouse tasted like a slab of sawdust. Maybe it would have been better if he'd never taken the job in Branson.

⌘

Addy breathed in the scent of the early summer afternoon as she drove her buggy up the lane toward Abby and Rafe's place. The kids had been high-strung today. She couldn't really blame them. They'd had a couple of accidents while gluing last-minute pictures on construction paper. But all ended well, and the walls of the room told the history of their hometown.

The children had been proud as they walked around the perimeter of the room and saw what they had accomplished. She hoped the parents would appreciate the labor of love they'd put into this project.

The final program practice had been a little rough, but she was sure the performance would go well. They knew their lines, and some of them were very good little actors and actresses.

In spite of all the busyness and excitement of the day, Addy had been restless. And for some reason, she had a strong urge to see Abby. She hoped her sister wasn't busy, but if she was, Addy would just pitch in and help her with whatever she was doing. They'd always worked well together.

Addy enjoyed the tomato canning season when she and Abby and Ma went to Aunt Kate's house and worked together to get tomatoes put up for the families and get others ready to sell to the tomato factory. It was always the highlight of the summer for Addy, in spite of the hard work.

But that was at least a month away. For now, she simply needed to see her sister's face and spend some time talking.

After three years, she should be used to Abby being gone, and she supposed it was easier than it used to be. But sometimes, like now, she missed her sister so much she simply needed that contact. She wondered if Abby felt the same. Probably not. After all, she had Rafe and their twin sons.

The farmhouse came into view, and Addy pulled up in front of the house, tying her horse loosely to the rail. She wouldn't be here that long, so no sense in unhitching him.

She tapped on the screen door and went on in. The aromas of fried pork chops and cooked apples tantalized her nostrils. "Abby?" she called out.

Abby's voice came from the kitchen. "I'm back here, sis."

Addy stepped into the kitchen and was greeted by four little arms encircling her legs.

"Aunt D, Aunt D." Their version of Aunt Addy.

She knelt down beside her nephews and gave them hugs, receiving sticky kisses in exchange.

"Uh oh. You boys have been scraping the apple bowl, haven't you?"

Abby laughed. "I always leave a little in there when I put them in to bake. For one thing, it keeps them occupied for a few minutes so I can get something done."

"You're very blessed, you know." Addy knew she sounded wistful and only hoped she didn't sound downright jealous.

Abby poured a cup of coffee and set it on the table. "Here, you look like you need this. And yes, I know I'm blessed."

Addy sat at the table while her sister washed the boys' faces and hands and then set them in the corner with their toys. Abby then sat across the table from Addy. "I'm glad you stopped by. Everything's okay, isn't it?" Abby scrutinized her twin's face.

"Yes, I just wanted to see you." Addy's eyes roamed to the boys again.

Abby reached over and placed a hand on Addy's. "You'll have children of your own one day, sis."

Addy nodded. "I hope so. I really do." She turned and looked at her twin. "Do you ever miss your old life? When you were with the band? And even before when we used to go with Papa Jack on the *Julia Dawn*?"

"Sure." Abby frowned a little. "I miss those things sometimes. But I wouldn't give up my life with Rafe and my boys for anything."

Addy nodded. She wanted to tell Abby how torn she felt. Part of her yearned to settle down with a husband and babies, but another part wanted to hop on a train or a boat and explore the world. But she couldn't say that to Abby. Her sister would think she was losing her mind.

Maybe she was. One minute she was dreaming of Jim Castle asking for her hand in marriage, and the next her thoughts took her away to strange and new places.

How could she be so double-minded?

Chapter 13

Addy peeped out from behind the curtain hung to separate the actors from the rest of the room. She almost giggled at the sight of proud mamas seated on the small chairs that usually sat behind the students' desks. Johnny's mother had somehow managed to fit her portly body on one of the chairs, albeit squeezed tightly against Clara May's tiny bit of a mother on one side and Mrs. Marshall on the other. Ma and Addy perched on their chairs, with Betty on Ma's lap. At last year's Christmas party, Addy had planned to ask folks to bring chairs but was informed by several students that the parents always managed fine on the children's chairs and they probably wouldn't like it if she tried to change things.

Most of the men were lined up against the back wall, including Pa and Rafe, who each held one of the twins.

She scanned the room for Jim, but he hadn't yet arrived. Perhaps he wouldn't be back in time.

When it appeared that everyone was there who was coming, Addy stepped out and smiled at the crowd. "Ladies and gentlemen, we are so pleased you could come tonight. Your children have worked hard on this presentation, which depicts the history of transportation in our region. When the play is over, please feel free to look over the essays and pictures that are posted on the walls. The front wall from side to side is our joint project and tells the same story that you will see performed live. The other walls contain individual illustrated essays about the first train into Branson. These contain your children's own thoughts about the events of that day. We hope you will enjoy your evening. At this time, I'd like to introduce our narrator, Miss Annie Brown."

Hearty applause sounded across the room as fourteen-year-old Annie stepped out wearing a long, pioneer-type dress with an old-fashioned bonnet atop her head.

The curtain was pulled back, and Johnny and Sam, faces painted and dressed in buckskins, stepped in through the door. Each of the boys wore a band around his head with a feather sticking up proudly. With solemn looks on their faces, befitting the stalwart race they represented, each led an Indian pony across the front of the room while Annie told the story of the native population of Branson many years ago and their mode of transportation.

Whistles and clapping thundered through the schoolhouse as the boys led the ponies down the side aisle toward the front door. The effect of their solemn expressions was spoiled as they gave war cries while leading the ponies through the door.

Addy closed her eyes and shook her head while laughter exploded from the men. But she grinned and breathed a sigh of relief that there'd been no accidents. She hadn't relished the thought of cleaning up horse manure.

Next a small covered wagon made of cardboard and sheets rolled across the room. Two boys dressed up like oxen pulled the wagon along. No one seemed to mind that instead of four wheels, eight feet stuck out the bottom.

Addy, directing things, still managed to keep an eye out for Jim. The covered wagon had just made its way through the front door when his tall form stepped inside. His eyes searched the room until they spotted her. Addy attempted to keep her delight and excitement from her countenance, but when he grinned, she was pretty sure she hadn't succeeded.

She made it through the rest of the program without too many glances toward the back wall where he stood.

The final mode of transportation to be displayed was the students' pride and glory. A huge black engine made of cardboard chugged across the stage followed by two freight cars. The audience showed its approval of the train and the actors by whistles and applause.

When the train had made its way outside, Annie explained that as soon as the two ends of the White River Line met and connected, they would have passenger coaches as well.

The curtain was drawn again as all the students made their way back inside through the back door. Then it was pulled open, and with Addy on the piano, the class sang the closing song, "I've Been Working on the Railroad." When the chorus began for the second time, most of the audience members joined in.

Addy glanced at the crowd. From the proud looks on their faces and the jovial comments they made to one another, it was apparent the program was a huge success. Once more she reminded the guests not to leave before looking at the projects on the walls.

She glanced around for Jim. He stood reading one of the essays with a smile on his face. Her heart thumped. Of course he would find the essays interesting. He had interests in the railroad coming into Branson.

Suddenly a thought popped into her mind. She had no idea what those interests were. They had never really discussed what Jim did for a living. They always seemed to talk about her. She blushed. He must think she was terribly self-centered.

She pursed her lips. She was pretty sure it had something to do with the railroad. Didn't it? Oh dear, somehow she must turn their conversation to him when they spoke again. Or perhaps she should ask Abby. That way she wouldn't have to admit she didn't know anything about him except that he was handsome, he was Rafe's best friend, and he thought she was pretty.

She started as he appeared at her side. "Good evening, Jim."

"A very good evening," he said. "Your students are talented."

"Thank you. I think so, too. Fenton Taylor is a fine artist, and Annie Bolton writes very well."

"Yes, I saw her essay. She shows a lot of promise." He smiled into her eyes.

Addy fidgeted under his scrutiny. She cleared her throat. "Well, I'd best get this room straightened up."

"I'll help."

"Oh, there's no need. I'll come in next week and put things away and do a thorough cleaning." She glanced at him and smiled. "But thank you for the offer."

"Then will you allow me to accompany you home? I'll just ride next to your buggy. That way your family won't need to wait for you."

"That would be kind. I'd like that very much."

A ride home in the moonlight? Was that really wise? She took a deep breath. Who cared if it was wise? Jim was a perfect gentleman, and she'd be quite safe with him.

⁂

What was he doing? Jim mentally kicked himself. He'd had every intention of watching the program then saying good night, having made the decision not to spend time with Addy until Sunday when he'd have a chance to talk to her. It wasn't fair of him to seek her out when she wasn't aware of the facts concerning his plans for the future. But one glance at the joy on her face when she saw him standing there and he could no more have left than he could have jumped in ice water.

Now as Jim held Finch back to keep pace with her buggy, his breath caught as moonlight danced in her hair and touched her brow. Inwardly he groaned. Every time he was near her, he felt the attachment grow. If something wasn't settled soon, would he be able to walk away?

Perhaps he should talk to her tonight. But no, he wanted to be able to focus his attention on her. To have a chance to read her face, in case she avoided revealing her feelings. Anyway, a road in the moonlight wasn't the place.

The silence had gone on too long. He noticed confusion cross her face and groped for a safe conversation. "So, has Annie Bolton shown an interest in writing before?"

"Yes, she showed me a tablet full of poems and stories she's written, starting with a little poem she composed when she was seven." She smiled. "It went like this. 'The moon is smiling from the sky. If I could fly so would I.'"

Jim laughed. "Well, I've heard worse. At least it rhymes."

"Actually, I think it shows a lot of imagination for a seven year old." She smiled at him, her eyes dancing.

Oh Lord, help me. He'd found himself speaking to God a number of times lately. His recent visits to church must have had more of an effect on him than he'd realized.

"You may be right. What do you plan to do about it?"

Surprise flashed in her eyes. "Why, I'm not sure. Of course, I'll encourage her to continue her efforts and see where it leads."

He frowned and shook his head.

"What?" she asked. "What do you think I should do?"

"Maybe you could try to find a mentor to help her."

"But where? I don't know any professional writers or even writing instructors. Do you?"

"Well, no. Perhaps you could try the nearest university. They may have some suggestions." Why had he brought up the subject in the first place? What did he know about writers?

She frowned. "Maybe."

He took a deep breath. "I'm looking forward to Sunday."

Her eyes brightened. "You are? Oh, I am, too."

His breath caught. If she was this excited about their dinner together, maybe there was some hope after all.

"I'm so glad you're enjoying church services. Reverend Smith's sermons are very uplifting." She frowned. "Most of the time."

He didn't know whether to be disappointed that she was speaking of church and not dining with him or amused that she was still miffed about the sermon from Song of Solomon. Amusement won, and he pressed his lips together to keep from smiling.

She glanced his way and caught his expression. Indignation crossed her face, and he quickly composed himself.

"Yes, the reverend is quite effective. He seems to know his Bible quite well, too." Realizing that might not go over right, he added, "I especially liked his sermon about the crossing of the Red Sea a while back."

She peered at him, probably to make sure he was serious, then smiled. "Yes, it was very good even though he did get quite loud a few times."

"I'm also very much looking forward to our dinner engagement." There, hopefully she still planned to accompany him.

She nodded and gave him a sweet smile. "It was very kind of you to invite me. I'm looking forward to it as well."

They turned onto the lane leading to the Sullivan farm. Lamps in the parlor gave out an inviting warmth. A twinge of sadness bit at Jim. He hadn't experienced that since his mother died when he was twenty. His father had passed on a few years before that, but somehow his mother had managed to keep home intact until she, too, was gone.

Could he ask Addy to leave a loving family and the warmth of home to travel from city to city, state to state? Even if she agreed, would she eventually hate him for it? And what sort of life would that be for children? The situation seemed to be growing bleaker. At the moment, it seemed almost impossible.

They stopped in front of the house. He dismounted and helped her down as Jack stepped out onto the porch.

"Don't worry about the rig, Jim," Jack said. "I'll take care of it later. Lexie told me to invite you in for a late supper."

"Are you sure it won't be an inconvenience, sir?" Did they see the needy side of him? Maybe they were taking pity on him. Nonsense, they knew nothing of his parents or his lack of family.

"If I thought it would be inconvenient, I wouldn't have invited you. Come on in, Jim." He held the screen door open and motioned them inside.

Grateful, Jim grinned and started up the steps. Whatever happened Sunday, he was going to enjoy this time with Addy and her family.

Chapter 14

"Could you let your own child die to save others? Even if an entire town or state was in danger? Could you?"

Jim sat at attention as Reverend Smith glanced at the tiny girl sitting on Mrs. Smith's lap on the front row. "I couldn't. I wish I could say if the logs of this church building caught on fire at this moment, I would grab the first person or two I saw and help them reach safety. But I know, as sure as I'm standing here, that my first thought would be to get my wife and child away from the flames. My love and concern for all of you would not be enough for me to endanger my sweet baby girl."

What honesty! Jim stared in amazement at the courage of the man who proclaimed to his entire congregation that his love for his child would allow him to let them all die.

"But God. . ." The preacher took a handkerchief from his vest pocket and wiped his face. "God loved you and me so much that He sent His only Son to suffer horribly and die for us, so that all we have to do is believe on Him and we escape the punishment we so deserve and spend eternity in heaven with our Father."

He paused and took a deep breath. "Yes, and it's only because of that great sacrifice made by the Father and the Son that we can even call him Father. Jesus died to reconcile us to His Father and ours."

A twinge of discomfort settled in Jim's chest. Was that true? He'd always thought Jesus died because evil men killed Him and wondered why God had allowed it. But if what the preacher said was true, then He died of His own choice to pay the price for everyone's sins. But surely just believing wouldn't be enough to make up for all that agony. Would it?

His thoughts went to a small white leather Bible stowed away in a box with a few other mementos from his old life. His mother's Bible. He'd look up the verses the reverend had quoted through his sermon. He'd see for himself. And maybe he'd talk to Rafe and see what he thought.

The congregation stood and burst into song. Startled from his thoughts, Jim stood. He'd missed the last of the sermon.

As soon as the final amen was out of the preacher's mouth, Jim glanced around in search of Addy. He spotted her walking down the aisle behind her mother. She turned her head, and their eyes met. Shyness and joy seemed to battle on her face. She smiled then turned and followed her parents through the door.

Jim's heart lurched. Would she look as favorably upon him after their talk?

He hoped so. But besides her parents and little sister, there was the incredibly strong bond between her and her twin sister.

He shook Reverend Smith's hand at the door then stepped into the churchyard. Addy stood talking to a group of young women. He walked over to Rafe's wagon and shook his hand, then greeted Abby, who sat with one of the twins in her lap and the other snuggling at her side. For a moment, he could almost see Addy surrounded by his children. But the vision only lasted a few seconds. As much as the two women resembled one another physically, their mannerisms and expressions were undeniably their own.

"We're going to Ma and Pa's for dinner, Jim," she said with a friendly smile. "Why don't you join us?"

"Thank you, Abby, but Addy and I are going to dinner in town." As an afterthought, he added, "You are all welcome to join us."

He didn't realize he was holding his breath until Abby burst out laughing and Rafe chuckled and said, "Don't worry, buddy. We wouldn't intrude for the world."

"Am I that obvious?" He shook his head and gave a little laugh.

"Afraid so, but we understand." He climbed into the wagon and, leaning over, gave Abby a kiss on top of the head.

Jim got the buggy and pulled up under the oak tree in the shade. He didn't have long to wait. Addy walked toward him almost immediately. He stepped down and helped her in.

"What were you and Rafe and Abby finding so funny?" she asked as they drove away.

"Oh, they were laughing at me about something." He smiled. "I made reservations at the Branson, so we'll be sure to have a nice table."

"Thank you, Jim. That was very thoughtful." She smoothed the skirt of her dress then folded her hands in her lap.

He wondered if she was thinking about her dinner there with the doctor. Jealousy seized his stomach, and he quickly got it under control. She'd sent the doctor packing. But who knew if he might not shortly receive the same fate?

There was little activity in town when they pulled up. The saloons were all closed, which helped quiet things down on Sunday. A few businessmen stood at the door of the hotel. They tipped their hats at Addy and moved aside. Families stood around talking in the luxurious lobby. The dining room doors were closed.

"I'm sorry," Jim said. "It'll be a few minutes before they open. Would you like to have a seat while we wait?"

"Addy!" A high-pitched voice sounded from across the lobby.

Jim turned to see a middle-aged woman bearing down on them. The banker's wife, Mrs. Townsend.

Addy smiled and held her hand out to the woman. "Good afternoon, Mrs. Townsend. How nice to see you."

"My dear, it's very nice to see you, too." She threw a questioning look at Jim. "And Mr. Castle. I didn't know you were acquainted with our school mistress."

Jim knew he needed to choose his words carefully. Mrs. Townsend loved to share every tidbit of news she could come by, and if it wasn't exciting enough to get the desired response, she didn't mind expanding on what she did know. It wouldn't do for her to get her hooks into Addy. "Yes, I've known Miss Sullivan's family for years. I was best man at her sister's wedding." He hoped that would be enough to curb the woman's curiosity, but from the gleam in her eye, he feared it wouldn't be. "We've just come from church and thought we'd sample the cuisine here. Perhaps you could suggest something. . ."

Before she could reply, the doors to the dining room swung open, and Jim spotted Mr. Elmer Townsend coming their way.

"A shame we have to delay our conversation, but I believe your husband is coming to fetch you, Mrs. Townsend." With a flourish he lifted her hand and leaned over just enough that his lips avoided actually touching the appendage.

With a girlish twitter, the woman took her husband's arm and pranced off to dine.

◦◦◦

Addy pressed her lips together, feeling a little faint as they walked to their table. The waiter pulled out her chair, and she sat, lifting her eyes to Jim. "Thank you. You may have saved my reputation and my job. There's no telling what she would have made of our being here together."

"You'd think that by now people would know better than to listen to her gossip." He shook his head. "But there are always those who want to think the worst and are quite willing to take part in shredding someone to pieces."

She looked at him for a moment before speaking. "Yes, but thankfully, not too many of that sort live here in Branson Town."

"Are you sure of that?" Addy gave him a quick glance, and he added, "Of course you're right. I apologize for being cynical. Hopefully we've averted her attention from you."

She looked at the menu. The waiter brought frosted glasses of water with ice. Addy glanced at Jim. "Would you mind ordering for me? Everything sounds so delicious I can't bring myself to choose."

She studied him as he placed their order. A lock of his hair had fallen across his forehead, and Addy longed to brush it back. She blushed at the thought, averting her eyes. The waiter left and Jim leaned back.

She smiled when his eyes met hers. "You seem a little nervous today, Jim. Is something wrong?" Oh dear, she shouldn't have blurted that out. He'd think she was terribly rude.

He smiled. "You are very perceptive. I am a little nervous."

She waited for him to explain. He'd just opened his mouth when the waiter appeared with bowls of steaming soup.

She bowed her head and waited. He cleared his throat, and she opened one eye. At the look of panic on his face, she quickly closed it again.

"Dear heavenly Father," he said, "we thank You for this food from Your bounty. Amen."

She lifted her head and reached for her spoon, determined not to mention his shyness about praying.

"I'm not used to praying out loud," he said.

"Me either. Usually Pa or Rafe prays. Sometimes Ma." She dipped her spoon into the delicious smelling broth-like soup. What was it?

He smiled and took a bite of his soup. "Delicious consommé, isn't it?"

"Yes, indeed. I've never had it before." She grinned. "Or even heard of it, to be honest. But it's sort of a fancy beef broth, isn't it?"

He chuckled. "You are absolutely correct."

They continued conversing during the meal. Addy was a little disappointed he didn't share with her his reason for being nervous.

"Addy." He gave her a serious look.

"Yes?" She waited. Maybe he was going to talk about it now.

"I asked your father if I could court you."

Her heart jumped and joy filled her. "You did?"

"But I'm not sure I should have."

Her heart plunged, and her spoon slipped from her hand, falling into the soup with a splash. "Oh." She grabbed her napkin and began to blot at the tablecloth.

"I'm so sorry, Addy. That was a clumsy way to say it. Please don't misunderstand. I'd like nothing more than to court you and perhaps pursue a long-term relationship."

Pain pierced her then anger. What exactly was he trying to say? Apparently he'd changed his mind since he talked to Pa and was trying to let her down gently. He felt sorry for her. How dare he? She placed her napkin on the table and took a deep breath. "Excuse me, Mr. Castle," she said. "What gave you the idea that I might welcome your desire to court me?"

"Why, I . . ." He looked at her in surprise. "Addy, will you please let me explain?"

Apparently he wasn't fooled by her question. Well, why would he be? Hadn't she been wearing her heart on her sleeve for weeks where he was concerned? "Very well, please do explain." Her forehead felt clammy, and her throat like sandpaper.

"Addy, my job takes me all over the country. I know how much your family means to you, particularly Abby."

What was he saying? Why couldn't he work with the railroad here? Didn't he care deeply enough to do that? She opened her mouth to ask him that question, but he was still speaking.

"This job will probably end sometime in September, and I'll be moving on to another location."

But. . .why couldn't he ask the railroad to keep him here? Surely they'd have something he could do. But again, she couldn't seem to voice her thoughts.

"So you see, my dear. If we pursue a relationship, it would mean that you'd have to leave Branson." His voice caught, and he stopped.

He didn't love her. He was telling her he cared more about traveling all over the world than he did about her. If she married him, she would have to be the one to give up everything. Well, perhaps she would have been willing to travel with him if he really loved her, but it was obvious he didn't. He wouldn't even consider settling down. He'd just given her an ultimatum.

She took a deep breath and gave a little laugh. Her voice barely even trembled when she spoke. "Jim, I thought we'd already agreed to be friends. Isn't it lucky we had this talk before we went and fell in love with each other?" She stood. "Perhaps we can talk about your very interesting job another time. I really do need to be getting home."

As she walked ahead of him across the room, the pain in her heart was like a weight trying to shove her off her feet. *Oh God, please don't let him see how he's hurt me.*

Chapter 15

Jim pulled up beside a bluff overlooking the river and jumped out of the buggy, mentally kicking himself for making such a mess of things. He wasn't quite sure how things got so out of hand, but he really wanted to kick himself for hurting Addy. When he'd seen the pain wash over her face, he'd wanted to take her in his arms and tell her he'd do anything she desired of him, including giving up his career.

The river churned and foamed below, as if to mock him for the turmoil inside him. If there was anything he could do in this area, any type of employment he was qualified for that would support a family, he'd take it. He'd even be willing to buy a farm like Rafe's and work it, but he didn't have the slightest idea how to farm. He knew one thing. He'd do almost anything to erase the pain he'd caused her with his bad handling of the situation.

He picked up a pebble and threw it into the river, barely missing a silver-colored fish that jumped and flipped before diving back into the water.

He'd already been in Branson longer than he would have been on most jobs. But of course, the hotel, the railroad, and the lodge were interconnected as far as his job went. His analyses and the proposal for the hotel were finished. But the final analysis on the lodge couldn't begin until it was completed and they saw if business turned out as he'd projected. If so, he'd give them an extended proposal for the next three years, and his job would be over. If not, then it would be back to the drawing board.

Well, he'd start looking in Kansas City and St. Louis before this job ran out. If he could find anything he had the skills for that paid enough, he'd take it. Maybe Addy wouldn't mind living that short distance away.

In the meantime, she'd at least expressed a willingness to be friends. Did she mean that? Or was it just a way to end the conversation?

He climbed wearily into the buggy and headed to town.

For Addy, the summer days dragged on and on. She kept busy helping Ma with housework and gardening, and a couple of times a week she went over and spent some time with Aunt Kate.

Her great-aunt was following doctor's orders most of the time, but every once in a while she'd have a spell of weakness that frightened everyone but her. She'd finally told them to stop hovering over her. When it was her time to go, she'd go and be a lot better off than those who were still down here.

She seldom saw Jim, and when she did, they would speak a few polite words and be on their separate ways. Even that small amount of contact was almost more than she could bear.

Addy breathed a sigh of relief when tomatoes were ready to put up. Abby came over, and it was almost like old times, except when the thought of Jim crossed her mind.

When her family had asked why she wasn't seeing Jim anymore, she'd simply told them it hadn't worked out and left it at that. Finally they'd stopped asking. But her mother sent worried glances her way every now and then.

She might have told Abby what had happened, but her sister was over-flowing with joy over the news that she and Rafe were expecting another baby around February. Addy wasn't about to spoil Abby's happiness with her own broken heart.

Once the tomatoes for the family were canned and the jars sat in double rows on the shelves at all three farms, they started hauling the remainder of the crop to the tomato factory outside Branson Town. Addy loved riding in the wagon with Ma to haul the tomatoes. Sometimes Abby and Sarah would take turns riding along while the other watched all the children.

As Labor Day approached, Addy looked forward to the town festivities, including a parade and a picnic on the river the day before school opened. She missed her students and the routine of preparing lessons and teaching. She tried to push aside the secret hope that she'd see more of Jim when she was in town every day.

After church on the day before Labor Day, she and Ma were cleaning up the kitchen after dinner. "Okay, Ma, that's the last one." She dried the serving bowl and put it away in the cupboard. "What do you want to make first?"

"Oh honey, let's get something to drink and sit out on the porch while Betty and your pa are napping." Without waiting for a reply, Ma got down two tall glasses and poured lemonade. "There's a nice breeze out today, but the house is still stuffy in spite of the open windows. We can cook for the picnic in a little while."

"All right, Ma. Here, let me take those." She took the filled glasses and followed her mother outside. They sat in matching rocking chairs, and Addy leaned back, relaxing for the first time in hours. "Oh, it does feel good out here. The breeze almost feels like autumn." If she closed her eyes she could imagine her favorite season.

"It'll be here before we know it, then winter." Ma sighed. "I hope we don't have all that ice again like last year."

"Me, too. I'd rather have a nice soft snow any day."

Ma chuckled. "Let's not ask for trouble before it's here. I'd rather sit and enjoy this wonderful September air and pretend it will last forever."

Forever. If only this moment could last forever. Or better, if time could have stood still when she and Abby were young and so happy here with Ma and Pa. Before life got complicated. Before everything changed. "I miss Abby."

Ma gave her a troubled look then took a sip of her lemonade. "I know you do, but life goes on, Addy."

"Why did God make twins to be so close when they were just going to be pulled apart when they grew up?" She could hear the self-pity in her voice but couldn't stop. Didn't really want to. "I feel sorry for Davey and Dawson. Look how inseparable they are. Just like Abby and I were. And someday that will all change."

"Change comes for everyone, not just twins. I could hardly bear it when your Uncle Will married Sarah. I'd always been big sister. Then suddenly he didn't need me."

"How did you handle it, Ma?" She'd never thought of Ma feeling that way about Uncle Will. It was strange to think of her tall, bearded, laughing uncle as her ma's little brother.

A dreamy look crossed Ma's face. "God was good. I fell in love."

"With Pa."

"That's right. I fell in love with your pa. And"—she reached over and patted Addy's arm—"I also fell in love with two sweet little rascally girls."

"I suppose we were rascals, weren't we?" She smiled at the memory.

"Well, Abby was a rascal." Ma chuckled. "You just couldn't bear to say no to her, so you went along with whatever she suggested."

"I felt responsible for her. I thought if I didn't stay close, I couldn't take care of her." Addy's heart raced. She still felt that way, only now. . .

"I know," Ma said. "Addy, your sister loves you very much, but she doesn't need you to look out for her anymore."

"I know, Ma. She has Rafe, and he would never let anything happen to her."

Ma rocked silently for a moment then said, "Your mind knows, but I don't think your heart does. Your heart needs to believe it, too, Addy. Then you'll be able to let go and have a life of your own."

⁓⁓⁓

Jim leaned against the feed store and watched the children down by the river as they ran through the spray from the waterwheel. He grinned, half wishing he could join them. The day, which had begun with a slight chill, had warmed up fast once the sun rose overhead.

He glanced a little farther down, where picnic tables had been set up. He squinted, searching for a mane of pale-gold hair among the women who were setting food on the tables.

He stood up straight. There.

On closer look, he leaned back and took his former stance against the building. It was Abby. The braids should have clued him in. He'd never seen Addy wear braids. When she put her hair up, it was always in some kind of roll or twist on the back of her head.

He was tempted to wander over in that direction to try to find her but didn't want to embarrass himself in case she snubbed him. Still, she had said they should be friends. Whether she'd meant it or not, she said it.

With determination propelling him forward, he shoved away from the building and headed down toward the picnic area. A space had been cleared for horseshoes, and he saw Rafe with a few other men lining up to take their turns.

"Hey, Jim, there's always room for one more." Rafe threw him a grin.

Jim paused and started to take a step in Rafe's direction, but a pretty blue dress with lace on the collar caught his eye. But the face above the dress wasn't the one he was looking for.

Idiot. Did you think she'd be wearing the same blue dress three years later?

"Hello, Jim."

His breath caught in his throat, and he turned at the sound of Addy's voice. He tried not to devour her with his eyes, but she was so beautiful and he'd missed her so much.

"Hello, Addy. It's good to see you." Oh, how good! If it were any better, his heart would burst through his chest.

"Hey, guess what, Jim?" Rafe grinned. "Addy learned how to fry chicken right good this summer."

"Cut it out, Rafe." Addy glared at her brother-in-law, who put his hands up in mock defense.

"How about going for a walk?" Jim said. "Some local artists have an exhibit down the street." Boring, but it was the first thing he could think of.

She smiled. "Maybe later. I need to help set the food out."

Jim watched her walk away.

"Man, you've really got a bad case of lovesick," Rafe said.

Jim glared. "Thanks for the diagnosis, Dr. Collins."

"Glad to help anytime." Rafe narrowed his eyes. "What happened with you two anyway? I thought things were going right good. I didn't want to intrude, but I've wondered."

"So did I. So did I." Jim glanced at his friend. He'd wanted to talk to Rafe about the incident with Addy before but hadn't wanted to sound like a love-lorn kid. Maybe it was time to stop hiding his feelings from his best friend. "I happened to mention the shortcomings of my job, such as leaving this place. That did it."

"You have to understand, Jim. The girls lost their real mother when they were babies, and their father was killed in a mining accident when they were eight. They sort of clung to their new family but especially to each other. They were stuck like glue." Sympathy crossed his face as he looked at Jim. "I'm afraid Addy hasn't let go yet."

Jim nodded. "I thought it might be something like that. But what do I do? I have to make a living."

Rafe shook his head. "I don't know. I sure wouldn't want to be in your place. But if she loves you, and I'm pretty sure she does, she'll come around eventually."

"Maybe. But on the other hand, that's a lot to ask of her. It's not like we'd be living a couple of farms over." And here he was again. Right back in the same place he'd started.

"Pray about it, Jim. God has the answer." Rafe headed back to the game.

Jim wandered off down the street, no longer caring about the festivities. She'd only been polite when she'd said they might be able to take a walk later. He wouldn't hold her to it, no matter how much he wanted to.

Chapter 16

S orry, Mr. Castle. Your qualifications are impressive except for one very important item. This position requires a degree in business. Perhaps you would like to place an application in our sales department." Mr. Fiferton, the head of employment services, waved a limp hand as indication the interview was over.

Jim stepped out onto the sidewalk. He'd be more than happy to work in sales, whether it meant store clerk or pounding the pavement and knocking on doors, but he knew too many salesmen who weren't earning enough to support themselves much less their families.

He stood on the sidewalk outside St. Louis's Herringdon's Department Store. This had been the last place listed in today's classifieds that sounded as though it might work.

Well, perhaps tomorrow. He hoped so. He had to be back in Branson in a couple of days to help with last-minute plans for the opening of the lodge.

Hardly a day passed that he didn't get an offer for his services, but so far he'd passed them all up in hopes that something would turn up that would be suitable. It was beginning to look less and less likely.

But he wouldn't give up. Not yet anyway. There had to be a way for him and Addy.

❧

Addy pulled up in front of the school building to find Bobby waiting with a grin to take her horse and buggy to the stable. A crowd of children had already gathered in the schoolyard and were engaged in a game of hide and seek.

"Howdy, Miss Sullivan. You glad school's startin' today?" Bobby held his hand out to help her down. Well, that was a first. The young man was growing up.

"Yes, I certainly am, Bobby. And so glad I'm done with tomatoes. I'm ready to turn that job over to someone else. I was beginning to feel like a stewed tomato."

He laughed and ducked his head. "Well, don't worry, ma'am. You sure don't look like one."

"Why, thank you, Bobby." When his face flamed, she hastened to change the subject. "Would you please check Ruby's right front hoof when you get back to the stable? I believe she may have picked up a rock or something."

"Sure thing. See you later." He waved and took off down the street toward the livery.

Shouts from the children drew her attention. She smiled and waved then stepped inside the school, removing her hat and gloves. She'd been here the week before to clean and dust and make sure the books were in order. Glancing around the room, she gave a nod of satisfaction.

She supposed it was a good thing she enjoyed teaching. It appeared she'd be doing it for a long time. Apparently she wasn't destined for matrimony and motherhood. Or even an adventurous single life. She straightened a stack of graded papers. Her dissatisfaction was probably the result of reading too many silly books growing up. She had a nice steady life and must learn to be content.

But Jim loved her, and she loved him. What if. . .

Before the thought could reach maturity, she shoved it away. If Jim really loved her, he'd ask that nice man with the railroad to keep him on here in Branson instead of sending him away. And she would never leave Abby.

She stepped outside and rang the bell more loudly than necessary in order to drive the traitorous thoughts from her mind.

She had planned some outdoor activities today, knowing the children would be restless after three months of freedom from the confines of the school.

A screech from the back of the room confirmed her decision. Carla Bright, a new student whose family had recently arrived from Kansas City, stood on top of her desk, a look of horror on her face.

Addy hurried down the aisle and looked up at the trembling girl. "Carla, what happened?"

Without turning her head, the girl pointed at Johnny. "That boy threw a mouse on me."

Whirling, Addy glared at the boy. "Johnny?"

"Aw. . .it wasn't a real mouse, Miss Sullivan. I thought she'd know. Anyone can see it's rubber." He held up the offending "mouse," which indeed was rubber and obviously so. He handed it to Abby.

She dropped it into her pocket and tapped on his desk with her ruler. "But perhaps it wasn't so clear to her that it was rubber when it came flying across the aisle and hit her. And I think you probably knew that."

He ducked his head. "Yes, ma'am," he mumbled.

Addy shook her head. "Look at me, Johnny." When he complied, she frowned slightly. "I believe you ended our last classroom session on the stool in the corner?"

He darted his eyes at the stool and back at her. "Yes, ma'am, but. . ."

"No buts. It's really a shame to have to start the year out this way, Johnny. But you must learn to think about other people's feelings. And especially a new student. I'm sure your antics didn't make Carla feel very welcome." She rested her hand on his curly top. "As soon as you can honestly say you're sorry, I'd like for you to apologize to her, Johnny. Will you do that?"

He stood and stepped over to where Carla still stood upon her desk and stared up at her. "I'm sorry. I really am. But you don't have to keep standing up there. It wasn't no real mouse." He turned and headed for the corner.

Addy glanced at the girl who still stood atop her desk. Addy was pretty sure that by now it was merely to keep everyone's attention. "Please sit down, Carla. There's nothing to be afraid of. As Johnny said, the mouse was only a toy made out of rubber." As the girl scrambled into her seat, Addy walked away but said loudly enough to be heard, "Of course, we do see a real mouse, occasionally."

When she got to the front of the room and turned around, she noticed Carla sat with a sheepish look on her face. "Well, class, I'd planned an outing this morning to the new hunting lodge. They'll be opening next week, and the owners very graciously agreed to let us tour the facility today. In fact, several mothers have volunteered to go with us and will arrive at any moment." At the outbreak of excited voices, Addy raised her hand. "But of course, we can't leave Johnny here alone, so I guess we'll have to have class instead." Disappointed murmurs arose but stopped when Addy once more raised her hand. "It's time for roll call."

Addy kept a surreptitious glance on Carla while calling roll. The girl was almost in tears. Addy was pretty sure there was more to the mouse story than had appeared on the surface. "Carla Bright," she said.

The girl raised her hand and said, "Here." She threw Addy a pained look. "Miss Sullivan, I'm so sorry. I knew the mouse wasn't real because I saw Johnny playing with it on the playground."

"I see." Addy bit her lip. "Then would you like to explain your actions?"

"I was mad because he threw it at me. I guess I just wanted to get even." She ducked her head then said, "I really am sorry. Please don't punish the class for what I did. I'll stay with Johnny."

The whole class stared. Addy wanted to take the girl, hug her, and say, "Bravo, Carla."

"Hey, I ain't no baby. I can stay here by myself."

Addy clamped her lips together to prevent a smile from popping out and glared at Johnny. "I can see you've forgotten proper English over the summer, Johnny. We'll have to work on that. But first, no more using 'ain't.'"

"Sorry."

"So, will you let me stay with him, Miss Sullivan?"

"Hmmm. Take your seat, Carla. We'll put it to a vote."

"Class, I'm going to pose three questions. After you've heard all three, I'm going to leave the decision up to you. The first option will be that we stay here today and try to reschedule our tour. The second option is that I allow Carla to stay here with Johnny. The third option is that we trust they have both learned a lesson today, we forgive them both, and we let them go with us."

As one voice, their decision roared across the classroom. But Addy made them sit and vote in an orderly way. After all, this would be a good lesson in civics.

Addy's heart lurched when she saw the huge log building, looking almost the same as it had at the World's Fair. It was startling to see it standing in solitude on the bluff overlooking their own White River. What changes had been made to the inside? Would it look somewhat the same? Probably not.

She swallowed and took a look down at the two lines of children waiting to enter the building. Ten volunteer mothers were interspersed along the line to keep them in order. Addy only needed two but hadn't the heart to turn them down. This would more than likely be their only opportunity to see inside this FOR GENTLEMEN ONLY establishment.

Yes, it actually said that on the cedar wood sign beside the door. She wasn't surprised, merely a little indignant. Why, pray tell, couldn't they bring their mothers, wives, and sisters along? Maybe some of them would like to go hunting.

She gave herself a mental shake. Well, maybe their women wouldn't want to go hunting, but there were other activities in the area they could enjoy while their husbands had their fun.

Just as she was about to lift the enormous knocker, the door swung open. Jim Castle bowed slightly as she gaped up at him. "Miss Sullivan, ladies, boys, and girls, I have the honor of being your guide today. Please step inside, and I'll show you the wonders of this historical edifice and also give you a glimpse of our plans for the future."

"Wow, look at that!" Sam's awe-filled voice rang out, almost echoing in the enormous room. "Is that a real bear?"

Jim turned and looked at the huge, brown animal that stood on its hind feet, fangs bared.

"Yes, it is, young man. Shot, stuffed, and put on display where it can't hurt a soul."

"But we don't have bears that big around here." Mrs. Allen's voice trembled. "Do we?"

"No, ma'am," Jim said quickly. "This magnificent animal was actually shot in the mountains of Wyoming."

Mrs. Allen's relieved sigh, accompanied by a few others, was audible to all.

"Perhaps we should get back to the tour, Mr. Castle," Addy suggested with a glare in his direction.

"I want to see some more bears," Sam said.

"Me, too." Johnny stared in wonder at the creature.

"Well, we'd better do as your teacher says, young fellows. But you'll see a few more stuffed animals along the way."

"You boys get back in line now." Addy shooed them with her hands. She met Jim's eyes and he smiled, an apology all over his face.

What in the world was he doing here anyway? Had he taken a job at the lodge? Did this mean he planned to stay in Branson after all? A surge of excitement rushed through her. She followed along, not hearing a word of his narration as he guided them through the building.

Jim had taken a job in Branson. He did care. But why hadn't he mentioned it to her? Had he changed his mind about wanting to court her? Pa had never said a word.

As they left the building, she gave Jim a very warm smile and offered her hand. "Thank you, Mr. Castle. It's been very interesting, and the building is perfectly wonderful."

He looked at her in surprise. "Why, thank you, Miss Sullivan. It's been my pleasure."

"Boys and girls, thank Mr. Castle for taking time to show us around and for the history lesson." Which she hoped one of the mothers could recite to her. Otherwise, how could she discuss this field trip with the students?

Among a chorus of "thank yous," the students lined up and walked down the hill to the school.

Addy's heart danced. He had decided to stay in Branson. And what other reason could there be except to please her?

Chapter 17

Jim wasn't sure whether to be elated or confused. The smile Addy had given him was warm and almost inviting. Wasn't it? He was more than likely imagining the whole thing. Or was it possible she'd had a change of heart and was willing to pursue a relationship even if it meant leaving her family?

He rode by the school at least half a dozen times that day. Then railing at himself for being an idiot, he took his horse to the livery stable. After that, he still managed to find errands that took him past the school at least once an hour.

Standing on the corner, Jim gazed toward the schoolyard then pulled out his watch. Almost three o'clock. He'd meet her when she came outside.

Suddenly he realized he had no idea what he intended to say to her. Was he crazy? He couldn't just come out and ask her if she'd changed her mind. He'd probably imagined she was having a change of heart. He'd better stay with his plan and continue to search for suitable employment. If and when he could come to her and offer a promising future, then the situation would be different. But until then, he was simply torturing himself.

He could see her on Sunday, perhaps, at church. That would be better than nothing. He'd been going to a church here in town for the last few weeks, and the preacher had given him a lot to think about. To the point, he'd recommitted his life to Christ. And he'd begun to look at life a lot differently. The main thing being if he and Addy were supposed to be together, God would work it out. But a sudden pang stabbed him. What if God said no? But that's what commitment to Christ was all about. Letting Him have His way in one's life. And knowing that He knows best. Perhaps he should continue with his present church for now.

Spinning around, he headed for his hotel. He had accounts to work on and needed to get on with it. Next week he'd head to Kansas City and see what was available there. It wouldn't hurt to help God out a little bit, would it?

∽≈∾

Addy searched through the cedar chest in the extra room that used to be Betty's nursery but was now used mostly for storage. Ma had sent her to find a shawl she wanted to use for a pattern. Addy's hand fell upon a soft bundle. A very soft bundle. Maybe a pillow? But it didn't feel like feathers. Should she look? But perhaps Ma wouldn't want her snooping. Still, who knew if the shawl might be inside? Guilt nibbled at her conscience. Ma had very clearly stated the shawl was folded up by itself.

Curiosity won. Addy lifted the bundle from the chest and laid it on the floor. Carefully she unwrapped the soft cotton sheet. A glimmer of red peaked out from the edge. Addy gasped. Excitement zigzagged through her as she lifted the bright red and green dresses from their protective sheet. "Ma, would you come here?"

"What is it, dear. . . ?" Ma paused in the doorway. When she saw what Addy was holding, a dreamy smile crossed her face. "Yours and Addy's Christmas dresses. I made those for you the year you came to live with me at Aunt Kate's."

"I remember." Addy swallowed past the knot that had formed in her throat. She smoothed her hand over the piney-green velvet. "I was so proud. I'd never worn anything so wonderful. I felt like a princess."

"You looked like a princess." Ma smiled. "So did Addy, even though she seldom wanted to wear dresses at all. I remember she was fussing about trying hers on, but when she saw the cherry-red velvet, she grew very quiet and didn't say another word."

"Yes, and she looked so pretty."

Ma gave her a knowing look. "So did you, sweetheart, even though you wanted the red for yourself."

Addy gasped. "How did you know that? I didn't say a word."

"No, you did not, because Abby's happiness was always first with you." For a moment a hint of sadness slid across her face. "I didn't know until I saw the look on your face that you wanted the red dress."

Addy smiled. "It's all right, Ma. I loved the green, and once we were dressed, I don't think I ever thought about it again." She laughed. "I'd never seen Abby primp before. So it was worth it."

Ma eyed the garments. "I should have used the fabric long ago, but I couldn't bear to cut into them."

"Look, Ma. The fabric is still in fine shape except for a couple of spots."

"Yes. You're right." She stooped down and placed a hand on each dress. Suddenly she stood, the dresses in her arms. "I'm going to take them in the parlor. Did you find the shawl, dear?"

"No, I'm still looking." Addy gazed after Ma. Now what was she up to? Shrugging, she began to search through the chest again. There it was. She removed the delicate shawl then closed the chest and stood up and carried it into the parlor.

Ma sat holding the dresses on her lap.

"I found the shawl, Ma. It's so beautiful."

Ma looked up from her rocker, her eyes sparkling, but ignored the shawl. "I have the most wonderful idea."

"Oh? And what is this wonderful idea? Tell me, please," Addy teased.

"Let's make Christmas suits for Davey and Dawson out of Abby's red and a dress for Betty from your green."

Addy stared at her Ma. She wanted to cut up their Christmas dresses?

Ma's eyes sparkled. "I thought I'd keep them forever, but we really need to do something with them while the fabric is still good."

"Really?"

Worry lines appeared between Ma's eyes. "Oh, of course not, dear. If you want to keep your dress, then certainly you may."

Addy closed her eyes. How silly could she get? Of course they needed to use the fabric.

"No, I think your idea is wonderful. I'll stop at the store Monday and get some white satin for bow ties for the boys and a hair ribbon for Betty."

Ma reached over and patted her. "We'll have enough from each dress to make bows for you girls to keep."

Addy's eyes swam. "Thank you, Ma. That will be perfect."

Ma's eyes danced. "Shall we tell Abby or wait and surprise her?"

Addy thought for a moment. "I think we'd better tell her. Otherwise she might take a notion to make Christmas suits herself."

"Very good idea." Ma laughed. "Let's tell her tomorrow at church."

"She'll probably want to help make them."

At least Addy hoped so. What if Abby didn't want her cherry-red Christmas dress cut apart?

Addy stepped out of the church. She'd hoped Jim might come this week, although he hadn't been there since the day they'd dined at the Branson Hotel. Abby had told her he was attending a church in town and had recommitted to Christ. The news had thrilled her. But after sending him what she thought was an inviting smile at the lodge, she'd expected him to be here today.

Oh! Maybe he'd thought she was too bold. Or maybe he'd found someone else, and that was why he'd gone to work for the lodge. Although, now that she'd thought about that, she couldn't help but wonder why he hadn't just stayed with the railroad. Surely they'd have found something for him to do. Maybe he'd had to wait for an opening.

Oh, what difference did it make? Apparently he wasn't interested in her anymore. Her face flamed as she thought of her actions that day. Why she'd been positively brazen, smiling at him that way. Her thoughts continued to race until she felt like putting her hands up and squeezing her head.

"Addy!"

At the sound of her sister's voice, she looked up.

Abby stood right in front of her. "What are you day-dreaming about?" Abby laughed and grabbed her arm. "Come on. You and Betty are riding with Rafe and me. Ma invited us to dinner."

"Oh, did they leave?" She glanced around and saw the wagon pulling out of the churchyard and onto the road.

"Yes. What's the big mystery? Ma said she wanted to show me something, but she wouldn't say what."

Should she tell her? But Ma would want to be the one. She only hoped Abby wouldn't be too upset. After all, her own first reaction had been a jolt of dismay. Maybe Addy should have tried to talk Ma out of the idea. She cleared her throat. "I think I'd better let Ma tell you. You know how she is about anyone spoiling her surprises."

Abby laughed. "Yes, how well I remember. Okay, come on. Let's go so I can find out what this is all about."

They climbed into the wagon and headed toward the Sullivan farm. Some of the trees were beginning to turn, and the varying shades of green, yellow, and bronze were breathtaking. Fall had always been Addy's favorite season. Abby's, too.

"Look at the color," Abby said. "A couple more weeks and they'll really be beautiful."

Addy grinned. "You read my thoughts again, sis."

A guffaw from the back revealed that Rafe had been listening. "I don't know how you girls can be so identical in some ways and so all-fired different in others."

"Tell me how we're different." Abby flashed a grin over her shoulder.

"Well, let's see, Tuck, my girl." Rafe held up one finger. "First, you're a whole lot meaner than your sister."

Betty giggled. "Tuck isn't mean, Rafe."

"Thank you, Betty honey," Abby said. "You tell him."

"Sure she is, Betty," said Rafe, with a grin. "And lots meaner than Addy."

Abby laughed. "Well, that's not hard. My sweet sister isn't mean at all. Tell me another one."

"I know one," said Betty. "Addy doesn't wear overalls."

Rafe howled. "I rest my case."

They pulled up to the house, laughing.

Addy inhaled deeply. If only these joyful moments could somehow be stored. If only things didn't have to change.

After dinner the men went out to look at a cow that Pa had purchased. Ma put the children down for naps while Addy and Abby cleaned the kitchen.

Afterward Addy bit her lip as she followed Ma and Abby into the parlor.

Ma patted the seat next to her on the sofa. "Come sit by me, Abby." She retrieved the bundle from a basket on the floor and removed the sheet.

Abby's eyes grew large. "Those are the first Christmas dresses you made for us, Ma."

"Yes, I've kept them all these years."

Abby grinned. "You're still sentimental, Ma. I'd have thrown them away a long time ago."

Addy stared at her twin. "You would? But Abby, you loved that dress."

"Well, sure I did. When I was eight." She laughed.

Ma smiled. "Then you won't mind if I cut your dress down and make suits for David and Dawson?"

"Oh, Ma. That's a great idea. They'll look so cute in little red velvet suits." She reached over and hugged Ma. "Can I help?"

Ma returned her hug. "Of course. Addy and I hoped you'd want to."

Abby reached over and touched the green fabric then turned to Addy. "What are we going to do with yours, sis?"

Addy smiled. "A Christmas dress for Betty. Won't she love it?"

"Oh, I'm sure she will."

"And we'll get white satin for bow ties," Ma said with joy in her eyes. "And enough for a hair ribbon for Betty.

As Addy listened to Ma and Abby chattering on about the project, she shook her head. Rafe had been right. She and Abby were very different in many ways. But the sad part was that Addy hadn't realized how much her sister had changed or how little she really knew her anymore.

Chapter 18

Addy jumped up from her desk. Was that a gunshot?

Voices cried out and a volley of shots followed.

By now the students had jumped up and headed for the frosted windows.

"Children, sit down!" She scurried around the room, corralling students and sending them back to their seats.

"But Miss Sullivan, maybe it's outlaws!" Johnny yelled. At least he had obeyed and was seated. The older boys still stood, their excited gazes darting from her to the door.

"Don't even think about it." She headed for the window and wiped her hand across the glass, then peered out, gaping at the throng that crowded not only in front of the schoolyard but, it appeared, all over Branson Town, in spite of the bitter cold. At least the snow had held off, which was unusual for the second week in December.

A man raised his arm, his pistol pointed in the air. Addy held her breath then sighed with relief when the sheriff appeared. She couldn't tell what he was saying, but from the look on his face, he wasn't too upset.

Torn between her desire to find out what was going on and her responsibility to her students, she finally turned to the boys. "Everyone, please be seated as I instructed. There doesn't appear to be anything wrong. It seems more like a celebration of some sort."

She started as the door flew open. The sheriff's deputy stepped inside, his fur collar pulled up against the icy wind, grinning like a schoolboy.

"Ernest! What in the world is going on?"

His grin grew wider. "The sheriff saw you lookin' out the winder. He told me to let you know everything's fine. The railroad crews have met, and the tracks are complete. The whole town is celebratin'. I gotta go." He waved at his younger brother at the back of the class and took off down the street.

The class exploded in an uproar. Addy put her hands over her ears as their shouts and whistles shattered the air, accompanied by the ones invading the room from outside. She quickly slammed the door and burst out laughing. Her students jumped up and down and swung each other around the room. She should probably put a stop to their cavorting, but why not allow them a few moments of celebration?

Finally she took a small round whistle from her desk drawer and blew three shrill blasts. The class quieted down immediately and looked in her direction.

"I know you're excited. So am I. Since it's only a half hour until lunch time, perhaps we'll cut our arithmetic lesson short and discuss this new event."

A roar of voices began to speak, and Addy blew the whistle again. "But first, I'd like for each of you to return to your seat."

One by one they dropped into their seats, breathing hard, the boys wiping their perspiring faces on their sleeves. Addy noticed a few of the girls pull out handkerchiefs and dab their foreheads. Who would guess it was so cold outside she'd had to break ice off the pump this morning?

"Charlie, would you please take my water pitcher to the pump and refill it? The rest of you get your cups out. I think you could all use a drink of water."

Heads bobbed in the affirmative.

After everyone had a few sips of water, Addy leaned against her desk and smiled.

"Maybe we'll have a new school project to talk about soon."

"Yes, ma'am," Johnny said with enthusiasm, "that play we put on last year was a lot of fun."

"Perhaps this time we'll focus on the workers who built the tracks and the excitement of this day," Addy said.

"Building the tracks through the mountains was really dangerous," said Sally. "My pa said some men were killed."

Addy nodded. "That's right, Sally. There were a number of accidents that resulted in injuries and, in a few cases, death. The White River Route wasn't built without a heavy price."

Margaret, who'd surprised everyone by growing three inches through the summer, raised her hand.

"Yes, Margaret?"

"Now we'll finally have passenger trains coming through, and Papa said he'll take Ma and me on a train ride."

"Aw, what's so great about that?" Johnny sneered in her direction.

"That was rude, Johnny," Addy said, her voice stern. Would the boy never learn? He'd spent a number of recesses on the corner stool.

"Sorry, but I like freight trains best. They carry all kinds of great stuff."

"Perhaps Margaret would like to tell us why she wants to ride the train so badly." Addy threw the girl a smile.

Margaret's eyes lit up. "They have real dining cars with white tablecloths and real silver. And when you look out the window, you can see fields and trees and farms flying by. Or so it seems."

"Farms and trees don't fly, stupid. And neither do trains."

"Johnny. The corner." Addy glared and pointed to the stool.

"I'm sorry, Miss Sullivan. I didn't mean to say it. It just came out. Really it did."

"The corner," Addy repeated.

A twitter rolled across the room as Johnny shuffled his way across the room.

"One more sound and some of you will be joining him. It's not nice to take pleasure in someone else's discomfort."

They quieted and, one by one, raised their hands and gave their take on the completed railroad and what they thought was best about it.

After a while, Addy found herself floating in an old daydream. She stood on the top step of a train, waved to her family, and then glided down the aisle to her seat. Beaming with joy, she waved and blew kisses out the window to friends and loved ones as the train pulled away from the station. Suddenly she realized something new had been added. Always before she'd imagined she was alone. This time, in her daydream, Jim Castle stood at her side, walked by her side, and sat by her side.

She took a deep breath. Why couldn't she get the man out of her mind? She hadn't seen him since Labor Day, except for an occasional glimpse as he rode past. She'd come close to asking Abby about him a few times. Was he still working at the hunting lodge? Was he courting anyone? But she couldn't bring herself to do so.

She forced her attention back to the child who was speaking.

"My pa says Branson will get a lot more tourists now that the passenger trains can run," Alice was saying. "Especially with the State of Maine Hunting Lodge here."

"And that writer guy that wrote that book," Tommy interrupted.

Harold Wright! Of course. He and his family were camped out near the old Ross cabin. What was the name of the book he wrote? Oh yes. *The Printer of Udell's* or something like that. Rumor had it he was writing a new one. About the Ozarks. Maybe he would have some suggestions for Annie and her writing. She supposed she should obtain a copy of his book and read it before she approached him. Jim would be happy to hear she had thought of someone to help Annie.

"Tommy, it's rude to interrupt when someone is speaking," she said, "but thank you for mentioning Mr. Wright. Perhaps he'll come and speak to our class someday."

⁂

Jim pushed the form through the window and paid to send the telegram. Spinning on his heel, he left the telegraph office. He'd spent the better part of November trying desperately to find suitable work in St. Louis, Kansas City, and the first two weeks of December there in Springfield. All to no avail. Now he had no choice. He'd accepted the offer from the Coney Island Park.

He'd completed his work in Branson the early part of October but kept hoping something would turn up. Most of the jobs that were suitable for him required a college degree, which he didn't have. When he'd started his own business, he'd been lucky to land that first contract that had set him up for success. He'd gotten pretty cocky. His future looked good to him. Well, he wasn't so great. Couldn't even get decent work. He'd never ask Addy to subsist on just enough to get by.

Now his options had run out. He had no choice but to get on the train the first week of January and head for New York, where he'd make a lot of money that wouldn't mean a thing to him.

He drove his rented buggy to a livery stable on the outskirts of the city, where he retrieved Finch and rode out of town. He'd carried the dream of being wed to Addy since that first day he'd met her. And after he'd gotten right with God, the feeling grew until he was certain she was the one for him. He thought they were meant to be together. But he must have been wrong. Apparently, it had merely been his own desires and not God's will at all.

All right, Lord. I give up. If You want us to be together, then work something out. If not, then okay. Thy will be done. There's nothing more I can do.

Peace washed over him, just as it had the day when he'd surrendered to God for the first time. Did surrender always feel like this? The pain of losing Addy was still there, but it was bearable. And somehow he knew they'd both be okay.

It was late when he arrived in Branson. To his surprise, people were still on the streets. He walked into the hotel and stopped. The lobby was crowded with men standing in groups, laughing and slapping each other on the back.

"Castle! This is a great day for Branson. Where've you been?" The portly man who staggered across the room had obviously been drinking for quite some time.

"Hello, Philips. I've been out of town. What's going on?" It must be big, considering the crowd.

"The tracks are complete. The White River Route is open for business. They'll be running the first passenger train next week." He hiccupped. "Lots of opportunity for us."

Jim turned away from the smell of alcohol on the man's breath. "You'd better go home, Philips, or get a room here and go to bed before you fall on your face."

A younger man came over and took Philips' arm. "Come on, Dad, the man's right. Let's get home."

"Oh, all right, son, all right. I'm coming. But I say again, it's a great day for Branson." He leaned on his tall son as they walked to the door.

Jim shook his head as he climbed the broad stairs to his room. Philips was right about it being a great day for Branson. But for Jim, it was the slamming of a door. Even though he'd had a hand in several enterprises directly affected by the railroad coming in, any happiness he felt for the town's success was snuffed out by a cold, dark hand that squeezed at his heart. He'd been so optimistic when he rode into town last spring. He'd had high hopes for his career and also for the lovely Miss Sullivan. Well, his career would be okay.

But it didn't matter a lot to him now.

He kicked off his shoes and unbuttoned his shirt. The sooner he got away the better for everyone. Maybe healing would even come, eventually. He'd stay until January because he had nowhere else to be before then. And he'd accepted several invitations for the Christmas season, including the Christmas Ball.

He'd hesitated about that one because Addy was sure to be there. Although, perhaps it wouldn't hurt to get one last glimpse of her before he left. It couldn't do any more than wrench his heart out.

He wouldn't ask her to dance. Because if he did, he might not be able to leave her.

Chapter 19

Jim dipped the pen in the inkwell and tried again. After scribbling a few words on the sheet of paper, he wadded it and threw it into the trash basket by the hotel-room desk. Leaning back into the slick leather of his chair, he drummed his fingers on the smooth cherry-wood desktop.

Writing Addy a letter probably wasn't a good idea anyway. What could he say except good-bye? Sorry it didn't work out? I love you but can't support you where you want to live? That would make her feel great.

The first rays of sun shone in the window. He'd been up all night, pacing the floor and trying to write a letter that had ended up as a trash can full of nonsense.

Better to leave things as they were. She'd probably put him out of her mind anyway. There had never been anything romantic spoken between them. Maybe a hint, but that was all. They'd been friends. He'd been an idiot to think there could be anything else.

He stood and gave the chair a kick. It rolled smoothly across the polished wood floor into the kneehole of the desk. Jim gave a short laugh. He couldn't even kick a chair over.

Striding to the door, he grabbed his hat and coat from the rack then went outside, locking the door behind him.

The lobby was empty except for a clerk behind the desk. He looked up and nodded.

Jim tipped his hat and stepped out the door onto the wood sidewalk. He stood and glanced down the street, having no idea why he'd come out in the first place. The novelty of having absolutely nothing to do was beginning to grate on his nerves.

He strode down the street, past the saloon and the new feed store. Ice stood in the horse trough out front, and gray skies promised snow. A good thing the railroad line was completed before it hit. There had been enough accidents while tunneling through the mountains and building trestle bridges over the river. A heavy snow would've shut them down completely.

He turned and walked past the other hotel. As he drew near the end of the street, he spotted Addy's buggy pulling up into the schoolyard. His heart raced. He had to admit to himself that he'd hoped to see her.

He quickened his step. Just as he approached the mercantile, Miss Martha Tyler stepped out. He tipped his hat and started to walk past the young lady. The touch of her hand on his arm stopped him in his tracks.

She tossed her head and gave him a saucy smile. "Why, Mr. Castle, you seem to be in a terrible hurry this morning." She batted her lashes and turned her green eyes fully upon his.

"Yes, I need to speak with someone." He took a step forward, but the persistent girl wouldn't turn loose of his arm.

"Will you be attending the Christmas Ball, Mr. Castle?" she asked with a simper.

"I haven't quite decided, Miss Tyler, but if I do perhaps I'll see you there?" He smiled and gently removed her hand from his sleeve. Speeding up his pace, he stepped off the sidewalk and crossed to the schoolyard, where Addy was handing the reins of her horse to Bobby.

As the boy walked away leading the horse and buggy, she turned and faced him, a strained expression on her face.

Now that they were face-to-face, he wasn't sure what to say.

She bit her lip and blinked hard as she looked at him. Were those tears?

He removed his hat. "Hello, Addy." The delicate scent of roses wafted over to him. Why did she have to smell so good? And look so wonderful?

She swallowed then ducked her head, causing the bluebirds on her hat to bob. "Hello, Jim. It's nice to see you."

"How have you been? It's been a long time." *Smart, Jim.*

"Has it?" She looked at him then averted her eyes. Why wouldn't she look at him? "Are you still working at the lodge?" she said.

"The lodge?"

"Yes, the State of Maine Hunting Lodge." She frowned. "You know. You were working there when I took the children for a tour. Right before the opening."

Why would she think. . . Oh. "I wasn't actually working at the lodge, Addy. I asked them to allow me to guide you on the tour. They did it as favor to me." He smiled.

A blush slid over her cheeks. "But I thought. . ." She shook her head and appeared confused. "Oh, never mind. How have you been?"

"Not very well as a matter of fact." He pressed his lips together, determined not to expound on his reply.

"Oh, I'm sorry." She bit her lip again and glanced toward the school. "Well, I need to get inside. The children will be here soon."

He gave a nod and moved aside so she could pass. "Will I see you at the Christmas Ball?"

"Why, yes. I plan to be there. Will you?"

"Yes, I promised Rafe and Abby. They tell me it's a grand event."

"Yes, it is. Everyone works hard to make it special. It's been held at Mr. and Mrs. Jenkins' old barn for as long as I can remember."

He nodded. "That's neighborly of them."

"Yes," she said a little too brightly. "The red bows and evergreen boughs are so beautiful, and of course there are dozens upon dozens of candles burning. And an enormous tree."

"It must be quite beautiful."

She took a deep breath. "I thought you'd have left Branson by now."

"I probably should have. I had a few things I wanted to look into first. Unfortunately, they didn't work out."

"I see. I'm sorry." She took a step toward the school. "Perhaps I'll see you at the ball, then."

"Addy, I'm leaving in January. I've accepted a job in New York." Would she care?

She stopped. For a moment she didn't move, and then she looked up at him, her face stiff. "Well, I'm sure Rafe will miss you. But after all, we did know this day was coming. I hope you'll be very happy in your new job. New York must be wonderful."

He watched silently as she walked away.

⌀⎯⎯⎯⌀

Addy leaned over her desk, her head on the hard wood, and sobbed. She'd known he would leave one day. Actually, she'd expected him to be gone long before this, but she'd had no idea how badly it would hurt.

She supposed Martha Tyler was the girl he was seeing now. Addy's heart had jumped into her throat when she saw the girl lay her hand on his arm so possessively. He hadn't said anything about getting married, but it was fairly obvious. So much for her silly dreams. Martha would be the one leaving on the train with Jim Castle.

She must pull herself together before the children arrived. It was a good thing she'd gotten here early. But then, if she had arrived at her usual time, she wouldn't have run into Jim and heard the news.

Addy raised her head and blew her nose on her monogrammed handkerchief. She patted her hair back into place and stepped over to her water pitcher. Removing a cloth from the shelf below the pitcher, she put a little water on it and dabbed her face and neck.

If the children knew she'd been crying, some of them would be upset. She wouldn't spoil their day. They were excited to get the results of the essays contest. She had given them free rein over their subjects, and their essays showed a great deal about their personalities.

She went outside and found the children lined up waiting for her. Smiling, she rang the bell in case of stragglers. And sure enough, Johnny and Sam came running from around the building.

After roll call she stood in front of her desk, a stack of essays in her hand. "This is an exciting day, students. I've read and graded your papers and was quite impressed at how well you did. I've chosen the top essay for each grade level, first through eighth, which I have in my hands in no particular order except for the top two, which will be last. When I call your name, please come to the front of the class and read for us." She glanced down at the top essay on the pile, a short history on the tomato canning factory and quite good. "Cora March."

With a beaming smile, the twelve-year-old stood and walked up the aisle. Her black hair lay in two long, neat braids in front of her shoulders. She handed Cora her paper, gave the girl an encouraging nod, and then took a seat.

Cora beamed when she saw the B+ at the top. Cora read without stumbling over a word then took her seat.

"Thank you, Cora. Next, Harry Porter." The third grader jerked his head up, and his face flamed as he jumped from his seat. He stumbled through his essay, which consisted of a how-to on making a lariat, then went back to his seat, a big grin on his face.

As the morning progressed, she could tell the students were beginning to get restless. She called a short recess, and they filed out with relief on most of their faces.

Funny the difference in people. Even twins like her and Abby. Addy had always enjoyed writing essays, especially if she was allowed to choose her topic. But anyone would have thought Abby had been sentenced to slave labor. Addy had always had to help her sister with anything writing related.

She was ashamed to remember that she'd even done them for her many times. She'd suffered a lot of guilt over the cheating, crying and repenting to God, while it never occurred to Abby that it was dishonest. It was just Addy keeping her out of trouble.

It had been a vast relief to Addy when they were in eighth grade and Abby decided to write her own essay. She wrote about canoeing down the river with Rafe. Of course, the seven fish they'd caught somehow grew to twenty in the essay, but at least she wrote it herself and did a good job.

Perhaps if Addy hadn't done so many of her assignments for her, she'd have been fine a lot sooner. The thought shot through Addy's mind seemingly out of nowhere.

The children came back inside and took their seats with a shuffling of feet beneath the desks.

Addy focused on the next essay in her hand. Ah, her pride and joy. "Johnny Carroll."

"Huh?" His red mop shot up, and his mouth flew open. "Me?" He frowned at the tittering of giggles and a couple of guffaws.

"Yes, Johnny." Addy smiled at the boy. "Please come up front."

He took his paper and stared down at the A- written across the top. A look of amazement crossed his face. "Wow, I must've done real good on this paper."

"Yes, you did very well, but if you don't rephrase that sentence right now, I might be tempted to reduce your grade, young man."

"Oh, oh. I meant to say, 'I must have done very well on this here essay.'"

Addy pressed her lips against the grin that threatened to ruin her discipline. "That's better, Johnny. Please face the class and read your essay."

"Okay, first of all everyone, you need to know this ain't, I mean, isn't a real happening. I made it up. But I wish it really happened." Johnny then proceeded to read his story of a boy who went bear hunting with his father and ten brothers. He ended up saving them all. The essay was written in perfect English.

The crowning moment was when Annie Bolton came forward and read her story of a young girl growing up in England. Where she got her information, Addy couldn't imagine, but she planned to ask her after class. It was almost as if the girl had been in London herself, and Addy knew for a fact that wasn't so.

She really must contact Mr. Wright.

Chapter 20

Jim rode Finch down the lane to Rafe's farmhouse. They'd planned to go hunting today, but sleet had begun to fall before he was halfway there. He supposed he should have turned back, but the idea of being alone with his thoughts today didn't appeal to him. He knew Rafe wouldn't mind him barging in on them. Abby either. She'd seem like a sister to him if she didn't look so much like Addy.

Rafe came out of the barn and motioned for him.

He rode Finch inside the large building and got off.

"No sense in the animal standing in the sleet when we've got this nice dry barn, now is there?"

"Thanks." He grinned. "I'm sure Finch thanks you, too."

"Might as well get that saddle and harness off him, too." Rafe shoved his hat back and grinned. "Tuck told me not to let you leave. She's making chili, and since we can't go hunting, we may as well play checkers or something, and you can eat dinner with us. Supper, too, if you've a mind. It'll probably be more of the chili."

"Can't ever get too much of Abby's chili. Guess I'll take you up on that."

After taking care of Finch, Jim helped Rafe toss hay down to the horses and mules.

By the time they left the barn, the sleet was coming down harder. "Maybe I shouldn't stay. It looks like it might get bad."

"Naw, it's just a passing storm. Won't last long." Rafe sounded pretty sure of himself, and he'd lived around here for a long time.

"Okay, if you say so." Jim chuckled and turned the brim down on his hat as he followed his friend inside.

"Jim!" Abby stood in the kitchen doorway, wiping her hands on her apron. "I'm glad you came. You may be holed up with us for a while from the looks of the sky."

"Naw. It'll blow over," Rafe said.

She placed her hands on her hips, and her apron pulled tight across her rounded stomach. "Don't be so sure. You never can tell, Rafe Collins."

"Now Tuck, don't be picking a fight with me in front of Jim."

She grinned and placed her hand on Rafe's cheek. "Sorry. You're more than likely right anyway."

Jim averted his eyes from the casual but intimate moment. A pang shot through him. If only things could have worked out between him and Addy.

"Okay, you rascals go on in the parlor. I'll bring you some coffee in a

330

minute." She turned to go into the kitchen.

"Hey, Tuck," Rafe said, "the coffee would sure taste good with a piece of that apple bread you made yesterday."

"Oh, all right." She tossed a laugh over her shoulder.

Jim frowned as he and Rafe went into the parlor. "Should she be waiting on us in her condition?"

Rafe grinned. "Don't let her hear you ask that. And don't worry. She knows what she can do and when to take it easy."

"I hope you know how lucky you are."

Rafe threw him a quick glance. "I do. But it's not luck. It was God who brought us together. Although, at the time, I probably thought it was my irresistible charm."

Jim laughed. "I seem to remember you had some tough times for a while, wondering if Tuck would ever see you as anything but her best pal."

Rafe quickly sobered. "Yes, that's why I know it was God. He straightened it all out for us." He grinned. "And now we're an old, settled-down married couple."

Jim nodded. "Yes, you have a great life."

"Okay, Jim. What's wrong?" He frowned. "It's that sister-in-law of mine, isn't it? She still giving you the cold shoulder?"

"I can't really blame her, Rafe. She loves her family, especially Abby. I've always heard twins have a special connection." He shook his head. "She won't leave. That's for sure. And I've about given up on finding a suitable job around here."

"Around here? You mean you'd consider giving up your business for Addy?" Rafe stared and then started setting up the checkerboard on a square table.

"Yes. I've scoured the job market in Springfield, Kansas City, and St. Louis. Anything I'm qualified for that would offer a decent income requires more education than I've had." He frowned. "I even thought of buying a farm somewhere near but realized that was stupid. I'd be broke the first six months. What do I know about farming?"

Rafe shook his head. "You'd also be miserable doing something you're not cut out for. I knew you were crazy about Addy, but I didn't know it was that bad. I don't know if I'd have even gone that far for Tuck." He paused. "Yes, I would've done anything for Tuck."

"I'm thinking about pulling out earlier than I'd planned. I don't know if I can handle seeing her at the dance in someone else's arms."

Abby came through the door. She carried a tray laden with coffee mugs and a plate of apple bread.

Her face looked frozen. Had she heard what he'd said? She put the tray on a small table and turned to look at Jim. "Does Addy know you've been trying to find work so you won't have to leave?"

"Tuck, were you listening at the door?" Rafe threw a frown in her direction.

"Not till I heard my sister's name," Abby shot back then turned to Jim again. "Well, does she?"

"I don't know how she would. I've never mentioned it to her. But I spoke to her a few days ago. Somehow, she had gotten the idea I worked at the hunting lodge."

"Oh." She frowned again then planted her hands on her hips. "You and Addy are pathetic. You love each other. There is a way to work this out. Don't you dare leave until after the ball. Give God a chance here."

Rafe frowned. "God or Tuck?"

"God, of course. Often on this earth He uses people, though." She turned and left the room.

Jim stared after her, dumfounded. What just happened here? She seemed pretty sure Addy loved him. He looked at Rafe in confusion.

Rafe laughed. "That's my girl. I'd listen to her if I were you, my friend. She knows her sister pretty well. And you never know what can happen when my Tuck gets on the trail."

⌒⌒⌒

Mrs. Bright passed out decorated sugar cookies, homemade coconut bonbons, and cinnamon apple cider then clapped her hands together. "Eugene," she scolded, "put that cookie down. We haven't thanked the good Lord for it yet."

Addy grinned as the boy dropped his cookie like a hot poker and folded his hands.

A tree stood in the corner of the room, nearly touching the ceiling. She and the children had made ornaments earlier in the week, and yesterday they'd decorated. Mr. Carroll had put the homemade angel on the tree's top for them when he'd come to pick Johnny up after school. The floor beneath the tree was covered with brightly wrapped gifts.

Mrs. Carroll sat at the organ and played Christmas carols. Addy was thankful she had volunteers today. A mix of sleet and snow had been falling since noon. She hadn't been sure they'd show up. But out of the six scheduled, Mrs. Bright and Mrs. Carroll had arrived with smiles on their faces and baskets of goodies to add to the ones Ma had sent.

As the children bit into the sweet confections, Addy attempted to keep a smile on her face, even though the scene she'd witnessed in front of the mercantile a few days earlier played over and over in her mind. It had been, ever since she'd seen the intimate moment between Jim and Martha.

She jerked her thoughts back to the classroom and her excited students. They would have the gift exchange in a few moments, and then Addy would pass out Ma's little treat bags before the children were dismissed for the Christmas holidays.

Ma had made brightly colored flannel bags and filled each with an apple, a handful of walnuts, ribbon candy, and a candy cane. The walnuts and apples were from their own cellar. Ma had purchased the ribbon candy from Mr. Hawkins' store, which she still preferred over the new mercantile, but the candy canes she'd made herself.

Johnny's shrill voice rang out in the last note of "Jingle Bells."

Addy clapped her hands. "All right, boys and girls. We're going to take a short break for whoever needs one. Please come back inside after you've been to the outhouse. The snow is getting harder. When we return, it will be time for the gift exchange."

They all scampered outside, several making a beeline for the outhouse, while a few began scooping up snow for a snowball fight.

"They're sure having fun, aren't they?" Mrs. Bright said, her eyes shining as she watched through the window.

"Yes, and I can't bring myself to scold them," Addy said. "This is the first real snow of the season."

Mrs. Carroll hurried to the window and peered out. "Oh, dear. Do you think we should go ahead and dismiss the children?"

"No, some of the parents will be here at two to pick their children up. If it gets too bad, Mr. Travis at the livery stable will hitch up a wagon and take the rest of them home." Addy was grateful for the kindly old man who'd volunteered his services a couple of years ago. So far, he'd only had to do it once, but Addy knew she could count on him.

When the children were back inside and their wraps drying near the stove, she smiled at them. "Who would like to help me give out the gifts?"

Annie's hand went up first. The girl took turns pulling out boys' and girls' gifts. She handed them to the ladies who passed them out.

"Aww. The snow's stopped." Sam's disappointment rang across the room.

Addy glanced at the window. Sure enough, only a few flakes fell, and the sky seemed to be lighter than before.

"Don't worry, young man," Mrs. Carroll said. "Before long you'll be complaining because there's so much snow you can't go out and play."

A smile tipped Addy's lips. That was so true. Early snow was fun, but around February, the winter could seem dark and long.

The children tore into their gifts, and soon the sounds of pleasure and "thank yous" were heard. Then the paper and ribbons were wrapped up to take home or throw away, depending on their condition. The smaller children squealed with delight when Addy passed out the bright-colored treat bags. And even the older children had grins on their faces.

The parents of the children who lived outside of town arrived promptly. Those students who lived in town yelled quick good-byes to their friends and took off toward their homes.

Mr. Carroll came inside and banked the fire while Addy and her two volunteers straightened up the room.

"Now, honey, will you be okay to drive home alone?" Mrs. Carroll stood in the doorway and darted a fearful look at the sky.

"Please don't worry about me, Mrs. Carroll," Addy said. "I don't have that far to drive, and there's not too much snow on the ground."

"But what if it starts up again?" She wrung her hands.

"Now, Polly. She'll be all right. Even if the snow does start, she'd be home before things got dangerous."

"Well, if you're sure." She patted Addy on the shoulder. "But you hurry up and get home, now."

"I will, Mrs. Bright. I'll be on my way in five minutes."

As Addy drove home, she forced her mind away from thoughts about Jim. After all, Abby was coming tomorrow to help Addy and Ma cut and sew the boys' little suits and Betty's Christmas dress. It would be a wonderful day.

She urged her horse forward, and the buggy picked up speed. She had her wonderful family and a community full of old friends. Who needed Jim Castle anyway? She'd been happy before he came into her life, and she'd be happy again.

Then why did she feel so torn inside? As though something had been ripped from her. Something that belonged.

Chapter 21

B rrrr." Addy rubbed her hands together as she stepped inside after looking down the lane for Abby's buggy. "I'm glad I don't have to go anywhere today."

"No sign of Abby yet?" Ma sat by the fireplace in her rocker. She and Addy had measured Betty for her Christmas dress the night before and cut the green velvet fabric, but they were waiting for Abby to bring her patterns for the boys' outfits.

"No, but I'm sure she'll be here any moment. She knows we need to get started." Addy hoped having her sister there all day would distract her from the disturbing thoughts of Jim that continuously ran through her head.

At the sound of horses and wagon wheels, she jumped up and ran to the door. Grabbing her shawl, she slipped out and shut the door behind her to keep out the cold. The wagon bumped up and down behind the running horses, snow flying beneath wheels and hooves. Her sister yanked on the reins at the barn doors.

"Land sakes, Abby," Addy yelled across the yard, her hands on her hips. "What are you trying to do? Have the baby before Christmas?"

Abby laughed. "I'll be in as soon as I take care of the horses."

Addy took off across the yard, reaching her sister just as she slid off the wagon seat. Addy grabbed the reins before her sister could and led the rig into the barn, handing the horses off to Pa.

Clutching her shawl tightly around her shoulders, Addy stormed out of the barn. "Abby, you need to start being more careful."

"Oh sis, I'm fine, but you're going to freeze, running out here without your coat." But she took the steps to the porch slowly.

Addy put her arm around Abby and opened the door. "Come on inside and sit down."

"Hi, Ma," Abby almost sang as she stepped into the parlor. "Am I late?"

"Not at all, dear." She lifted her cheek for her daughter's kiss and smiled. "You did remember to bring the patterns, didn't you?"

"Yes, ma'am." She slipped them from her coat pocket. "I'll lay them on the kitchen table for now."

"Tuck!" Betty ran in and grabbed Abby around the legs. "You're here."

"I sure am, little Betsy Boo." Abby patted the three-year-old on the head."

"Betty, you mustn't grab Abby around her legs like that." Ma frowned. "You might trip her and cause her to fall."

"I'm okay, Ma." Abby reached down and gave Ma a kiss. "Is that coffee I smell?"

Without waiting for an answer, she headed for the kitchen with Betty trailing behind.

Addy followed. "I'll help. Ma, do you want tea or coffee?" she called back over her shoulder.

"Neither, dear." Ma's voice trailed after them. "If you girls need help cutting the suits out, call me. I want to start basting the top of Betty's dress to the skirt."

Addy poured coffee for her and Abby while her sister laid the fabric out on the table. Last week Addy and Ma had carefully removed the stitches from the dresses and removed the sleeves and collars. Now she helped her sister pin a pattern to the soft velvet.

Betty rubbed her hand over the fabric. "Pretty."

"Yes, it is pretty, sweetie. But you mustn't touch now. Soon it will be full of sharp pins."

"Okay." She perched on a stool behind the table.

"I never used to like sewing," Abby said. "But I just love making things for my little sugars."

Addy glanced at her twin, and a pang of envy shot through her. Quickly she pushed it away. She was happy for Abby, and even if she should never marry and have children of her own, she would not allow jealousy to raise its ugly head and come between her and her beloved sister. "Who wouldn't love sewing for those two little darlings?" she said around the pins in her mouth.

"Be careful, silly. You might swallow one of those things." Abby frowned. "Use the pin cushion."

Addy removed the pins from her mouth and stuck them in one of the pincushions scattered around the table. "When did you get so bossy?" she asked.

Abby grinned. "When I got married. You weren't around to boss me, so I decided to try being the boss. Rafe didn't take to it though."

"So I guess you'll have to settle for bossing Davey and Dawson."

Abby shrugged. "Half the time they try to boss me. But I'm attempting to put a stop to that."

Betty giggled. "Davey and Dawson don't boss you."

"No, but they would if I let them." Abby flashed a grin at Betty.

They finished pinning and cutting the tiny trousers.

"I hope Rafe won't think these look sissified," Abby said, cocking her head with a frown.

Addy laughed. "Sissified? They're just babies."

"I know. I was teasing. But he'll have them in boots before you know it. Just you wait and see." Abby picked up her coffee mug and took a drink. "Cold already." She poured it back in the pot and moved it to the hot part of the stove.

"We probably need more wood in there," Addy said. "We'll need to start cooking pretty soon. It's eleven o'clock."

"Pa'll be hungry as a bear after splitting wood all morning. I'd have helped if he'd have let me."

"Oh, you were going to split wood in your condition," Addy said. "That would have been a sight to behold." She picked up one end of the fabric, being careful of the pins.

"I thought Pa was hiring someone to help out around here," Abby said, picking up the other end and helping Addy carry it into Addy's bedroom.

"Everyone's been so busy on their own farms, he hasn't been able to find anyone."

"I'll tell Rafe to ask around. Pa isn't getting any younger."

Addy laughed. "He's not that old, silly. He can outwork a lot of younger men."

"I know. Still, it wouldn't hurt for him to slow down a little."

Ma came into the kitchen and started preparing the noon meal. Soon the aroma of pork chops filled the entire house.

After lunch, Pa went back to splitting wood, and Ma put Betty down for a nap.

After Addy and Abby had cleaned the kitchen, Addy said, "We'd better get the fabric and take it into the parlor. We have a lot of sewing to do."

"Wait a minute, sis. Let's step out on the porch where we can have some privacy. I need to talk to you about something."

"What is it? We need to get busy or we won't get done."

"We don't have to finish today." Abby said. "I can work on finishing up the boys' suits in my spare time. This is important. It's about Jim."

On wooden feet, Addy followed her sister to the front porch. They'd grabbed their coats, but Addy still shivered. She stared at Abby. "If you're going to tell me he's leaving town, I already know."

"I know you do. But did you know he's been riding all over Missouri for weeks trying to find work so that he won't have to leave you?"

Addy gasped. "What? What do you mean?"

"Just what I said. Jim knows you won't leave home, and he loves you so much he's searched high and low for a job, but nothing turned up that paid enough to take care of a family. He even considered buying a farm, but the man can't even milk a cow. He'd be broke before a year was out."

Jim loved her? That much? Confusion beat at her mind. But why didn't he stay here in Branson and work for the Missouri Pacific?

"But. . .Abby, why doesn't he talk to his boss about staying here and working for the railroad? Surely they have something he can do in this area."

"What? Jim doesn't work for the railroad, you silly thing. He has his own business."

Addy laughed. A sick sounding little half sob that wasn't a laugh at all. "Of course he works for the railroad. He has business meetings with them all the time."

Abby shook her head. "That's what I thought, too. But it's not so. He's some kind of consultant, and he helps people get their businesses in shape so they make more money or something. He's been on a job, which included the White River Line and the Branson hotel and some other businesses. They pay him to do this, and when the job is over he goes somewhere else."

"But why didn't he tell me?"

Addy's hand pressed her shoulder. "I guess he thought you knew."

"Then he was going to give up his business for me?"

Abby shrugged. "Looks that way. Rafe told me Jim has turned down at least four or five offers since his job here ended in September. But he can't wait any longer. And he's about sick from having to leave you."

Addy closed her eyes against the tears that filled them. "Oh, Abby," she whispered. "What have I done?"

"The important thing is what are you going to do?"

"But what can I do? He's going to New York."

"Go with him. You love him, don't you?"

"Yes," she said. "But you're telling me to leave you, Abby."

Abby groaned. "Addy, you've been taking care of me all your life. Now it's time to get one of your own."

"But. . ."

"Listen, sis, I love you, and I know you love me, but you don't need to take care of me. I have Rafe. And more important, I have God." She stopped and bit her lip. "I don't mean to sound mean, sis, but if Rafe were going to New York, I'd leave you in a minute."

"I never thought we'd be apart," Addy said. "Ever since Ma died, then Pa's accident, I felt like I needed to watch over you."

"I know. And I thought we'd both get married and live right next to each other and raise our babies together."

A cold, hard fist seemed to shove itself into Addy's heart. "I don't know if I can do it."

Abby took her hand. "The train comes right into Branson now. It's not like we can't visit each other."

"That's true." A little glimmer of hope sparked in Addy. "Do you think Jim still wants me to go with him?"

Abby laughed. "I wish you could have heard him. Of course, if he'd known I was listening, he'd never have opened up to Rafe the way he did. Aren't you glad I snooped?"

How could she have been so stupid? She'd thought he was putting his job before her when all the time he was willing to sacrifice a career he loved for her. "I don't know what to do."

"You'll see him at the ball Friday night. Talk to him," Addy said.

Horror stemming from humiliation washed over her. "I can't just go up to him and say, 'I changed my mind. Take me with you.'"

Abby laughed. "I would, if it were Rafe."

"I think your memory is a little faulty," Addy said. "You thought Rafe wanted to marry Carrie Sue, and you almost had a conniption fit trying to decide what to do."

"Hmm. I guess you're right. I'd forgotten about that." Abby thought for a minute. "I guess you should just go and leave things in God's hands."

Now why hadn't she thought of that?

Chapter 22

Nostalgia engulfed Addy as she sat on her bed and sorted through a box of mementos. She took a deep breath and let it out with a ragged *whoosh*. Matching gold wands represented the fifth grade school play when she and Abby had played identical fairies. A sound halfway between a sob and a laugh erupted from her throat. She'd had to practically drag her sister to school that night.

"Addy, you haven't even started dressing for the ball." Ma stood in the doorway. Her deep-blue dress deepened her eyes until they appeared almost as if one were gazing into a midnight sky. Her black hair, with only a few white strands at her temples, was arranged softly around her face with the back pulled up in a smooth chignon.

"You're so beautiful, Ma." Addy whispered the words. No wonder Pa was still so much in love with her. Not that looks were everything. Ma was a wonderful woman, too. But Addy hadn't realized just how physically beautiful Ma was until this moment.

"Oh, you just think that because I'm your mother." She smiled. "Come now. Get dressed or we'll be late. I want to get your pa on the dance floor as early as possible so that he can't use tiredness as an excuse."

Addy rose. "What should I do about Jim?" She'd shared with her mother what Abby had told her about him. But Ma hadn't yet offered any advice.

Ma brushed a lock of hair back from Addy's face. "No one can tell you what to do. That's your decision."

"But what do you think I should do?"

"Are you in love with him?" Ma leaned back and looked closely at her face.

"Yes. I love him so much I've been in agony for months."

"Well, there is your answer. Of course you must let him know that you're willing to go with him."

How could Ma speak so emphatically? Like that was the only answer. What about leaving family? What about her job?

"But Ma, I'll be far away from here most of the time. Jim travels all over the country. Even to foreign lands sometimes." At the words, her heart raced, and a jolt of excitement ran through her.

Ma smiled. "You have a love of adventure in you, Addy. I've always known that."

Addy sobered. "Ma, if I go, I'll be so lonely without you."

"Probably. In the beginning. But God will replace the loneliness with a brand-new life. And brand-new people. A husband. Children. New friends."

"How can you be so wise, Ma? You've hardly been out of Missouri."

Ma's eyes sparkled. "I always wished I could go downriver on the *Julia Dawn*."

"You did? Really?"

"I really did. And as happy as I was when your dad sold his boat and took up farming, I'd have gone to the ends of the earth with him, if he'd asked."

"Oh, Ma. What about Abby? How can I leave her?" She picked up the box she'd been going through. "Look. Every memory I have includes Abby. Sometimes it's like we're one person."

Little furrows appeared between Ma's eyes. "You are a whole person, Addy. You don't need your sister to make you whole. Only God can do that. And as for your memories, we all have them, sweetheart. Some good and some bad. But in order to follow God's will for our lives, we must be willing to leave some things behind."

"I know. I know Jesus said that many times. But how do I know God wants me to go with Jim?" This was a question she'd asked herself for days. She knew it needed to be settled in her heart before she could make a decision.

"God isn't deliberately keeping you in the dark about His will for you," Ma said. "The Bible says, 'If any of you lack wisdom, let him ask of God, that giveth to all men liberally, and upbraideth not; and it shall be given him.'"

As Ma spoke the familiar scripture verse, peace washed over Addy. "Thank you, Ma."

"You are welcome, daughter," Ma said with a smile. "And now, I think you had better get ready. You know we have to drop Betty off at Rafe's parents' house on the way."

Jim leaned against the wall inside the Hawkins' old barn. Red bows decorated fresh green boughs, and the pine and cedar gave a festive look as well as aroma.

Jim scarcely noticed any of it. His eyes were on the wide, festooned double doors.

Rafe and Abby had arrived a few minutes ago, decked out in finery. He'd started at the first sight of Abby. Dressed in a green satin gown, with her hair all fancied up, for a moment, he'd thought she was Addy, and his heart had almost stood still. Then she'd turned, and the oversized shawl couldn't hide her growing stomach. Plus the movement and the expression on her face were all Abby. They'd said hello in passing and headed for the refreshment table.

The Packard brothers were tuning up their guitars, so Jim assumed the dancing would start any moment.

"Hey, Jim," Rafe said, coming to stand by him. "I need to talk to you before Addy gets here."

Coldness ran over Jim. What now? More bad news? Had she met someone?

"I thought you should know that Addy thought all this time you worked for the Missouri Pacific."

"What?"

"Tuck told her how you'd been job hunting because you didn't want to leave her, and she wanted to know why you didn't just keep a railroad job here in Branson." Rafe grinned. "She asked why you needed to hunt for a job when you were already working for the railroad and all you needed to do was ask them to assign you to Branson. Or something like that. Anyway, Tuck told her about your business, and now she's feeling bad about the way she treated you."

"Are you sure about this?"

"Yes, she's still pretty squirrely about not wanting to leave her family, especially Tuck. But she's softening some." He slapped Jim on the back. "Just thought you should know."

"Thanks, I appreciate it."

Rafe turned away, and just then, Jack and Lexie walked through the doors. Jim stood straight, his eyes glued on the entrance. He took a sharp breath as Addy stepped inside. Moonlight streamed in, bathing her in its glow. Her pale-blond hair cascaded in loose curls down the back of her deep-scarlet gown. A gold locket rested on her throat.

She turned, and her eyes met his. They widened and shock filled them. As though in a daze, she turned and followed her parents across to the refreshment table.

◆

Shock hit Addy as her eyes rested on Jim. As though through a tunnel, his voice resounded in her head, telling her he'd loved her from the moment he saw her. As though looking through a kaleidoscope, she saw his tenderness toward her and the revelation that he loved her enough to give up a career he'd worked and fought for. Indescribable happiness pierced through her. Her legs trembled.

What had she been thinking? Of course God had brought Jim into her life. This was a strong man. If not for God and the love He'd put in Jim's heart for her, he'd have swept her out of his mind months ago. Joy swelled up in her, and she knew she needed to find a chair before she ended up on the floor.

Addy accepted a cup of punch from Carrie Sue's little sister and went to one of the tables. As soon as she was seated, she turned slightly and met his watching gaze. She averted her eyes and pressed her lips together but couldn't keep them from tilting upward at the corners.

Horace Packard stepped up to the raised platform at the back of the room. "Ladies and gentlemen, everyone line up for a lively, toe-tapping Virginia reel."

Among laughter and catcalls, couples, young and old, formed two lines. Addy groaned as she saw Dr. Fields head her way from the front of the barn. Just before he arrived, a tall shadow crossed her vision, and she looked up to see Jim bow.

"May I have this dance, Miss Sullivan?" His smile was uncertain as though he half expected her to refuse.

"I'd be delighted, Mr. Castle." She placed her hand in his and stood.

The next few moments of toe-tapping fun flew by with no chance to speak.

The dance ended, and the couples all reunited, some waiting for the next dance, others falling into their chairs.

"Addy."

"Jim."

Before either could continue, a sweet, sweet sound started low and muted and then grew, almost heart-wrenching in its intensity. Startled, Addy looked toward the platform. Abby sat, her bow held high. Their eyes met for a moment. Then Addy closed her eyes and let the haunting notes of Abby's violin caress her soul.

As the sweet strains of a waltz filled the room and Jim took her in his arms, the thought crossed Addy's mind that her sister must really want to get rid of her. She smiled to herself and relaxed in Jim's arms.

"You are so beautiful tonight, you take my breath away." Jim's voice was soft on her ears, his words tender to her heart.

"Thank you," she said, her voice trembling.

Weakness washed over her, and she prayed he wouldn't let go because she'd surely land right on the floor. But in spite of the weakness, a peace she'd never known washed over her.

Oh God, thank You for straightening out my thinking. Abby never really needed me. I was the one who needed to be needed.

The music came to an end. Jim asked, "Would you care to go outside for some air? It's quite stuffy in here."

They walked across the room, and Abby grinned at them as they walked by. On the way out, they stopped to get cups of hot cider. They strolled across to the fence and leaned against it.

Addy shivered, and Jim reached over and adjusted the shawl she'd thrown around her shoulders.

"Why didn't you wear a coat?" he said.

She laughed. "You sound like my sister. She said the same thing to me a few days ago."

"Your sister is very wise." He smiled, and the crinkling of his eyes made her knees go weak again.

"Yes, she certainly is, but as a matter of fact, my coat is in our buggy. And must we talk about my sister?" Oh no. Had she actually voiced that thought?

He laughed. "As a matter of fact, I do have some things I'd like to talk over with you. I was going to ask if I could take you for a drive tomorrow."

"Yes, I'd like that." She looked up at the night sky. "Of course, it looks as though we might have snow."

"Snow won't keep me away," he said. "What I have to say is much too important."

A gust of icy wind hit them suddenly, and Addy shivered again.

"Let me get your coat."

"Thank you, but we should probably go inside."

Disappointment clouded his eyes, but he nodded. "Of course."

She laid her hand on his proffered arm, and they went inside.

Within a few moments, the wind had increased and roared against the barn, shaking the sturdy walls and roaring down the chimneys.

The guests hurried to get their things together.

Ma appeared at her side. "Dear, we need to go home now. Pa thinks a storm is coming. Abigail and Rafe are going to take Betty home with them, or if the wind gets worse they'll all spend the night with Rafe's folks." She nodded at Jim. "Good night, Mr. Castle. Please be careful on your wayback to town."

Jim walked Addy to the wagon. She turned and watched as he saddled Finch and rode away.

Chapter 23

Addy wiped the frost off the parlor window and peered out at the deep drifts piled high against the house and outbuildings. Would he show up? He'd said snow wouldn't stop him, but surely he hadn't realized how much would fall in the night. The only way he'd get through this was by horse or sleigh. When the snow stopped earlier this morning, Rafe had brought a bundled-up Betty home in his sleigh.

She was almost beside herself with nerves. Now that she'd come to her senses, what if he didn't ask her to marry him and leave Branson with him? After all, he couldn't know that all she wanted now was to be with him, even if he took her to the other side of the world. Would she dare bring up the subject?

"I hear sleigh bells." Betty ran to the window and looked out.

"Are you sure, Bets? I don't hear them." Addy squinted and peered again through the frosty pane.

"Yes, I'm sure." Betty said. "Maybe your ears don't work as good as mine."

"Maybe they don't work as well as yours, sweetheart."

Betty hunched her shoulders and grinned. "That's what I said, silly."

Wait, maybe Betty was right. Addy ran to the door and flung it open. She heard the jingling of bells just before the single-horse sleigh came around the bend of the lane. Quickly she shut the door before Jim could see her. After all, it wouldn't do to appear too eager.

Betty gave an impatient little stomp. "Why'd you close the door, sister? He's almost here."

"Well. . .umm. . .I didn't want to let cold air in."

"Oh." She wrinkled her brow and gave Addy a suspicious stare.

At the knock on the door, Betty flung it open. "Hi, Mr. Jim."

"Well hello, Miss Betty," Jim said with a bow. "It's mighty cold out here. Is it all right if I come in?"

Addy blushed. "Please come in, of course. May I take your hat?"

"I'd better take care of it myself. I dropped it in a snow bank a few minutes ago, and it's wet." He hung it on the hat rack.

Pa stepped out into the hall. "Come in and sit by the fire, Jim. I think Lexie just took cinnamon rolls out of the stove."

"Thank you, sir, but if you don't mind, I'll wait until Addy and I get back from our ride." He gave her a questioning look. "That is if you'd still like to go. I have a pile of warm blankets for you."

"Yes, a sleigh ride will be fun. Let me get my coat and gloves."

"And a hat," Betty piped up. "Don't forget your hat, Addy."

"Oh, thanks, Bets, but will a wool scarf do?" She smiled and gave her sister a kiss on the cheek before she and Jim walked to the sleigh.

He helped her in then tucked blankets around her before getting in himself.

The sleigh glided smoothly across the snow, and Addy leaned back against the seat in satisfaction. "Are we going any place in particular?" she asked.

"I thought we'd go down by the river or maybe over to the churchyard so we can sit and talk," he said. "Unless there's someplace else you'd like to go."

"No, that would be fine." She licked her lips, suddenly nervous again.

Snow began to fall in soft white flakes as they pulled into the churchyard.

"Oh, dear." Addy pulled her collar closer around her neck. "I hope it doesn't get any harder."

"I can take you back home if you'd like. I suppose we can talk another time." The disappointment in Jim's voice would have made up her mind, if she'd needed it.

"No, that won't be necessary. It's not snowing that hard. And look how beautiful it is." Addy took a deep breath as she glanced around. Snow draped the trees that surrounded the church and yard, and drifts billowed up against the weathered logs.

"It almost looks like a picture, doesn't it?" she said.

"Yes, it does. I feel like singing 'Jingle Bells.'" He grinned.

She giggled. "Me, too."

He reached over and wiped snow off the red wool scarf she'd placed over her hair. Then he paused and looked deeply into her eyes. Her breath caught, and she lowered her lashes.

"Addy, look at me." He lifted her chin. "I love you. That was the first thing I wanted to say."

She couldn't contain the happy sigh that escaped. He loved her. Her heart beat rapidly. Could she say it? Should she? Casting caution aside, she whispered, "I love you, too."

Joy slid over his face, but immediately he sobered. "I tried to find work, so we could be together without your leaving the home and family you love."

"I know. Abby told me." She raised her eyes and met his. "Jim, I didn't understand. I've been behaving like a child hoping everything would work out the way I wanted it. But life doesn't always work out the way we have it planned."

"Does that mean. . . ?"

"It means I've realized sometimes God's plan is different than ours, but His is always the right one." She trembled as she allowed her love for him to shine from her eyes. "I want to go wherever you go. If you still want me."

"Still want you? Oh my darling girl. . ." he said. "And we can visit often now that the railroad is complete. Who knows? Now that those Wright brothers have had a successful flight, we might even fly here someday."

Addy giggled at the ridiculous remark. "I think I'd rather stick to the train."

She gasped as snow began to come down heavily. "Jim, this isn't light snow anymore."

"You're right. I need to get you home. But first, I have a very important question to ask, and I don't want to wait any longer. Addy, will you please marry me?"

"Yes," she whispered, "I will."

As a curtain of snow fell, Jim bent his head and kissed her waiting lips.

⁓

Addy stood on the top step of the train and waved, feeling the comfort of Jim's chest behind her.

Ma wiped the corner of her eye with her handkerchief but managed to throw a tremulous smile Addy's way.

Little Betty clung to her mother, sniveling and waving. " 'Bye, Addy," she said for about the umpteenth time. "Don't forget to write me a letter."

"I won't forget, Bets. I promise. Good-bye." Addy's voice cracked, and tears rushed up, threatening to overflow. She averted her eyes from her little sister just for a moment, then forced a big smile and turned her gaze back on her family.

Pa appeared stern, but Addy knew he was fighting back tears. Funny how men thought they had to be so brave. He cleared his throat. "Take care of my little girl, Jim."

"I will, sir. I promise." Jim's voice was deep with emotion.

Rafe and Abby stood to one side. Worry rose up in Addy as she looked at her sister. Abby stood stock still, a smile frozen on her face. Grief filled her eyes.

Addy touched her hand to her lips and blew her a kiss.

Jim pressed gently on her waist. "We need to find our seats, sweetheart."

Addy waved again then walked down the narrow aisle at her husband's side. She scooted into her seat next to the window while Jim put her hatbox in the space above. Waving to her family, she examined each face.

The train lurched and began to roll slowly forward.

Addy hung on to the arm of her seat and continued to wave.

Suddenly Abby broke loose from Rafe's protective arm and took a step after the train. "Addy! Good-bye. I love you so much!" She continued to wave as the train crept slowly forward.

"I love you, too, Abby. I love you, too. Don't worry, we'll visit!" She blew another kiss.

"I know. I. . ." The rest of her sentence was drowned out as the train whistled loudly and the wheels picked up speed. Abby grinned and blew a kiss back then buried her face in Rafe's shoulder. The train picked up more speed, and Abby leaned back against Rafe.

Addy put her hand to her throat. Her sister would be all right. She had her husband, and they both had God. Peace flowed through her as she turned around. She looked at Jim and met love in his eyes.

"I love you, Mrs. Castle," he said.

Suddenly amazement washed over her. It was just like her dream, from the moment she stood on the train step then walked with her husband up the aisle and sat beside him as the train left Branson. "I love you, too, Jim Castle."

A ripple of delighted laughter escaped her throat. Life would be one grand adventure with her handsome, dashing Jim. And she didn't need to worry about leaving home. She'd heard the phrase "Home is where the heart is." And her heart was right here where it belonged.

Jim eyes crinkled as he smiled down at her. A lock of almost-black hair fell across his forehead as he bent and kissed her tenderly on the cheek.

Epilogue

Addy stepped through the gate, holding onto Jim's arm, then stopped and stood still. Closing her eyes, she inhaled deeply. The smell of wood smoke tantalized her senses, taking her back in time to the Sullivan farm and Ma's old wood stove. She could even smell chicken frying.

Her eyes flew open, and she glanced up at her husband. "It smells just like the old homeplace, Jim. I even smell chicken. You didn't tell me. Is this the surprise?"

Her husband grinned. "No, it may be a surprise, but it's not *the* surprise. But come on now, you don't want to stand here and get knocked over. They'll be opening the gates to the public any minute now."

"Should we wait here to see it?" After all, she was here to see the grand opening.

"Nah. You see one crowd, you've seen them all. I want you to see the place before anyone else gets here." He winked. "Especially your surprise." Gently he looped her arm through his and stepped forward.

"Oh look, Jim. A blacksmith shop." Her eyes wide, she pulled away from him and walked by herself to see the brawny man with his sleeves rolled up above his elbows pounding on iron with his anvil in front of an old wooden structure. Sparks flew and Jim pulled her back a step.

She wrinkled her nose. The wonderful aroma she'd experienced had been replaced by an acrid smell. Still, the shop reminded her of long ago, so even the smell was yet welcome and somewhat familiar.

As they walked on, the rest of the family trailing behind, she stopped again, her gaze following two women clothed in long dresses that would have been in style in Branson a hundred years ago. "Why, Jim. You didn't tell me the workers wore period clothing."

"I thought you'd like the surprise," he drawled with a teasing look in his eyes.

"Oh yes. And that's my surprise. A wonderful one."

Jim chuckled, that deep laugh that still curled her toes. "Nope. That's not it."

Craft stalls lined the dirt streets of the town, and Addy took her time examining expertly handmade quilts and tatted scarves. A wood shop filled with old-fashioned, handcrafted furniture drew her attention. Over in one corner of the shop stood a horsehair chair. A pang shot through her. "Look,

Jack. Your Uncle Rafe's pa used to make chairs just like this."

Jack walked over and examined the chair. "Even the bottom?"

"Of course. He made cane-bottomed ones, too. Now there's a renewed interest in caning." She ran her hand over the smooth seat. "But I don't think anyone makes horsehair chair bottoms anymore."

They strolled down to a stand where vendors made candles and displayed them for sale. Addy ran her hand down the smooth wax of short and tall tapers. The other side of the shop displayed old-fashioned oil lanterns and lamps. Some were intricately made with flowers painted on the side. She closed her eyes and allowed nostalgia to wash over her.

Jim squeezed her arm. "Just like the old days, aren't they?"

"Yes," she whispered. "Most of ours were plain, but Ma had a rose-patterned one very similar to the one on the shelf there. It's very beautiful, isn't it?"

"Yes, it is." He motioned to the middle-aged shopkeeper. He paid and asked her to wrap the purchase and have it sent to the gate to be picked up when they left.

"Thank you, darling." Addy beamed at him. "I'll cherish it always."

"And I will cherish you always." He leaned in and gave her another peck on the cheek.

She giggled. "That tickled. I think the mustache needs trimming."

"Your wish is my command," he said with a droll expression. "I trust you won't mind if I wait until later."

"I don't mind at all. But I might not let you kiss me." She wrinkled her nose.

His laughter roared across the little mountain town. "Just try to stop me."

"Now, Jim, you have me all curious. Where is my surprise?" She batted her lashes, teasing.

He shook his head. "No, no. You can't work your wiles on me, young lady."

Addy heard subdued laughter from behind them and turned to see her son and grandson shaking their heads at one another.

"Hmmph. So you don't think I'm a young lady?"

"I absolutely do, Mother," Jack said with a serious face. "You are undoubtedly the most young-at-heart lady I know."

"And don't you forget it." She smiled and gave a short nod. "All right, if I can't have my surprise, how about some of that fried chicken that's torturing me. I know it's here somewhere.

"Right this way." Jack took her other arm, and the two of them led her to a shack with a cut-out window. From inside, the tantalizing aromas of chicken and barbecued pork and beef wafted to her nostrils.

"Oh dear, now I don't know what I want. You decide, Jim." She bit her lip. "It all looks and smells so delicious."

"How about the beef on a bun?" he said. "That way, I won't have to worry about your choking on a bone while we're walking."

"Walking?" She waved toward rustic tables and chairs that sat invitingly beside the café. "Why can't we eat there?"

"Because I want to get to your surprise before the crowd finds us."

"Oh, I almost forgot the surprise. Everything is so wonderful. I'm so glad I got to come."

"I am, too. It would not have been the same for me without you here." He handed her a sandwich and then got one for himself, letting the rest of their group fend for themselves.

She took a bite and rolled her eyes with pleasure. "This is the best food I've had in years."

He laughed. "What about the fine dining we did in Paris last year?"

"No, this is better." She wiped the corner of her mouth with a paper napkin.

Jim laughed and waved to the rest of their party, who were all taking their food to the tables.

Good. She'd rather be alone with Jim.

They strolled over a bridge that crossed a creek and continued over a hill. Suddenly she stopped, and stillness enveloped her. "Oh, Jim," she whispered.

Before her stood a small log building. A rustic sign across the door said WILDERNESS CHURCH. Except for the sign, the building looked exactly the way it had seventy years ago, when she saw it for the first time at the age of eight. But there was a deeper reason for the tears that filled her eyes and overflowed onto her cheeks.

Cupping her face in his hands, Jim brushed his thumbs across her cheeks and wiped away her tears. "And this, dearest, was your surprise."

She took his arm. "Thank you, my darling," she whispered as they walked inside.

Standing in the darkened building, Jim took her in his arms, and they shared a kiss that was every bit as wonderful as the one they'd shared when they'd been joined in marriage in that very church fifty-five years ago.